PRAISE FOR THE

INCEPTIO
"Brilliantly plotted original story, grippingly told and cleverly combining the historical with the futuristic. It's a real edge-of-the-seat read, genuinely hard to put down." – Sue Cook

CARINA
"This is a fabulous thriller that cracks along at a great pace and just doesn't let up from start to finish." – Discovering Diamonds Reviews

PERFIDITAS
"Alison Morton has built a fascinating, exotic world! Carina's a bright, sassy detective with a winning dry sense of humour. The plot is pretty snappy too!" – Simon Scarrow

SUCCESSIO
"I thoroughly enjoyed this classy thriller, the third in Morton's epic series set in Roma Nova." – Caroline Sanderson in The Bookseller

AURELIA
"AURELIA explores a 1960s that is at once familiar and utterly different – a brilliant page turner that will keep you gripped from first page to last. Highly recommended." – Russell Whitfield

INSURRECTIO
"INSURRECTIO – a taut, fast-paced thriller. I enjoyed it enormously. Rome, guns and rebellion. Darkly gripping stuff." – Conn Iggulden

RETALIO
"RETALIO is a terrific concept engendering passion, love and loyalty. I actually cheered aloud." – J J Marsh

ROMA NOVA EXTRA
"One of the reasons I am enthralled with the Roma Nova series is the concept of the whole thing." – Helen Hollick, Vine Voice

THE ROMA NOVA THRILLERS
The Carina Mitela adventures
INCEPTIO
CARINA (novella)
PERFIDITAS
SUCCESSIO

The Aurelia Mitela adventures
AURELIA
INSURRECTIO
RETALIO

ROMA NOVA EXTRA (Short stories)

———

ABOUT THE AUTHOR

A 'Roman nut' since age 11, Alison Morton has clambered over much of Roman Europe; she continues to be fascinated by that complex, powerful and value driven civilisation.

Armed with an MA in history, six years' military service and a love of thrillers, she explores via her Roma Nova novels the 'what if' idea of a modern Roman society run by strong women.

Alison lives in France with her husband, cultivates a Roman herb garden and drinks wine.

Find out more at alison-morton.com, follow her on Twitter @alison_morton and Facebook (AlisonMortonAuthor)

· PERFIDITAS ·

ALISON MORTON

To John,

Happy reading!

Alison Morton

PULCHERIA
PRESS

DRAMATIS PERSONAE

Mitela Family
Carina Mitela – Captain, Praetorian Guard Special Forces (PGSF), nicknamed 'Bruna'
Conradus Mitelus – 'Conrad', legate, head of the PGSF
Aurelia Mitela – Carina's grandmother, head of the Mitela family
Allegra Mitela – Carina and Conrad's eldest daughter
Antonia and Gillius – Carina and Conrad's younger children
Helena Mitela – Carina's cousin
Superbus – Undistinguished family member
Lucilla Mitela – Student

Household
Junia – Steward of Domus Mitelarum
Galienus – Under-steward / housekeeper
Marcella – Aurelia's assistant

Military
Lucius Punellus – Adjutant, PGSF
Daniel Stern – Major, PGSF
Julia Sella – Colonel, PGSF, Training & Personnel
Drusus – PGSF strategy group
Fausta – PGSF strategy group
Aburia – Major, head of Intelligence Directorate, nicknamed 'Tacita'

Sepunia – Senior captain, Intelligence Directorate
Petronax – Head of Internal Security
Somna – Colonel, head of Interrogation Service (IS)
Volusenia the Younger – Retired legate
Rusonia – Legate's executive officer
Longina – Lieutenant, IS

Carina's PGSF Active Response Team:
Paula Servla, Flavius, Trebatia, Maelia, Novius Livius, Atria

Bad guys
Caeco – A heavy
Sextus – An ingénue
Trosius, Pisentius, Cyriacus – Conspirators

Palace
Silvia Apulia – Imperatrix
Stella Apulia – Silvia's eldest child
Darius Apulius – Silvia's second child
Hallienia Apulia – Silvia's third child, 'Hallie'
Caecilius – Silvia's physician

Pulcheria Foundation
Apollodorus – A career criminal, turned mostly legitimate
Pollius – Doctor, ex-member of the Foundation
Hermina – Recruiter and provider/organiser of people
Philippus – Master at arms and logistics
Albinus – Technical genius
Cassia – Financials/accounts, ex-Censor's investigator
Justus – Informer and intelligence gatherer

Other
Mossia Antonia – Owner of prestigious gym
Adianus Hirenses – 'Aidan', psychotherapist and part-time masseur
Cornelius Lurio – Commander, *Custodes* XI Station
Dania – Bar owner, Carina's protégée
Paulina Carca – Intimate friend of Lucius Punellus
Claudia Vara – Lawyer

PART I

CONSPIRACY

1

'Captain Carina Mitela?'

'Yes,' I said. 'Who is this?'

'*Custodes* XI Station. An emergency token with your code has been handed in. We're holding the presenter.'

Juno.

I dropped everything and headed for the tunnel connecting our headquarters to the police station. The duty sergeant, with a typical cop's bland expression but trying to conceal a speculative gleam in her eyes, handed me the token without a word.

As we walked to the interview rooms, I stared at the thirty-nine-millimetre diameter disc, made to imitate a casino chip, indigo blue polycarbonate shielding the tiny microprocessor. The last one I'd had in was from an informant handling incoming diplomatic baggage at the airport; her sharp eyes had spotted a very undiplomatic cargo of compact assault rifles. Sure, Roma Nova was a small country, hidden away between New Austria and Italy, but we weren't stupid or sloppy. Working with the Intelligence section, I'd traced the weapons back to their Balkan Republic origins and led a covert service unit to destroy their warehouse.

The figure I saw today through the smartplex observation window of the public interview room was slumped over, elbows on the table, hands braced her under her chin, her long black hair looking like it hadn't seen a brush for days. Mossia Antonia. She owned and ran one of the toughest, and most exclusive, training gyms in the country. Right now, she looked like a street vagrant.

I shucked off my uniform of beige shirt and pants and black tee and pulled on the casuals the *custodes* duty sergeant had found in lost property for me, ignoring the smell of stale food and cooking fat clinging to them.

Mossia jerked her head up as I entered the room.

'*Salve*, Mossia. What's the problem?' I plunked myself down on the other chair, crossed my arms and waited.

'Bruna?' She blinked and shook her head like she didn't believe what she saw.

I opened my hand in a gesture inviting her to talk.

'Aidan has disappeared,' she said, looking down and rubbing the table with her index finger. Inlaid with coffee rings from careless mugs, the plastic surface reflected the impacts of hard-tipped pens and handcuff scrapes.

'Are you sure?'

She nodded.

'How do you know? Maybe he's been called away or gone on vacation. He does have other clients apart from yours. Maybe he's working for one of them.'

Her head came up at that. 'His first duty is to me – I pay him a good retainer to look after my clients.'

'So what makes you think he's not coming back?'

'This.'

She pulled out a folded piece of paper with black, sloping writing. I read it, laid it down on the table, and leaned back in my chair. Then I picked it up and read it again. I couldn't believe it. He wrote he couldn't bear it any longer; he'd had enough of her unfair working practices. He resigned with immediate effect and would make sure her clients knew exactly why he'd done it. I pinched the bridge of my nose to make sure I was awake.

'He took nearly a thousand *solidi* from the cash drawer and my gold pen.' Mossia jabbed the air with her finger. 'Whatever. What really bugs me are those lies.' Her face was rigid and her eyes blazing. 'I could kill him for that.' Her chair crashed backwards to the ground with the force of her jumping up. She started pacing around the room like a lion in the arena.

4

I wasn't surprised at her anger. She worked her people hard, but looked after them. I knew her employment packages were first-class; as an anonymous shareholder, I'd seen her accounts.

'You've reported him to the *custodes* as a missing person?'

'I'm reporting it to you.'

'Why? I'm not the *custodes*.'

'Well, you're something like that.' Ninety-eight per cent of my colleagues in the Praetorian Guard Special Forces would take offence at that, but I let it pass.

She came to rest by the table and looked down at me.

'What?' I said.

'It's personal.'

'Were you sleeping with him?'

Her shoulders slumped and she crossed her arms across her chest.

'Silly sod.'

She pulled a small moue.

I stretched over and touched her forearm in sympathy. I shot a side glance at the watch on my outstretched wrist. Hades!

'I'll have the *custodes* log it,' I said and stood up. 'You go home now or, better, back to the gym. The *custodes* will let you know of any developments.'

She took a full stride toward me, so near that she was all but touching me. 'What do you mean? Aren't you going to do anything about it?'

'Okay, it's bloody annoying, it's hurtful, whatever, but it's hardly a case for an emergency token. Leave it with the *custodes*.'

I stepped away and pushed my chair under the edge of the table.

'Come on, Mossia, time to go. Think of the money you're not making while you're wasting time here.'

She shot me a vicious look. The anger was rolling off her. She took a deep breath, gazed unseeing at the dirty beige walls for a minute or so.

Had I been too harsh? A stab of guilt prodded me. I'd known Mossia for years, but my schedule was crushing and I was behind already.

I knocked on the door which opened inwards revealing a blue-uniformed *custos*.

'We're finished here,' I told him.

5

I looked at Mossia's taut, silent figure. 'The *custos* will see you out. I'll stop by the gym if I hear anything.'

'Well, screw you!' She turned her back to me and stalked out without another word.

'Everything all right, captain?' the duty sergeant asked me as I changed back into my uniform.

'Yes, thanks,' I said, and pinned my name badge and insignia back on. The Department of Justice *custodes* were both wary and polite with us. Back in Eastern America I'd grown up in, city cops had never liked feds either. Many of my PGSF colleagues sneered at the *custodes* and used the public's name for them – scarab, or dung beetle. I'd been a DJ *custos* once.

'Thanks for sending the alert through – I hope it hasn't been too disruptive.' I smiled at her as she escorted me back to the tunnel door. 'I'm not so sure myself what that was about.'

'No problem, ma'am.'

As the tunnel doors swished open, I felt my irritation at Mossia unwrap itself and flood back. What in Hades was she playing at? By the time I arrived at our end, I was annoyed for not being able to figure out whether she'd told me something significant or not.

The PGSF general office was plain, cramped and a mess. With the new regime, the whole floor was due for a refit. None of us could wait for it – I'd been tempted to heft a paint brush myself. Back at my desk, I checked my presentation but couldn't concentrate as I went back through the interview with Mossia. What had I missed?

'What's the frown for?'

'Um?'

'Deaf again?' came the mocking voice. Daniel.

'Funny,' I said in a sour tone. His ready, attractive smile reflected in his brown eyes. He could usually lift me out of the dumps, even though he irritated the hell out of me the other half of the time.

'I think I stepped into an alternate universe earlier on. Or maybe I'm losing it in this one. I just can't see the problem, but I know there is one.'

'Tell me,' he encouraged. Daniel Stern was a tough operational type, but he wasn't dumb. And, when he tried, he could listen. 'Why don't you think it's boy meets girl. After a while, he wants out, he grabs the cash and scarpers, leaving girl behind, hurting badly?'

'Scarpers? What's that?'

When we spoke English together, Daniel sometimes used weird words from his early days. Something to do with his uncle being brought up in England.

'Leaves, decamps, does a flit, vamooses.'

'No, it doesn't fit Mossia. She doesn't make emotional bonds. Ever. She's not cold-hearted – just desperate to protect herself. Her parents divorced and dumped her in the gladiator training camp when she was fourteen. Apparently the *lanista* was more than keen to take her after he'd seen Mossia scrapping in her school playground. Can you imagine how hard that was?' I shot a glance up at him. He shrugged.

'No,' I continued, 'it's not the personal so much as the lies he wrote.'

'Okay, so what about the boyfriend?'

'She gets a lot of clients via his counselling practice. It brings him into direct access to the great and the good.' I looked away for a moment. 'I've used him on several occasions for contacting all sorts of people. He's a very discreet intermediary. That's why I gave him a token. He's the most cynical and egotistical person I've ever met. Shell harder than Aquae Caesaris granite and about as much emotion.'

'I thought everybody liked him, you included.'

'Sure. He's beautiful, sexy, charming, fun to be with. But I've never seen or heard of him partying with anybody but clients. He gives them the physical and emotional attention they need.'

Daniel smirked.

'Whatever,' I said. 'But it's always on a commercial basis. And they pay. I've seen him sometimes when he thinks nobody's watching and, while he doesn't sneer, I'd say he was pretty cynical about the whole thing. That letter was completely off. It conflicted with everything I know about Aidan.'

'Don't worry.' Daniel chuckled. 'The ransom note will be along soon.'

'Maybe, but you know what? It was his token she brought in, not hers.'

7

· · ·

I played around with some final notes for the big meeting that afternoon but couldn't concentrate. I looked around the office at nothing in particular and chewed my el-pad stylus.

After five minutes, Daniel looked across the room at me. 'You're not going to let this go, are you?' He gave me an exasperated look. 'So, where's the letter?'

'Mossia grabbed it back as if her life depended on it. I've made a copy from memory.'

'Yuk!' said Daniel, after reading it. 'He's really putting the boot in.'

'Exactly. He'd never write so melodramatically. But then, do we really know him?'

'You know what? You're starting to sound like a cross between an agony aunt and Sigmund Freud. Let's grab some lunch.' Daniel liked eating. A lot.

The mess hall was packed. Grabbing our food from the hatch, we couldn't find anywhere but at the end of one of the long tables with Daniel's Active Response Team. All outrageously fit, and boisterous, they acted like high schoolers. In reality, they were magnificent soldiers; they could have been the model for the Hollywood stereotype. Daniel called them his boys (even though half were girls). They followed him without question because he was as crazy as them.

'So when are you going to give up all that mental stuff and join us, captain?' Galla, one of the senior NCOs was grinning at me. She'd helped rescue me in New York seven years ago when I'd been hunted by a government-sponsored killer.

'I have so much else to do than run around on open moors, climb up sheer rocks, wade through mud firing a weapon and shrieking like a banshee.'

'We don't shriek like banshees, ma'am!' said Galla. We leave that to Daniel; I mean Major Stern.'

Laughter broke out with a lot of mock punching, elbowing and shouting. How anybody didn't get a headache being around them, I didn't know. But they had more honours, decorations and awed admiration than any other team.

I preferred a silent approach. Daniel called it sneaky; I called it effective.

'Carina?' I looked up. Julia Sella, our training major – no, newly appointed Lieutenant Colonel Sella, no less. 'Everything ready? Let me know if you need anything.' Even her brown hair was soft and wavy, in tune with her personality. My mentor during my first confused days in the PGSF, and my friend now.

'Thanks, ma'am,' I said. 'I think I'm set. If it all falls apart, I'll just wing it.'

She smiled back ruefully. 'Yes, I know you probably will, but don't try it too often. Both you and the unit have a lot riding on this.'

2

Three hours later, after the last guard had left, I perched on the front row of seats in the empty hall. The zoned hall lighting that ruthlessly excluded any pooling or dark corners had been switched off except for an overhead spotlight above the rostrum. No longer shimmering under the light, the cherrywood panelling shaped to give maximum acoustics was inert.

I shut my eyes and breathed deeply. The adrenalin flow that had surged through me half an hour ago was still pulsing around my body. I could have gone out and climbed both peaks of the Gemina, without mountain gear. I'd won my new job as head of the strategy section against ferocious competition. Sure, I'd been nervous before my first presentation today as *strategos*. Who wouldn't be? It had brought back the anxiety of that first advertising pitch I'd done in New York when I was still Karen Brown – the catalyst that brought me here seven years ago.

Now I was in the place I had yearned for, where I could share my passion for strategy, play games and have fun. Hours of thinking, challenging, arguing, teaching, learning. I saw models, 3-D imaging, live intranet games, holographic battlefields, not forgetting the traditional sandbox...

So why the tape running in my head, its hum getting louder like some damn mosquito? Mossia! What *was* wrong there? I decided to pass by Aidan's later and check it out. More than likely, he had some new lover or was tied up in a poker marathon. But why that vicious letter?

The shadow of a tall figure fell over the seats beside me.

The legate. Our new chief. He'd radiated confidence that afternoon in front of four hundred alert, cocky and critical pairs of eyes. But I'd seen how he rubbed his fingers along the hairline by his temple more times than usual – his signature tell.

The previous legate, Valeria Vara, had been a political appointee, some said due to horizontal influence. She'd appointed her family clients to several positions, with really bad results – one had tried to kill me. But the troops had listened carefully today to the new legate; he commanded respect, and not a little fear. When he was deputy, he'd been frustrated under the treacherous fog of Vara's rule, but he'd succeeded in protecting and inspiring troops despite that. Some murmuring had run around the hall after he finished, but it had sounded both surprised and positive to me.

'Ready to go home?' he said. 'Do you want a lift?' He didn't need to move his lips to smile; it was in his eyes. Hazel with unfairly generous lashes, set in an angular, sculpted face. Sure, he looked good: tall, dark blond hair, the fit build of a professional soldier, but that wasn't it. Fortuna had blessed him with the gift of charm. When he smiled, every man wanted to be his friend, to have his respect and companionship; every woman wanted him in her bed.

But when he was angry, his face shrank back onto its bones, the tilting eyes tilted more, and his lips almost disappeared. When I saw that expression, I was sure there had to be a Norseman or Hun in his gene pool.

But now he was smiling. Now he wasn't the legate. He was my husband, Conradus Mitelus. Conrad. I still used the English form. That's what I'd called him when I'd met him in New York. That's how he lived in my head. And heart.

'Yes, that would be great,' I said, coming back to the real world.

'I thought they were going to eat you when you threw that challenge at them,' he teased. 'You don't hear stunned silence like that every day. But you had them like cats lapping milk out of your hand at the end.'

'Well, I hope I can live up to their expectations.' I glanced at him. 'And yours.'

He smiled again but said nothing.

At the door, we passed through the biometric scanner, collected our side arms, and stepped into the fresh air. Despite state-of-the-art environmental systems in the headquarter building, I preferred natural warmth and the breeze on my skin. Even rain was good. I turned towards the parking lot, but Conrad's faint touch on my arm stopped me. He nodded at the car approaching us. Of course, now he was the legate, he was chauffeured around. A guard stepped out from nowhere and, as the driver opened the back door for Conrad, slipped into the front passenger seat. Being a mere captain, I had to walk around the other side of the car. This was too formal. I was riding in on my Ducati tomorrow.

The early evening rush hour was hardly starting so we made good speed along the Decumanus Maximus – Main Street. In earlier times, it had been two-way, which had to have been a nightmare.

As we crossed over the Cardo Max by the forum, Conrad touched my arm. 'You look preoccupied. What's up?'

'Nothing, really,' I said. 'Well, it should be nothing. A contact sent in an emergency token today, for something trivial. Not trivial to the players' personal lives, I suppose, but definitely not justifying a token.'

'Want to run it past me?'

'No, I'll work on it for a bit first. I'm not seeing something I should,' I almost growled in frustration.

'Do I know the person or people concerned?'

'No, I don't think so.' I sighed. 'Sorry, I'm being grumpy. I don't mean to, especially today.'

I studied his face: brown shadows around eyes that had drooped back into their sockets, deep lines each side of his mouth. Away from his audience, he finally relaxed and the fatigue of the past weeks showed. I brought my hand up to his cheek. He smiled back.

Just for a second, he glanced into the rear-view mirror.

Hades. The driver and guard. I whipped my hand back down.

Conrad chuckled and whispered into my ear, 'You'll get used to it.'

I shot a sour look at him and sat back like a prim librarian.

As we approached the house, he laughed softly, like he was determined to be in a good mood. At the entrance in the high wall, I rolled my window down and held my hand against the bioscanner. We swept under the golden stone arch into the wide courtyard, tall gates closing behind us. We were home.

3

Domus Mitelarum was an imposing house, occupying the whole block and beyond. The golden stone glowed in the late afternoon sun. Conrad directed the driver to manoeuvre the car to place my side to the house entrance. The guard and driver exchanged a quick glance. As heir to the most senior of the Twelve Families, I outranked Conrad in civil life by several steps. So far, we'd been able to keep the work and civil contexts separate, each of us studying to stay in the correct bounds. Some days it was more of a strain than others.

Although my door was opened by her teenage son, Junia, the steward, greeted us herself.

'Good evening, Carina Mitela,' she said, face impassive as usual. 'Legate', she added, nodding to Conrad. 'Countess Aurelia would like you both to join her in the atrium.'

'Thank you, Junia. Straightaway?'

'Yes, lady, she was clear on that.'

Conrad started giving the driver and guard instructions for the morning.

'Um, Junia, could you put the legate's driver on the bioentry system, please? Some sort of limited access?'

Junia rescued me. 'Of course, lady, I'll arrange it immediately.' Without seeming to hurry, she was beside the car, had the driver out and was escorting her and the guard into the domestic hall door by the time Conrad and I had a foot on the first shallow step to the main entrance.

Crossing the vestibule, past the entry to our wing, the only sound came from our leather boots as they creased and relaxed with our foot movements across the marble floor. Eyeless *imagines* looked down on us from both sides of the hallway, some coloured marble, some painted. I still found them spooky, like running the gauntlet. Conrad didn't give it a second thought, but I'd been raised in the Eastern United States. The average Eastern American home didn't have rows of ancestor statues in the hallway, especially one of your mother at the end. The sculptor had caught an air of wistfulness in her face; drooping eyes, tendrils escaping from the thin ribbons around her head and curling down around the hollows of her neck, emphasising the hesitant expression – an other-worldliness. She'd run away to Eastern America at twenty, married my father, and produced me within the year. I found it hard to imagine how this descendant of a hundred generations of warriors had become the model Eastern American housewife in the few photos I had. Maybe this conflict was why she'd driven herself off a cliff into oblivion when I was three.

'Any idea what Aurelia wants?' Conrad asked me, breaking into my thoughts.

'Not a clue. Somebody's birthday?'

'Whatever it is, I hope it doesn't take long.' He ran his fingertips down the side of my upper arm onto the back of my waist. As they ran over my rear, he smiled. I returned it, holding his warm look with my own.

A burst of laughter from the atrium broke our mood and Conrad dropped his hand.

The atrium rose up for three storeys. Light from the late summer sun shone through the central glass roof onto luxuriant green planting at the centre of the room like rays from an intense spotlight. A dozen or so people were scattered around a table covered with white linen, glasses, fruit and honey cakes, olives, nuts and cheese. At the centre stood the tall, spare figure of my grandmother, Aurelia Mitela. Now over seventy, she looked twenty years younger and carried herself like the soldier she'd been thirty years before. My cousin Helena, standing next to her, had the same angular look as Aurelia, but her bones were overlaid with softer, immaculately groomed skin. How Helena balanced in those designer shoes was a mystery to me. She was talking to Conrad's uncle Quintus Tellus and his two teenage sons who hovered close by their father. Conrad groaned softly before we approached the group.

'*Salve*, Nonna.' I kissed my grandmother's cheek. Her blue eyes gleamed.

'Good evening, Aurelia,' Conrad added, lifting her hand and passing his lips over the back of her fingers. He winked at Helena who winked back, turned to his uncle with genuine pleasure, grasped arms and then remembered to nod to his two cousins.

'What's going on, Nonna?'

'We're having a drink to mark Conradus's appointment. It's over a hundred years since a Mitela has been appointed legate in the PGSF,' she said. 'A good excuse!' she added, with a mischievous smile. She'd ambushed us after a hard day, and knew it, but I forgave her easily and grinned back.

Junia's son, Macro, offered glasses of champagne around, his face serious with concentration in his anxiety to get it right. He was only sixteen, barely an adult.

We duly drank Conrad's health. I reached up and kissed him lightly on the lips. He encircled my waist with his arm and turned to the group.

'Thank you. It's been a heady few days. When I was called to the palace on Monday, I was genuinely surprised to be named legate.' His face became solemn. 'I need to ask for your patience and forbearance. Without a doubt, the work in front of me means strange hours and domestic disruption. And, yet, it's a great honour that brings credit to both families.' And he raised his glass to include his uncle.

I loved Quintus as if he were my own uncle; well, a great deal better if I compared him to Uncle Brown whose family I'd been fostered with in Nebraska after my father's death. Quintus had raised Conrad in the hard school of rural poverty after the rebellion had been defeated. Thirty years ago, Conrad's stepfather, Quintus's half-brother, Caius Tellus, had launched a coup and imposed a brutal regime that lasted barely eighteen months. But, starting years before, he'd destroyed Conrad's innocence.

I watched Conrad as he circulated, talking to Aurelia, Helena and the other guests. 'You must be so proud of him,' I said to Quintus.

'Yes.' He smiled at me. 'He's worked hard to overcome his poor start.'

'You've not done too badly yourself, Uncle Quintus.' I laughed.

In the aftermath, Quintus was lucky to have escaped with his life, exiled to the east as a country magistrate. He'd fought his way back, gaining a compassionate patron – some say lover – who'd brought him back into the circles of power. He'd sent his tough little nephew into the legions. Conrad had thrived, risen meteorically, was invited to join the PGSF as a young officer, and had now reached the top.

Quintus let his hand rest on Conrad's shoulder. Conrad half-smiled back at him. Quintus's own two sons were young and, although legally belonging to their mother's family, were often in their father's company. To me, they looked cosseted, vulnerable, softer somehow – part of Quintus Tellus's later more prosperous years.

'Will you eat with us or do you have other plans?' Aurelia asked me.

'We'd love to, but I must change,' I insisted. 'I want to see the children.'

'That's cool, cuz,' Helena chirped in. I laughed at her using the English word. She made a face back, a contrast with her poise and Vogue-like smoothness. Although she'd been a successful teacher, she'd given it up, escaped, she claimed, and now cared for my children. 'They're all ready for you,' she added. 'But Allegra will eat with us downstairs as a special treat.' My eldest was only six, but she loved to be included with the grown-ups.

'I have to step out later and run an errand,' I murmured to my grandmother, 'but I don't need to go until after dinner. It's work.'

She shrugged, somehow making it an elegant gesture. 'I understand. I'm just grateful we can all come together like this now and again.' She indicated the others with a light wave of her hand, but her gaze lingered on them. Although head of an extended tribe, Aurelia Mitela had been without close family for years. I knew she relished having one now.

Conrad and I went up to the nursery, to see the twins and bring Allegra back down with us. She walked confidently, with a secret little smile on her face as she took her place at the table. Dinner was light-hearted, even mildly boisterous, conversation pleasantly superficial. The older generation went off to the library afterwards to let my grandmother fleece them at cards and the younger one to the pool tables downstairs. Allegra pouted as Helena grasped her hand to take her up to bed but, at the door, she turned, pulled away from Helena, raised her free hand, shook it sideways in a cartoon wave, and sent us a smile that squeezed my heart.

I left Conrad and Daniel at the table, arguing some point about field tactics, and hurried across the hallway into our apartment. Rummaging in my closet, I found some old running sweats and worn sneakers. I released my hair from its plait; it was red-gold but not frizzy. Pulled back in a ponytail and secured with an elastic band, I could hide most of it at the back of my head so the colour wasn't too obvious. Shoulders slumped forwards to look younger and poorer, I checked myself in the long mirror. I slipped a thin nylon rope into my hoodie pocket along with a set of miniature tools on a ring and scanner, and grabbed a special packet of small cards from a drawer and stowed them in my pocket.

Down the back stairs and into the domestic hall. I tapped on the door. I could go anywhere in the house at any time, but I wouldn't dream of barging into the domestic hall without some form of preliminary. Even after seven years.

My father must have had help when we lived in New Hampshire before he died. Aunt and Uncle Brown had no time for anything like that, thinking it was "pure vanity".

Macro opened the door. I passed through the spacious hall, painted in pale blue with racks of hooks, open shelving on one wall and two shallow but long wooden tables, one with two terminals. Two of the younger female house servants giggling and pushing against each other exited their dining room. One cast her knowing eyes at Macro who blushed but, as soon as they caught sight of me, they looked down and hurried off toward the sleeping areas. I glanced up at the large control panel for the domestic system, seeing a cluster of biosignatures in the small drawing room and a smaller group in the games area.

The panel bleeped as I downloaded the entry code for after midnight into my ID. Down the basement stairs and out the service exit in the garage door. It was dry now, cool, but not yet chilly. You could see snow on the mountains in the distance, but only on the peaks, like in jigsaw puzzle pictures.

After twenty minutes, I crossed the Dec Max making my way to where Aidan lived. His end of the Via Nova was less busy, less well lit, mildly louche, to be honest.

At his building, I bent down as if to retie my sneaker. As I stood up, I passed my reader over the scanlock, captured the code and was in. On his floor, I fished in my pocket for the packet of cards. I glanced up and down the brick-faced corridor. No signs of company. I kept it simple and knocked at Aidan's door.

The spyhole darkened. I smiled and waved. The door opened a few centimetres. Aidan's face filled the gap. Hair mussed, his face was pale with a green-grey tinge; a line of sweat had formed above his lips; his pupils were dilated in red-rimmed eyes. He was completely still. No, rigid.

He shrank back.

Trouble. Not a doubt.

I held up a card with the words *My name is Amaelia*. He dipped his eyes down to it.

'Hey, Aidan, did you forget our run this evening?' I sang out like a cheery co-ed.

'Hi, Amaelia. Great to see you.' His lips made a painful, tight line.

Nobody else in immediate view. Was there somebody else behind him? Or to the side?

He opened the door a few more centimetres, but his body blocked the view both in and out. I couldn't see anybody over his shoulder, or any mirror. So I showed the card that said *Help needed?*

'Oh, yes,' he said. 'Umm, I forgot about the run, sorry.' His voice was on the edge of cracking.

I held up another card *Phone you?'*

'No,' he continued. 'I really can't.'

'Okay,' I said, showing the card with *Work*. 'That's too bad,' I continued. 'Do you want to reschedule?'

'Yes,' he answered, nodding his head.

'Maybe next week?'

He shook his head almost imperceptibly.

'Sure. Same time or something different?' I asked. I needed a time. He had to give me a clue.

'Same time is fine.' His Adam's apple bobbed as I saw him swallow hard. He narrowed his eyes like he was concentrating on

19

something. He glanced downwards. 'And bring Decima Amorack – we can go through the park and she can have a real run.'

'It's a date.'

He winced. His body jerked forward a fraction towards me.

'Must go,' he said and shut the door. I stared at it for a few moments, turned and bounced off along the corridor and down the stairs.

Well, that was weird. Aidan looked sick. Something, or someone, had stopped him inviting me in. He'd had the presence of mind to play along with my pantomime, but he couldn't speak. He'd looked shit-scared.

On my way back home, three things became obvious: firstly, Aidan was in real trouble; secondly, he didn't know how to dig himself out; and thirdly, I didn't have a clue what 'Decima Amorack' meant.

Still racking my brains, I jogged back to the house. How come a personal services worker, a therapist, basically a civilian, had become caught up in something that would scare him that much? He worked in a clean industry, helping people resolve problems, making people feel good, giving them a good time. The most brutal thing to happen to him would be a clamped car or a noisy neighbour playing music at full blast.

People consciously or subliminally filtered out anything that looked threatening, and rarely stepped over that invisible line. A little tax evasion here, petty theft in the office there, or not reporting something valuable found in the street formed the total of most people's experience of flirting with the dark side. I'd noticed that these upright citizens were the first to complain about law and order and public integrity. Hades take them and their hypocrisy.

I waved at Junia as I went back through the domestic hall. She smiled and called, 'Night,' in reply as I made my way through to our apartment.

'Hi.' Conrad raised his eyebrows at my dishevelled appearance. He was lying on the bed in his robe, reading his netbook, a folder shedding papers all over the quilt. I showered quickly and towelled my hair as I came back into the bedroom. I gave him a quick rundown.

'What made you think of using the cards?'

'Gut feeling. If you get it wrong, the other guy just thinks you're crazy but, in this case, it was a hundred per cent right. He's under constraint. That's obvious. He wants help but can't ask for it openly.'

'Why don't you hand it over to the *custodes*? They're perfectly capable of sorting it out.' He shrugged.

'I feel responsible. He's one of my informants, and he's given me some good stuff in the past. I can't drop him.' I glanced at Conrad. 'I won't use official hours.'

He waved his hand, dismissing my offer.

'I have to talk with Aidan away from his minders. He nodded at the *Work* card, so I guess it means a client meeting at his office, minders or not.'

4

"Amorak" was still on my mind at breakfast next morning. I mooched around silently, helping myself to food from the side, nearly putting eggs on the same plate as my fruit. I studied the caramel patch from the drops of coffee I'd spilled on the linen tablecloth as it seeped into the fibres.

'Something we said?' asked Daniel.

He'd lived with us since Conrad had sponsored his formal transfer to the PGSF. He occasionally visited his family in the Near East, but he was so firmly entrenched into Roma Nova life I think he forgot them sometimes.

'Sorry, something on my mind and I know I should know it.' I sat down beside him. 'Daniel, what does "amorak" mean to you?'

'You mean like anorak, a coat, or anorak a nerd?'

'I don't think so. Aidan said "Decima Amorak" all in one, like it was a name. Decima is tenth, but amorak isn't a Latin word.'

'Put it into Quaero Vox then,' Conrad said without looking up from his paperwork.

I bit my lip. Why hadn't I thought of that?

I tapped on the keyboard of my netbook lying at the side of my place. We were early to breakfast and my grandmother wasn't down. She forbade anything but eating and talking at the table. I sighed. She was right: it *was* bad manners fiddling with work stuff at mealtimes, but we lived in the real world.

Daniel made a face at me as I spoke into the mic. I tried a second time, avoiding his eyes. The two words together gave a "Not found", but the second word alone gave the perfect result.

'Well?' said Daniel.

I panned my smile between him and Conrad. 'Aidan is third generation Irish, isn't he?'

Daniel did an impatient twirling thing with his hand.

'Decima obviously refers to the tenth hour but, in Gaelic, "amárach" means tomorrow.'

Coffee in hand, I plunked myself down at my desk in the main office at just gone seven thirty and ploughed through messages. After reducing them to half, I glanced at my watch. Aidan should have arrived around eight so I dialled.

'Good morning.' I said in an older, accented voice, 'is that Hirenses Associates? I have an appointment around ten o'clock this morning. Could you just check, please, dear?' Then I pretended I was talking to somebody else at my end so she couldn't ask my name.

'Caterina Mac—,' she stumbled, 'Macatari?'.

'Hallo, yes, sorry. That would be MacCarthy, dear,' I corrected. 'Irish name, you know, like dear Aidan.'

Daniel mimed a vomiting gesture beside me while I listened to the receptionist's confirmation. I looked away, ignoring him, and focused on the far wall.

'Thank you, dear, and goodbye now, until later.'

'Gods! Is that the best Irish accent you can do, Carina? It was pathetic!'

'Oh, shut up and go play soldiers!'

He grinned, gave my plait a gentle tug and took off.

I had a while before the appointment, so I gave my team their orders for the day. Getting the strategy room equipped meant going up to bat with the quaestor. I groaned inwardly. Anybody responsible for issuing equipment and resources was mean with them, but the quaestor used the cunning of Mercury to guard his stores. I'd give the first shot to Drusus, a young logics graduate; not the most aggressive or even competent soldier, but the owner of a scissor-like brain. His team buddy, Fausta, had a mixed past as a black hat hacker, but only I knew that. When she'd realised she could play with the entire national encrypted security system, she'd reformed on the flip of a gold *solidus*.

I tasked them with listing and costing. Fausta belonged anonymously to several strategy gaming groups on the web so had the expertise to find what we needed. Kid-in-a-candy-store syndrome might break out, though. Drusus would pour a cold draught of realism on her enthusiasm and I would end up with a balanced requisition list.

In the field room, I selected clothes and accessories, packed them and made for the south concealed exit.

'Going somewhere interesting, captain?' the guard called out as I headed for the great outdoors. I was dressed in my preppy shopping outfit, complete with designer carrier bag.

'Yah, people to see, lunch to do.'

He smiled and gave me a quick salute.

I entered the largest department store in the Macellum quarter from the eastern street side, changed in the restroom upstairs, and rolled up my preppy kit into a plastic holdall of the type used by more mature citizens. Back on street level, I exited through a cloud of perfume in the beauty department into a large outdoor square.

Colonnades built in the sixteenth century provided shelter, encouraging shoppers to linger in front of faceless models wearing twenty-first century suits, weekend casuals and impossibly elegant gowns, all encapsulated in a fantasy world behind glass. The pillars supporting the colonnade were perfect body-width for watching people. Unfortunately, perfect also for the bad guys to loiter behind.

The large plate-glass windows on the south side reflected my disguise as a middle-aged woman dressed in a beige pleated skirt, green corduroy jacket and sensible shoes. The shoe inserts gave me a genuinely painful hobble. The worn stone sidewalk wasn't helping. I reached the office of Hirenses Associates, took a deep breath to steady myself and went up to the first floor.

'Good morning, dear,' I said as I approached the receptionist. He wore that gawky, unfinished look of late adolescents, so no more than eighteen, I guessed. 'I'm Catherine MacCarthy. I've come to see Aidan.' I gave him an anxious smile over the top of my spectacles and hovered in front of the reception counter.

'Oh, yes. He's nearly ready. Please take a seat.'

I scanned the small room. The leather couch offered a soft landing, but I chose a plain upright chair. Parallel windows let in light through bamboo-slatted blinds. Landscape prints, mostly mountain scenes, hung on all four walls. Even down to the lifestyle magazines overflowing over the edge of the little table, everything looked as menacing as a packet of vanilla cookies.

'Have you been long with Aidan?' I asked. 'He must be a lovely man to work for.'

He glanced up, looked across to Aidan's door, then back to me. Nervous rather than wary.

'His auntie, my cousin,' I continued, 'said I should look him up if I became a bit lost when I moved here. Is he very busy?'

'He's occupied with a special client now, but I'm sure he was happy to fit you in.' The boy looked flustered, seeming not to know what to do with his eyes. He looked down again, his fingers tapping on the desk, not his keyboard.

The inner door opened, and a compact, muscular man emerged and crossed to the reception counter. He knocked the pen off with the edge of his jacket cuff, glanced down at it, but ignored it. When the boy said a few words to him, the man tilted his head up and looked down his nose at him. His deliberate movements and fixed gaze as he looked over carried an intensity which to me radiated menace, but the boy didn't react in any way. I heard him make another appointment for the afternoon, a double. Was that usual? Aidan worked at Mossia's gym every afternoon as well as some evenings.

I coughed and the man's head whipped around. He focused his pale-brown, almost bleached, eyes like lasers on my face. I dropped my gaze, clutched the holdall on my lap and shrank back, as a normal person would. Through my lashes, I saw him assessing me. A second later, he dismissed me, turned and left.

I released my breath, with a little 'Oh'.

'Are you all right?' the boy asked.

'He was a bit scary, don't you think? Why did he look at me like that?'

'I'm sure everything's fine. Perhaps Martinus Caeco can be a little abrupt but he's a very good client.' Suddenly, the expression on his face stiffened. He stopped speaking, and a faint red tinge spread over his cheeks. His head went down, and he fiddled with the appointments screen.

When I called under two hours ago, the receptionist had been female. When had this kid taken over? He clearly wasn't a trained receptionist. And he hadn't answered my earlier question about how long he had worked with Aidan.

'Catherine! Welcome.'

Aidan came out of his inner office, walked up to me and kissed my cheek. I whispered in English. 'Your Auntie Marie's cousin.'

'How are you getting on? Settling in?' he replied, his English a weird combination of Irish and Latin accents. 'How is Auntie Marie? I owe her an email, you know.'

His skin had lost the grey look, but was still pale. His smile was wide and fresh. But it didn't reach his dark eyes. He drew me into his office and shut the door behind us. The smile vanished as his face crumpled. We sat down in two of the leather easy chairs clustered around a small oak table set off with a vase of tiny, perfect white roses. Looking straight at him, I started prattling, showing him a letter, supposedly from Auntie Marie but on which was written *Camera – blink once, listening bug – blink twice.*

He blinked twice.

'I know I came to see you about feeling homesick, Aidan, but can you also help me first with my new mobile phone while I'm here? It's quite confusing, and I can't switch it over to English. You have no idea how useless you feel when you're old.'

'Please don't worry, Catherine, or feel embarrassed. I'll sort it out.' He looked at me as if I was insane.

'Here it is then.' I laid a cellphone on the table, then a small cloth-covered shape. I moved the roses away, opened the shape to reveal a crystalline pyramid and placed it exactly between us.

'Okay, Aidan,' I reverted to Latin, 'this pyramid device confuses sound waves. We probably have five to ten minutes before laughing boy out there comes in with a coffee, urgent message or whatever. Any way of shaking them off so we can talk more?'

'No.'

'Okay. So what's all this about?'

He stared at me, saying nothing. I saw he was finding it difficult to process the difference between what he was seeing and what he was hearing.

I touched his hand. 'C'mon, Aidan. Talk.'

He swallowed. 'Gods, where do I start? In short, I got into debt gambling. Poker.'

My turn to stare at him. I only hoped my mouth hadn't fallen open. Aidan was known for his uncanny luck with cards. Some said he used a complex system or cheated or could read minds.

'They must have some really sophisticated system – I couldn't see it. They gave me a week to pay. Three days later, they said I could cancel the debt if I found out some information for them from inside the PGSF. Somehow they knew I had a number of clients who were scarabs or military, but I told them I didn't know their real names or what unit they were in.'

True, we all used nicknames at the gym; Aidan only knew me as Bruna, also my nickname inside the PGSF. With a membership ranging from the prominent and powerful to anybody who could pay the fees, Mossia insisted on aliases for all members. If you recognised somebody, you had to act as if you didn't know them. Weird, but that was the price of membership.

'If I didn't come up with it, they said they'd kill somebody I knew and make sure I was blamed. Right now, one of my clients is in hospital with a broken leg and collarbone from a car accident. As a demonstration, they said.' His body didn't move a muscle, but from the agony in his eyes he was burning up inside.

'So who did you target?'

'You and your friends looked like good prospects. I worked out you had to be something. Too bright – and bossy – to be an ordinary foot soldier. I didn't know whether to tell you the lot, or do what these thugs wanted me to, but when they started minding me twenty-four seven, I was trapped. I had to get somebody's attention – I was desperate. I wrote that letter to Mossia, put the token in and posted it in among the bills. I knew it would make her explode. I hoped enough to try and find you.'

'But who did you target specifically?'

'Tacita.'

Tacita? Merda.

A knock at the door. The next second, the handle moved and the door started to open. I grabbed the pyramid, stuffed it in my pocket and quickly replaced the perfect roses in the centre of the perfect table.

I picked up the cell and smiled at Aidan. 'Thank you so much, dear, for stopping that awful whine. You have no idea, it was driving me mad. Is there any chance I could have a glass of water now?'

'Of course, Catherine.' He smiled. 'Yes, what is it, Sextus? You know I'm with a client.'

'Of course, Aidan Hirenses, I apologise for interrupting you, but there is an urgent call from your afternoon appointment. He insists on speaking to you now.'

'Well, I'm not finished with my client. I'll have to call him back.' Aidan was childishly defiant. So was this Sextus one of the minders? If so, Aidan couldn't afford to rile them.

'Don't worry, dear,' I said. 'I'll wait outside while you take your call; then we can finish afterwards. You must look after your important clients. Your Uncle Brian always said so. And he was forty-five years in business! Your young man can find me a drink while I'm waiting.'

Sextus looked more than annoyed, but he was in a corner with no escape. In the reception area, he stomped over to the water machine.

Five minutes later, Aidan emerged, paler and shaken. He gave me a quick, nervous smile. 'Catherine, I'm so sorry, but we'll have to finish for today. Let me book you in for tomorrow.' With his back to Sextus, he gave me a pleading look.

'We're rather busy tomorrow, sir,' said Mr Helpful.

Aidan pulled the screen round so he could see for himself. 'Does eleven o'clock tomorrow morning suit you, Catherine?'

'Well, that would be wonderful, if you're sure that's convenient.'

'It is. Let me see you to the door. That's the least I can do.'

Sextus rose and tried to intervene, but Aidan was already walking me downstairs. He paused in the tiny lobby before the street door, breathed 'Thanks' and pressed my hand. He glanced at the door, then back up the flight of stairs. Sextus was standing at the top, arms crossed like a parent when a child comes in past midnight. Aidan's face closed, his shoulders dropped, and he dragged himself back up the stairs.

. . .

But Tacita?

Her nickname meant clever or silent. In true life, she was Major Marcella Aburia. We'd recently gotten to know each other; I'd introduced her to my battle practice group at Mossia's gym. Although not a natural action woman, she'd surprised herself, and me, by enjoying it. At least, that's how I'd interpreted her huge grin and bright eyes at the end of the session despite her gasps to recapture her breath.

At the big meeting yesterday, she'd looked nervous, almost brittle as she'd walked up to the lectern. Her notes wavered in her hands. She wasn't tall, or commanding, but she'd spoken in a clear voice and kept her poise. She was a bright cookie and, when describing her new Intelligence section in detail, she'd thrown out a few challenges. I'd seen thoughtful looks on several faces.

No, not Tacita.

After leaving Aidan's, I trudged down to the station and caught the next suburban shuttle. I couldn't see a tail but, two stops later, I left the train and made for the public library where I fussed around the fiction shelves for a quarter-hour. Nobody was following me that I could see. I glanced around and headed for the connecting door into the local curia office. In the bathroom, I released my hair, changed into jeans and tee, stuffing everything else into a nylon backpack. It was the last layer of my disguises for today. A scruffy-haired teenager, rucksack on back, trotted down the steps of the curia main public entrance, across to the shuttle and was soon in the city centre.

Back at my desk in the PGSF main office, I sorted through my messages and tried to tune out other voices: fourteen people insisting on being heard. Why did they have to shout across the room? I could hardly wait until the strategy room was equipped when I'd be able to sit quietly in front of my screen and think.

I searched the internal and allied security bases for Martinus Caeco. To be honest, I didn't expect anything so I wasn't disappointed. I went to the secure room to search PopBase which contained every piece of known data about every citizen. After the double door scanner and the optical check, the sour-faced duty information officer grunted as she entered an access code for me. She pointed me to a cubicle with a keyboard and terminal. I knew PopBase was, and needed to be, well-guarded with secure protocols, but she acted like it was her personal property. And she could have tried turning the corners of her mouth up just to see if she was able to.

I tapped away for an hour, entering different permutations, but the result was a big fat zero.

Back in the general office, I distracted myself by looking through Fausta and Drusus's shopping list. I smiled when I found a hard copy wedged firmly between the second and third rows of my keyboard with "In confirmation" written across the envelope. It was ambitious, but well-argued. All it needed was another couple of arguments for the holographic simulator, so that the quaestor couldn't find any excuse to refuse it. I messaged back to Drusus to finalise it for Friday morning.

Writing up the morning's events, I puzzled about who had sufficient resources to field a professional heavy plus minders, one as receptionist, the other at Aidan's home. With reliefs, they would need at least six. That didn't come cheap.

And how was Tacita involved? As the new head of Intelligence, she could access everything. I closed my eyes and shuddered. Had Aidan asked Tacita for any information yet? And had she passed anything to him? We could have the biggest security breach for years on our hands.

5

I arrived at Aidan's office a little before eleven. Sextus was playing at receptionist again. I hadn't used the "Cousin Catherine" character for several years, so it was unlikely anybody would recognise it. By anybody, I meant somebody with their eyes tuned, alert for something odd. Most people were preoccupied with their daily lives – children, job, taxes, sex, cat – and didn't notice anybody or anything else. Unlike television cop shows would have you believe, trying to find useful witnesses was a nightmare: nobody saw anything because nobody was looking.

Sextus was looking now, but trying hard not to. He had to be a player, but on whose side?

I delivered my best nervous smile. 'Good morning, dear, and how are you today?'

'Good morning, Mrs Macarti,' he said. He hadn't used my name to me before. He couldn't say the 'th', so he had to be Roma Novan. 'I will tell Aidan Hirenses you are here.'

Aidan greeted me as before and, as we sat down, he blinked twice.

The pyramid on the table, I started. 'What information was Tacita supposed to provide?'

'About the new legate.'

My turn to blink. 'What precisely?'

'His family, his contacts outside work, his current concerns, his vulnerability to corruption, and anything else she might find on the way.'

'And did she?'

He looked away.

'I guess that's a yes.' I glanced at the little gold clock in Aidan's cabinet. We had another fifteen minutes if we were really lucky. 'How much did she obtain?'

'She gave me his contact details, what he was working on, but she doesn't know him well enough to know the other information, but she was digging. She's doing her best.'

Doing her best to reserve a long-term stay in the central military prison.

'Have you passed it on?'

'What do you think?' He sighed. 'It was that or have my hands broken bone by bone.' He pulled his shirt out of his pants waistband. Purple bruising below his right ribs was fading to a dull yellow. He bowed his head, the blond hair falling over his forehead, his face flushed with embarrassment. 'I'm sorry, so very sorry.'

He was a normal person caught in an abnormal dilemma. Despising people for not standing up to the threat of extreme violence was easy in theory, but when faced with it, the average person was shit-scared. I'd been in that place myself. You just wanted it to go away. If pushed, most people would run away to survive. Aidan didn't have that option.

I skipped lunch. Stowing my disguise kits in the field room gave my hands some busy work. Thank the gods Aidan didn't know Tacita's and my real names to pass on to his persecutors.

A wave of cold washed through me. Tacita surely didn't disclose them? Well, whatever she'd said, it was too late now. As I pulled my uniform back on, I gritted myself for an unpleasant hour reporting a colleague to the internal security office. I trudged back upstairs but, on my way, bumped into the adjutant, Lucius Punellus.

'Got a minute, captain?' That was too formal.

'Of course, sir.' I followed him back to his office. He favoured a traditional style, eagle and flags in the corner, unit photos, comfortable but plain dark wood meeting table and chairs, all placed with military precision. Yet in his display cabinet, among the various awards and plaques, there were some childish pottery pieces and a tiny ivory finger ring – mementos of his dead daughter, I guessed.

'Now, Carina,' he said, giving me an avuncular smile. My heart sank. I knew I was going to make a rude reply. 'Have you been up to anything you shouldn't have?'

'Sorry, sir?' I didn't remember being especially insubordinate. I hadn't "borrowed" anything without signing for it or led recruits astray recently.

'Don't bullshit me!' he growled.

'No, really, I can't think of anything.'

'Hmm. Well, I overheard Petronax in the security office talking into his screen about an internal trouble. And he wasn't moaning about his bowels. He was saying something along the lines of "I'll have to rein her in before she causes any trouble". He clammed up instantly when he saw me but somehow I thought of you.'

'Huh.'

He shrugged.

Nobody liked internal affairs departments. Ours was staffed by regular military *custodes* who relished listing our faults. Maybe it was just human nature to point out other people's deficiencies. I put it down to boredom and jealousy. Unfair, I suppose; they had a job to do. Daniel wanted to take them all out on a rigorous training exercise and give them what he called a beasting. I didn't want to know what he had in mind, but I knew it would be unrelenting and exhausting.

Their chief, Petronax, didn't like me. It was personal. He sniped at me in front of others when he could. He watched me all the time whenever we were in the same room, like he was a predator waiting to pounce. Let him try.

I searched Lucius's face for further clues. He frowned, the two lines above his nose ploughed deep with worry. He played with an el-pad stylus, scratching little circles into the polished surface of his desk.

'Well, you'd better cut along now. Thanks for confirming.' He looked relieved.

I glanced back as I left He was staring down at his desk with a sombre look. Something was going on, but no way was Lucius going to give me a clue. Tempting as it was, I wasn't going to short-circuit him and ask Conrad. That was an invisible but immovable line we'd set when we started working together. I wasn't prepared to cross it. Yet.

6

Drusus and Fausta's shopping list for the strategy kit-out was now perfect. I signed it off and sent it on its way, marked urgent. I would stop by the quaestor's office in a day or two and sweet-talk him. With any luck, we might have some of the network in at the beginning of next week.

I ducked the security office visit for an hour and decided to go for a run. The locker room was deserted. A shower was running in the restroom area. It cut out while I was changing into jog pants and shoes. As I reached into the locker for a water bottle, a prickly sensation crept along my shoulders into my neck. Somebody was hovering nearby, watching me. I stretched up to the top shelf in my locker like I was searching for something. I silently counted *one, two, three*, swung my arm down hard and grabbed warm flesh.

'Ow, gods, Mitela,' came an anguished cry. Tacita. She squirmed in my grip. I had caught her upper arm and clamped her radial nerve with my fingers. My thumb pushed down hard. Something fell from her hand. I kicked her nearest leg out from under her and forced her to the ground. She gulped air. I stood over her, my foot and leg jamming her up against the lockers.

'What in Hades do you think you're doing, creeping up on me like that?' I glared down at her.

Fear, embarrassment and resentment mixed together in her face, her eyes tight and narrowed. A flash of anger there. She tried to pull back from me.

'Let me go,' she shrieked. She drew her free hand back into a fist and aimed for my knee. Before she could strike, I lunged and grabbed her wrist, jerking her arm up. I hoped I hadn't dislocated her shoulder, but she gasped like I had.

Catching my breath, I spotted something on the floor: black skeletonised metal handle, part serrated blade – a tactical folder, not a true combat knife, but deadly.

She'd meant to injure or maybe kill me.

Given what I'd discovered this morning, I didn't wait. I reached down for the knife, picking it up at the pivot between my thumb and forefinger. 'Up. You're coming with me.'

I shifted my weight to my back leg while she struggled to unfold herself from her awkward position on the floor, but gripped her arm again when she was upright.

'Where are you taking me?'

I didn't bother replying.

I dragged her along the corridor and reached the adjutant's door. I knocked and entered, pulling her in. Lucius looked up with a wary expression and flashed his eyes to the side. I followed his glance. The slight figure of Petronax, the section head of the internal security office, was leaning against the door wall, arms crossed. His fine-boned face looked like he was smelling rotting spinach.

Hades.

'Sorry, sir, we'll wait outside,' I said and attempted to withdraw.

'No, no, captain,' said Petronax, his mocking expression travelling from Tacita to me. 'I was about to leave. We're done, Adjutant, I think. Please don't let me interrupt a nice little cat fight.' He smirked at us as he went out.

One of these days, I was going to kill him. I closed my eyes for a second.

'Now what?'

'Adjutant, I am here to make a complaint to you, the senior tribune, against Marcella Aburia who attacked me with a weapon, without cause. I ask you to instigate a formal investigation, prior to summary judgement by a senior officer.'

Stunned silence. Tacita looked at the floor. I released her arm and carefully placed her knife in the centre of his desk.

'Is this true?' he asked her. His look would have scoured the coating off a non-stick pan.

She said nothing, looked away, then back down.

He stared at her for several minutes. We were like three silent statues. I could hear nothing but my own heartbeat and a faint vehicle sound outside. I saw specks of dust falling in the sunlight by the window.

Eventually, still looking at Tacita, Lucius leaned forward and pushed a button. 'Sergius, get in here stat and take a statement.' *Testis unis, testis nullus* – Lucius was very careful about procedure. The adjutant's exec slid into the office, scarcely making any noise on the wood floor. He glanced at us, hesitated for a moment, then came to rest at the side of Lucius's desk.

Lucius waved his exec and me over to the meeting table. 'Sit over there and you,' he jabbed a finger in the direction of Sergius, 'take Captain Mitela's statement.'

When I had no more to say, Lucius beckoned me towards him. He flicked his fingers at Tacita to take my place at the table. As we passed, she shot me a venomous look. She gave Sergius her name and refused to say anything else.

Lucius wandered over to the other side of the room, arms crossed, the first two fingers of his right hand tapping on the shirtsleeve of his left upper arm. He stared into the display cupboard. The afternoon light fell on the folds of his face, casting shadows, highlighting the tensed muscles in his face.

After another minute, he turned abruptly and strode over to Aburia. 'If you don't defend yourself now, in the face of your accuser, I'll have no other choice but to arrest you.'

She looked up, blinked and shook her head.

He came back to his desk and growled into his commset. 'Adjutant. Security detail to my office, stat.' He dismissed Sergius, instructing him to message the statements back the second they were finished.

He looked at Aburia like she was an insect to be stepped on. 'Gold eagle and rank badges on the desk, and empty all your pockets.'

We were all silent until the detail arrived. I watched the hands on

Lucius's old-fashioned clock as it ticked away a long five minutes. He was dedicated to the PGSF. He'd defend you to the point of stupidity if he thought you were doing the right thing, but he wouldn't tolerate any deliberate act of disloyalty. Two guards arrived, and he instructed them to take Aburia into close custody until further notice. They showed no reaction as they marched her away.

I couldn't say anything. I just stood there, feeling blank. Lucius had been tapping on his keyboard for several minutes when I took half a step sideways.

'Stay where you are.'

I froze.

'Right,' he said, looking up when he'd finished, 'now kindly explain what in Hades this is about.'

'I don't have a clue,' I said. 'One minute I was changing into sweats, the next fending off a crazy trying to stab me with a lethal blade.'

'I've requested the medics to carry out a substances test immediately she arrives in the custody suite.' He paused. 'They'll also do blood just in case it's a bad attack of PMS.'

Gods, what a patronising comment!

'Take that look off your face – it happens.' He tapped a few more keys then fixed me with his eyes. 'Sure there isn't any trouble between the two of you?'

I was tempted for a few seconds to disclose the Aidan situation. The only reason she could want to attack me was to stop me reporting her to Petronax for a security breach. But I'd told nobody. Sure, I'd made general notes on the central registry about visiting Aidan undercover, but details would be held securely in my case lock box on the system until formal charges were framed. She couldn't have known what was said, unless she'd overridden the privacy control. Damn! As head of Intelligence, could she have done that?

Whatever, Aburia was neutralised now so there could be no further leaks. I wanted to investigate further. I needed to find out exactly why these people wanted such personal information about Conrad.

I shook my head, and Lucius let me go. My complaint would grind through the internal security office bureaucracy. I groaned at the pleasure it would give Petronax.

I absolutely had to go see Mossia now. Not only did I need to rebuild my friendship with her but she was my only open lead to Aidan. She wouldn't have gotten over the other day yet. I'd be in for a workout that she'd ensure was punishing.

Scanning my gym pass at the door, I nodded at the receptionist who gave me the false smile he gave everybody unless you were young, male and beautiful. I hesitated in front of the archway leading to the changing rooms. Today, it reminded me of a lobster pot. I went back to the reception counter and booked a full hour massage for after Mossia had destroyed me.

The gym formed only part of the complex. A superb set of hot, cold and warm rooms on the traditional Roman pattern was complemented by a Japanese massage pool and an Olympic-standard swimming pool. The gym itself consisted of a large hall with various sets of machines for torturing flabby and not so flabby bodies, a small indoor arena and a series of practice rooms. The fun part was the laser tag battle zone, the one I'd introduced Tacita to. For the sheer adrenalin-pumping exhilaration of stalking opponents and unleashing a volley of laser fire in a battle of wits and fitness, it was unequalled. Well, for the thirty or so minutes it lasted.

Around a dozen other women were pulling on gym wear in the changing room and chatting. My foot on the bench, I was bending over tying my sneaker when the babble cut. Mossia. I straightened up and smiled at her.

'Come with me,' she said with gritted teeth and turned, stalking off. At her office door, I studied the worn indents on the old-fashioned keypad lock. Anything to distract my mind from what was coming. Inside, it had everything you'd expect, plus a wall of around twenty photos of Mossia in her arena competition days. One with a gilt frame predominated and showed her triumphant, magnificent sword in her hand, her long, black hair loosened, curling down her back. She was receiving her prize in the Circus Maximus on a sunny day several years ago. She stood now, arms crossed, with her back to them so that I faced a horde of dangerous and armed Mossias.

'I hope you have a good explanation for how you treated me.' Her mouth was a tight, puckered line. I saw anger in her eyes, but also embarrassment in the red patches on her cheekbones. 'I was upset and you cared less than if I was a dirty arena fly.'

She turned her back to me and took her time running her fingers over the pommel and down the creamy wire-inlaid grip of a ceremonial *pugio* dagger in the open glass display cabinet. The grooved, waisted blade was flat and wide with razor-thin edges. It was twenty centimetres of meanness.

I walked over to her desk, away from the knife, willing her to follow.

'I want to show you something.' I pulled out the crystalline pyramid from its velvet cover and placed it in the centre of the desk. 'Now we can't be overheard.'

'What's that?'

'It scrambles sound waves within a fairly tight area around itself. It sounds like gibberish on surveillance bugs or recorders.'

'You think my office is bugged? Are you paranoid?'

'It's unlikely, but something strange is going on, and I'm not taking the least chance.'

'What do you mean: "something strange"?'

'That's the problem – I haven't worked it out yet.' I waited for a few moments then took a deep breath. 'Mossia, I'm sorry if I upset you the other day. I had so much else on my mind. I didn't mean to put you down.'

I let my words settle in and waited for her reaction. She frowned at me, her dark eyes mobile, unreadable. After a few moments, the red faded from her cheeks. The tension swelling her face lessened and her jaw relaxed.

'Oh, for Hercules' sake, get on with it,' she said and plunked herself down on her red leather chair.

'Just how close were you to Aidan?'

She shrugged. 'We got together about three months ago,' she said, 'but it's a very open relationship.' She sounded defensive. 'We're both professionals with personal clients we can't neglect.'

So, the bottom line was still important. A lot more like the Mossia I knew.

'We agreed that if we needed to give a client personal attention, then that was how it had to be.' She grimaced.

'It goes back to that night you brought your new group here. Aidan was helping out as part of the massage team for your lot after your game. One of the girls had gone off sick, so he stepped in. It was a while since he'd worked as a masseur, but he remembered all the moves.' She rolled her eyes. 'He and your friend Tacita seemed to hit it off. I think he saw her a few times after that. One night, she was leaving in a hurry and looked upset. She looked as guilty as Hades. I wondered if she'd left without paying. The next day, I got that letter from Aidan. He put it in an envelope with another note saying I was to take his lucky gaming chip to the scarabs and ask for Bruna.'

I raised my eyebrows at that. Tokens were personal, not transferable.

'I threw it in the bin with the letter. But when I calmed down, a little, I thought about how he would always keep it within reach. It was the last thing out of his pocket at night. He'd put it carefully on the bedside table. Telling me I had to take it to the scarabs was weird so I rescued it from the bin. I hadn't seen you for days so I took it to the central *custodes* station. I knew they'd make sure it reached you.'

She paused, looking over my shoulder, plainly not wanting to meet my eyes.

'Then you were so cold-blooded.' A hard edge crept into her voice. 'Perhaps it was good. It made me stop feeling sorry for myself. I wanted to kill you, but I knew I couldn't do it there, surrounded by scarabs.' She gave me a calculating look. 'I knew you'd come here eventually and I'd get my chance.'

Juno! I tamped down a stab of fear. I was considered an efficient fighter. I'd even beaten Mossia occasionally, but she had been a professional gladiator. Although they never fought to the death these days, she was perfectly capable of terminating me without a moment's second thought.

'Don't worry, Bruna.' She grimaced at me. 'I'm not going to kill you today. You're too valuable a client!'

7

I arrived home after an exhausting round in the indoor arena with Mossia. The massage and a restorative session in the baths had eased the muscles, but not the tiredness. But now I knew why the token had been cashed in: Aidan had no other way of calling for help.

I hung around in the main house making conversation with my grandmother about the upcoming family day, the fall holiday at the farm with the children, her travel plans.

'Stalling, darling?'

'Whatever do you mean?'

She snorted. 'I know a delaying tactic when I see one. You'll have to have it out with him sometime, but if it's about work, try not to quarrel before sleeping.'

I tipped my head sideways, gave her a half-smile and conceded. 'Something trivial is becoming more of a problem than I thought. It's like chasing spaghetti around a plate with a knife. Then, today, I was attacked by another guard.'

'You're unhurt, I presume?' she asked in a calm voice, knowing how I hated a fuss.

'I'm fine. But let's say I was more than surprised.'

'Did you tell Conradus?'

'Not directly.' I looked away. 'I reported it through the proper channels,' I said to the floor.

'Ha!' She looked at me with a sardonic gleam in her eye. She folded her hands, the thumbs interlocking. 'Have you considered that restructuring the land forces, including the PGSF, may have upset people at a political level?'

I stared at her in surprise.

Then I realised I was being naïve. Apart from discomfort felt by individuals within the unit, the changes could have upset the delicate client/patron system that dinosaur families like the Varae still practised.

After retiring from active service in the PGSF when her mother died, my grandmother had served abroad as a diplomat and, later, as senator and foreign minister at home. She knew how to swim around the oily political sea, and which fish would bite.

I kept forgetting this sort of thing was instinctive to home-bred Romans like my grandmother and Conrad. I'd studied hard and read everything I could grab hold of to catch up since that waiting time in the legation in Washington, but the delicate stuff of the political system still flowed way over my head.

Drained mentally and physically, all I wanted to do was fall into bed. My limbs were aching with tiredness when I arrived at the door to our apartment.

Inside, Conrad was waiting for me.

As soon as I came through the hallway and made for our bedroom, he followed me in. He leaned his shoulders against the wall and crossed his arms. Only his eyes moved, tracking me as I threw my gym clothes in the wash basket, cleaned my face and brushed my teeth. He didn't say anything, just stared. This was stupid. I wouldn't allow myself to feel like a deer caught in headlights. I hadn't done anything wrong. He could stand there looking dangerous and enigmatic all night for all I cared. I was going to bed.

'Something you might possibly think you should mention to me?'

'In what connection?' I replied, equally coldly.

'Like nearly getting yourself killed this afternoon.'

'Oh, that.'

'Yes, that. I nearly choked when Lucius sent the report through. Didn't you realise that I needed to hear it direct from you? Yet I learned second-hand you'd swanned off to the gym. What in Hades were you playing at?'

'Sorry,' I said sullenly.

'Not good enough.'

'I followed the correct procedure and the report came through to you. I only did what any other guard would have done – I filed my accusation through the senior tribune.'

'So I'm supposed to ignore the fact that you might be lying in the mortuary with a knife sticking out of you?'

I took a deep breath. 'We agreed a long time ago you can't give me special treatment. It works both ways.'

The expression on his face hardened. He launched himself from the wall, reached me in one stride and grabbed my wrist. The outer edges of his eyes seemed to tilt upwards. Copper brown flooded out the green. and his eyes blazed as they bored into mine. I shivered inside. He was scary as hell when he lost his temper. And his grip was hard, pinching my skin up into folds.

After a minute, he swallowed and dropped my wrist. He turned sideways to me, poured himself some water from a bottle. The surface of the water in his glass trembled with his hand.

'There's also the inconvenience,' he said as he turned back to glare at me, 'of having no head of my Intelligence section.'

'Oh, good, now we have our priorities sorted out. I'm glad that's clear.'

Neither of us moved a muscle. We both raged: he from deep concern, me from his over-protectiveness. I despaired. Would we ever hit the right balance?

'All I'm saying is that I'd have preferred you to come and see me,' he said sullenly.

'I couldn't come running to you like teacher's pet.' I glanced at him. 'If it helps, I was blindsided. One minute, Aburia and I were colleagues; the next, she's trying to split me open with a knife.'

'I hate seeing you threatened in this way.' He came over and took my hand, cupping it in his. 'You were right to go to Lucius.' He let a deep breath out then kissed my forehead. 'I know it's not easy for you,' he said. 'Or me.'

I wrapped my arms around him and pressed my face into his neck.

'Drink?' he offered, a little later.

We sat on the balcony, not quite warm enough in our robes, but

44

friends again as well as lovers, his arm resting along the back of the teak bench, his fingers playing with my hair. We sipped wine, letting our eyes rest into the distance out over the backyard as the sun gave out its last light. A pretty garden with walkways, now illuminated, it gave way to lawns which sloped gradually down to the river. Tall cedars and oaks provided welcome shade in summer over part of the parkland; the result of my great-great-grandmother's time in England as a diplomat. She'd obviously visited too many big piles over there and fallen in love with the Capability Brown look. Luckily, another more capricious ancestor with a sense of humour had planted a maze as well as secluded intimate gardens on the south side.

'So how far are you along with your investigation?' Conrad asked.

I was relieved to tell him everything I'd discovered. He listened carefully; his face tensed when I recounted my second heart-to-heart with Mossia earlier that afternoon.

'Well, in light of Aburia's attack, this is looking far more serious,' he concluded. 'Let's extract Aidan and have a chat with him.' He glanced at me. 'You'll lose your anonymity over this one.'

I shrugged. 'It'll be all right with Mossia – she doesn't give a damn about status. As for Aidan, he's been a useful source – I've had my money's worth out of him. I'll see how things work out once we've finished.'

'Your op. I'll advise Lucius and Daniel. I presume you'll want to use your own team as core?'

'We'll start rehearsing tomorrow.' I was already playing different tactical scenarios through my mind.

He nodded. How illogical he was. He was perfectly happy for me to lead a dangerous operation, but had gotten more than uptight about Aburia's attack.

We sat for a few more minutes in silence, before I asked the question at the centre. 'So why do you think the thugs holding Aidan wanted this particular info about you? Not your military role but the stuff about your attitudes, corruption and your wider family.' Which of course, meant his former partner, the Imperatrix Silvia and their three children. But that was public knowledge; it was recorded in the imperial family records.

'Sounds like standard intelligence gathering to me,' said Conrad. 'But go through the threat board tomorrow. Nothing came up on the joint watch report today, but worth checking if Justice and the *custodes* have anybody on their radar at the moment. It's starting to sound political, and that could mean terrorists.' His voice hardened. 'I won't tolerate anybody's active service units operating here. Any we find will be terminated.'

Next morning, I took off for the office straight after I'd showered and dressed. As I rode through the streets on my new toy – a Ducati – I was fuelled by the blood-adrenalin mix pounding through me. I took that extra risk sliding into gaps in the traffic, stopping a little too quickly, edgy to storm away the second the red light flashed to green. I loved the strong surge of energy when faced with a new challenge, a "call to action high", Daniel called it. It would power me through until the operation was finished.

I messaged my Active Response Team to assemble in my unfinished strategy room for 13.00. Fausta and Drusus had rescued two folding tables and a dozen stacking chairs that didn't from the recycling pile. I darted between the hard plastic chair where I sat when attacking my netbook keyboard and the easel where I scribbled diagrams on my flipcharts. Where in Hades were my network and large electronic touch displays?

I shook off my irritation and started. After an hour, I had fingers stained with red, blue and green ink, but I had the whole thing pulled together. I sat back and shut my eyes for a few minutes.

The heavenly aromas of fresh brewed coffee and just-baked rolls. I opened one eye. Fausta smiled down at me. 'I thought you might like to eat something, ma'am, as it's nearly ten o'clock.'

'Fausta, you are wonderful, thank you.' Especially as I'd discovered that she regarded coffee as a recreational drug of dubious choice. 'Can you fix me an appointment ASAP with the legate, please? And ask Major Stern to attend.'

I ran my plan past Conrad who grilled me for a full twenty minutes. Daniel listened quietly and added a few tactical and equipment suggestions. He was the operational expert and transformed into a cool, analytic commander when something serious was going forward. He thought my Active Response Team would be more than enough to carry it through. When I suggested using some of the Intelligence section for the first stage, I glanced speculatively at Conrad.

'Yes, of course, you'll need them,' he answered, his voice downbeat. He looked preoccupied for a few moments, and then came back to us. 'I'll put Aburia's number two, Sepunia, in charge for the moment. Liaise with her.' He handed me a signed operations order, gave me a quick nod and went back to his desk.

As Daniel and I walked back to the strategy room, he said, 'Do you want me to sit in the team briefing session?'

'If you like,' I answered automatically, momentarily distracted by Conrad's sombre mood. I could see how stricken he was by Aburia's betrayal, particularly as he was trying to rebuild morale in the unit. Dishonour of core Roma Novan values was offensive, particularly in a military officer sworn to state service. Despite the lack of them around them in the late fourth century, Apulius and the founders knew upholding values was critical to survival and had hammered them into every part of life in their new colony.

'Sorry, Daniel, that wasn't very gracious of me. Yes, of course.'

'Tough times,' he said.

'Really?' Livius said. 'This is a simple extraction, surely?'

A fast-tracker because of his military skills and ability to think, Livius was already an *optio* waiting for his promotion to centurion. But sometimes he was a little too confident.

I looked at him and tipped my chin up. 'If it was, do you think I'd be wasting my time trying to herd you bunch of prima donnas into line? No, it isn't that simple,' I continued. 'We not only need to rescue the hostage, but take all the hostage-takers alive and uninjured, and immobilise booby traps without triggering any remote systems. Anybody with these resources has to have a remote warning or surveillance system.' I jabbed my index finger at the probable enemy capabilities and threat list on the flipchart.

'The extraction must not be seen as such, or as an arrest from the street, either before, during or after. The opposition will be watching.

We also have to assess both work and home locations, and plan for both.'

Something in my expression kept them quiet for a few moments, even Trebatia, who could have won prizes for wholesale chattering. Of all the team, Flavius looked the most serious, eyes creased but unfocused. I remembered that expression from my first undercover mission seven years ago when I met him. Novius chewed his lip, already sketching some overlapping line diagram for the technical framework.

'Is there a particular reason for this level of stealth?' asked Paula Servla.

'There's always a good reason – just take it as read,' I said, drawing breath to move on to the next subject.

'Yes, obviously,' retorted Paula. I could see from her sceptical expression that she didn't buy it. She saw too much. When I'd transferred into the PGSF, she'd been the first to work me out.

'What I meant was,' she continued, 'is there a wider security or even political aspect here?'

The others gaped at her except Flavius who smiled to himself. He knew me too well. As always, Paula detected the underlying dimension. Was it simply experience, intuition, or was she borderline telepathic?

I glanced sideways to Daniel, who nodded. I pulled out the pyramid jammer and placed it on the table. Seven other pairs of eyes looked down at it, some diverting glances to me.

'This might sound a tad melodramatic or even paranoid...' I began.

'Oh, surely not?' came a sarcastic female voice. Atria.

'...but I cannot stress enough, the secrecy of this operation. We don't know who our opponents are, whether they're friendly or hostile.'

'Surely, hostile?' Flavius looked up. He sounded surprised at having to ask.

'Well, not necessarily. The thing that bugs me is that Aidan isn't dead.'

'True,' Flavius said. 'That's quite strange, even benevolent.'

'Precisely. Given the level of threatened violence and the opponents' professionalism, it's illogical.'

'We're not crossing somebody else's operation, are we?' Flavius asked.

'Not that we can see,' confirmed Daniel from the side. 'We've checked the whole spectrum, other agencies, everything. Absolutely nothing on the joint watch net. Intel are running a box at the moment, tracking everything at home and office. Maybe they'll come up with something.'

Somebody snorted.

'We don't know if they're foreign or home-grown,' I added. 'But from what I saw and heard in Aidan's office, my money's on home-grown.' I caught some angry looks at that. If the bad guys were so competent, they could only have come from within the intelligence or law enforcement communities.

'Gods, this is a blind one,' said Atria.

'Totally.' Just that word unsettled my audience. None of us was used to this. We practised scenarios concentrating on the fundamentals, banking the experience so that when the tactical situation fell apart, as it did on occasion, and you didn't have time to think about what to do, the training clicked in automatically. We trained hard to make drills mirror operations to the extent that live operations ran like drills, but with added intensity, sometimes regrettably with blood. We knew how each other thought, so could adapt fluently when the situation was different from the intel to hand before the start of an operation. Here, the problem was that we had nothing to hand apart from the plan of Hirenses Associates' offices.

'Right,' I said, 'let's pull this together. Firstly, no breath of this operation to anybody outside this room. We act as if we are running a training session. Although we have a go from the legate, this operation does not exist.' No reaction.

'Next, I've drawn up a plan with allotted tasks.' I messaged their el-pads. The puzzlement in their eyes changed to concentration as they read and absorbed their instructions.

'So, Phase I must be completed by tomorrow afternoon; reports by 16.00, please. Those not already in the field meet outside the back practice room tomorrow at 17.00 when we will appear to go for a run in the woods with suitably filled backpacks. If there are no other questions, we'll break until tomorrow.' I turned to Novius. 'Nov, I'd like you to stay, please.'

49

They pulled themselves out of their seats and left. I smiled my thanks at Daniel, and he went off to find out if Intel had uncovered anything.

'Right, Nov, how do you see this working? Tell me what you need.'

'Well, you know this instant cut-off you want, we can—'

A knock at the door. I grabbed the pyramid and shoved it in my pocket.

'...so that's how I see the new equipment for the team,' he concluded in a slightly tense voice as the quaestor strode in.

'Sorry to interrupt, captain, you seem to have an outage. I've been trying to contact you for the past thirty minutes.' He didn't look at all sorry and glared when I didn't react. 'I need to test your comms unit,' he growled. 'Now.'

'Quaestor, we are in the middle of a meeting here.'

'The quicker I test it then the quicker you can resume your meeting.'

'Of course, I would be delighted to cooperate and support your efficient approach,' I said. 'Will my equipment requisition be treated with equal dispatch?'

'Humph!'

He scanned my ear and mouth units. He grunted and left with the same grace as when he'd arrived, not quite closing the door. I just hoped he didn't need to scan anybody else who'd been at our meeting and see the same outage: using a pyramid within the Praetorian building was forbidden. I pushed the door closed and jammed a folded wedge of flipchart paper under the lower edge.

'Right, Nov, let's have a look at your ideas,' I resumed, pyramid back on the table.

8

Everything was in place. I hoped Aidan could hold out. I thought about calling by as "Amaelia" the jogger, but she wasn't due for another couple of days (and with the infamous Decima). I could go back to the old stand-bys: pizza delivery, neighbour seeking help, courier drop-off. But Intel were watching and I didn't want to cross their operation.

Back home, I went for a swim. We had a beautiful pool in the basement. Irrationally, I regarded it as my personal property and, more rationally, tried to use it every day. The hypnotic rhythm of length after length, back and forth, in the warm, moist atmosphere settled my thoughts as well as calming my body. Water flowing intimately over my skin always gave me physical pleasure. Dappled light dancing on the mosaic walls enhanced the seductive dream-like ambiance in the pool area. I felt myself blending with the water and drifting...

My semi-stupor was broken by a discreet cough.

'Sorry to interrupt you, lady, but the Countess would like us to meet in half an hour's time to discuss the family day.'

Crap! I swam over to the edge where Junia stood like some implacable messenger from the gods.

'We've postponed it twice.'

Hours of talking nicely to, let's be honest, fairly boring people who all they shared with you was a name and a few genes. I should have felt ashamed at feeling like that, but didn't. I tried to stare her out, but she refused to budge.

'Very well, Junia, you win.'

Sitting in my grandmother's office, making faces at Helena who'd also been dragged in to help, I tried to be constructive, but it was boring. Nonna and Junia had it zipped up so all we did was drink wine and make rude comments about family members.

'Where on earth shall we seat Lucius Mitelus Superbus?' Junia frowned over her table plan.

'Not next to me!' No danger, really. I was on the top table and he was a nobody. His wife Valeria was nearer as a second cousin.

'Nor me,' squeaked Helena, realising she was much more vulnerable. 'Gods, if anybody had an appropriate *cognomen*, it's him!' She was right: he thought his branch should be senior with him as head of the family. He was a pretentious, arrogant jerk with bad breath and a creepy smile. Although I knew this social stuff was important to the family's powerbase, I didn't need it when I was trying to concentrate on the operation. I yawned.

My grandmother looked down her long nose at me and said briskly, 'Well, I think we'll finish for now – Carina Mitela looks as if she is falling asleep. We'd better not disturb her.'

Junia and Helena sat there immobile and silent.

'I apologise, Nonna, I did not intend to be impolite.'

'We sometimes have to turn our efforts to less welcome areas and carry out duties towards others which we would rather avoid.'

She frowned at me like Mr Olsen, my high school principal, used to when I'd failed an easy exam. I felt fifteen years old and just as embarrassed.

I was still smarting from my grandmother's reprimand as I gulped down my coffee. I hated being in the wrong. It overshadowed all the right things you'd done and crippled your judgement of things you still had to do. But she was right. I had a privileged position and needed to pay some attention to the balancing obligations and responsibilities. But I didn't have to like it.

When I decided I'd beaten myself up for a sufficient time, I went along to the nursery to see the children as they went to bed. Conrad was already there, tickling Tonia's toes while she giggled hysterically. Around the corner, Allegra was combing her hair in front of her mirror. She stared intently at her reflection; her mouth was set in a straight line. Such a solemn face for a six-year-old. She'd inherited my bright blue eyes, but the red brown hair came from my mother. I picked Gil up, kissed him. He smiled. My heart fluttered. He giggled and burrowed his head into the fold of my arm. Allegra broke her gaze and, still carrying Gil, I went through into her room.

'Hello, darling,' I said. 'You look as if you have some serious thoughts in there.' I stroked her forehead.

'Great Nonna says I'll have a long tunic and *palla* for the family day and must behave myself with grace and decorum. What's decorum?'

Where to start? I was in no way qualified to answer, but I tried. 'I see it as doing the right thing, in a polite way, but not allowing yourself to be pushed around by anybody else. But, hey, Allegra, if you do it wrong, just smile. They'll forgive you.'

Helena looked over at me and frowned.

'Oh,' Allegra said, 'I thought it meant standing there being bored, not saying anything while the grown-ups commented on how much you'd grown.'

I burst out laughing, which set Gil off giggling into my chest. I stroked his soft hair. 'Well,' I replied, 'I'm not very good at it, either. Nonna told me off earlier for not behaving properly.'

Allegra's eyes came out on stalks. 'You?'

'Yes.' I chuckled. 'Here's the thing, Allegra, let's you and I watch out for each other on the day and make a secret signal to each other if we think the other one is losing it.'

'Deal,' she said, using the English word.

'Deal,' I confirmed.

When they were all tucked up, passing through drowsiness on the way down to sleep, Helena waved off the light and ushered Conrad and me out .

'Honestly, you two are a piece. I settle them for bed and you come along and hype them up.' She waggled her red-lacquered finger melodramatically.

Helena had given up, she said escaped from, teaching other brats and now educated my brats. She said she could shout at them without

53

censure as they were family. This was an act she put on. My children were wonderfully looked after. Allegra delighted everybody she came into contact with. She was quick, and charmed her way into and out of anything she wanted; maybe something to watch as she got older. The twins were just hitting the terrible twos, but Helena was a past mistress of the art of distraction.

She paused, turning to look at me. 'Are you all right? You seemed only half there this afternoon. Aurelia was really pissed with you.'

I made a face. 'No, everything's fine. I just have a difficult training exercise coming up and I have to impress the new legate,' I said, glancing at Conrad who gave me a little smile. 'I heard he's a real horror, so I'm shaking with nerves.'

'Yeah, right.'

9

"Catherine MacCarthy" rang Hirenses Associates next morning about her missing umbrella.

'I'm sorry, Mrs Macarti,' said Sextus after a brief pause, 'I can't see one anywhere. Perhaps you left it on the shuttle?'

'No, dear, I'm sure I had it when I came to see you, and I've lost track of it after that.'

He sighed. Silence.

'Oh, well, I'll drop in later or tomorrow morning. Please give my love to Aidan.'

I was in the field room checking kit for the operation when a priority message with a caution tag came through from Sepunia. I didn't know her that well: she'd sat quietly in meetings offering careful supplementary remarks like a good number two when Aburia was giving her reports. For her to use a caution tag was really something, which is why I sauntered down the corridor to Sepunia's open door in the Intel room like I was on a casual Sunday outing.

'*Salve*, Sepunia.' I knocked on the door frame and smiled. 'Anything for me to brighten up a dull day?'

'Hello, Carina, nice of you to drop in. Come in and sit down,' she chirped at me. We were like a couple of girls sorting out our social calendars. I closed the door and she flicked the smartplex windows to frosted. Her face dropped from bright and breezy to one hundred per cent serious.

'The surveillance team reports that Aidan is travelling in his normal pattern between home and office,' she began, 'but he's either in the company of, or in direct sight of, a minder. We've identified four other definites, plus another two possibles. I can't confirm the last two, but they appear more frequently than they should if they were the general public.' Sepunia handed me printouts with photos. 'I've run these images from the public surveillance feed and the box against our database and the *custodes* one and found no matches.'

'So who are these guys?' I studied the images. 'Wait a minute, they're all guys – there are no women.'

'Exactly. How do you think that's relevant?'

'Not a clue, but it's weird, and weird almost always means something. Okay, that's really helpful. Thanks, Sepunia,'

She looked at me, obvious curiosity in her eyes, but didn't push it.

Reports came in from about three onwards: Livius was *in situ* and would remain there until the start; Novius's framework was ready; Atria was serving coffee with a smile across the road; Flavius had already mended a pipe, taken in mail and cleaned the hallway in Aidan's office building – the perfect concierge.

We were ready.

By 11.00 the next morning, Aidan was sitting in the PGSF barracks, looking pale, drinking tea and recovering his breath. Both his apartment and office were secure and guarded, a new receptionist installed in his office, and a note on the website about family bereavement.

My report would detail how a middle-aged woman walking awkwardly (those inserts nearly crippling me), accompanied by her attractive niece (Maelia wearing her best spoiled pout), had called at Hirenses Associates earlier that morning, looking for the aunt's umbrella. The minute after the two women entered the reception area, Sextus, the receptionist, was suddenly overcome by a coughing fit. The niece, wearing a figure-hugging, electric blue dress that barely included a skirt, made straight for Aidan's consulting room. The occupants – Aidan and Caeco – were stunned, momentarily by her smile and body, then by gas. The building security and comms lines had inexplicably blipped, but everything was back on line within three seconds.

The only exciting thing was outside. Two cars had collided. The drivers cursed and threatened each other; it progressed to a full-blown fist fight. One passenger had hysterics, and the coffee shop server ran out to help. A uniformed concierge tried to separate the two fighting drivers. The *custodes* arrived and arrested everybody they could lay their hands on. A number of people exiting Hirenses Associates were caught up in the *custodes'* sweep along with several interested bystanders. Soon after the custody vans disappeared, a car transporter and city cleaning detail cleared up the mess, and the district went back to sleep.

Daniel was waiting for us with a security detail at the *Custodes* XI Station. Caeco, Sextus and the three bystanders were bundled into a secure vehicle and driven back to the PGSF. We were at the back garage door, about to clamber into an unmarked truck to follow them, when I heard an echo from the past.

'Ha! I heard a rabble had been brought in, but I didn't expect it to be this scruffy.' A tall, bulky figure with a grin breaking up his harsh-featured face stopped in front of me.

'Hello, Bruna.'

'Hello, Lurio,' I replied, grinning back.

'Love the outfit,' he snorted. 'But you'd be so much better out of it.'

Everybody snickered. Daniel looked offended. He didn't know that Lurio and I had briefly been lovers several years ago.

'Aren't you going to introduce me to your team?'

'Everybody, this is Commander Cornelius Lurio, DJ inner city commander.' But I signalled them to move out. Shielding their departure, I turned to Lurio. 'You remember Major Stern from the Pulcheria operation.' I shot a warning glance at Lurio. Daniel didn't know the inside secrets from that operation.

'Yes, of course.' He scanned Daniel's face, nodded at him. Daniel gave a taut smile. 'And your other friends…?'

'Oh, they're a bit shy.'

'Well, you'd better get going. We'll need to give this garage a good sweeping out now.' His face suddenly dropped into solemn, and he ran his finger down my cheek. 'Give me a call sometime if you're ever fed up playing secret soldiers and want to rejoin a proper service.'

'And up yours, too, Lurio.'

He burst out laughing.

'What the hell was that about?'

'Just a bit of inter-service banter,' I said. 'You know we worked together at the Department of Justice when I was a *custos* in his section.'

'Yes, well. But he—'

'Just keep your eyes on the road, Daniel!'

Surprisingly, we reached the PGSF barracks in one piece. I went down to the custody area to brief the Interrogation Service team who were to deal with Caeco, Sextus and the three bystanders. IS had already run the three against Sepunia's images. So we'd missed one, possibly two other bad guys. I batted the wave of irritation away. They'd have gone to ground by now. Maybe the IS would sweat the names out from the three we'd bagged.

I heard Paula's low voice at my side, asking if I wanted to start Aidan's interview now.

'Yes, let's do it. You and me in the room; Atria and Flav to observe.'

A quick glance through the observation panel before we went in. This was the "friendly" interview room, furnished with two couches set at right angles to each other, a low table, two easy chairs and the standard water cooler. Bland chocolate-box pictures hung on three walls, a plain mirror on the fourth. The remains of a sandwich lay on a plate, and Aidan clutched a mug in his hand. Shoulders slumped, he was staring into the far distance as if his eyes had lost the ability to focus.

He jumped when we came through the door, spilling some of his drink on his pants. His Adam's apple bounced as he swallowed hard and he switched his gaze between Paula and me. And then the apprehension in his eyes changed to something else – surprise.

'Bruna?'

'Hello, Aidan. How are you feeling?' Probably wanting to throw up, I thought as I looked closely at him. 'This is Staff Sergeant Paula Servla who is going to sit with us.'

He stared at me. His gaze flickered over to my gold eagle pocket badge, the black tee showing at my neck, and then my face.

'You're a Praetorian! Jupiter save me.'

'That much of a shock?'

'I thought you were a scarab.'

'I'm called "Bruna" sometimes, but my correct name is Captain Carina Mitela and I belong to the special forces section.' I let that sink in.

'Does Mossia know?' he asked, processing this information.

'No. She knows I'm something in law enforcement, but not which unit, nor my rank and name. I need you to keep that to yourself. Can you do that?'

He nodded, but continued to stare at me.

'Now, we only had a few minutes to talk before. I really need you to expand on what you told me then.'

'Bruna – no, sorry, captain,' he stumbled. 'I'm very sorry, but I haven't thanked anybody yet for rescuing me. I've been trying to get my head around it.' He looked at me. 'I must be feeling better. I'm starting to analyse myself now. Gods! I'll be in therapy for years!'

'Don't worry, Aidan,' I said, touching his arm. 'Everybody feels a bit weird after this kind of experience. Call me Bruna if it's easier or more natural to you.' I smiled at him. 'Tell me everything in as much detail as you can. Everything, however trivial you think it is.'

Paula made notes while I listened, watching Aidan's face and prompting him.

'...so I asked Tacita to give me information about your legate. Mossia had mentioned that Tacita worked in the military, possibly in the PGSF.'

Juno. Aburia's security was crap letting that out. Why didn't she pretend to be a scarab like the rest of us did?

'Caeco said I must have somebody among my clients I could use.' He looked down at his hands. 'I thought Tacita was my best bet. She'd taken a liking to me.'

Not very glorious behaviour, but I could follow his logic.

'But why did she do it?' I asked. I'd see the report from Petronax later. His internal security team had started interrogating Aburia yesterday. But I wanted to hear it first from Aidan.

He looked directly at me. 'She did it for me. I think she felt sorry for me. I used her to protect myself from Caeco.' He dropped his head in his hands. He looked racked. 'It was only afterwards I realised how deeply I loved her.'

In the meantime, he'd dumped Mossia. Bastard.

I stood up and walked over to the water cooler, almost wrenched the tap off, and filled a cup with water. I stood with my back to him until I'd finished. From the side, Paula shot me a warning look. I crossed back to him, stopping barely centimetres away, forcing him to crook his neck up. 'So what did you pass on? About the legate?'

Aidan looked at me. My name badge was in his face. He stared for a few moments then shrank back. 'You're related to him, aren't you?' he whispered. He covered his face with his hands.

'What did you pass on, Aidan?' I repeated.

'How do I know you won't lock me up and melt down the key?'

'You don't. But you'll find out if you don't give me more.'

He was caught whatever he did. He wiped his hand across his face, looked at me, then at Paula. His gaze came to rest on the table.

'Tacita told me about the reorganisation, the new staff appointments, his assessments of people, his tough attitude to corruption.'

All standard intelligence gathering.

'Then I had to ask her for other stuff – his wife,' Aidan glanced in my direction, 'her family, her children, his children and imperial connections.'

Not so standard.

'So how did Caeco react when you delivered?'

'He wanted more – attitude to the throne, loyalty, any resentment or bitterness about his first family's punishment.' He looked at me, but I didn't move. 'But Tacita didn't know. Then I didn't see her again.' His voice dwindled to a whisper. The deep hurt and bleakness in his expression kept me from being too hard on him.

'Okay, Aidan. Let's leave it there. I want you to think about the whole time from when you joined that poker game to now. Divide it into separate days and write everything down that happened each day.'

'So am I a prisoner?'

'Let's just say it's safer for you to be in here at the moment.' I signalled to Paula to pack up.

'And Tacita?' Aidan said.

'She's not your concern any more.'

He jumped up, eyes blazing, and took a step toward me. 'What have you done with her?'

'She's alive and well – that's all I can say.'

He opened his mouth to say something.

I looked back at him with a steady gaze.

He dropped his eyes, and Paula and I left.

'That was a fun interview!' We walked into the observation room and saw Flavius looking sombre and Atria apprehensive. Both were silent. I frowned, not understanding; then I turned around and saw Conrad, shoulders leaning against the wall, not happy.

'You three, go write your notes up.' I glanced at my team and nodded towards the door. They were out in an instant.

'What in Hades is going on?' Conrad asked, almost to himself. 'Those were some damned intrusive things they wanted. How did they expect Aburia to know?'

I was momentarily distracted by the obs screen blanking. I took a few moments to log off the session.

'Would you mind if we left it until later?' I said. 'This is more than just putting pressure on a soft target. It's becoming a personal and family matter for us.'

One eyebrow went up and a question in his eyes, but I was relieved when he gave a short nod.

10

Beyond the maze lay a secluded part of Domus Mitelarum's grounds. A three-metre high wall enclosed a private garden full of lavender, sage and rosemary, edged with mulberry and fig trees between walkways festooned with trailing vines. Across one corner lay a triangular wooden summer house, with honeysuckle chasing all over it. The rich scents of the plants released by the warm evening drifted and swirled around inside the confines of the golden stone wall. A large myrtle tree stood at the centre with a teak bench circling it. Myrtle for Mitela. I stretched up my hand and crushed its leaves between my fingers. You could get high on the rich scent released.

There was only one gated entrance, so it was totally private. Nonna had handed me the heavy, spiral-headed key when I'd first arrived in Roma Nova like she was handing on an heirloom. After the break-up with Conrad years ago, it had been my haven. Now I shared it with him.

'This afternoon,' I said, not looking at Conrad, 'after Aidan's interview, I know I stepped across the line. I apologise.'

'We're still waiting for various reports so it wasn't crucial. I appreciated that you didn't pull the family card in front of others.'

I stared at him. Well, obviously not. I sometimes wondered if I was more aware of keeping a professional distance at work than he was. But now, despite being in our intimate retreat at home, he was still in work mode.

'So what did you think of what Aidan gave you? What's your general analysis?'

'My instinctive reaction is that you, and by extension all of us, are being challenged in some way, personally, as a family.'

Conrad raised his brows. 'Reaching a bit, aren't you?'

I made a moue but said nothing.

'Things like the reorganisation, new staff appointments and my attitude to corruption are pretty much open book,' he said. 'It's the sort of standard information any intelligence agency would have on record. Fair game – we have it on others.' He smiled. 'I suppose that both our imperial connections are interesting,' he admitted. 'But what the Hades is this "attitude to the throne, loyalty, any resentment or bitterness about his first family's punishment" to do with anybody? I thought that was all behind me.'

I saw the shade of Caius Tellus flit across the garden and shivered. Nearly thirty years after his death, Conrad's traitor stepfather was still reaching out to taint us. I remembered Conrad's haggard face the day he'd revealed what had happened to him. We'd been at Castra Lucilla, our summer home in the country, lying on a rug drying in the sun after a vigorous swim. He wouldn't detail the personal abuse Caius had imposed on him. He stayed silent for a few minutes at that part, his breath light and eyes unfocused.

After the city had been retaken by imperial forces and Caius's brutal rebellion defeated, Quintus had discovered the nine-year-old Conrad cowering, filthy and terrified, in a locked cellar in Caius's suburban villa.

During the journey to the derelict farm in the east that the ruined and disgraced Tella family had been allowed to keep, Conrad remembered pulling the blanket over the back of his head and huddling on the seat of an old utility truck, refusing to let go of Quintus as they drove through the night. He remembered the headlights shining through the rear window panel from the escort vehicle and blinding him whenever he glanced back.

I'd held Conrad quietly in my arms that day by the lake while he wept at the memory of his ruined childhood.

'I don't think it's to do with that,' I said. 'Uncle Quintus is surely more vulnerable as the imperial chancellor than us if that were the case.'

Conrad looked thoughtful, his gaze fixed on the far wall. Without turning, he asked, 'What do you think about consulting Aurelia? She has excellent instincts.'

My grandmother operated these days as a consultant to the Imperatrix Silvia. But they were even closer; Silvia's father had been Aurelia's youngest cousin. More importantly, Aurelia Mitela headed the most senior of the Twelve Families, so knew everybody, and everything about everybody.

'I don't think I want to involve her – I feel it would endanger her.'

'Why on earth do you think that? She's not as strong physically, granted, but inside she's as tough as old boots.'

I took a few moments to watch the light playing on the stone wall through one of the fig trees. Strange how the pattern chopped and changed, yet the light stayed essentially the same. Too bad life wasn't like that.

'Do we need to take any special precautions here, at the house, do you think?' he asked.

'The building itself is pretty secure with the scanlocks. And they have regular security staff and CCTV. What more could we do? The only way in is with the access codes.' I glanced up at him. 'Maybe this isn't the moment to mention it, but I had Flav and Livius try to break in last month.'

'What?'

'I bet them a crate of beer, but they couldn't crack the scanlock codes.' I wasn't going to say that Fausta had programmed the codes for Junia. 'They failed, but I gave them the beer anyway.'

He tugged my hair, but gently, and shook his head. But it made him smile.

'The children are well-protected. Helena will ensure they don't go anywhere at the moment without her, plus one of the house servants. But I'll talk to Nonna anyway about increasing security.'

'We should have preliminary results from the interrogations tomorrow and the intel reports, so should have a clearer idea then,' Conrad said.

'You know something?' I took a deep breath. 'I've had it with not seeing it. I'm going to try a deep state analysis.'

11

I'd always been able to switch off – daydreaming, Uncle Brown had called it and snorted when I'd misplaced a whole afternoon once. I'd never connected it to how solutions to my girlish problems appeared soon afterwards.

One warm day, seven years ago at my training camp, I was slumped over on the grass, recovering after a strenuous trail run. I'd been trying to puzzle through a problem and thought a hard run would help. I closed my eyes to relax and woke only when a small bird chirruped near my ear. In a clear, almost overbright moment, I had my solution. More importantly, I knew how I'd done it. I'd been slow making the connection, but now I had it.

With practice, I could access this dream state at will to analyse any problem. But forcing it wasn't always good. Sometimes my head stung like it had been scoured out with coarse-grade tungsten carbide sandpaper. And my hearing and vision became super-sensitive. But it was a great gift. And gave great results.

Next morning, just before the first debrief started, Conrad came over and gave me an appraising look.

'Any good?'

'Oh, yes, and then some.'

'My office, then, lunchtime.'

. . .

My debrief with Petronax in the internal security office was as wonderful as I'd anticipated. During her interview, Aburia had been composed and had said very little.

'She just sat there and wouldn't give a reason beyond that it was personal. Did you girlies fall out about a new frock or someone you fancied?' Petronax smiled, nastily. I knew he was trying to bait me, but I ignored it. I couldn't tell whether or not Aburia had accessed my lock box for information about my meetings with Aidan, but I wasn't going to mention that to Petronax. Besides, that was pure speculation.

He was perfectly aware he had an unpopular job and that most people instinctively avoided him. Lucius said he was meticulous and disciplined in everything he did, but regretted that Petronax couldn't resist the temptation to take his obnoxious attitude out for an airing whenever possible. If he were more professional, more people would forgive him for existing.

Looking disappointed I wasn't going to provide him with any fun, he pulled his lips together as if attacked by lemon juice.

'She strikes me as being completely distracted, he said. 'We pushed her hard, but she wouldn't budge. That's the problem trying to deal with you lot – you're all too well trained in resisting interrogation.' He snorted. 'Her initial profile was of a steady, hard-working and reasonably keen young officer.' He looked at her file on his desk. 'She's never had any disciplinaries, even when training, unlike some people,' he said snidely. He half-threw a stapled bunch of paper at me, 'Here's the transcript. Make what you will of it.'

'What happens now?'

'We'll commission psych reports on her and she'll have a judgement hearing in due course. If proven, she'll get between five and eight years.' He looked straight at me. 'I don't like you, Mitela. You're said to be a popular officer, and sharp as all hell. I think you're disruptive. I won't have this kind of incident on my watch.'

I waited to see if he had any more golden nuggets to offer. Apparently not.

'I've got nothing more to say to you – dismissed.'

Back at my desk, an urgent message was flashing on my screen ordering me to Colonel Somna's office in attendance on the legate.

Juno.

Somna, the Head of the Interrogation Service. What in Hades did she want? As I rushed through the IS general office, I almost collided with Daniel.

Before I asked, he shook his head. 'Not a clue.'

I rolled my eyes at him and trooped in after him to find Conrad already there along with Sepunia.

Somna's office looked fairly standard, with bookshelves the dominant feature. She seemed to have more on philosophy and history than applied harassment. Around forty-five, Somna looked like a tax inspector, complete with glasses, thin lips and ordered hair. Although the rest of her face didn't show any hostility, her pale grey eyes were cold. I knew how formidable in action she was from the receiving end. Maybe she could have got more out of Tacita. But Petronax protected his internal security jurisdiction like a vampire defending his source of blood. Sharing did not occur to him.

Somna was handing out sheets of hardcopy and gestured at us to take chairs from her meeting table.

'I want to show you some interesting footage from the public feed, but first I'll bring you up to date on the interviews. We haven't had a great deal of luck with Caeco. Our language psych says he's a native speaker, from the western provinces – he thinks perhaps Aquae Caesaris – but he's spent a lot of time in the city. He's a self-confident individual, convinced of his abilities. Although he looks like a standard muscleman, he has a very solid internal core. He may well turn out to be ideologically motivated.'

'In what way ideological?' Conrad asked.

'We don't know,' Somna replied. She looked at us all. 'I understand that's frustrating for all of you. We're trying some other things in the meantime, but it would be helpful to know, Legate, how quickly we need to crack him.'

'It's becoming more important. There are no individual DNA matches, which I find astounding. We must find out who Caeco and his people are, and why they held the therapist hostage. He's a nobody, but they put considerable resources into their operation. At a guess, I don't think they realised we would discover them so quickly.'

'I see,' said Somna. 'You'll be pleased to know we've done better with Sextus. He's a local boy. Sepunia's intelligence section has been invaluable in liaising with my team. Their staffer has been able to cross-check instantly and advance our interrogation considerably. I hope this new interdeployment will continue.' She flicked a glance toward Conrad who nodded back. 'Anyway, Sextus. He's had a couple of warnings, nothing serious. Living with his father, who took him away from his family when the boy was four years old. Sextus is his real *praenomen*, but his mother's family is a branch of the Corneliae.'

One of the Twelve! I wonder what snooty Livia Cornelia would think of their wandering boy?

'The father is a middle-ranker, with his own small business, and has supported them both since the split with the family. DNA testing done years ago proved the father-son relationship. The certificate has been lodged as a public record. The boy uses the father's surname only.' Conrad and Sepunia looked shocked. As foreign-born, Daniel and I were less anal about these things.

Somna continued, 'The Corneliae had official custody – we found the court papers. The mother married some years ago and made a financial settlement on Sextus, but he hasn't touched a *solidus* of it. He refuses to see his mother. He has an original view on the role of women and men.' Somna paused and looked up from her report. She didn't meet Conrad's eyes, but glanced away for a few moments and scratched the back of her neck with her index finger. I'd never seen her betray a moment of unease like that. She rubbed the top sheet of paper between her fingers.

'In what respect?' Conrad prompted.

'He is a patriarchalist.'

Sepunia gasped. I heard a sharp crack. Conrad's hand was holding the remnants of a stylus. He stared at Somna with an intensity that should have incinerated a block of Aquae Caesaris granite, a tense, frozen expression on his face despite the angry flush. Somna's grey gaze flickered back at him, but she refused to give way. Daniel stared at Conrad but said nothing. Muted vehicle noises from outside and a footfall outside Somna's door gave us some kind of anchor in the real world.

Conrad cleared his throat. 'Is this a personal opinion or do you think Caeco shares it?'

'At this stage, we don't know. Do you want me to push this line of investigation?'

'Given that you think Caeco must be ideologically driven, I think it's highly relevant.'

After a full minute's awkward silence, Somna signalled to her aide who started playing the footage from the public surveillance feed.

'Watch the figure in the pale jacket,' Somna instructed. I recognised Caeco entering a bar on the Dec Max: he walked with that same smooth, purposeful movement he'd used in Aidan's office. The images speeded up to ten minutes later, and three more men arrived at three- to four-minute intervals. The date was a month ago. Fast forward to a week ago and we saw Caeco enter the main Macellum colonnade and sit in one of the outdoor cafés. Same men, but much clearer pictures.

'This one,' Somna highlighted a tall, brown-haired man, 'is a provincial curia employee called Cyriacus from Brancadorum; next to him is one Pisentius originating from Castra Lucilla.'

Conrad and I glanced at each other. Our summer villa was at Castra Lucilla. A coincidence, surely?

Somna looked directly at me with her unnerving stare. 'Is he known to you, captain?'

'No,' I replied, feeling pinned down in my chair like a dead butterfly in a museum case. 'No, I don't know the name at all. I'll...I'll ask our steward, just to be sure.'

Her gaze swivelled back to the screen and I relaxed. 'We haven't ID'd the last one yet, but I feel we've made good progress.'

Nobody moved for a few seconds.

Sepunia coughed and broke the tension. 'We'll dig out a bit more on Sextus and run a full check on these two,' she said. 'It'll be interesting to see if they have any ideological stance.'

Conrad moved at last, reaching over to pick up his el-pad from Somna's desk. 'I suggest we meet the same time tomorrow to check progress,' he said in a low voice. 'My office, unless you have any further screenings of the local low life for us, colonel?'

'Thoughts?' It took me a minute to register Conrad was addressing me, not Sepunia or Daniel, as we walked back to his office. His face was pale, but otherwise he appeared to have recovered from his earlier shock. Apart from the revulsion any Roma Novan would have, it must have hit Conrad deep inside and unleashed the horrors of his childhood; his rebel stepfather had been the arch-patriarchalist.

'Well,' I glanced at Sepunia, 'if the IS comes up with information suggesting they share ideology then we're playing in a different ball game altogether. Ideologicals are historically both ruthless and blind. They're convinced of their cause and don't mind destroying anybody else on their way to achieving it.'

As soon as Conrad had disappeared along the corridor, and Sepunia trotted back downstairs, Daniel grabbed my arm and half-dragged me along to his new office.

'What?' I asked, once he had closed the door. I rubbed my arm, exaggerating a little.

'Why did they all go into retreat-into-the-cave mode back there? And what the hell happened to Conrad?'

'Ah.' I could see the curiosity raging in his eyes. 'Tell me, Daniel, what do you understand by the word patriarchalist?'

'Something about the role of men and them taking the lead in the family, I suppose.'

Like me, Daniel had been raised with standard Western values, but more so as his first family was very traditional. His Uncle Baruch was the head of the family and Daniel's widowed mother, even though she'd been the elder brother's wife, deferred to him when the chips were down. Being a sophisticate from New York, I'd thought it was old-fashioned and repressive until I thought about Aunt and Uncle Brown with their Midwestern family culture.

I caught myself staring out of the window. Like that was going to help. How could I frame this so it'd make sense to Daniel? When Apulius had left Rome in the fourth century with his daughters and followers and headed out from Italy into the mountains, they needed to make radical changes to survive. So women took over social, economic and political life, and the men fought to ensure the colony survived. In the end, both sons and daughters put on armour and picked up blades in the struggle to defend their new homeland.

Inevitably, reversing values was a struggle. It took several generations to become entrenched, but Apulius the founder, his daughters and granddaughters enforced it. He'd married a Celt from Noricum, where women participated in decision-making, fought in battles and directed families' property. Her four daughters had inherited her qualities in spades.

I sighed. None of that would help explain to Daniel how threatening the patriarchalists were. I went for the summarised version. 'You know Roma Novans have lived almost since the founding with women running the families. It's not just their history; it's in their heads, their blood. Apart from that, they've seen how poorly other cultures have treated women and children over the centuries. Patriarchy is abhorrent to them, as a system and a personal value. That's why they wouldn't let Christians or Muslims in. For them, patriarchy is close to a perversion. They've fought hard to defend their way of life, and rejected anything that threatened it.'

'I can follow that, but why did Conrad have that weird turn? I know he's big on doing the proper thing, but I thought he was going to pass out.'

'So did I.' I chewed my lip. 'Keep this confidential, okay? Some of it's common knowledge, some not.'

He nodded.

'About thirty years ago, when Conrad's stepfather Caius launched the coup and made himself the so-called First Consul for a year, he introduced a pretty brutal male-dominated regime. Quite a number of women didn't survive it. Three female heads of family were executed on trumped-up charges within the first few months. My grandmother nearly died and was in hospital in Vienna for six weeks. Eventually, resistance groups united with exiles and retook the country piece by piece. I don't know how they found the courage to do it.'

I paused and looked down at Daniel's untidy desk.

'Conrad was only nine at the time and had been living under Caius's roof six years before that. He was beaten by Caius every day to "man him up". That was his personal pattern of men in control. The gods know what other abuse he suffered. That's why his reaction was so strong.'

Daniel leaned against the edge of the desk, looking puzzled. 'I never thought about it. I don't feel particularly disadvantaged as a man.'

I just laughed at him, lightening the mood. 'You have too much fun to notice!'

He looked relieved to be distracted and drop the subject. When

Conrad and Nonna started discussing politics or some philosophical theories on winter evenings at home, Daniel usually closed the door and left them to it.

Finished with my history lecture, I went to check on Fausta and Drusus in the strategy office and found chaos. Surrounded by boxes, some half-opened, piles of racking struts, shrink-wrapped cupboards, chairs, cabinets and a cabling crew, they were beaming. Drusus, el-pad in hand, was directing another arrival – two of Manlius's people with a huge situation screen. This was more than good. I told them to carry on with it; they were perfectly competent.

'Just message me when it's safe to come back in.'

12

Promptly at 13.00, I knocked on Conrad's door.

'Come!' He was frowning at the screen, tapping on his keyboard as I entered. He finished and looked up at me. The fine lines fanning out from where the upper and lower lids of his eyes met seemed deeper in the strong white sunlight, as if digging in for the long haul. A sign of getting older? He had a good eight years on me. Today wouldn't have helped.

'Are you okay now?' I asked.

'Stop fussing, or I'll pull rank on you.' He wouldn't, and I wouldn't care if he did. And he knew it. But his semi-joke reassured me. A little.

'So what can you give me from your analysis?' His voice dropped a half-tone.

'I strongly suggest that you visit the palace and check out the security for the children, that you meet with Silvia and advise her of a possible threat.'

I dragged out drinking my water.

'Next,' I said, studying the arm of my chair, 'whatever you do, make sure there's at least one, preferably two independent people who can see you at all times when you are in the same place with her. Write everything up in detail, not just your personal digital diary, but hard copy. Store a copy of everything in your lock box.'

'Are you serious?'

Nobody had a higher security clearance than he did or was trusted more. He was responsible for the personal and political safety of the head of state. More binding still, Silvia Apulia was not just the imperatrix to him; he was the father of her three children.

'Completely.'

'Oh, come on! You can do better than that.'

'No, I can't,' I blurted out. 'Juno help me, I don't know how to describe it. I saw you threatened, in danger, but I can't tell how. You were also seen as a possible threat.' My voice fell to a whisper.

He said nothing. He picked up a pen from his desk tidy and tapped the end on the dark leather top. The repetitive staccato became unbearable. Then he turned it and started on the other end. His face was hard like a concrete mask. I cleared my throat.

'Any more?' His voice was clipped; his features showed him to be in professional and analytical mode again, but his face was flushed with anger.

'You know DSAs don't always give results on demand.' I started to feel resentful. Sometimes they were a little obscure, but so far in my life they had proved one hundred per cent true. Some appreciation would have been good.

Looking for an outlet for his fury, something in my expression must have kept him from making me the preferred target. He flung back into his chair and murdered the roller-ball.

I knew everything was wrong, all wrong, and I had an almost uncontrollable urge to run.

'Very well,' he said. 'I'll go up to the palace now and check the security thoroughly. I'll take the *primipilus* with me and Paula Servla.' He gave me a sardonic look. 'Do you think they're sufficiently credible babysitters?'

'Well, having all three of you descend on them all at once will frighten the shit out of the guards there.' I tried to keep my voice light, but wasn't too sure I'd succeeded.

'You know something?' He fixed his gaze on me. 'You're a real Cassandra sometimes.'

Itching to move, I went to the gym downstairs for some hard circuit training, followed by a kilometre on the outdoor track. Despite pushing my pace so my breath seared through my lungs, making my eyes water, it didn't distract what was pounding through my mind. My gut instinct was to keep running. Now.

As I sweated back inside, one of Sepunia's staffers found me. 'Captain Mitela? Captain Sepunia would be grateful if you could call by her office this afternoon,' he said. 'She said it's not urgent, just interesting.'

What had Sepunia dug up that she couldn't leave until tomorrow morning's meeting? And what exactly did she mean by interesting?

Half an hour later, I knocked on the door frame of her office, a friendly smile on my face.

'Hi, Carina. Come in and sit down,' she said, as cheerful as I appeared. I shut the door and waited for her to speak. She dropped the happy look, glanced at me almost furtively, then glued her eyes back on the paper in her hand. She wasn't very tall, and fidgeted around like a little brown mouse in front of a stalking cat.

'When we were searching the safe in Sextus's house, we found an envelope marked "Sympathisers". One of my people was logging the contents – mostly letters and message printouts – and putting a list together. She was somewhat taken aback to find these. Any comments?' She shot me a speculative look.

Two photos showed a group of people in full formal dress filling a magnificent hall. Domus Corneliarum. I recognised it from the last gathering of the Twelve Families. In the foreground were my grandmother, Livia Cornelia, Laetia Volusenia, her daughter Marcella and Claudia Sella, Julia Sella's aunt, and me. A rough circle had been drawn around my head in red marker. In the top photo, I was slightly turned away, accepting a drink from the waiter who was…Sextus. No. The second photo was similar, but included Imperatrix Silvia Apulia. My face was turned at a more direct angle as if I was in serious conversation with Sextus.

Hades.

'I don't know what to say – I don't pay attention to each and every servant that hands me a drink,' I said coldly. That probably sounded snooty, but that was how it was. Maybe Sextus had wormed his way onto the staff list for the big bash at Livia Cornelia's. Maybe he was curious about his mother's family after all. I hadn't had the slightest murmur of recall about him when I first went to Aidan's office. And my memory was pretty good.

'The photos look like part of the batch taken for publication. Anybody could have accessed them via the public pages of the Twelve Families' site,' I said. 'C'mon, Sepunia, this is the kid fantasising with some fancy graphics package.'

'And the letter?'

She stretched out, but held on to a single sheet, handwritten in blue ink. The sloping, hurried scribble looked exactly like mine. I read it through, twice. A big lump of lead landed in my middle. It was supposed to be from me saying that Conrad and I had been impressed by Sextus and wanted to hear more about his interesting ideas. Would he please like to contact me and arrange a time to meet?

I stared at the letter, caught somewhere between dismay and shock. Why in Hades would Conrad be remotely interested, with his history?

'Would you believe me if I said this was a forgery?' I asked Sepunia when I had recovered my voice. 'I always use black, when I write something. Not something I do often.' I shrugged. 'And we have our own hand-milled paper, not this everyday stuff.'

'Perhaps so, but you understand I have to submit it to full forensic examination.'

A shiver ran through me. I felt a noose tightening, not only around my neck but Conrad's too.

'Of course,' I agreed. What else could I say? Somebody was mounting an attack on the Mitelae. Nonna and I thought it would be financial or digital, and she'd had yet another layer of BI security programs installed. I hadn't anticipated anything from the inside, or so personally directed. My heart started to thump as the adrenalin responded to the threat.

'I need you to write this out in front of witnesses so we have a comparison,' she added. She gave me a typed version to copy from so I couldn't make a deliberate effort to miscopy. For all that Miss Innocent look in her green eyes, she'd prepared this well. She couldn't, or wouldn't, look directly at me.

Whoever was running this operation had done an excellent job. I had to assume the letter would be a good forgery, too. But who wrote a letter by hand these days? And in ink? I heard the door open, and a senior staffer set paper and ink pen on the desk in front of Sepunia then stood to the side, watching me. She headed it "Agreed witness copy – comparison only" and pushed it towards me.

'Now what?' I asked as I put the pen down ten minutes later.

She bagged the copy letter and handed it to the staffer who went off to process it.

'I'm sorry. I can't say any more until I see the results in about an hour. Please return to your office and wait until I contact you.'

She couldn't have spoken more coldly if she'd tried. If it were me, I would have had me suspended from duty and confined to barracks.

Her mistake.

I hurried up the corridor to Conrad's office. Empty. Of course, he'd gone to the palace. I stood there, chewing my lip, not knowing what to do. I needed to warn him. Conrad's exec, Rusonia, was impassive, as usual. I didn't know her well enough to leave a message – she'd think I was crazy. I gave her a tight smile, slipped back out into the corridor. I texted him in encrypt: 'Code 5. Get out now. Meet me stat fav resto.'

I prayed he'd pick it up immediately. If I was being paranoid, the worst result would be embarrassment. If not, I wasn't going to wait for a trap to close on us.

I went to the locker room, gathered some things into a small backpack. I walked up to my old desk in the general office which, miraculously, had not been reassigned. I leaned up against the inside curve and spent two precious minutes talking and laughing with the guys there and, still bantering, felt behind the vinyl edging strip. It was still there. I broke a fingernail easing the tiny chip out. No reaction from any of the others. I sat down on the chair and logged on to my account. It hadn't been barred, but I had to assume the Intelligence section was already monitoring it.

I slipped the chip into a card carrier and initiated a timed destruct sequence on the whole account. It was a cute little program Fausta had made up for me when I worked undercover with Apollodorus. The bonus was that it would eat itself up once it had finished its work. Normally, nobody would notice, but what was normal now? I reckoned I had a safety margin of eight minutes left.

Back in the locker room, I abandoned my uniform. I stowed my gold eagle badge in my pants pocket. I needed it to clear security at the exit. I sauntered down the corridors as casually as I could manage, my heart in my stomach. Normally three and a half minutes from locker room to exit, each second seemed ten times longer. I was sweating as I approached the security gate – the last barrier. My heart thumping, I put my hand and eye up to the readers and waited for the take-down.

Nothing. The reader pinged and I was out.

'Hold a moment, captain,' the security guard called. She was porting a bullpup and stood two metres away.

I took a breath, and forced myself to turn back. 'Yes?'

'You forgot your side arm.' She stretched out her hand with my Glock.

'Thanks.' I stuffed it in my leather jacket pocket as casually as I could manage, hoping she couldn't hear how loud my heart was pumping. 'Sorry, it's my daughter's birthday today, and my mind was off on a trip.'

'No problem, ma'am,' she said. 'Got my own.' She smiled. 'Hope it goes well.'

I faked an answering smile, collected my bike from the garage and, piling on the revs, fled the barracks.

PART II

PULCHERIA REDUX

13

I found the nearest parking garage, slipped into its blind spot and changed. I dug out a long curly wig from my backpack. It wasn't wonderful, but enough to deceive the passing eye and, more importantly, the public CCTV. I unclipped the surface panels off my bike and threw them under the trader's van in the next bay. Levering the false tooth containing my mic took a minute or two. I could hardly see in the bike mirror in the poor light, but I felt the stab of pain as it came away. I wiped away the blood dribbling down my chin. The earpiece was easier to extract. I stuffed them, my cell and my gold eagle badge – all trackable – into a digital franked mailer addressed to the PGSF office and threw it into the first mailbox I found. It would be confined in the automated mail system for a day or two.

I barrelled along the inner ring road to a suburban post office. In their private box room, I collected the contents of my safe box: four thousand *solidi* in cash, a special cellphone made by Brown Industries in Eastern America, and a thin metallic mesh cloth which I carefully pinned in place under my tee to shield my left shoulder and upper arm. I raced back to the city centre to a third post office and deposited the unwanted items in another lock box. By now, my bike was too exposed and, regretfully, I dumped it in a parking lot in the middle of the Dec Max.

I trembled with the tension rippling through me as I completed each step of my escape route, but enjoyed a guilty frisson of excitement at playing hooky. Maybe Lurio was right that I'd been born to be either a great counterspy or a great criminal. Both had their attractions.

Filled with numbers the scarabs would love to have, my BI supermobile was now recharged from the bike. BI – Brown Industries – was the specialist defence electronics firm I'd inherited from my father, something that had triggered me running for cover in Roma Nova seven years ago. As majority shareholder, I had full access to the candy store, and I'd taken my pick. After the deep cover operation a few years ago finished, I'd packed my handset in a shielded bag and hidden it in the safe deposit drawer. I'd deactivated the network but, being paranoid, I'd kept the ultimate control key. This was not something I had shared with either the DJ or PGSF when I transferred in. I had to hope the encryption level was still good. I breathed out as the screen showed "Activated" when I entered the key code. It had been seven years. I dialled.

'*Salve*, Pollius. How's your knife?'

Silence. A cough.

'Pulcheria?' A voice croaked.

Was he having a heart attack?

'Live and kicking.'

'Gods! What can I do for you?'

'Can I come over now? I need a small procedure done, urgently.'

'Now? Are you alone?'

'Yes and yes. Problem?'

'No. Just surprised.'

At his door, I repressed the instinct to turn my head and scan for watchers. I just trusted my peripheral vision which was pretty near 180 degrees. Besides, I had changed my appearance yet again and now wore a red leather jacket, taupe chinos and a scarf bandeaued around my head.

Pollius came to greet me himself. 'Delighted to see you again,' he gushed, faking it. He instructed the bored receptionist to hold all calls and ushered me into his ultra-chic consulting room.

'Pulcheria,' he stated simply. The smile dropped off his face.

'I hope I didn't startle you.'

'I was told they'd put you away for good.'

'Hmph, it sometimes felt like it!'

His deep-set eyes didn't hide his curiosity, but I knew he was too cautious to push it.

'I'm not going to disrupt your new life,' I said, careful to reassure him. 'I'm pleased to see you're prospering, though.' I panned around his room.

'Your severance payment was very generous.' He showed me his office with mini-operating room attached. 'I do small surgery, fine cosmetic work mostly – it's very lucrative.' He smiled, gradually relaxing. How many patients had sat at the Italian grained oak desk in his elegant office, wondering how much their consultation would cost? Did they know Pollius was expert at digging bullets out of bleeding bodies?

'I need a small favour. Can you extract a tracker?'

He tensed. 'Not a penal one?'

'No, personal security.'

'Let me see the site.' He slid into medical mode as I stripped off my jacket and white tee. He raised an eyebrow when he saw the mesh. I quickly slid it into my jacket pocket.

'In the fold under the shoulder joint.'

He had me lie down on the operating table, found the tiny tracker with his scanner, and daubed the area with an incredibly cold liquid. I felt the scalpel slice my flesh, but with no pain, followed by a sucking sound. He gel-sealed the wound, padded the area and we were done. Ten minutes flat.

'I've never seen one of these,' he commented as he cleaned and bagged the tiny thing before handing it over.

'Yes, well, forget you ever did,' I replied. 'Do you have a protective mailer I could have and a plain envelope to put it in?'

I thanked him and left. I had been under twenty minutes. I walked three blocks and posted the tracker back to Domus Mitelarum. How easy it had been to slip back into that efficient camaraderie with Pollius. All he said when I went was 'Go carefully', our old valediction.

I made my way to the Onyx, Conrad's and my favourite restaurant, where I'd told him to meet. I walked past on the opposite side of the street, then dove down a side alleyway but stayed in line of sight of the restaurant's large plate glass window. Using the scope from my pack at nearly max focus, I could see into the restaurant.

Nobody apart from the server. I leaned back against the plasterwork. No message on my cell from Conrad even to tell me I was wrong. Had he received my text? If he had, he would have been here or at least called or messaged. Although I'd sent the text from my other cell, the one I'd mailed back, the system was cloud-based. I would have received his reply. Just to be sure, I double-checked I'd reconfigured the supermobile correctly, but I knew I had.

I didn't dare call into the PGSF building, even with the reactivated supermobile. Who knew if the encryption was still unbreakable after seven years? Unlikely. They'd track me within minutes. I glanced at my watch. It wasn't two hours since I'd left. It could hardly be classed as desertion. Yet.

This was a trap, I was sure; a really clever one where somebody had gone to a heap of trouble to make sure it was well-sprung.

I had to find somewhere safe and contact Nonna. She would protect the children. She would let Olympus collapse before letting them come in harm's way.

I found Dania, in her bar just off the Via Nova. I raised my brows at its new look: stylish indigo and silver decor, with beautiful glass and ceramic mosaics. She must have given in and taken professional advice this time. The bar area was starting to fill up now the sun had set. I wandered up to the marble counter, perched on a stool and ordered a dry white wine. I heard a few foreign accents: tourists soaking up the Roman atmosphere. No sign of security or scarabs.

After a few sips, I made my way to the back, pretending to look for the bathroom but I snuck upstairs. I passed the rooms, looking for the office. Red LEDs on old-fashioned swipelocks showed some were occupied. Ah, a codelocked door. I knocked and smiled at the spyhole.

The door opened two centimetres to show part of an elaborately dressed blonde head.

'*Salve*, Dania.'

'Venus's tits! Pulcheria!' Dania's jaw dropped open so far I thought I'd have to apply first aid.

'Can I come in?'

She flung open the door, grabbed my arm and pulled me into a welcoming hug. Unlike the cautious Pollius, she beamed with genuine pleasure to see me. Thank Juno. But then, Dania knew exactly who I was.

'I need a place to hide out for a bit. Do you think—'

'Well, obviously,' she replied, cutting me off. 'What have you done now?'

My narrow room at the end of the corridor was painted in a nauseous shade of pink with pictures that would have made an old Imperial Roman blush, but it had a unique advantage – it gave onto the fire escape at the back.

After Dania closed the door, I threw my pack on the chair and dropped down onto the bed. I didn't stop shaking for some time. The adrenalin had worn off and I was cold, tired and hungry. But I couldn't face the risk of going down to the kitchens to forage for something. I lay back on the bed and closed my eyes.

In the pitch-black of the night, I woke in a sweat exactly twelve hours after I'd left Conrad's office. Gut churning, I replayed every detail in my mind. The frown on his face had been so deep, almost stamped into his skin when he'd heard my DSA results. Surely he'd had my message. Why hadn't he joined me at the Onyx? We could have worked this thing out and cleared it up together. Half of me wanted to slink back and take the harsh consequences, but the other half hoped to the depth of all Hades that I'd been right to run.

The next morning, I'd patched my split self together. I went down to breakfast and caught an odd look or two. None of the girls and neither of the two live-in male staff said anything beyond *salve*. They carried on reaching for food, drinking coffee and swapping dubious remarks. Dania had found me a plain tunic and skirt; my newly-dyed hair fell loose on my shoulders. She announced with a casual wave of her hand that I was her cousin from the country who would be staying a while, but not joining the team. I endeavoured to sound innocent and unworldly. I helped clear breakfast away, trying to blend in as grateful poor country mouse happy to do domestic work for richer, more glamorous cousin.

I stayed hidden upstairs for the rest of the day, logging on via Dania's system, scouring the newscasts, blogs and public portals for the *custodes* and PGSF. I sent one innocuous-seeming email fixing to have coffee with a friend. As I hit send, I sat back, hoping it would still work. In desperation, I then sent an email to Conrad's personal account from a web-based encrypted account. I didn't dare risk it being tracked back to Dania, but I had no reply. I hardly slept that night.

The next morning, I murmured I was going to look at the market and did she want anything? Dania raised an eyebrow, but said, 'Go carefully.'

At the *macellum*, I browsed one or two stalls in the outside market, bought a cheap scarf, a linen bag and another pair of sandals. A scruffy market porter leered at me from between two booths. I responded with a nervous smile – he was just perfect. He beckoned, and I slipped in to join him. He squeezed my waist and pulled me into a room at the back, looking for all the world intent on a quickie.

'Really, Flavius, you don't have to look as if you're enjoying it so much.'

'Oh, come off it,' he said. 'It has to look authentic.'

'Just behave,' I warned and pulled myself away. 'You have no idea how relieved I am that the fallback system still works.'

'Isn't that the point of the coffee messages?' He raised his eyebrows.

'Sure, but still... Okay, report.'

'When you hopped it two days ago, the legate said you must have gone home. When you didn't turn up the next morning, you were posted AWOL.'

'That was quick,' I said. 'Too quick.' I frowned at him.

'Well, they've ramped the alert level up to red plus. They all came out of the emergency senior staff meeting with thunderous faces yesterday. Petronax is crowing like the arse-ache he is. He took over because your going AWOL was classed as a massive internal security breach. The legate has a personal guard tagging along with him everywhere at Petronax's insistence. One of the internal security lot I've never seen before. Sepunia's people are working under the direction of Petronax's tribe and nobody's happy.'

Gods! Was Conrad under suspicion? I swallowed the sour taste in my mouth. 'What's happening on the investigation?'

'Nothing that I can find out. There are no leaks, no gossip. Nobody from the legate's or Major Stern's response teams is on the investigation and your ART has been dispersed and reallocated. Paula's been posted to the palace guard, and I've been put on standard guard detail.'

Again, that was fast, like it was planned. Twenty-plus of the most effective guards were excluded. Tainted by association?

'Isn't there anybody we could pressure?'

'No, I've been through them all in my mind. C'mon, be serious, you know they won't leak. You wouldn't, would you?'

'Okay.' I sighed. 'We'll have to do it the traditional way.'

I rubbed my face to heighten the colour, mussed up my hair a little and stumbled into the street and back to Dania's.

Back in my horrible little room, I worked at correlating the past twenty-four hours with my deep scan analysis.

Fact number one: I'd been ambushed by the photos and letter obviously planted at Sextus's house – a trap designed to throw me off the investigation, discredit and immobilise me, preferably in an uncomfortable jail like the Transulium.

Fact number two: it had worked to a certain extent: I was on the outside but, on the plus side, I was free.

Fact number three: I'd had to reactivate some of the old Pulcheria network. The suspicion entered my mind that maybe this was the objective so it could be exposed and caught. Not very likely, but I kept it on the table.

Fact number four: three of the best teams had been taken out of the loop, including my own ART which had successfully caught Sextus and "Martinus Caeco". That was beyond bizarre.

Fact number five: my analysis had projected a threat to the imperatrix, not just personally but in her function. And Conrad would soon be in the frame. Was he under guard or protection?

Although I should, I didn't follow the political trends closely. Voting in the Representatives and Senate elections was the extent of my political activity. But one thing I did know was that the military was subordinate to the civilian administration – that went back centuries. Sure, there are always whiners and moaners, people with unrealistic aims or non-orthodox views – that was normal and, I guess, healthy – but nothing had shown up on the security screen

87

before I'd left to point to any movement to overthrow our political structure.

Gods, I could use talking to Nonna, but not just for her political input. Desperate to reassure her and worried for my children, I'd dashed off a text to her from the supermobile. All she'd replied was "Mitela protects its own". Was I still included in that?

I chewed another nail down to the quick. I was conscious of hovering on the edge of a dark void. Normally, I relished the buzz of going undercover on an operation. But no adrenalin raced through my body now. I had no doubt I'd been on the brink of being arrested as a conspirator; I'd been trapped into deserting my post so would be pursued; I was cut off from my family, my children and my love. A cold wave washed through me. Deep down, I had never felt so alone.

14

But I had no time for the luxury of feeling sorry for myself. I had to clear my head and think logically. Aside from finding out who and what were after me, I needed to know why. Martinus Caeco was the only lead I had at the present moment. Too bad I couldn't access Somna's file on him.

My last sighting of him was at Hirenses Associates office, so next morning I took up position on a bench across the way to see if anybody came snooping around. I drew a magazine out of my bag and pretended to read it. My companions were a black cat sniffing around the flower bed and a couple of older guys on another bench, talking in a desultory manner.

Before I'd left, Caeco hadn't figured on any database we had; and the model citizen hadn't jumped up on the DJ system either, nor his el-fit given any image result. I imagined Sepunia had some unlucky staffer pull an all-nighter and slog her way through PopBase. Maybe she'd find more than I did.

After half an hour's reading, looking as if I was waiting for somebody, I couldn't drag it out any longer. Maybe I was more than usually sensitive, but I was sure there were more *custodes* on the street. Two pairs had passed in the last twenty minutes; one *custos* with his nightstick in his hand instead of buckled on his belt. If one of them got bored and started ID checks, I'd be in trouble.

I trudged off around the corner, quickly darted into a doorway.

Fortuna was smiling on me – it was a thrift shop. My eye was drawn immediately to colourful tees and shorts for kids, just about the twins' size. I swallowed hard and forced myself to search the adult rails. I grabbed a dark hoodie top with a worn overprint design and a pair of frayed jeans from the rail, and picked a pair of plastic sneakers from the rack. The startled sales assistant took my tunic and some *solidi* in exchange.

Slouching like a teenager, my hair down and tied back, I wandered back along Aidan's street, browsing the shop windows. I went in a mom-and-pop electrics store and bought a budget music player, dropping the packaging on the grass. The two seniors chewed me out, but I ignored them. I sat on the bench, bouncing my head back and forward, pretending to listen to music and talked into my cellphone once. After nearly an hour, I shambled off, mumbling about "the aged".

Another visit to the thrift shop for a bulky coat, shoes, and a scarf for my hair. I offered to substitute for the woman running the kiosk at the intersection. The kiosk holder, whom I'd seen shuffling from foot to foot like she had collapsed arches, was more than pleased to take a break when she saw the size of the tip I gave her.

Selling papers, nicotine, toys and condoms was not that entertaining. Business was slow, the customers rude, and nobody wanted to chat. Boredom was starting to creep in and drag me into brain-fade when I spotted a homely guy, dark hair, medium height, regular clothes and walking too slowly past Aidan's office, trying not to look at it. He returned five minutes later. I caught him on my cell camera the second time. He started to come over to me. I stuffed my cellphone in my pocket and smiled.

'Gazette, dear?'

'Er, yes.' As he handed me the coins, he hesitated.

'What is it, dear? You look a bit lost. First time in the big city?' I asked in a patronising voice.

'Oh, no. I'm just wondering what happened to the therapist. I thought I must've got the address wrong when I saw it was closed.' He showed me a folded street map. 'This is the right place, isn't it?'

I took his map, opened a couple of folds and saw Aidan's office was marked. 'Yes, that's the right place,' I said. 'There was a bit of a crash here a few days ago, and the drivers went at it like a couple of gladiators. You should have seen them! The caretaker tried to stop the fight, but one of them bashed him in the face. Serve him right, pompous git! Some girl was screaming her head off. I saw Mr Hirenses come out with his lovely young receptionist.' I half-leered. 'An ambulance turned up, then the *custodes*. There were people rushing everywhere.'

'But why is the therapist still closed?' he persisted.

'Oh,' I sounded bored, 'I don't really know, dear. I think somebody said there'd been a death in the family.' I sighed, trying to sound bitter. 'Nobody tells me anything, you know.'

He thanked me, and I watched him go off down the road. He looked so nondescript, he just faded into the street scene. I waited half an hour in case he came back or somebody else was watching. I dug the old woman out of the café and gave her back the kiosk keys. I reminded her to forget I was here, hinting she was playing an important role in a national security matter. She looked both excited and flattered.

Right on time, Flavius turned up at our new meeting point.

'Anything?' he asked.

'Yes. A completely beige man turned up at the kiosk opposite Hirenses, trying not to appear interested in Aidan.' I transferred the photo to his phone. 'He looked depressed, melancholic, somehow.'

'Gods! Don't start feeling sorry for them.'

'Oh, please!' I threw a scornful look at him. 'He looked so atypical for a bad guy, that's all. Maybe he's one of the bystanders we missed during the extraction?'

Five hours later, we met in the palace park. Crouching in a tiny clearing full of cigarette butts, Flavius gave me not only a name – Trosius – but an address, fixed number and place of work. We hurried over to the central civic buildings just in time to spot this Trosius leaving the *Biblioteca Publica* where he worked. *A librarian?* Librarians involved in fomenting revolution? My brain seized up. Now I *was* on another planet.

'Actually, he's their IT specialist, which is interesting,' Flavius said. Glasses perched on our noses, we read the noticeboard like a pair of avid culture-vultures, only turning away to follow Trosius when we saw him exit the library and disappear around the corner.

We were tracking him into the old part of the town, narrow lanes with overhanging timber-framed houses from medieval times, when he disappeared. Flavius was on point ten metres forward of me and on the same side as Trosius. I crossed the road and closed the gap in seconds. Flavius stood back a half-metre short of the entrance to a narrow passageway between two of the houses. Unfortunately, it was nearly straight: no jutting corners on the houses, no wood uprights to block the view. You could see and so be seen all the way along.

We bunched together like a sightseeing couple. Flavius fished out a gaudy map from his back pocket and started folding the pleats back on themselves. I'd often laughed at his lost tourist technique, but had to admit it made for a great cover. Lucky for us, Trosius wasn't the least aware he was being followed. The passageway opened up at the end into a plaza beyond which was the Via Nova. We ambled on like good tourists, exchanging admiring and inane remarks in semi-loud English. I looked at Flavius like I was following his every word, but kept our target in view over his shoulder.

Trosius headed for the cluster of tables in the centre of the plaza, joining two men drinking from white cups at one of the middle ones. The maroon umbrellas not only kept the sun's heat off the eaters and drinkers, but in the bright light they shaded faces from view.

Although there were a few other people browsing shop windows or walking across the plaza, there weren't enough. We couldn't get nearer to the three men without drawing attention to ourselves. Trosius and the others were absorbed in their conversation, but we watched them the whole time as we moved along into the shaded side of the square. While Flavius gazed into a shop window, I shifted around and made a face at him like I was cajoling him to buy me something, and fired off a few quick-shot photos of them over Flavius's shoulder. Then I crouched down and gestured as if I wanted to take a shot of Flavius from a worm's eye view with the old buildings as backdrop. I fired off a few of Trosius's table. Thank Juno the lens had a polarising lens and auto balance.

Huddling together, Flavius's arm around my shoulders, we stared at the images on the screen. Neither of us could say anything. But I'd seen the faces with my own eyes. I could hardly believe it then. There was no doubting the thickset figure of Caeco nor his short, wiry companion: Petronax.

'Bloody hell!' hissed Flavius. His eyes bulged as he flicked through the pictures for a second time.

'Move along to the next window,' I whispered back. I grabbed his arm and we shuffled along to a high-end ceramics shop. The glossy faïence and replica samian ware in the window failed to make any impact on us today.

'Where's Petronax's security team?' I murmured.

As head of Internal Security, he took a minder or two with him everywhere he went. Flavius recovered enough to scan the plaza. He unfolded and refolded his map, frowning like he was lost, but he checked every metre on the ground. I covered the upper storeys and roof. Internal security people were drawn from regular forces, so they were usually pretty easy for us to detect, sometimes even recognise.

'Nothing,' Flavius muttered.

'Me neither.'

Crap. Either Petronax was supremely confident and was alone or he was using unknown civilians. Not only couldn't we see them here, we didn't have a clue what they looked like or what their capacities were.

'A large brandy, please.'

I gulped it down and ordered another. I drank the second one more slowly. We'd retreated to the covered area of a bar on the Via Nova, the green awning darkening the bright sunlight. Sports photos were scattered around the walls inside, famous faces showing full-teeth grins. The bartender was intent on a screen at the end of the counter, and sneaking a cigarette. Flavius pretended to read the paper, but I knew he'd been equally shocked.

In the seven years I'd served in the PGSF, I'd seen instances of greed, power hunger and bitterness. Even elite force personnel were human. But betrayal? Rarely. The last time I knew about was Robbia seven years ago. She'd been on the take from drug dealers and tried to kill me when I'd found her out. Tacita's attack was a curveball, I thought, but now Petronax of all people was meeting clandestinely with Trosius and Caeco, two known conspirators. And Caeco was supposed to be in custody under interrogation. How in Hades had he gotten out? Petronax, the scornful side of my brain replied.

It all slotted into place – Petronax must have been the one who planted that letter and the photos of me. But why? I knew he didn't like me – an understatement – but this was beyond the personal.

'I have to get back.' Flavius's expression was flat, his eyes drained.

'Sure.' I nodded. 'Go carefully. And watch that bastard Petronax.'

I took a circuitous route back to Dania's, exercising extreme caution.

I was sneaking in the back when she caught me on the stairs. 'Gods! I've been so worried! Where in Hades have you been?'

'What do you mean?'

'Wandering around the big city by yourself like an idiot,' she said in a raised voice, making a face at me. 'Whatever will I tell my aunt?' Her fingers twisted and flicked, signalling silently: *Scarabs. Unknown plain clothes.*

Crap.

'Oh, Dania, I'm so sorry, I didn't mean to be a bother,' and I started some sobbing noises. *Find anything?* I signalled back.

She shook her head in response to my mime. 'Well, go up to your room and get some rest. We'll talk in the morning.'

I stumbled along the corridor like I'd been in the arena all day, unlocked the door, slammed it shut, but I remained outside. I crept back along the corridor. Dania pulled me into her office and switched on the news channel. I fished out my pyramid and placed it on the table.

We stared at each other. I took a few long breaths to steady myself.

'Thank you,' I began. 'I really, really did not want to bring down any trouble on your head.' I hesitated, watching Dania, carefully evaluating her reaction.

She replied with a very rude word, which roughly translated as 'Don't be such a fricking idiot'. 'Just tell me what you want me to do,' she added aloud.

'Look, Dania, a small affair has completely run out of control. The worst thing is that I don't know who the good guys or bad guys are any more. How in Hades did they think about coming to look here?'

'They're searching for you under your real name.' Her voice was stone-cold sober. I saw an uncharacteristically nervous look on her face as she showed me a leaflet with my face staring out. I grabbed it and read through. I started shivering. She guided me to her couch before I fell down. My hand clamped over my mouth, I shook my head at her. I thought I was going to throw up.

I'd been proscribed.

Shit.

I was stripped of my citizenship and excluded from all protection under the law. It was open season on me. With attitude. Anybody informing on me could be paid a reward plus a portion of my assets; the state would take the rest. Nothing would go to Allegra, Gil or Tonia; they, Nonna and all the Mitelae would be blighted. Conrad. He had to divorce me, and immediately, or he'd be dragged in. I should count myself lucky they didn't decapitate proscriptees and stick their head on a spear in the Forum any more.

'They've said all the usual crap about desperate criminal, threat to national security and so on,' Dania said. She snorted, snatched the leaflet from my nerveless hand and threw it in the corner. She tipped her chin at me, encouraging me to finish the glass of water she'd thrust at me.

'You're not on the news, the Internet or the vidchannel, which is odd,' she said. 'With them taking these leaflets round, it'll get out anyway.'

'Yes, but this'll be slower. Why are they doing it that way?' I said, mostly to myself. I couldn't move. My brain was still numb. I took some deep breaths and concentrated for a few moments, running my tongue inside along my teeth. 'I have to leave here immediately.'

'Very clever. That'll be so easy!' Dania replied with awful sarcasm.

'I will not stay here. You know the penalties for helping proscriptees.'

'Don't be silly.' She said it forcefully enough, but I saw a flicker of fear. She'd taken six years of solid hard work and little sleep to build her life up from nothing.

'End of discussion,' I said. 'I'm out of here.'

Early evening, the shouting, raucous laughter and bumping of bodies on furniture from loudmouth, borderline drunk young profis swamped the restaurant. Dania had put a sign outside *'Happy hour for the under thirties'* and caught a load of office workers. She'd drafted in extra staff, and they were handling it with good humour. Then in came some definitely drunk students and it all went to hell.

She called the *custodes*, but she and the bar staff tried to throw the rowdies out in the meantime. The twenty or so drunks started to fight in the street, testosterone flowing freely. The girls stood there egging them on; some joined in. When the scarabs arrived, they broke up the fight, gave Dania a mouthful about irresponsibility, and shoved the happy crowd into blue vans to spend a night in the cells. In the confusion, I slithered off down a side alley. Around the corner, a battered pickup truck was waiting, its engine idling, throwing out diesel fumes. I pulled open the passenger's door and slid into the seat.

I sat in silence, breathing slowly to reduce my heart rate. The truck engine rumbled and coughed. I was bone weary. I glanced at Flavius as he concentrated on innocent-seeming evasion manoeuvres as he drove out of the centre. He wore a coarse-weave shirt and jeans and looked exhausted. I didn't ask where he'd found the students. I was just grateful.

He paused right by the river and threw his cellphone and comms set over the parapet. We drove into a block of lock-up units in between an old apartment block and a junkyard. Flavius killed the lights. A metallic clash and thud made me jump. Another from nearby. I leapt out, knife ready. Flavius rolled out and crouched, his back to mine. We hardly breathed as we circled and scanned.

Nobody. Nothing.

'Some bloody cat,' he said under his breath after a few minutes. The thin metal door of one of the garages swayed as he jerked it open. He drove the truck in. I ran in and dragged the door closed behind us. We stood in the safe dark for a few seconds.

'The shit's hit the fan,' he started. 'I'm out now, too.'

I stared at him, but only saw the reflection from the dashboard lights in his eyes.

'What happened?'

'Paula received a text warning from an ex that they were coming for your ART team. She told us to run.'

We slept in the back of the truck, wrapped in prickly felt blankets, but grateful for the respite. I woke early, cold and startled by the Stygian blackness and smell of metal and sweat. I turned over on the ridged truck floor. My body ached, but not as much as my mind. I was being hunted with maximum effort. And one of my most loyal colleagues was a fugitive with me. And where the hell was Conrad in all this? I'd called him repeatedly on the encrypted supermobile I'd retrieved at the post office. There was no reply. But I wasn't entirely sure he would talk to me if he did pick up.

Flavius woke, eyes wary in a tense face, and dragged himself up. We gathered our things and walked down to the river to find coffee and something to eat. After a night in a dirty truck, we blended perfectly into the dockside canteen. I tried not to gag on the heavy smoke as I swallowed scalding coffee and attacked a wonderful bacon roll dripping with grease. The exquisite salt flavour burst in my mouth and I tasted heaven. Maybe I was just hungry.

'We have to find a secure base,' Flavius whispered. He pretended he was reading a curled-edged tabloid. I glanced at him, stifling my surprise. Why had he said something that obvious?

'We can't go to Dania's,' I said. 'She's already had the scarabs in. I won't endanger her any more.'

'There's one place,' he suggested and stared at me, his eyes searching my face.

I caught my breath. I realised where he was going. I hadn't been happy when I'd contacted the other two "old friends" but I figured it would be brief and temporary. Now he was suggesting something much more dangerous.

'No,' I almost hissed at him. 'No way. I am not involving him in this.'

'Do you ever listen to yourself?' he retorted. 'You talk the biggest load of balls sometimes!' I heard his voice harden and saw the cords in his neck stand out. 'He probably knows all about it anyway. You left him with one of the best information networks around. Being his efficient self, he's bound to have refined it. Pollius and Dania have probably reported your contact. Moreover, he's got the resources we need,' he added, brutally frank. He sat there watching me chew this over.

I was tired and, to be honest, discouraged. Not easy to make balanced decisions when your thoughts and feelings are floundering like beached eels. Flavius made perfect sense, but could I face disrupting a life I'd carefully left protected? Apart from the dubious legality of it all, I would be treading on some extremely sensitive personal ground. I drank another cup of coffee to think about it.

I tried Conrad again. Nothing. I risked a second call, this time home. All I heard was a voice recording with a strange voice, saying nobody was available and please to leave a message. Who in hell was that? I knew every member of our household, and that voice didn't belong to any of them. I cut the call and stared at the blank mini-screen. My hand started trembling. Hades. They'd already intercepted and diverted comms to the house.

By now, the *custodes* would be on full alert, my picture on every patrol person's el-pad. They couldn't track me, now I'd ditched the tracker and badge. I hoped the supermobile shielding still worked, but they'd slog at it in the traditional way. The PGSF were more dangerous. It would only need one scanner to pick us up from an image captured from the public feed and a squad would be rousted to grab us. And only Jupiter knew who Petronax had in his private army.

More urgently, I had to find out what was going on at home; if the children were safe. And Nonna and Helena. I shut my eyes for some relief but opened them again almost instantly to block out terrifying images of my family in danger forming in my head.

'Enough.' I wiped the grease from my fingers, threw the rest of my coffee down my throat and stood up. 'We have no other workable option. Let's do it.'

The docks were compact. Swinging cranes and forlorn industrial warehouses petered out, giving way first to open fields, copses and, two kilometres or so upstream, individual houses dotted along the bank, all with private landings. Ideal if you needed an alternative escape route. We marched in silence, staying under cover of the trees and diving for the ditch whenever we heard a vehicle. The familiar stone house came into sight. The high gate, metal but clad in innocent wood, was closed.

Behind that graceful stone arch with the coded entry system lay a gravel area and another gateway with metal barred gates curved to fit the archway, finials a breath away from the stone. The Venetian scrollwork disguised how solid they were. I shivered at the flow of memories in the house on the other side.

Flavius and I hid behind shrubs across from the house, a little to one side and settled down to watch the entrance gate. Two things worried me. Easy one first: Dania's. There must be a leak somewhere. Although I mailed and wrote her about business stuff, I only went there occasionally; with my job and family, there was too much else to do. Had Pollius spilled? Unlikely, but remotely possible. Was the rest of the network penetrated? If we made it inside, I guessed we'd find out soon enough. I was turning to the difficult question when Flavius shifting his weight caught my attention.

His fingers signalled he couldn't see anybody watching. I confirmed the same. Ironic, in light of later events. The only excuse was that we were tired and desperate, but still a pretty poor one.

A delivery truck drew up, and the gates opened to let it in. We leapt up, coming sideways at the gate. Flavius scrambled onto the rear fender and stretched his arm out. My hand was an inch from his, fingers flexing to grasp it when a shot rang out from behind. Flavius fell off into a crumpled, inert heap at my feet. I seized him, heaved with all my strength. Inch by inch, I dragged him over the gravel through the gate while the truck driver stared, literally with an open mouth. The porter, much more alert, started to block me and my burden when another shot burst out. A kick to my head, searing heat, and I went out.

15

The first thing I noticed was the smell – fresh linen, slightly antiseptic, vanilla even. Next, I heard tiny regular bleeps. I went back to sleep.

'She's progressing well.' A quiet voice and warm breath, somebody bending over me and resting a hand on my forehead. Juno! My head. No way was I going to open my eyes with a headache like this. I heard his low, rich laugh. Absolutely no way, I thought as I drifted off.

I must have known subconsciously I was safe, so I attempted eye-opening next time I woke. I looked around warily. Although it was painful, my head stayed on my shoulders. I was lying half-propped up in bed in a pale blue room, flowers on a table in the corner, bedroom furniture, window, blue drapes. So not a prison. No, of course not – I'd heard that laugh. We'd made it.

'Ah! You've decided to wake up,' came the first voice again. I turned my head very carefully and saw gold-rimmed glasses, greying hair and a sardonic smile above a white lab coat shining too brightly. He gave me a sip of some lemony drink, and I lay back exhausted.

'I'm not going to ask how the head feels – that would be fatuous,' he said. 'But like Hades, I suspect?'

'Yes.' I swallowed. 'Tell me,' I whispered, 'how's my comrade?' I feared the worst. He had been so still, lying there shot.

'I operated on him personally and sewed him together. He's up and pestering to see you.'

Thank the gods. I tried to focus on the man's face above me.

'Something to eat?' he said. 'You've been out for nearly two days.'

My stomach replied forcefully.

He chuckled and disappeared.

I closed my eyes and went back to sleep.

'Come on, lazy, you can't lie there pretending to be asleep. Besides, your sandwiches are getting warm!'

I smiled at him. 'Hello, Flav.'

Flavius found me some extra pillows and I eased myself up gingerly. I munched my sandwiches slowly, my jaw tight, and the muscles pulling the skin on my skull. Each bite hurt, but my hunger overrode the head pain. Flavius told me how he'd been badly winded when he fell and couldn't move. The shot dug a trench through the flesh in his left shoulder but, apart from that, he only suffered some bruising. The porter had slammed the big gates shut and rung the alarm. Guards had run out the house, pushed through the service gate and scoured the approach road, firing off a few rounds. But they'd found no sign of our attackers.

The second round from the unknown shooter had grazed my head, barely scraping my skull. I shuddered at the near miss. I had a hell of a headache but nothing more serious. A hanging basket had suffered an untimely death from the onward travelling bullet, Flavius said drily.

I looked at him, my loyal comrade in arms. He was smart, aware and physically tough. He wasn't a pretty boy like Livius: his light brown hair and mid-brown eyes together with the other standard features you got in a face made a pleasant, but not outstanding combination. This was a great asset for a spook as nobody remembered the average. But, when he smiled, his soul shone out through his eyes. I'd known him seven years; he gave me balance, sometimes quite starkly, other times humorously, always as a true friend. I would've been devastated if I'd lost him.

I was dozing again when I heard the quiet laugh.

'Hello, Pulcheria,' he began.

'Apollodorus.'

He sat on my bed, holding my hand and completely still. It was an old trick of his. He could move as fast as a deadly panther if he wanted. His tall, slim figure was, as always, dressed in black; his black hair, brows and eyes a contrast to his lightly bronzed skin. His smile didn't diminish any of his powerful and dynamic presence.

'Why didn't you come to me straightaway?' he gently chided me. His black eyes were warm and inviting.

'You know why,' I said. 'We split and went in opposite directions. Flav and I only came to you because we were in a desperate situation.'

'So I gather,' he replied in a voice straight off the Arctic Desert. He pressed my hand. 'My dear, you know very well it would give me enormous pleasure to help you in any way I can. To be honest, I'm a little bored.'

Even the half-smile I pulled was not a good idea for my head.

I owed this man a great deal – he'd been my mentor, my faithful servant and my more-than-friend. He'd run my organisation with absolute efficiency, knowing it had been built on deceit. He'd organised the exit strategy, severance payments, retained the network, and built up a new role for himself after my departure. The Pulcheria Foundation was a business organisation these days, generally dealing in property and entertainment. That it was mostly legal, but not always, was irrelevant.

He looked at me with polite curiosity, one eyebrow raised in his mock old-world way.

'So tell,' he commanded.

I smiled wryly. Our positions were reversed, as if he were the patron and I the supplicant client. He caught my expression and smiled back in reassurance. He listened intently until I'd finished.

'I will not have anybody indulging in a shooting match outside my front door, particularly when it is targeted at my colleagues, whether former or current.' He spoke so gently that it made the words much more threatening. I remembered how effective that polite, but deadly voice could be.

'So are you happy now, running around catching what you charmingly call "the bad guys"?'

I'd known, of course, that he would be following my activities, from personal as well as professional interest.

'Ecstatically,' I replied. 'No, really. I can't think of anything I'm better suited to. But this current crisis is bizarre. I'm being caught on the wrong foot most of the time.'

'Unusual,' he remarked.

'An understatement!' I said. 'I figure I'm usually at least one step ahead of the opposition, but here, everything keeps shifting. I never imagined I'd see the Head of PGSF Internal Security letting a dangerous extremist like Caeco out.' I studied the far wall. 'What in Hades has happened to the rest of them? Why didn't they stop Petronax?'

Flavius knocked on the open door. His eyes were shrunken; deep lines ran from the side of his nose to a mouth pulled down. Was he sick? He came over to the other side of my bed.

'What?'

'The legate.'

My heart contracted and flooded with pain.

'No.' His hand shot out and grasped mine. 'He's alive. As far as I know.'

I closed my eyes for a second or two.

'I used the secure comms room here. They've stripped Conradus Mitelus of his command, arrested him for treason and thrown him in the Transulium. My contact doesn't know anything else.' He shook his head and turned away.

I felt sick to think of Conrad labelled as a traitor. It had to be because of my proscription. Tainted by association. What a bloody mess. He had to disown me, divorce me. That would clear him.

Who was I kidding? I'd known somebody was targeting him when they'd forced Aidan to push for that information from Tacita, but I'd never dreamed it would go to this level. The only tiny comforting thought was that he would have given Petronax's people a seriously hard time when they took him.

'My dear?'

Apollo's voice pulled me out of my paralysis. I took some deep breaths to clear my head.

'Okay,' I said. 'This is the situation. The chief bad guy is a rat-faced traitor who has access to everything. The expert personal teams have been disbanded and reassigned. The central command structure is penetrated and effectively paralysed. And this is the unit supposed to be responsible for the safety of the imperatrix and the country.' My voice rose despite my best efforts. 'A total fuck-up.'

'Not, I think, a very glorious state of affairs,' Apollodorus conceded. He was kind to leave it at that.

'The worst is that none of us saw it coming.'

'Ah! Vanity. You really must overcome that tendency, Pulcheria. It's so limiting, you know.'

I glowered at him.

His ironic glance landed on me. I knew he was provoking me to break the blister of my emotion. But I turned away and refused to look at him.

'The doctor says you can get up tomorrow if you feel like it. Then we can assess everything and plan accordingly.' In such bland words, he dismissed a world of chaos, terror and despair.

A steaming drink materialised, brought in by one of Apollo's silent house servants.

'You are to drink this before going to sleep,' Apollodorus said. I looked at him, thinking of refusing on principle, but my nerves were shredded, my head throbbed. I had no strength left to fight him.

I woke the next day feeling groggy, but with no headache – a blessed relief. I stumbled into the shower off my room. Drying my hair, I looked around for my clothes. No sign of my jeans, but Pulcheria's trademark red and black clothes were laid out for me, and the black boots. It took me several minutes to decide to put them on. They fitted perfectly.

Nothing had changed in the house, absolutely nothing. I walked to the dining room as if it were only seven minutes ago I had left it, not seven years. Sitting eating breakfast, Apollo and Flavius were talking quietly. Both looked up as I entered the room. Flavius gasped at my appearance, Apollo showed no reaction. I didn't look either in the eye. I had hardly taken my place when fruit, yoghurt and eggs were put in front of me with a cup of coffee, white, one sugar. I glanced up, searching for the clock, and there it was, exactly where it should be. Even the cutlery was the same fluted design. I ate in silence. I was slipping straight back into a shell waiting for me to inhabit it.

'Shall we go through after you've finished?' Apollodorus

suggested, or was it a command? A meeting table was set out in the atrium. Nothing had changed: the large open area, not as big as at Domus Mitelarum, but more elegant, minimalist even, with white upholstered benches running around three sides and alcoves placed along their length to provide more intimate seating areas. I looked up at the bull's eye glazed centre in the roof. Sunlight poured down making artificial lighting superfluous.

Apollo insisted I take the head of the table. Others joined us, some familiar, but older, some I didn't know. From under my eyelashes, I caught some speculative looks and one or two guarded ones.

'If I may?' Apollo looked at me. I nodded.

'I am delighted to advise you that Pulcheria is once again part of our lives. Some of you will, of course, have fond memories of the previous work we achieved together. Others of you have that pleasure ahead of them.'

I'd bet any money they were wondering what the Hades Apollo was springing on them.

'Hermina, you know, she remains our administration manager.'

She nodded at me, half-smiling. I did the same. I'd always liked Hermina, although she was a bit of a control freak.

'Albinus is our technical genius – he was trained by Dolcius, now sadly equipping the next life.'

I took in Albinus's jet-black head, dark eyebrows, dark eyes. Somebody clearly had a sense of humour, or maybe irony, given his name meant white. He nodded, his face impassive, but eyes appraising.

'Justus, our informer, you know. His network tends to cover, ah, economic opportunities rather than political ones, if you recall.'

What I remembered was how incredibly tough Justus was. Likeable no, efficient yes. I nodded in his direction. A smooth, knowing half-smile glided across his lips leaving absolutely no trace on the rest of his unremarkable face.

'Cassia runs the financial aspects of the foundation. She worked previously as Censor's investigator in the tax service.'

Her symmetrical features were spoiled by a sullen expression dulling her light brown eyes. She didn't smile. The investigators were renowned for their tenacity, resourcefulness and utter ruthlessness. I think the expression "killer Rottweilers" came into Junia's vocabulary if a visit from them was threatened at Domus Mitelarum. She and our legal team burnt the midnight oil to prepare. Cassia looked at me without a trace of emotion; she didn't even muster a smile.

'Hello, Pulcheria,' came a cheery voice as a relief to the serious faces. I'd known Philippus as assistant to the old master at arms. 'Just let me know if you want anything that goes bang,' he said. I'd always loved his lively, almost boisterous manner, like an overgrown high schooler, but I saw he now had a few grey hairs peeking through at his temples.

'Hi yourself, Phil,' I threw back. 'Well, you know what I like, just the usual service.'

He grinned.

'And of course, Flavius, our tactical expert, whom you know so well.'

Flavius stared down at the table and rubbed the fingers of one hand across the back of the other. The irony was painful. I tapped my nail twice on the table surface, forcing him to meet my eyes.

'Thank you, Apollodorus.' I looked at each face, appraising them in turn. Most had settled into a wary look, Justus and Philippus neutral.

I turned to Apollo. 'Now, could you please update me on what you have?'

'I'll let Justus lead on this,' he said.

'We have confirmed Flavius's information about the PGSF legate. He's being held in maximum security, in solitary, in the Transulium military prison.'

My heart thumped.

'Command devolved temporarily upon the adjutant.' He checked his el-pad. 'No, for a day only. A replacement has been appointed: one Lucius Mitelus Superbus.'

'*What?*' I shrieked. 'Please tell me that's not true.'

They all stared at me, startled by my outburst.

'What?' Justus said. He raised his eyebrows.

I exchanged glances with Flavius. I swallowed hard. 'I'm sorry, please continue.'

'Superbus doesn't seem to be fond of his family. He had them all arrested and carted off, even the old lady, Aurelia Mitela, and her grandchildren. No,' he looked at his notes, 'they're her great-grandchildren – the granddaughter, also PGSF, has disappeared. She's been proscribed. Maybe she's in the Transulium as well – we don't know.'

The first I knew I had bitten through my lip was when blood dripped onto the table. Through the red fog of my anger, I tried to reassemble my scattered brains. What did Justus mean by "carted off"? Not to a prison. No, not the children. Gods, no! Even Superbus wouldn't do that, would he?

'Where are they now?' I managed to ask.

Justus looked unhappy, almost apologetic. 'I don't know. I haven't been able to get at anybody inside the Mitelae. They're as tight as a duck's arse, so I can't confirm anything.'

My hands trembled, not only with fear, but rage that such a horrifying thing had been done to my family. I knew Nonna could tough it out. But the children, and Helena? I pictured the concrete cell walls, the solid metal door clanking shut, enclosing them, the terror of being wrenched out of their home by shouting, unknown and uncaring strangers. If any of them was hurt – in any way – Superbus was dead meat; and the butchery would be slow.

'Petronax is really running everything. He's quite strange,' Justus mused. 'He's not married, has no mistress, girlfriend, boyfriend, companion. He visits a *hetaera* twice a month and that's it.'

'Same one?' I asked, thinking of possibilities.

'No, he rotates around three, but in a random pattern.'

'We need to get a hold over each one and bleed them.'

'Of course.' He looked surprised at my callousness. 'I'll arrange it as a priority.'

'Anything else?'

'Well, these "patriarchialists"…Sextus Decius aka Cornelius has a couple of warnings: pilfering when twelve and public disorder at seventeen. He was at a demo for parental rights which turned violent.' He smirked. 'The scarabs were their usual understanding selves. Martinus Caeco – there's a challenge. We can't find him anywhere, but you say he's definitely native-born.' He looked at me, doubt all over his face.

'He's a heavy,' I said. 'Probably a bodyguard, enforcer, numbers runner, possibly procurer, something like that.'

Justus gave me another sceptical look.

'I know one when I see one, Justus.' Why was I explaining this to him? He was that undermining sort – I didn't need to rise to his bait.

'He's going to be hard to find again, but I'll see what I can do. He and Sextus were released without charge along with three others arrested at the same time. It would help if we had some images, but even Albinus can't penetrate the PGSF net.'

'I can help you there.' Six pairs of eyes focussed on me. 'With the pictures,' I emphasised.

Cassia went next, her hard features showing little animation. 'I've started enquiries about this group's financing. You say they're ideologically driven, but they must have considerable undeclared resources to have funded their actions to date.'

She even talked like a tax form.

'Creativity always costs,' she continued. 'There will be an audit trail somewhere. Once we have some more names verified, we can go through their tax files. If there is anything hidden, I will find it.'

I twitched at her hard tone and empathised with Junia.

'Now, the two names we do have…Trosius, your librarian, I've found his return. All appears in order – he's paid the proper tax due on what he's declared. But I conclude he must engage in some undeclared self-employed work as his expenditure is high for his reported income. The other known name, Sextus, has no tax history, but his bank account shows quarterly credits from PFPP, whatever that is. I'll let you know when I have identified the source.'

'Well, that's a reasonable start.' High praise, from Apollo. 'Report back at five this afternoon.' He concluded the meeting and dismissed them all. He ushered me out to the veranda.

'How did you feel that went?' he asked. He smiled pleasantly, but not warmly. His voice was at its most urbane.

'Well, I thought.' I wondered what was coming.

'Justus is looking into the two disconcerting incidents we discussed earlier,' he continued. 'I am unhappy that Dania had a visit from the *custodes* specifically looking for you. I have had a little talk with Pollius.'

I shivered.

'He assures me he said nothing – I believe him. Now, we've identified the two plain clothes – Department of Justice Organised

Crime Unit.' He looked me right in the eye and asked, 'So how are they involved, do you think?'

I took a couple of breaths. Did he think I had instigated a sting? Hades, I hoped not. I was coffin-fodder if he did.

'Not a clue – really,' I assured him. 'The only DJ *custos* who I know has been anywhere near this case is Commander Cornelius Lurio, at the XI. He was there when we mopped up after the Hirenses extraction. I've known him for years.'

'Slightly better than in a comradely way, I think?'

'Correct.' I knew my colour rose as the heat flushed through my face.

'Hmm. Well, we found two cases from the shooting here, and they turned out to be standard *custodes* service issue.'

I digested this slowly. 'So you think the DJ is involved? Maybe it's a small group or just one or two with access to situation reports and/or sensitive information,' I speculated. 'Yes, and they must be able to direct more junior officers to do the legwork.' I pushed further up the path. 'Which means we can narrow it down to a small number. So we have to search through the organisational charts. Do you still have access to the DJ database?' Seven years ago, I'd been appalled to discover he had. Now I just needed it.

He handed me an el-pad. 'Your account has been reactivated, full access. You'll find what you want on there.'

Juno only knew what else I'd find.

'Philippus will arm you – he's probably working on it now, and Albinus will update your mobile. I suggest you discuss your personal security requirements with Hermina this morning.'

I closed my eyes, took a deep breath and then looked him straight in the eye. 'Apollo, I am not slipping straight back into my old role.' I indicated my clothes. 'I think I should like something else to wear.'

'My dear Pulcheria, how can you be so distrusting?'

'Oh, come on. I know a trap when I see one.'

'Do you really?'

16

Apollodorus's organisation started to deliver. Despite the name – The Pulcheria Foundation – it was his. I'd made everybody a lot of money through it, but I'd relinquished control when the old structure had been dissolved. Despite his hard exterior, Apollodorus was a romantic. He felt he owed me for "saving" him from a squalid existence at the edge of the criminal world. Personally, I was sure that a man of his talents would have thrived anyway, but maybe I'd given him his break.

How easy it would be to slip back into this life, this parallel existence. I would have the power of total command, a complete lack of legal restraint, the ability to have an untrammelled, instant effect on people's lives. Seductive. I consoled myself that I was only "borrowing" the organisation until the crisis was over. But I wondered if this was what an addict says to herself when confronted with temptation to indulge in an old habit? Only a little? Just one last time?

These unhealthy thoughts were interrupted by Philippus bringing me a personal armoury. I selected one firearm, a couple of knives and some gas pellets.

'That's a bit bare, isn't it?'

'Not all of us like clanking along setting off every metal detector.'

He grinned and shrugged.

'These are nice,' I commented on the military-issue pellets. 'Where did they come from?' I looked up at him, all innocence.

'Don't ask questions like that, and you won't get disappointing replies.'

I said a very rude word as he collected up the surplus weapons and strode off laughing.

I escaped to the veranda for some fresh air. Bordered by tall, waving trees casting flickering shadows, the back garden stretched down to the river edge where Scots pines and cypresses obscured the house from any prying eyes from the other bank. A cool drink appeared on the table the instant I sat down. Really, Apollo's staff was even more efficient than Junia's team.

Crap.

I had told myself not to think about home. My palms hurt from my fingernails pressing into them. I could do nothing. Nonna would hold them together, but the children would be so frightened. And my strange, sensitive Allegra – how would she get through it?

After lunch, Albinus took forever personalising my supermobile with some mind-altering update.

'If it doesn't detect your biosignature after a set time, it'll shut down and melt the insides into a lump of metallic plastic.' He showed me how to vary the trigger time. Hermina fidgeted nearby waiting him to finish. She had her schedule and hated it being disrupted. She never actually said anything; she just kept looking at her watch. As Albinus left, she unclipped a punched sheet from her diary folder with the schedule of my personal security detail.

'It's a waste of resources. I can look after myself.'

'Sorry, no. These are strange times. The last thing we need is you to be picked up by some over-eager DJ scarab or, worse, PGSF.'

'Why do you think PGSF is worse?'

'They always seem to be one step ahead. You know yourself how single-minded they are. Look how they dragged you off last time.' That had been Daniel, leading the raid on the Goldlights Club and arresting me as a major drug dealer, not knowing I was an undercover DJ *custos* at the time.

'The scarabs give us plenty of hassle, but the PGSF are more dangerous. I don't want to meet trouble halfway up the street. At the moment, they've been hijacked by this Petronax and have that idiot Mitelus Superbus as nominal head. The other Mitelus was tough but professional. This one is a total prat. They're unpredictable at present, so we'll keep you well clear of them.'

'Got anybody inside them?'

'Be serious. Nobody has enough of a suicide wish to volunteer for that job.' She thrust the sheet into my hand. She wasn't going to give way.

'Thank you, Hermina,' I said formally.

'My pleasure.' She gave me a full-on smile and patted my upper arm. 'It's lovely to see you back. I miss the buzz of the old days.'

As I watched her bustle off, my mind started to sketch out a few objectives. Firstly, it was crucial that I take some positive action instead of sitting here waiting for the next bad thing to happen. Secondly, the imperatrix and her family had to be secured and guarded. Thirdly, we had to stop the rot spreading into civil organisations. How deep did these patriarchalists' influence go in, say, the Senate, Curia, the media? Where did the people's tribunes stand? Fourthly, that having restored the situation, my colleagues – wherever they came from – and I would hunt down the traitors with extreme prejudice.

'Report.' I looked at Justus first.

'The palace is quiet, no outward sign of any disruption. I understand a large detachment of PGSF has replaced the regular Praetorian guards. They marched in, completely unexpectedly and sealed it. They're headed by a Major Stern from their Operations branch. We rate him as dangerous, gives no quarter. Is he that good?' he queried.

'Yes.'

Justus waited for me to elaborate. He was disappointed.

'Well, to continue…Your pictures were very helpful – we think we've found Caeco.' He sounded smug. I ground my teeth. How?

'It's only a sixty-five per cent match, mind you, and, I have to admit, it was pure fluke.'

I felt a lot better.

'If this is the same man, he originates from Folentia, near Aquae Caesaris and his family name is Apnia. His father was a self-made man who married into a middle-class family. Lovely dysfunctional family, this. The mother's brother did a stretch for embezzling his sister's investments. The father felt unaccepted by the mother's snooty family so started blackmailing them for, let's call it, personal misdemeanours.'

I hated to think what that meant.

'Caeco, or Apnio, whatever you want to call him, has form for running a numbers game as a kid and later for two counts of aggravated assault. He disappeared from the radar after his release. Possibly radicalised in prison?' he ventured. 'He met up with a Pisentius in Castra Lucilla the other day. One of our outliers was visiting this Pisentius because he's been a naughty boy, not paying his gambling debts. Our man got warned off by a heavy, possibly Caeco.'

'Has this outlier been shown the images Pulcheria provided?' Apollodorus said.

'Yes, and he reckons it could be the same man.'

'Good. Try and increase beyond sixty-five per cent. Now, what about Petronax and his monthly visits?'

'We can squeeze two of the three, and I'm working on the third.'

'Soon as you can, Justus.'

Cassia looked smug, so I invited her to go next.

'Interestingly, PFPP turns out to be a short form for Paterfamilias Patria Potestas.' She let that hang in the air.

Albinus broke first and murmured, 'Each to their own.'

Philippus snorted derisively.

Flavius looked grim.

'Who in Hades are they?' I asked. I knew it wasn't going to be good.

Justus chipped in like the know-it-all he was. 'They're a fundamentalist group, believing literally in the original Roman tribal values. They're only two and a half thousand years out of date, stupid bastards.'

'So they live like retards – is that a problem?' Cassia asked.

'There've been rumours,' Justus said, 'but there's been no court case recorded for killing or selling children. One or two battered women have turned up in refuges, and slightly more than the average number of young girls between twelve and nineteen have committed suicide, but nothing too far above the radar. It's all in the countryside. The scarabs report they've looked into these cases, but they don't push it. According to their records, these people are law-abiding and behave impeccably – no drunkenness, no thieving, so no problem.'

Cassia seized the limelight back. 'The PFPP is registered as a charitable group to help children, particularly male, abandoned by their mothers' families. Their funds are considerable, but the number shown as given financial support is low. My conclusion is that it's a front organisation, albeit an unsavoury one.'

'What's the source of their income?' I asked.

'Credits are shown as a lot of small monthly amounts, so subscriptions I would say. There are just under two hundred and fifty. There are one or two larger donations, which I am tracing.'

'Anything else?'

Heads shook.

'Thanks for the progress report. Same time tomorrow, please.' As they filed out, I glanced over at Flavius.

He nodded and kept his seat.

I turned to Apollodorus. 'I have an idea I want to run past Flavius – he knows the personalities involved.' Apollodorus's black stare fixed on me. I held it with my own. After a minute, he rose and left.

'That took balls, biting the hand that just took us in.'

'Yes, I know,' I said. 'But you'll see why in a moment.'

I fished out the crystal pyramid and plunked it on the table.

Flavius couldn't stop his mouth falling open. 'How in Hades did you smuggle that out?'

'Wrapped it in aluminium foil.'

'That simple?' He grinned in appreciation.

'Have you anything for me?'

'Yes, some good. Major Stern has indeed sealed the palace. They'll have arms, food and water for a considerable time and their own power supply, but they don't have any comms as Petronax has cut the lot.'

I fished my supermobile out of my waist bag, grinned at Flavius and dialled.

A pause. 'What do you mean, who is this? Who in Hades do you think it is, Daniel?' I growled into the mic.

Another pause. 'Taped under the bottom of your top desk drawer.'

Daniel had no imagination about where to hide stuff.

Pause. 'Your cousin Hannah in a shed on the orange farm when you were sixteen. Uncle Baruch beat you into a pulp – pun intended.'

Flavius smirked at that.

'Because I am fabulously clever and well-connected,' I continued. 'Need to know, but I'm safe and active. Are you alone?'

I heard footsteps and a door slam.

'Yes, that's what we heard.' Pause. 'Flavius.' Pause. 'No. Yes, probably.'

I let him carry on for a short while.

'Right, Daniel, here's the thing. We're working on it and I have resources.' Pause. 'Don't ask. Tell no one you've been in contact with anybody outside or even that you can. Juno knows who we can trust at the moment.' I gave him my number – the phone's internal program wouldn't let it register on his cellphone. 'I'll call again in seven hours.' Pause. 'Because I am not an idiot who gets their ideas from James fucking Bond! Out.'

17

I was sitting in a slatted chair on the veranda, my mind on idle, watching the surface of the river rippling and reflecting the early evening light. I closed my eyes for a few moments and imagined myself immersed in it.

'Probably be smashed into and sunk by a waterskier not looking where he was going,' said the cool voice.

I jumped at the sound of Apollodorus's voice. He was a powerful man, heading a powerful organisation, and I'd snubbed and excluded him. Time to pay. But for all he was an expert manipulator, Apollodorus was fatally weakened where I was concerned. Our relationship was hard to define, but at the crucial point he'd always deferred to me. I thought I'd now regained my touch, but I didn't want to hurt his feelings. Laughable, if you looked at it logically.

But I smiled as I looked up at him and accepted the glass of wine he held out. He smiled back, humour reflected in his black eyes. A little older now, the creases around the eyes had deepened and multiplied. I'd never known his age or, for that matter, his true name.

'I'm sorry I couldn't include you in that little chat with Flavius. I have to take account of other commitments and I—'

His finger pressed my lips closed. 'Don't act like the idiot I know you not to be.'

How could he just accept it? I could deflect most harshness, but this constant understanding was unsettling.

'Apollo, if we win, I may not be in a position to reciprocate in a way you hope or maybe expect.' His eyebrows rose. 'If that's a factor in helping us then Flavius and I should go.'

He sighed. 'My dear, I really should have taken more care not to leave the pomposity pills out where you can find them so easily. I suppose I should feel insulted that you think I expect a *quid pro quo*, but I can't make the effort to work myself up to it. The most ridiculous thing you have just said is "if".'

From his reaction, I must have looked puzzled.

'Have you so changed that you think you won't win?'

For once, I couldn't think of a thing to say.

'I like having you here. I like having something different and absorbing to work on. Don't start spoiling my fun.'

Fun?

Yes, in a weird way, it had been fun seven years ago. Apart from the grim business of stopping organised criminals from the West pushing drugs on an industrial scale. We'd been comrades who worked hard and achieved something purposeful together. We'd shared danger, some laughs, and we'd survived. We even made good profits.

I gave up on looking at the river and brought my focus back to the cones on the pines, then down to the red petals on the geraniums in pots on the veranda. I kept my voice low. 'It's not fun now, Apollo. This attack is on everything, not just my family, my cousin and our children, but on the Imperium and its survival. You know the last rebellion like this killed thousands and nearly destroyed the country.' I slammed the glass down, just missing the table edge. It shattered on the stone slab. 'All the time I'm alive, I will not let it happen again. Period.'

Next morning, I was up at four and thinking. It was cold and I sat huddled in a heap of blankets on the grass river bank. The river moved hypnotically in the semi-dark. In the half-light, I saw Silvia and her second child, Darius, almost too good, unlike the atrocious Stella, the eldest, who I could cheerfully strangle. Darius was only ten but already serious, with large, enquiring eyes. And Hallie, only eighteen months older than my Allegra. And their father, Conrad, flowed into my mind. No, he lived in my mind, my heart, my soul. Something in my core knew he was still alive. A blood and bone Roman, he was tough as Hades. What horrors had Petronax prepared for him? I jammed my lips together but the tears fell down my cheeks.

My conversation with Daniel the previous night hadn't been long, but we'd established a comms schedule. If I wasn't available, he would talk to Flavius. Back in my room, I called Daniel and told him to be especially careful of Darius.

'You have to go through all Darius's staff and contacts again, especially the men. And do it now.'

'God! You've become so bossy!'

'Oh, well, sorry. Hey, Daniel, who's the one out here trying to sort things out? Like you're in a position to do something?'

'Don't get used to it,' he grumped. 'I still outrank you.'

'Oh, right. Yes, sir, no, sir!' I retorted. I picked at the embroidered edge of the duvet cover. 'Have you…have you heard anything about Conrad?'

'With our lack of comms?'

I could almost hear him thinking my brain had fallen apart.

'Don't worry,' he said much more kindly, 'he'll get out of this. He's tough as hell and he's survived one rebellion.'

Apollodorus and I talked over breakfast.

'Do you still have that secure facility over by the industrial park?'

'Of course,' he replied, looking surprised.

'Good, I want the librarian, Trosius, plus Pisentius, Cyriacus and Sextus picked up, held separately and prepared for a little talk with me and Justus. We'll let Caeco run for the moment. Tell the troops ditto for Petronax. If they see him, they must exercise extreme caution – he's a mean little shit.' I smashed the top of my egg. 'It's only a remote possibility, though. I'm sure he's holed up inside the PGSF barracks.'

'You're very focused this morning.'

'Yes, well, we've spent enough time dithering around.'

I looked at the table with its impeccable silver cutlery and white porcelain, and my fingers twitched on the damask cloth. I swallowed some coffee and looked directly at Apollodorus. 'Do you have any contacts at the Transulium?'

'Ah! I wondered when we might come to that.'

'I'm not going to pretend an attitude or play any little games. I will beg and plead if you want, but I must break him out of there, Apollo.' I looked across the room at the buffet with its arrangement of white and yellow roses, glass jugs, bowls, and preserves, and back to Apollodorus. I rubbed the back of my left wrist with the fingers of my right hand and stared back down at the tablecloth.

'Yes, I think so, too, or you won't be able to concentrate.'

How strange this man was. He always managed to surprise me with his curveball comments. What on earth could his real motivation be? Such an operation would take resources and time. It could lead to injury or death of one or more of his people.

'Leave it with me,' he said. 'One thing: I will not have him running round afterwards, playing soldiers in an operation where my people are involved. The best I can offer is to put him somewhere neutral. I hope you understand that.'

Neither Justus nor I was too bothered by the summer heat reflecting inward from the sheet metal walls of the old warehouse on the industrial park: we'd both opted for light tunics, but our guests weren't so comfortable waiting in their locked, windowless cubicles. I insisted on giving them a water bottle each, despite Justus's protestations.

We started with Sextus, who was young and less experienced. Two of Justus's heavies had plunked him on a chair in the middle of the empty cavern. Sextus's eyes were covered by a black cloth and his hands strapped to the edges of the chair. Justus and I played Nisius and Nisia, a delightful pair of siblings. Standing just within earshot, we discussed ways of breaking bones, specifically kneecapping. We ranged through whether to use a gun, knife, a crowbar or sledgehammer, and whether from back or front was most effective and painful.

'I don't know, Nisius,' I moaned, my tone nasal and whining. 'I don't know why we don't just pump him full of the chemical stuff and wait for the verbal diarrhoea to start.'

'Or the real thing!' Nisius/Justus laughed nastily. 'You know it makes the veins in their dick rupture and go septic. Remember the mess last time?'

'Oh, all right, we'll go for the physical then.'

Sextus was trembling by now. Our boots resounded on the concrete floor as we approached the seated figure. The metal tools we carried clanked loudly. They were, in fact, assorted lengths of domestic pipe.

Sextus had a deepening bruise on his cheek and a dried blood dribble at one corner of his mouth. Sweat soaked his front hairline, and his forehead glistened. Maybe it was the heat, but probably not.

'Oh dear, dear...What happened to you? You didn't try to pick a fight, did you?' My fake sympathy was a long way from the nervous tones of old Catherine MacCarthy. 'Now, we need to have a little talk and you're going to do most of it.' I tapped his knee firmly with one of the pipes. He shivered. Sweat broke out above his upper lip.

'My boss is a bit cross with you and your friends – you've interfered with an operation he was running.'

I paused, waiting for the fear to soak in.

'You just tell me everything like a good boy and we'll part friends. You screw around and what's left of you won't be able to limp back into your little hole.'

He gulped and then started.

Caeco had recruited him after the demonstration he had been involved with. He'd been barely seventeen and was only nineteen now. Jupiter! Corrupting a cross, frightened kid was classic fundamentalist tactics, but purposefully damaging an already fragile soul looking to strike out at something was worse.

Sextus had been assigned to Aidan Hirenses' office as receptionist as he was presentable and well-spoken enough to divert clients' enquiries while still watching Aidan. As Novius had found when we'd raided, they'd had a remote alarm installed that Sextus could easily trigger from his desk.

Aidan had been targeted by the conspirators because several PGSF used his practice or his services at Mossia's gym. Sitting inside the PGSF building, surely Petronax could have accessed any information they needed, including personal stuff about Conrad? Then my brain started up. Of course, Petronax wouldn't have cleared access to the personal records for somebody as high-ranking as the legate. None of the PGSF would dream of saying anything to Petronax unless absolutely necessary professionally, and then only if he threatened to pull teeth. He was a bare rock stranded in a sea of information, and no boat ever landed there.

'Now, Sextus, I have this bad feeling you're not telling me everything. Maybe I'll have Nisius think up a way to remind you.'

Justus rubbed two of the pipes together as if he were sharpening some tool.

'No!' Sextus all but screamed.

'Fine then, you tell me right now what information they wanted and why, and I might be able to persuade Nisius to fetch you a cup of water.'

Growls of "spoilsport!" came from Justus. I glared at him.

'They said they had to take the PGSF legate out. Eliminate him.'

My turn to tremble.

'Now, why was that?' asked Justus.

'Because he is the child's father.'

I froze. I glared at Sextus through a red haze that had welled up in front of my eyes, tensed my muscles ready to spring, and brought both hands up ready to tear him apart. Justus grabbed me in time.

'The child's name?' Nisius's whiny voice asked, a little short of breath. He was struggling to hold on to me.

'Darius, the so-called Imperatrix Silvia's son. The whole line is tainted but, with a male child at least, we could restore the normal order of things,' he shouted with some defiance.

I gave him his due. That was a courageous thing to say in the circumstances.

Justus took over while I tried to pour water into a plascard cup with shaking hands.

'How is that to happen?'

Silence.

Incredibly, Sextus appeared to be sulking. Had he found some grit deep in his being? Was he reverting to the stubborn Cornelia type at last?

Justus slapped his face. 'I asked you a question, sonny. Now answer me.'

'The woman and two female children will be disposed of in the traditional way and the boy put in her place. We have enough supporters in the Senate to make a Council of Regency until he matures.'

'Nice,' hissed Nisius. 'Kill a popular ruler along with two of her children. What were you going to do, strangle the six-year-old and rape the teenager to death like in ancient times you love so much?' He spat in Sextus's face, shoved the chair to the ground and gave Sextus a vicious kick.

I was astounded. I didn't know Justus had it in him.

We left him there. I ran outside and threw up.

'Do you need a few moments before we do the others?' Justus asked and made me finish the cup of water I'd fetched for Sextus.

'I need to make a phone call. Back in five.'

'Nice delicate fingers, Trosius. Shame if they got broken and healed crookedly.' Nisius put a little backward pressure on his right-hand forefinger. By the time we'd acted out the preliminary pantomime, Trosius had turned white, a contrast with the black cloth covering his eyes. He started to tremble once Justus bent down to whisper the threatening words in his ear.

'Now, now, Nisius, you're going to make him scared,' I cooed from the other side. 'Trosius, be a good boy and tell me about what you've been doing for Martinus Caeco. And don't say "Martinus who?" or I *will* have to let my brother loose on you.'

'Please,' he moaned. 'Don't break my fingers, please!'

Justus bent one more back, a little more than was necessary, but didn't snap it. I frowned at him.

He shrugged, but relaxed his grip a little.

'Well, let's start with your messaging lists and protocols, and see how we do.'

He spilled the lot: names, e-addresses, protocols, system passwords, schedules and more.

Cyriacus proved a little more stubborn. His was quite a sad story: his son had been taken away by his dead wife's mother who'd somehow rescinded the settlement her daughter had made on Cyriacus. He was left destitute and childless, virtually a beggar until he had some luck gambling. Then, of course, he'd run up debts. Caeco spotted the opportunity, stepped in, paid them off and recruited him into the patriarchalists. From that moment, Cyriacus felt he'd found a purpose in life, strongly motivated by his earlier misery. I felt sorry for him until he started saying he'd be proud to be a martyr attempting to kill the women heading the Twelve Families starting with the old Mitela bitch. I kicked him. Hard. After that unprofessional spurt of temper, I settled down with Justus to interview Pisentius.

Another one with gambling debts. Was there a type emerging, I wondered? What we really wanted was his dealings with Caeco. He looked pale, but determined. This was not going to be easy, or pleasant.

'Now, Pisentius, your friends have been very cooperative. You're not going to spoil the pattern, are you?' I asked reasonably. He told me to go and do something very rude, and anatomically impossible, so I stamped hard on his upper instep with the heel of my boot.

He shrieked.

'That was the wrong answer, Pisentius. You lose ten points.' Tears streamed from his eyes. He flinched as I placed my heel on his other instep.

'Now, let's start with an easy one – tell me when you last saw Caeco.'

'Last week,' he mumbled.

'And you talked about…?'

'Things.'

'Oh dear, you are trying to give yourself a hard time, Pisentius.' I sighed.

I walked away as Justus brought his right arm up to start the lesson in behaviour. Although I heard, I couldn't watch.

A little while later, I intervened. Justus was enjoying himself too much.

'Now, Pisentius, let's see if you're in a mood to be a bit more chatty. Caeco came and saw you. Tell me what happened.'

'He saw off that bastard trying to put pressure on me for some money I owed. We should've finished him off.' He took a deep breath and spat out a tooth and gob of blood. 'Martinus said we had better things to do. Shame.'

'Then?'

'He had a list of senators who supported our cause – he'd picked them out himself. He knew they were right thinking.'

'So where is this little boys' fan club meeting?' I sneered.

Justus shot me a warning glance and stepped in. 'Never mind her, she gets a bit over-excited. Just tell me, between us men.' Justus smirked at me.

He was irritating, especially when he was right.

Justus tapped Pisentius on the knee as a reminder.

'They're meeting in three days' time at the Senate, before the formal quarter day. He's going to do it as a charity petition.'

'So which senators are we talking about?'

'I don't know – Caeco never said.'

'Oh, please! Do you really want that injection? No bother to us which way we go,' I said in my coldest voice.

'No! Really, I really don't know. Please.' He started pleading.

'You do know that Caeco is only after power, don't you? He doesn't care a minim about your cause.'

'That's not true. He embodies the cause.'

'Oh really? None of you means anything to him.'

'You're just saying that, you lying bitch.'

Justus slapped him hard.

'If you talk to my sister like that again, I will put your eye out.' He pressed lightly through the blindfold on Pisentius's eyelid and spoke in an over-gentle voice. Pisentius shrank back.

'Sorry to disappoint you, Pisentius, but why do you think Caeco and his boy, Trosius, met with the Head of Security at the PGSF. Not exchanging flower arranging tips, I think.'

Silence.

Justus handed me the photos and we stood behind Pisentius's chair. I curled the lower edge of his blindfold up so he could see.

'Manipulated,' he mumbled.

'Gods, you are ignorant. Look again. See the pixels, how the pattern's not disturbed? Didn't you learn anything at school?'

'No. Not possible.' I could hear the desperate hope in his voice that it wasn't true.

. . .

Justus's troops took him back to his cell. All four would stay locked up for the duration. For operational security, I calculated Petronax would have forbidden Caeco to contact any of them before the Senate meeting.

Back at the house, Justus poured me a large brandy. 'Here, get this down your neck.'

'Thanks,' I muttered.

'You don't like this side of it, do you?' Behind the curiosity in his eyes, I saw unexpected sympathy. 'I remember from before, you preferred to trick them.'

'I'm realistic enough to know we don't have time now,' I conceded. 'But no, I don't.'

I'd given up counting how many laws I'd violated.

18

Next morning, I woke feeling optimistic. We had identified the conspiracy's principal targets, neutralised several key plotters, and accessed their comms. We would move on Caeco at the pre-Senate meeting and Petronax was entering into my sights. But we had one serious vulnerability, or rather I did.

I was peering over Albinus's shoulder at the screen displaying the richness of the comms info we'd gained from Trosius.

'You know, this guy was very meticulous,' he said. 'His organisation and filing are immaculate. It's also his weakness.'

'He's a librarian!' I snorted.

'Somebody has to be – my father was one.'

The heat spread up my neck. 'I apologise. I didn't know. I shouldn't have been so judgemental.'

He swivelled around on his chair. 'Gods! Don't go all formal on me, Pulcheria – you shouldn't be so sensitive.'

'Now who's being judgemental?' But I gave him a smile.

He turned to the screens again. 'I'll send you a list of the main correspondents when I've teased them out. You'll want them before the Senate meeting, I suppose?' He moved his head up and down by a few millimetres at a time as his eyes followed the scrolling data down the screens.

'Please,' and gave him an encouraging pat on the shoulder.

Apollo materialised behind me and scanned the screens for a few minutes. He bent down, his mouth brushing my ear and whispered, 'He's not quite the sorcerer that one of my former employees was. How is the delightful Fausta? Still using her nimble fingers to delve around in forbidden places?'

I kept my eyes on the screens. 'She's settled in very well.'

'I was more than a little annoyed when you poached her. But, on reflection, I have to acknowledge she had finished her most important project for me, so it wasn't such a loss.'

Technically, I hadn't poached her. The *custodes* had pulled her in on suspicion of hacking a bank, a private project of her own. When her name came up on the watch report as a Pulcheria Foundation employee, it generated an alert in my mail. I knew how talented she was, so I gave her the choice: a crushing length of imprisonment as a cyber criminal or a career as a cyber cop with access to the most powerful security systems in the country.

She gasped once then almost immediately reassumed a nonchalant pose. But I'd seen the fire in her eyes in response to my offer. She flipped from a truculent teenager into a keen recruit faster than I could have spun a *solidus* coin. She'd worked hard to prove that the best defenders were former pirates. And to my surprise, and I think hers, she was an excellent soldier.

I shrugged and followed him into his study.

'These are the schedules for the maximum security wing at the Transulium,' he said, handing me several sheets. I glanced up, but his face was impassive. I studied the pattern of shift changeovers and personnel, and found one or two possibilities where the coverage was a little weaker.

'The main problem is the confirmation call from the governor,' Apollodorus commented. 'I understand it doesn't go to the new legate but to his deputy, the unlovely Petronax.'

Shit.

'I don't know Governor Sentoria,' I said, 'but she's supposed to be a careful individual, a bit of a cold fish, She keeps out of inter-service bickering by not cultivating anybody in any branch. Fence sitter.'

'Well, we can't all be action heroes with attitude problems,' he teased.

'So, we're not going to have any leeway there, are we?'

'No, even though she's likely to lose her job under the Petronax regime,' he speculated. 'I think she'll go by the book, especially with such a high-profile prisoner. Even Justus has nothing on her.'

'So, we need to divert the call she'll make to Petronax to somebody willing to impersonate him without that somebody being killed.' I fetched myself a glass of water and waited until I'd drunk it all before continuing. 'There's one obvious candidate in place: he's one of Conradus's oldest friends and comrades. We'll have to bring Albinus in on this.' I looked straight at Apollo. 'You'll have to forgive the question, but can you reassure me that Albinus can be trusted one hundred per cent?' I winced internally as I asked this.

I saw a flare of light in his black eyes as they narrowed. His index finger touched his forehead creased in concentration as his mouth tightened in a straight line. He paused for a second or two.

'How can I put this?,' he said. 'People in my organisation would think long and deep before contemplating a foolish step such as talking to inappropriate outsiders. The consequences would be unpleasant. And permanent.'

'I knew you'd be annoyed.'

I glanced at the luminous display on at my watch. Eight thirty. Our target trudged into view. That was weird. A strong, self-confident man, he usually strode along, clearing everything and everybody before him. He reached the door of a tasteful, but fairly modest, apartment block, slid his card into the reader and slipped inside. He must have some kind of additional security clearance under the current curfew. Justus reported earlier that evening that the authorities had "reluctantly ordered that citizens should act responsibly and stay off the streets at night". The official line was that criminal elements were rampant. Well, that was right, but from whose angle? I'd noticed there were far more *custodes* around – we'd dodged several patrols on our way here.

By now, our mark should have gotten to the apartment on the top floor. I'd give him another five minutes to settle down in a comfortable armchair with a glass of beer and start chatting to his hostess. They'd known each other for several years and were established lovers.

Oh, well, I thought, as we hacked the entry code and followed his route up the stairs, time to interrupt their friendly pre-sex banter and ruin their evening. I knocked on the door.

'Evening, Adjutant,' I whined in my nasal Pulcheria voice. 'Mind if we come in?' I pushed in past him before he could object, followed by Albinus and two bodyguards.

Shock and anger passed across Lucius's face. For a second, he stood there, speechless, immobile. Then he recovered and took half a step towards me, but one of my bodyguards had a muzzle in his chest before he could reach me. The other one grabbed Lucius's belt and side arm from the hall table and slung it over his own shoulder in case the adjutant felt tempted.

'What in Hades do you want? Who the fuck are you?' He moved instinctively to screen his companion from view.

'Tsk, tsk, language!' I pulled my side arm out, motioned him through the hall, away from the others into another room. I closed the door. It looked liked the bedroom. Lovely cut-work sheets, I thought. I kept my weapon trained on him and waited.

'Who are you?'

'Look more closely, Lucius,' I said in my normal voice.

Several seconds passed. He frowned but, as suspicion gave way to disbelief, his eyes opened wide.

'Gods! Mitela? Is it really you?' I gave him a cheeky smile like I normally would. I was incredibly pleased to see him. He was a direct connection to Conrad.

'Jupiter's balls! Where the hell have you been since you deserted? Give me a fucking good reason not to arrest you here and now!'

I moved my weapon up a centimetre. 'Look, Lucius, I'll explain, but it's crucial you don't mention my name in front of the others. Or that I have any involvement with the PGSF.'

'That won't be hard, once internal security has finished with you.' He stared at me, still looking like a sullen volcano, but past the point of erupting. 'Gods, Carina, you've had us frightened stupid. Conradus hid it well, but I know he was worried shitless. Mind you, he's got more problems right now than a renegade junior officer.'

'Stop bitching, Lucius. That's why we're here – to get him out.'

He looked me up and down. 'Well, you and your monkeys out there don't exactly look like a rescue team; more like the Mafia.'

'Nice,' I retorted, but appreciated how near Lucius had guessed. 'I had no option once I was proscribed.'

He said nothing.

'And how have you been doing in your efforts to spring him?' He couldn't fail to hear the hard edge in my voice.

He flinched. 'Point taken,' he said. 'But I've been desperately trying to stop Petronax destroying us.'

I looked closer. The shadows around his eyes were deep, an unhealthy brown. Although he thrust his chin forward, his skin was taut, showing the strain he was under.

'What happened? What did he do?'

'When Conradus was taken away, Petronax pulled the national security card to summon the entire unit on parade in the courtyard. To update us, he said. Of course, all our personal weapons were in the safe boxes.' He looked away.

'His private army was waiting outside. He segregated the men and made them stand separately from the women. He gave the men the option to join him in his "glorious enterprise", as he called it.' Lucius snorted. 'Of course, nobody stepped forward. Petronax sneered at us, calling us ball-less. He ordered all the women to be locked up in the cells or the secure interview rooms, and the men back to their desks. His associates would be guarding us. They had enough weapons to start an arms fair. All outside comms had been cut. He told me I was answerable for any disobedience. For any breach, he'd decimate the unit, starting with the female officers and NCOs. And then, as an example, he said, he walked up to Galla, put his pistol to her head and shot her point-blank.'

His voice had almost vanished. He croaked the last bit out, sat down heavily on the bed, and dropped his head in his hands.

'Thank Mars, Daniel Stern had taken off with his group to the palace.' He let a breath out slowly. 'Galla should have gone with them. She'd still be alive if she had. But fucking Petronax would have chosen somebody else.'

I turned away, grasping hold of a chair back. Sour fumes rose up my throat and I ran for the bathroom.

I rinsed my mouth and wiped my face. I gripped the edges of the fluted porcelain basin and stared into the mirror. Blood oozed from where I'd bitten my lip. I swore into the glass I would kill Petronax, if nobody else got there before me.

Back in the bedroom, Lucius handed me back the pistol I had dropped.

'Fine terrorist you make.'

My hand shook as I took it from him and stowed it in the holster. I dabbed at my lip. 'Lucius, I have to ask you something personal.'

With all his problems and the sickening brutality he was trying to contain, it might not have touched his radar.

'Do you know where my grandmother and the children are?' After Galla, I braced myself for the worst.

'Yes, I do. They're at home, under house arrest, but they're safe.'

My legs gave way. I dropped down onto the bed.

He laid his hand on my shoulder and smiled. 'Nothing to do with me, I'm afraid. Paulina knows a friend of Helena Mitela's through the teacher mafia. She and Helena were supposed to meet, but the curfew torpedoed it. This friend couldn't get anything but a voice message, so she went round to your house, but it was bristling with *custodes*. They said no contact was permitted with any of the Mitela women and children inside.'

Back in the hallway, Lucius's friend, Paulina, was frozen out of her wits at the immobile, but obviously menacing, Albinus and guards. The two bodyguards, now porting arms, watched everything without emotion or reaction. Not many teachers come across such disturbing figures in their professional lives. A few rambunctious teenagers annoying the rest of the class didn't count in comparison.

I went forward, holding out my hand in greeting and smiling. 'Paulina Carca, I am so very sorry to burst into your home and interrupt your evening. If it were not for the extremely serious circumstances, I would not have dreamed of doing so.'

She was taken aback by my top-drawer manners, completely at variance with my raffish appearance. Her middle-rank social conditioning led her to deny it was any trouble, and she asked us whether we would like any refreshment. Lucius pulled her into the bedroom, shut the door, curtly nodding his head to the rest of us to go to the main room.

He emerged after a couple of minutes, a scowl on his face. A faint sound of quiet sobbing in the background stopped the instant he shut the door.

'I should flog you, Ca— What the hell am I to call you?' he asked, glaring at me.

'Nothing.'

'Sit down somewhere, but don't make a mess.'

The two bodyguards stationed themselves behind me, weapons ready, but Albinus sat with me.

'Well?'

I'd forgotten how formidable he could be. I took a breath and started.

'We have a plan to extract the legate from the Transulium, but we need a little help from you.'

'How are you—?'

'You don't want to know.'

'Very well.'

'What do you know about what Petronax and his friends are up to?'

Lucius looked around at us all. 'I can't tell you that.'

'I don't want to be a bore, Adjutant, but we probably know a great deal more than you do,' I said. 'I just want to know how much I need to fill you in about the situation.'

'You go first.'

I waded straight in. 'You know there's a conspiracy by patriarchalists to overthrow the imperatrix, kill her female children, and put Darius on the throne with a Council of Regency made up of traitor senators?'

His eyes goggled. 'No,' he croaked. His face had gone white. I thought for a moment he'd stopped breathing. I was fascinated. I'd never seen Lucius so obviously upset. It made his reaction to Aburia look like a lover's kiss.

'Once they have the imperatrix, their intention is to execute her. The legate, as the boy's father, would naturally protect him if his mother were dead as well as be a focus for opposition, so he's high on their hit list. They need to remove him early to pre-empt any action he might take. We're fighting time here.'

I took a deep breath. I was nearly reverting to Carina. Time to swap back.

'That bastard Petronax finessed all your lot,' Pulcheria's voice gloated. 'I mean, you have to admire him for his tactics.'

Lucius was coming to the boil again, but he contained it.

'Have you any proof?' I could see him pleading silently with me not to have.

'Shedloads. Confessions, electronic, witnesses, documentary – the lot. But before we can start drawing the loop tight, your legate has to be out of there.'

'I'm in, obviously.' Lucius started to breathe again.

'We don't want to expose you yet – you're too useful where you are, containing the fallout from Superbus. Petronax is not stupid, so our timing has to be ultra-precise.'

'Tell me what I need to do.'

Albinus ran through the procedure with Lucius. They rehearsed it several times until they were second-perfect. Lucius would have no problem imitating Petronax's voice: he'd entertained us several times with his impression of the latter's ratty little squeak.

I took Lucius aside for a few minutes to outline the next phase to him privately. He found it difficult to accept at first and grumbled that it would take hours afterward to reset everything, but of course he would be ready as soon as he received the operational order.

'I trust you, Carina. You scare me shitless with some of the risks you take, but I admit you've never had an operation fail yet.'

'I'm touched, Lucius.'

'Yes, I know.'

Later that night, we assembled in the basement garage at Apollo's house. The troops were all ready, to be led by Flavius dressed as a senior centurion. Weird to see him back in his uniform. Well, it wasn't his, of course. Philippus had an excellent source of military matériel. Flavius and

I exchanged looks as we inspected the security vehicle. It was absolutely genuine. Somebody had a nice little operation selling off military property. This was starting to bug me; something to look into afterwards.

I could hardly bear watching them go off without me, but I knew Flavius and his team would do it. I walked all around the house, up and down both sets of stairs, into every room. I walked around the garden twice. Apollo came and fetched me, pressed me down onto the white cushion seat in the atrium. Without saying a word, he handed me a small glass of brandy and stood over me while I drank it. He made me eat a plate of tiny, exquisite bites prepared by his chef. In the end, he sat with me and waited.

Eighty-seven minutes after they'd left, the interphone rang. I jumped up and ran down to the underground garage. The long wheelbase came to a halt by the service door into the house. Flavius leaped out. He nodded and grinned. I ran to the back and tore at the door. I couldn't open it. My fingers were numb. A strong hand gently removed mine and tugged the door open. Somebody brought a flashlight. A still figure lay slumped on the floor of the vehicle, light catching on the chains on his wrists and ankles. I held my breath.

'No, he's alive.' Flav's voice cut through the fog that had invaded my brain. Somebody brought a stretcher and Conrad's body was gently lifted out.

The medic hovered over him doing checks. 'Take him upstairs to the sick bay,' he said, ignoring everybody. I followed, determined to see and know everything.

The medic did a more detailed examination, grunting as he read the screen on the scanner he ran over Conrad's unconscious body. He gave him a shot and fixed up a drip. He pulled a blanket up over Conrad, turned the light out and shooed us out.

'Well?' asked Apollodorus.

'He's dehydrated, undernourished and exhausted,' the medic answered dispassionately. 'They've worked him over systematically and I would say over several days. General bruising, concentrated to kidney, stomach and groin areas. Two cracked ribs, though. I can't find any major internal injuries. I'll leave him to rest tonight and examine him again in the morning. He should sleep at least twelve hours. Leaving the chains on tonight won't hurt him. You'll disturb him more trying to remove them now.'

I moved from foot to foot; I fidgeted with everything near my hands; I bit the skin either side of my nails. I wanted to touch Conrad, to feel he was alive. I was so wired I could have sprung on anybody. I caught a movement out of the corner of my eye as Apollodorus nodded to the medic, but it was too late to do anything about it. I felt the needle prick then fell unconscious.

I woke up early the next morning in my own bed. My eyes struggled open in a head full of cotton balls. I shook it to clear it and reached over for a drink of water. The black writing stared out of the white paper; one word: "Sorry".

Sorry? I'd kill him! How dared he?

I leaped up, threw on my clothes and rushed along to the sickbay. The clock showed just gone seven. The nurse looked startled as I pushed in. Conrad was still out cold. His skin colour had improved from grey to white emphasising the bruises. The cut and burn marks were livid, but starting to pucker. I stroked his forehead gently and kissed it. He didn't stir. I sat by his bed, right by his head and waited.

Somebody brought me a tray with coffee, pastries and fruit. I devoured them – I hadn't eaten since yesterday lunchtime. Flavius looked in after nine, but there was no change.

I felt Apollo first rather than heard him. 'Don't say it,' I said between my teeth.

Silence.

'What were you playing at?' I growled, not looking at him.

Silence.

'Well?'

'You commanded me not to say it, so I didn't.'

'Gah!'

'I'm sorry to have tricked you, but I knew you would have stayed at his bedside awake all night to nobody's benefit. If you weren't so cross, you must admit it was the logical thing.'

I rolled my shoulders further inwards and drew my face in, my lips tightened.

'Don't,' he said, running his finger across my cheek. 'It spoils your face, and it wouldn't be the best thing for him to see when he wakes.'

I came near to hating Apollo when he was so reasonable and so right.

A little while later, Conrad stirred. I leapt up, but he was still fast asleep. Around half ten, the medic came in. I turned my shoulder to him, trying to look offended. He just ignored me and did some checks. I must have looked desperate.

He took pity on me. 'Don't worry, he'll be fine.' He smiled at me. 'I mean it. Sleep is the very best thing for him right now. If he wakes, just buzz me.' He handed me the remote.

I was dozing when I heard a noise of stirring plus clinking of chains. His eyes opened, blinked at the light, chased around, scanning for danger. He found me and settled there. His pupils were tiny in the hazel irises.

'Carina?' he whispered.

I leaned over and touched an unmarked patch on his face with my fingers. A dark red-purple bruise with an open diagonal slash covered most of the right cheek. I couldn't say anything. He gave a ghost of a smile and winced. Involuntary tears fell out of the outside corners of each of his eyes and streaked down the sides of his face.

'Drink,' he rasped.

Juno, I was a fool. I grabbed the closed plascard mug of water and raised it to his lips. His mouth was torn. He sipped carefully through the straw. What had they done to him? I felt the soft roll of a tear escape my own eye and quickly wiped it away. Conrad would need me strong.

He closed his eyes and took a deep breath. He stopped abruptly halfway, grunted and let it go slowly. I took a square from the pile of gauze on the bedside table, poured water on it, and gently patted his eyelids and lips.

'I thought they were going to kill me,' he rasped.

'They were, and soon,' I said and turned my face away. I didn't want him to see my agony at that thought. I cursed Governor Sentoria for letting this happen. She was such a coward, sitting on the fence. Well, she'd be out of a job soon, I vowed.

He stared at the ceiling. 'We've been well and truly had, haven't we?'

'Yes. They were clever and determined. They must have been planning it for months, even a year.'

He tried to move and found the chains.

I laid my hand on his arms to stop him pulling against the shackles.

'You needed the sleep first,' I said. 'I'll ring and have them removed, if you're up to it.'

'Who? Where are we?'

'Don't have a hissy fit, will you?'

'Tell me.'

'At Apollodorus's house.'

He closed his eyes and said a very rude word.

I buzzed and people descended. The medic, whose name I eventually learned was Balius, came to do more interminable checks. He asked all kinds of questions. Justus took notes of every answer Conrad gave. Flavius hovered at the bedhead, a grim expression on his face, like he was Conrad's bodyguard. Conrad managed to sit up but even though Balius and the nurse were careful, he couldn't help but wince. The pink that had started to reappear in his face vanished back to white, and sweat broke out on his forehead. Somebody brought sandwiches which I broke into tiny pieces and he devoured despite his ruined mouth followed by another full cup of water. Blood oozed from the deep crack in his lip. After that, he looked tired but better. Balius refused to take the drip out.

Apollodorus arrived shortly afterwards with Philippus, who carried a bag of tools and piece of solid wood clad with metal on one side.

'Welcome to my house, Legate Mitelus,' drawled Apollo at his most urbane. I nearly threw up at his smugness. He didn't spare me a look, but focused on Conrad like a prize he'd won. He waved to shoo superfluous bodies out. Flavius and I stayed put.

'No doubt you will be a lot more comfortable *sans* manacles. Philippus will deal with this now, if you are up to it.' He raised his eyebrows questioningly.

'Please proceed,' Conrad answered, barely concealing his chagrin. He radiated anger and awkwardness in equal proportions.

Balius wiped some coloured liquid around the flesh under Conrad's manacles which I later learned was a local anaesthetic. Philippus inserted pads under the metal rings. Using giant bolt cutters, he cut the steel chains which made a loud cracking sound, and then approached the first wrist.

'I apologise if this is painful. I will be as quick as I can.'

Conrad nodded curtly.

He didn't show any reaction during the grim procedure, but I saw the blood weeping from the inevitable cuts and abrasions. Balius came back and bound up the wrists and ankles and gave Conrad another shot. Thankfully, he drifted back to sleep.

'Well, I'll give it to him, he was courageous during what must have been a very painful experience,' Philippus admitted to me shortly after. 'Most would have screamed or fainted. Those bastards at the Transulium are using a new armoured steel.' He rubbed the metal almost admiringly. 'I wonder how they cast that for restraints?'

'Nothing like practical research on a half-comatose beaten-up victim is there?'

'Aw, give over, Pulcheria. Bitter doesn't suit you.' He grinned at me, trying to cheer me up, I thought. 'We got him out. What more do you want?'

I tried to ignore the heat of the flush invading my face.

'Ah, is that how it is?'

He burst out laughing as he walked away.

19

Conrad woke later in the afternoon. I buzzed, and Flavius appeared with a tray of minced up food. Dried bloodstains showed through Con's wrist bandages. He moved his arms and hands stiffly like somebody miming a robot. His jaw worked slowly as he ate. It must have been agony. Some of the purple bruises were starting to turn dull yellow. He looked less haggard, but wore a tense, wary expression on his face.

When we'd finished, nobody spoke. I fished the pyramid out of my waist bag and settled back for the storm to blow.

'How in Hades did you get that out?' Conrad growled.

He narrowed his eyes when I described how I'd used simple aluminium foil.

'I extracted the tracker chip, obviously.'

'Gods, you are a piece.' He looked away, studying the cream wall. I didn't know if he approved my ingenuity or condemned the theft.

'So, report.'

I gave him a rundown, including my proscription and Flavius's escape. He shut his eyes momentarily and winced when I'd told him how narrowly we'd escaped being shot right outside Apollodorus's gate. 'So,' Conrad said, 'How deep are you two in here?

His expression was grim. Flavius and I exchanged a glance.

'It was my decision to reactivate the Pulcheria contacts,' I said, 'and I accept that I may by now be beyond—'

Flavius interrupted, 'No, you're not taking the blame. It was my idea to ask Apollodorus to help us.'

'Maybe, but I accepted it on our behalf.'

'Very entertaining, but what payback have you committed to?' Conrad asked dryly, now back in full legate mode.

'There is none,' I said softly.

'Don't be so naïve, Carina.'

'Why don't you just accept it?' I flared. 'Sir,' I added.

'Oh, please!' He looked at me as if I were five years old.

I took a breath to launch another volley, but Flavius interrupted me. 'If I may?'

My turn to shrug. I stood up and walked over to the corner of the room, plunked myself on the upright chair, crossed my arms, and glowered at both of them.

'Apollodorus is a complex individual,' Flavius began. 'His motives are not always as you would expect.'

'He's a criminal, heading an illegal organisation,' shot back the legate.

'Undoubtedly yes, and certainly no.'

'Explain.' Conrad looked suspiciously at him.

'You know, Legate, that the Pulcheria organisation was a construct to flush out the drug pushers from the West seven years ago.'

'A fact I was not made aware of until the end,' Conrad remarked.

'Nevertheless,' Flavius continued, 'that was its *raison d'être*. However, it proved very profitable on its own account, especially the fully legal side of the house.' I saw him pause, smile, and shake his head in memory. 'In fact, the, er, more dubious activities, while giving us the essential street cred, were in fact cross-subsidised by the legal ones. I admit there were some short cuts and infringements, but the core business was not criminal.'

'So I am to infer that instead of it being dissolved, as ordered,' Conrad said, looking across at me, 'it continued?'

Silence expanded to fill the room.

I cleared my throat. 'I couldn't abandon my people like that, on some freaky whim. They worked hard for me and trusted me.'

'A bunch of criminals? How very touching!'

'Well, screw you.'

Flavius looked horrified and took a step towards me, but I waved him away.

'This bunch of criminals just saved your ass. And not a nanosecond too soon. Why can't you accept that other people and organisations can do some good when they're not official or military? You've been in uniform too long.'

'And you've forgotten how to wear yours.'

Flavius busied himself with finding a drink and taking frequent sips from the glass. He must have thought he'd entered a war zone. Wisely, he carried on as if nothing had happened.

'The exit plan had been in place for some weeks, and Apollodorus carried it out impeccably. All our people received severance payments for a new life, but a number stayed to help build the new Foundation. It *is* a powerful organisation, but it pays its taxes, settles its disputes behind closed doors and doesn't cause any political ripples.'

'You defend it so well, Flavius. I presume you're thinking of resuming your career here?' came the sarcastic question.

'No, Legate, not at all. We parted ways at the end of the operation when I joined the PGSF. But it doesn't make me blind to either the organisation's capacities or my good memories of that time.'

'And you, Carina?'

'Are you crazy?'

He raised an eyebrow and looked down his nose at me.

'Sorry,' I muttered. Trying to fight down the flush creeping up my neck, I said, 'If I still have a place then naturally I want to stay with the PGSF. Like Flavius, I can't deny I found certain attraction in the values and ways of doing things here. I'd be lying if I didn't admit it.'

He looked at me as if I were a poisonous snake.

'But it's not my way now. Everything changed after the original operation. I've followed due process for too long.'

'So you damn well should,' he answered in a terse, but not hostile tone. I couldn't read his expression. I didn't say anything, but I sensed the storm had blown out.

'Very well. So what do we know and where are we?'

I glanced over at him, met his eyes briefly, but he merely nodded to me as a senior to a junior. No sign of anything more. I guess it was safer for us both at present.

We slipped back into PGSF formal operating procedure: I gave him a SITREP but, as I progressed through status, intelligence, transport, effective, personnel and so on, it sounded more and more bizarre. He absorbed the threat against the imperatrix and the state almost without reaction: it was what he was trained for, what he would die for. He struggled to tap notes into a small el-pad Flavius had handed him. I could almost see his mind working to analyse and propose counteraction.

'As for their plans after deposing Silvia…it defies all logic,' he said. He looked into the distance, and I saw from the way he narrowed his eyes he was processing the implications and struggling with them.

'Setting Darius up as a puppet with a Council of Regency would be unstable politically as well as cruel to him personally,' I said. 'Can you imagine how frightened and lonely he'd feel with both you and Silvia gone?'

'Bastards.'

As he brought his hand up to his face, I saw it was shaking. I wondered if he was thinking back to his own brutal political baptism at that age.

'Conrad, I…'

'What?'

'I'm not sure I can find the right words for this next thing, so forgive me.'

'There's more? Well, spit it out.'

'The girls, Stella and Hallie…' I reached for his hand.

'Yes?'

'They were going to kill them in the ancient Roman way of disposing of daughters of political enemies.' I couldn't say the word rape. I looked away, tears running down my face. I'd seen Conrad furious on many occasions, but this time his face hardened into something else. For a second, he looked like a savage beast. It vanished and a cold, smooth shell spread over him.

'Petronax is mine,' he stated flatly.

I waited for a few moments. 'What happened to due process?'

'Operational accidents happen,' he replied curtly. Nobody would reproach him for that, whatever Petronax's body looked like afterwards.

• • •

I glanced at my watch, a vanity of silver and diamonds set in a black leather wristband. 'Hades, I'm three minutes late for our schedule.' I walked over to the far side of the room and dialled Daniel. It was a relief to move on.

'Hi.' Long pause. 'Good. Look, I may have a solution, but I have to run through it with some people.' Pause. 'Yesterday.' I could feel ears in the room straining to listen. 'Much as usual, only grouchier.' I couldn't keep from glancing at Conrad, hard as I tried. 'Fine, Daniel. Keep the four-hour rota going and let me have any names. I'll be issuing operational orders within the next twenty-four hours.' Pause. 'Yes. Out.'

Conrad opened his mouth but, before he could say anything, the doctor strode into the room.

'We need to change the dressings, so if you're ready we'll start. Your fan club can take a hike.' I grabbed the crystal, praying that Balius hadn't seen it.

As we trudged towards the atrium, Flavius said, 'Have you thought through the consequences of putting Apollodorus's orders before the legate's?'

'Yes, but Apollodorus is adamant on this. He suspects the legate's motives, understandably so. He won't let his people be exposed or end up on some PGSF alert list.'

Flavius shrugged as if conceding the point. How difficult it was to walk this tightrope.

'I understand your concern, Flav. But the legate is unfit for duty. Lucius can't make any kind of move, we know Somna and Sepunia are locked up, and Daniel's holed up in the palace.' We reached the atrium doorway. I stopped and looked at him. 'You have any better ideas?'

I wanted to update Apollodorus on the next phase. I couldn't find a natural opening in our conversation – I was sure he was avoiding it – so I plunged straight in.

'I plan to move straight after the Senate meeting tomorrow, so I'll issue orders this evening. I need to have the legate primed and into the palace after the orders meeting. Can we be ready?'

'My dear, all you need do is ask and it will happen.'

I giggled.

'What?'

'I'm sorry, Apollo, but you sounded like the genie of the lamp.'

His eyes glinted. 'One day, *ma chère*, you will push me too far.'

So Apollodorus knew French and used it naturally.

'Sorry – that was impertinent. Forgive me, please?' I peeked up at him in the most appealing way possible.

He sighed. 'You know I always do.'

'Where would I be without you?'

'Floating in the public sewer, probably, or tucked up in a nice little prison somewhere. Not that you don't deserve it.'

Apollodorus swept into Conrad's room with me in his wake. Flavius was already there, sitting by the bed, notepad in hand, discussing something with Conrad. I regretted wearing my trademark black leather and long boots. Despite the air conditioning, I felt warm and uncomfortable. Apollodorus was in black, in an over-elaborate stitched business suit. Organ grinder and monkey, but which was which?

Conrad looked coolly at us both as we sat down.

'Balius tells me you have made excellent progress, Conradus Mitelus,' Apollo said. 'This is naturally to be celebrated. However, he is concerned about your general debility and recommends continuing rest and recovery.'

Conrad drew breath to speak, but his words didn't get out of the starting blocks.

'Naturally enough,' Apollo continued, 'you will wish to be involved in events going forward, and I wonder if you could help us out with a delicate matter?'

Patronised, but curious, Conrad bit. He completely ignored me and looked only at Apollo. 'What are you proposing?'

'No doubt Pulcheria has explained the difficult situation at the palace. It is an unpleasant thought, but no one, not even the inestimable Major Stern, can be completely sure of Darius Apulius's safety in these, shall we say, treacherous times.'

All three PGSF in the room winced.

'The child needs a competent adult he trusts and who is tied to him, preferably by blood, to be with him twenty-four hours a day, particularly as the operation steps up. Somebody prepared to die or kill for him. Pulcheria tells me you are the only person whom she trusts to do this.'

Conrad wouldn't look at me. Stubborn Tella pride.

Apollo spread his hands in a self-deprecating manner. 'Are you prepared to do this?'

'And if I'm not?'

'Then we will continue to care for you here until you are completely well and beyond, if required.' I shivered at Apollo's slow and deliberate delivery, radiating quiet menace. He could be so unpleasant so politely.

Watching them staring each other out reminded me of when they met for the first time on the floor of Goldlights, the club I'd built for the undercover operation seven years ago. Even then, they'd been instantly mutually hostile.

'Apollodorus, would you and Flavius please leave the legate and me to talk for a few minutes?'

'But of course.' He closed the door silently as he and Flavius left.

'You've served me up nicely on toast, haven't you? Proud of yourself, are you?' Conrad said bitterly. 'Either way, you've pushed me out of it.' He slumped back in the bed, exhausted after battling Apollodorus.

I had to get him out of here, to safety if there was such a thing now. Against everything I knew, some gut instinct made me distrust Apollodorus as far as Conrad was concerned. It would only take one more spark of antagonism between the men, and Apollodorus would snap.

I sat on the bed and took Conrad's hand in mine. 'Conrad, listen to me.' I waited until he opened his eyes. 'You're unfit for duty. I'm no medic, but you look like shit. You can hardly walk to the bathroom, and your head is full of sedatives and painkillers. Would you consider yourself capable of exercising proper judgement? We're up against a crucial time window and you're not ready for it. If you know of any other available operational officer or unit, maybe you could let me have their details?'

Silence.

'No, I thought not. I'm running this operation with a very

competent team, but that has a different approach from PGSF. Apollodorus is under no obligation to help me, you or anybody else. However, he has been my friend for many years. I'm sorry if you don't like it, but there it is.'

'I don't trust him.'

I laid my hand on his arm. He didn't shrug it off. 'Look, Darius needs you now and so do the girls. The next forty-eight hours are going to be hugely disruptive. They *must* have somebody with them they trust, who is exclusively dedicated to them. Silvia may have to act and not be able to look out for them. You can't leave them to their staff, however loyal.'

He stared at me, the green washing out the brown in his eyes. He searched my face then sighed. 'Oh, all right, I'll dance to your tune. Tell me what to do.' He was a proud man and had conceded a lot.

I kissed his forehead – his lip was too sore – and opened the door to let the others back in.

20

Minutes before the curfew started, Conrad, Flavius and I were dropped off at a stone-built row house a block away from Imperatrix Silvia's home, the Golden Palace. More of a substantial house than a palace, the imperial home had been rebuilt several times on the same site since they'd abandoned the old fortress on the clifftop.

Earlier that evening, Conrad had let us into the secret of some interesting additions to the Golden Palace introduced several centuries ago during one of the rebuilds. 'There's a system of underground service tunnels that runs under the city, connecting strategic locations. Very few know the extent of the network, or how to access it. Let's keep it that way or I'll have both your hides.'

Although Conrad was using a cane, Flavius helped him up the steep stairs of the row house to the portico. I entered the keycode Conrad gave me and we slipped in.

Flavius and I eased Conrad down on an unpadded wood settle – he looked white as death and was breathing heavily from the effort of the short car journey. A dim light shone through a faded pink plascard shade onto a blue floral woven rug that had been new a hundred years ago. Conrad nodded at me.

'Hello, the house?' I shouted out.

After a minute, a figure emerged bearing an antique, totally illegal, double-barrelled shotgun. Jupiter! She was slight, very old and grey, but she looked incredibly fierce, and there was, of course, the gun. If it still worked, I'd bet it could still blow a good-sized hole in anybody or anything.

'Good evening, Marcella Volusenia,' Conrad said. 'I'm sorry to disturb you, but we need to use the tunnel.'

'Tellus? Conradus Tellus? What's wrong with you? You look terrible!'

'Thank you,' he said, making the tiniest bow. He smiled.

She cast an eye over Flavius and me, decided we weren't worth the favour of an introduction, and ordered us to follow her. We descended into a stone-lined cellar which looked centuries old. Although stale, the air wasn't musty. Volusenia glided past wine racks and storage shelves, and between boxes, old furniture, boots and general detritus. We had to push stuff to one side as Conrad couldn't manoeuvre easily. In the last alcove, almost hidden at the side, she pointed to a lightweight, empty, metal-backed shelving rack.

'Move that aside, if you please,' she barked. We abandoned Conrad and hurried to obey, revealing a wooden door, plain and clearly old. She unlocked it and pulled it open. 'I'll lock it behind you.' She nodded to Conrad. 'You know where the return key is?'

He nodded.

She gave him her flashlight, turned on her heel, clanged the door shut and left us in the corridor. We heard the lock mechanism turn behind us.

'Who was that scary woman?'

Walking slowly along the tunnel, Conrad explained. 'She's Volusenia the Younger, Marcella Volusenia, if you will, and was the second deputy Legate after Caius Tellus's rebellion. She was my mentor within the PGSF – I owe her so much. There was no favouritism.' He half-smiled at his memories. 'In fact, she was quite hard, but she stood up for me when I was treated unfairly because of my name. Most of all, she taught me how to endure.'

'Then you can understand a little how Apollodorus and I stand.'

He didn't reply.

We reached a long flight of steps hacked out of the rock. The stone walls were rough, but dry. Lights were strung along regularly and triggered by movement, so we couldn't see much ahead. I thought they'd never end. Conrad leaned on me heavily, the cane taking the rest of his weight. We needed to stop several times to let him rest, but he kept waving us on. I was more than glad when I saw a fixed light glowing in the distance: even in the limited light, I could see Conrad was exhausted.

'Just remember that Daniel doesn't know I'm Pulcheria,' I said. 'I told him you'd be delivered by an unexpected person.' I glanced back at Flav. 'Flavius will stand back in the shadows.'

'Do you think he'll fall for it?'

I heard the scepticism in his voice. 'Yes. People, even trained ones, only see what they expect to see. Look at me.'

He saw long, dark brown curls, tight black leather clothes, black leather boots, black eyes, all stitched together with a bad attitude.

'When I alter my voice, he'll see what his brain and his anger want him to.'

At the wooden door decorated with tapered iron fittings and a metal sign XIV, Conrad fished out two heavy keys from a wall box. He stretched his hand out to Flavius with one of them. 'This will open the door at Volusenia's end.'

Just as Flavius reached out to take it, it fell from Conrad's fingers and clanged on the ground. Flavius bent down and grabbed it. We'd be trapped without it.

Conrad fumbled at the lock and I nearly took over, but he managed to turn the key and the tumblers grated, releasing the door. Flavius swung it open, carefully stepping back into the shadow. Daniel, flanked by three PGSF in full battledress carrying heavy weapons, stood there, legs braced, one hand resting on his pistol holster.

'Good evening, Daniel,' Conrad said casually, like he was at a smart evening party. Then he wilted. I caught him and came in full view.

'Don't go and die on me, commander,' came Pulcheria's irritating voice. Within seconds, metal clashed. Three sub-machine guns were trained on me, Daniel's pistol centimetres from my head.

'Diana's tits, it's the boy Daniel! I remember you when you came sneaking round my club. You always have to go off too early, don't you, sunshine?' I said. 'One of my girls would have sorted you out in no time.'

Daniel's eyes boiled. I thought he was going to have a stroke.

'You little cow! I thought they'd put you away permanently and walled you up. Fuck me if I don't shoot you here and now!'

'Enough!' Conrad's voice cracked but it reached through the fog that seemed to have invaded the space between Daniel's brain and mouth. 'Strange times bring strange allies, Daniel.'

He stared at Conrad as if he were crazy. 'Sir, can we be in such trouble that we need the help of this sort of parasite?' He spat on my boots.

'You misjudge the situation,' Conrad said tersely.

'If you say so, sir.'

'Well, we'll be getting along before your boy here does something silly.'

'Thank you, Pulcheria, for your help. Our ways part here.' He looked solemn and held out his hand. I squeezed it then cheekily kissed him on the lips. I flashed a rude arm gesture at Daniel and slammed the door, relieved that Conrad was out of harm's way.

Quarter days were a strange mix of Western European and Roman customs, solstices and equinoxes really, but in the West the Christians hijacked them and made them religious and legal days. For Romans, they meant ruptures and new beginnings through the year.

Traditionally, charities could petition the Senate in the morning before the latter's formal meeting. Silvia Apulia usually attended on these days, not as imperatrix but taking her place like any other senator. She also attended the Representatives' sessions regularly, as an observer. Apart from it making good political sense, she was genuinely interested. I wondered if this was part of the reason she was popular. My grandmother would normally have taken her place in the front row at the Senate, too, on quarter day, but what was normal now?

The open public forecourt of the Senate building was covered and wide steps rose towards the formal entrance. Inside, the vestibule was dominated by the ancients' Altar of Victory on which a statue of a winged woman stood, holding a palm and leaning down to present a laurel wreath to some victor or other. Founder Apulius had smuggled it out of Rome as the old Empire was falling apart. The superstitious insisted that while it sat in the Senate, Roma Nova would never fall. I made my offering: a quick pinch of incense and a muttered prayer for success. I'd take help from anywhere.

I sidled in, dressed in my usual black, but covered with a long white *palla* drawn up over my head in a semblance of modesty. It was also a pretty good disguise. Inevitably, Hermina's drones were not far away from me, but she herself was standing right by my side, also in *palla,* posing as my companion.

'How long do we wait?' she whispered.

'Until his petition is drawn from the ballot, which we know it will be. He'll have fixed that simple a detail.' I scanned around and saw a number of familiar faces go into the main chamber. It was surreal: everything seemed so normal despite the frisson of excitement caused by the curfew. I always said life existed on different layers like a pile of pancakes, one sitting on top of another. The top pancake was certainly not clued into the gooey mess bubbling up at the bottom of the pile.

'Oh, here we go!' I whispered to Hermina.

The Senate officer drew the paper out and announced, 'Martinus Apnius from Folentia begs leave to present…'

'Gods, he's using his real name!' hissed Hermina.

'Yeah, Caeco would have been too obvious.'

We moved forward through the crowd and slid into Committee Room 3 where his petition would be heard. Around twenty senators were seated on one side. Opposite them, separated by the waist-high public barrier, we managed to stand just behind the people's tribune. Justus and two others were already there, dressed as Senate orderlies.

Justus had placed his troops strategically to catch as many of the delinquent senators as possible on covert video and stills so that the *custodes* could arrest them with due process. Justus thought we were being far too nice. I'd given up trying to explain. I gave him his orders and told him to just do it. Stopping and capturing Caeco was our main objective. Justus could do what he liked with Caeco as far as I was concerned. All I wanted left was something to interrogate.

A bored Senate officer signalled Caeco to begin. He stood and faced the Senate rows. He looked much the same as before, but was impeccably dressed in full toga. He drew his squat figure up to its full height, his arm thrust out.

'Gentlemen of the Senate.' He paused and scanned his audience. 'And Lady,' he added as an afterthought, inclining his head to the single female senator almost as a concession. Who on earth *was* the woman senator? I didn't recognise her. With her fancy necklace and white face, she looked like a ritual sacrificial offering, or maybe it was just anxiety.

'I come here to enlist your help,' Caeco declared. 'I speak as head of the Paterfamilias charity. For centuries, there has been unequal treatment of half the population. My group aims to rectify this. We petition you today to restore the traditional Roman way that led to a thousand years of greatness.'

Oh, for Jupiter's sake! Caeco had watched too many swords and sandals epics as a kid.

Shouts of 'Well said!' came from the Senate rows. Justus had better be picking this up – nobody would believe us if not.

Caeco went on to describe various injustices, proposed the reintroduction of the *Leges Juliae* and asked for the group's endorsement. He finished with an impassioned plea, which was straight out of a bad movie.

Leges Juliae. Not merely the Augustan ones, but the harsh anti-female update brought in by that Greek idiot Justinian in the East. None of them had *ever* applied in Roma Nova. I could hardly believe it. In the twenty-first century, for fuck's sake.

In a boring and bored voice, the official asked the people's tribune if anybody wished to address the Senate group on this subject. Usually these things went through on the nod, but he was legally required to ask. He'd picked up the agenda to pass to the vote, when I raised one hand and tapped the tribune's shoulder with the other. The clerk stared at me, not believing what he saw. The tribune's mouth dropped open in surprise.

'I'd like to speak,' I whispered directly in her ear.

'You're not serious?'

'Yes. Is there a problem?'

She ran her eyes up and down me as if she was searching for signs of craziness or wondering if I was going to be a bunch of trouble, or both. Deciding I wasn't either, she nodded at me, stood and advised the official that the people wished to address the group.

Stunned is how I'd describe the general reaction. The senators looked wary, some shocked. Heads bent together in urgent whispers and questions. Caeco's face was a dream: surprised, thunderous, murderous.

'What's the name?' hissed the tribune at me.

'Pulcheria.'

'That's it?'

'It's enough.'

'The people present Pulcheria to speak on its behalf,' she announced.

I let the fold of my *palla* fall to my shoulder, revealing some of the black underneath and stepped forward.

'Lady and Gentlemen,' I began, bowing to her. *I*, at least, knew the precedence rules. 'Martinus Apnius has made an eloquent case to you. Indeed, he has brought forward many intriguing arguments. His oratory is clear and convincing.' I graciously inclined my head in his direction. He glared at me. 'However, before you make your decision to support his cause, I would like to make a few comments. We must, of course, be certain of our grounds for considering these arguments. We must peel away any emotion coating rational arguments for and against. Lastly, we must weigh up the consequences of our actions for future generations.'

The audience listened politely. They must have thought it was amateur night.

'Let me ask you to consider some concepts: absolute power in the hands of one individual with no popular, historic or democratic support; economic and social breakdown with collapse of a prosperous, stable and advanced scientific civilisation; and lastly, the murder of female children.'

Uproar. Two men started in my direction, obviously intent on shutting me up. Hermina's drones surrounded me in seconds. Tall, muscular and radiating attitude, they would beat anybody off.

'Next,' I continued, once the babble had eased up, 'allow me to introduce one or two facts. Firstly, the man addressing you, Martinus Apnius, known as Caeco, is a convicted criminal. Secondly, he is joint partner in a conspiracy to overthrow the imperatrix, dispose of her and her female children, and set up her son with a puppet Council of Regency to be drawn from your honourable ranks.' I paused and panned around the twenty senators who were starting to squirm.

Cries of 'No!' and 'Murderers!' came from behind the public rail beside me.

'Thirdly, he has corrupted youth and embezzled over two hundred naïve supporters. And finally,' I heard my voice hardening, 'he and his partners in the conspiracy have blackmailed, subverted and imprisoned members of the security forces responsible for the imperatrix's and the state's safety. All these facts are supported by documentary, image and witness evidence, now in the hands of loyal members of the security forces.'

My voice became bleak. 'You may, therefore, wish to reconsider your support of his cause.'

The room erupted. People jumped over the public barrier, hurling abuse at the senators, some intent on attacking them physically. Others watched, mouths open. The Senate orderlies struggled to hold them back.

I stood there and enjoyed the ensuing pandemonium for a few moments before Hermina dragged me out, two drones guarding my back. I had seen Justus's troops grab Caeco amid the flurry of fleeing senators. I laughed all the way back to Apollo's house.

21

I called Daniel to report what had happened at the Senate.

'Hades! But good result. How did you make that little cow, Pulcheria, do that?'

'Don't try and outthink yourself. Just accept that I have my ways,' I answered him smugly.

He snorted, but didn't say anything.

I broke the silence. 'How is he?'

'Getting on well. He's stopped using the stick now and only limping a bit. I think eating, drinking and sleeping are all he needs. Those bastards really worked him over.' His voice was grim. 'He hasn't said much, but I saw him in the pool this morning with Darius and he's covered.'

Well, I'd seen that during Balius's checks.

'He's strong,' Daniel said. 'Just give him a week.'

'We don't have a week. We have to move now. He'll have to sit this one out.'

He grunted.

'At the expense of teaching my grandmother to suck eggs, can you be extra alert for some kind of retaliatory or asymmetric strike against the family?'

He made a rude but funny comment about over-protective nannies.

My last words to him were: 'Phase Three: execute.'

. . .

Now we had to move on Petronax himself, and fast. He was a tricky bastard. It was the one part of the operation I wasn't a hundred per cent sure about, but I kept that opinion to myself. I made the call to Lucius: 'Phase Four: execute.'

The PGSF headquarters had a bland exterior; the front pedestrian entrance looked like any government office with a small public reception area. Most PGSF guards used the side service door next to the tall vehicle gates. You had to pass through a short tunnel which opened onto a courtyard parade ground. Both vehicle and pedestrian access was controlled by a bioscan, voice and video system so, unless you ripped out an authorised person's eyes, cut off their hand for the fingers and could simulate their voice, you stayed out. If the system registered any kind of anomaly, shutters crashed down either end of the tunnel trapping the offending vehicles and releasing paralysing gas. When you recovered consciousness, you would wake in the cells with a thumping head, if you hadn't been shot by an annoyed security detail. Flavius and I were barred out the system with a shoot-on-sight alert which could only be rescinded by the legate.

Now kitted out in PGSF fatigues, with standard-issue side arms, we were too wound up to talk as our vehicles approached the gated entrance. We stopped in front of the tall gates. I glanced at my watch. I counted down the seconds in my head.

'Come on, Lucius,' I muttered. Ten seconds stretched like an eternity. The sweat ran down between my breasts and my throat dried to bone. Miraculously, the gate swung open.

I couldn't speak as we drove in, but remembered to breathe. Flavius parked our vehicle, the other two juddered to a halt either side. We peeled out and grouped into four squads of twelve within ten seconds. Counting slowly to fifteen, we crossed to the building entrance and the door slid open. He would have kicked himself if he'd known, but Petronax helped us by having his armed supporters stationed inside the building. The surround sensors were switched off and didn't react to our weapons.

We crept along the wood floors. Justus and Flavius broke off,

Flavius leading his group downstairs, Justus his upstairs. I nodded at Philippus to go further down the corridor to the back rooms and annexes. I gave them two minutes.

'In position?' I whispered through my mouth mic.

Three affirmatives.

'On my mark. One...two...three...mark.'

The surprise was total. Petronax supporters, heavily armed, stationed in every room to control the building and people, were quickly neutralised. I marched to the command centre, ignoring stares from stunned PGSF. Just as they started to react, my bodyguards trained their weapons on them, discouraging further reaction.

At the legate's office, I grabbed the handle, burst in with my two bodyguards and stuck my assault rifle in Superbus's face. His jowls wobbled almost comically as I snarled, 'On the floor, you bastard! Now!'

His face contorted with hatred. His eyes darted all over, desperate to find some way out. I readied my weapon. I longed for him to make the tiniest sign of resistance. Even if he only moved his fingertip to push an alarm device.

'I said NOW!'

To my intense disappointment, he complied.

As he lay face down being handcuffed, he rasped, 'You bitch! You're dead!'

I couldn't be bothered to answer him.

As I finished detailing somebody to guard him, I kicked him with my steel-capped boot. Full strength.

The click of a weapon being cocked. I turned and found Drusus, of all people, standing in the doorway, pointing a pistol at me, his eyes intense. His hands trembled. Poor kid. Although fully trained, he was in no way an operations soldier. He was much happier driving his keyboard. The last time he'd used a live weapon was on the fitness-for-task field exercise several months ago. Behind him, I saw one of my bodyguards cock his weapon in turn, ready to take Drusus out. I shook my head.

'Hello, sweetheart,' I said in a nasal voice and smirked at him. 'You're not really going to shoot me with that great big gun, are you?'

Drusus stared at me, hesitated and so lost his advantage. A hand came over his shoulder, grabbed the weapon and spun him to one side.

'Of course he's not, although some might not blame him.'

'Adjutant to the rescue,' I murmured.

'It's okay, Drusus, stand down.' Lucius gave the younger man a quick smile to reassure him. Lucius quickly emptied the weapon and handed it back, and stowed the little magazine in his own back pocket. Drusus looked bewildered then stepped back.

'Gnaeus, Adjutant,' Lucius snapped into his commset. 'Get the damned security system back up, stat, including the surround sensors, for Mars' sake.' He lifted his head. 'Somebody take this piece of filth out from under my feet and lock it up.' Two guards came forward and dragged the unfortunate Superbus out of the office. Destination: cells.

He pressed a button on the legate's desk. 'This is Lucius Punellus, Adjutant. All personnel to secure their work areas to protocol six and report immediately to the strategy room. Duty centurion, down to the cells, stat, and ensure the female personnel are released. All there within ten minutes, please.'

He turned to me. 'You and your lot not included. Group them in the courtyard and stay there.' He looked at his watch. 'You have three minutes before the surround sensors reset.' He turned his back on us and marched off.

I relayed the order to my four commanders and signalled our group to make their way outside. Flavius looked glum and not a little chagrined.

'Did you expect to be greeted as a conquering hero?' I asked.

'I didn't think we'd be excluded like that. The adjutant looked at us as if we were dirt. We're stuck here in the courtyard like a herd of animals.'

True. Now the full security was reactivated, we couldn't get back in the building or out of the gate. I laid my hand on his forearm.

'Let the adjutant sort the troops out first, Flav.' I told Sergius to let the groups relax, have a drink, smoke if they wanted. We sat down in a corner under the canopy by the garages and waited.

A little over twenty minutes later, four fully armed PGSF approached us. My group of twelve immediately stood to and formed a protective circle around me.

'Your commander plus one to come with us. Weapons to be left here,' ordered the centurion. She looked straight through me. Being rescued by a bunch of dubious characters like us had to have been humiliating. I stepped out of the circle, beckoning Flavius to come with me.

Lucius sat in Conrad's chair and was talking to an orderly with a max el-pad, whom he dismissed when he saw us at the door.

'Come in and shut the door behind you,' he commanded, his voice flat and neutral. I was surprised to see a pyramid appear from his pocket. He set it on the desk and looked up at us, his eyebrows raised. I wasn't sure what was supposed to happen next either.

'Oh, sit down, for the gods' sake!' He waved his hand impatiently. 'Right, anything else before you clear your lot out?'

I knew we had to be a bad smell under their noses, but I resented being thrown out so abruptly.

'A few words of thanks to the people who rescued you would be nice,' I said sarcastically.

'Food and drinks are being taken out to them now. A "thank you", we don't have time for.'

'Not good enough,' I said. 'They put themselves on the line for you. They're part of a private business team, not a formal military force of the state.' My breath shortened and anger pushed up through me. I looked him straight in the eye. 'I won't have my people neglected like this.'

'Oh, really?' Lucius leaned back in the chair, his eyebrows raised. 'Perhaps a few nights in the cells will deflate your little tantrum.'

'Tantrum isn't in it,' I said, trying to calm down. 'Can't you see how positive an effect it would have just to be gracious? Conradus would have done it automatically.'

He said nothing.

'Look, we're wasting time, bickering like this,' I said, moving on. 'We saved the day – deal with it. You have Superbus in custody. It's my right to prosecute him in the Families' Court, as a delinquent member of my family, but it'll be too civilised and follow formal process. I want a session with him here first.'

'We'll be holding him in close custody for the statutory twenty-eight days,' Lucius conceded. 'But after that, who knows...' He shrugged like he was unsure of his next step in a fluid situation. He wiped his fingers across his chin and stared into space for a few seconds. He blinked, stood up, seeming to gather himself together. He thrust the pyramid into his pocket and opened the door. 'Right. Let's go and see your monkeys.'

I had a tart answer for him, but suddenly remembered one vital thing. 'You have secured Petronax, haven't you? We didn't find him.'

Lucius pressed the guard alarm and shouted down the corridor 'Duty NCO. Stat.'

A centurion appeared within seconds. Lucius barked questions at him.

'I was on my way to you, sir. No trace of him,' he reported. 'We've searched the whole building. Nothing. His vehicle's gone from the basement garages.'

Shit.

I stabbed the numbers in on my supermobile. 'Daniel? Petronax is on the loose.'

'Yes, I know,' he replied. His voice was bleak. 'He's here.'

22

'Details, please.'

My fingers played with the zipper on my fatigues jacket as I walked around Conrad's office. I stopped and told Daniel to repeat the last thing he said.

'No,' I said and sat down.

Lucius frowned at me, mouthing, 'What?'

I waved the back of my hand at him and bent over, pressing the cell to my ear, hoping I could hear something different.

'How in the depth of black Tartarus did that happen?' I asked. 'I thought that was all in hand.' I listened some more. 'How badly?'

I batted my reactions out of the way and started assessing all the possibilities. There was only one. 'Okay, we'll use Strategy 8. Give me twenty.' Pause. 'Too bad. Execute.'

I closed the phone and faced Lucius and Flavius. 'Petronax has Hallie.' They both looked at me, appalled. Hallienia Apulia was the youngest imperial child.

'He's killed one of the nursery staff – a kid of sixteen, for fuck's sake! The guard he knifed is in surgery and is touch and go. Conradus was downstairs with Darius and didn't hear a thing. I've initiated Strat8. We have to kit up and go. Now.'

Strategy 8 was an emergency plan developed as a result of Caius Tellus's rebellion. Selected officers were authorised and trained to take decisive action under Emergency Order. Mars knew why they'd included me. I figured it went with the strategist job. It was an uncomfortable honour. If you fouled up, who wanted to spend the next ten years in the central military prison?

Lucius, to his credit, didn't blink. 'The pack will be in the garage within ten minutes,' he assured me. He went to the safe, opened it, and handed me my insignia and personal tracker. 'You'll need these.' He also handed me a sealed envelope. 'And this.'

Written on the front were the words: *Additional protocol in the event of Strategy 8 implementation.* I looked at it in surprise. We'd practised Strat8 until we'd covered every scenario we could imagine.

'Open it and read it. Do not tell me the contents.'

I read it through several times, committing it to memory. Then I shredded it and pressed the burn button. I drew my hand across my forehead, closing my eyes as I did. Juno! The fallback instructions were beyond grim. I wasn't sure I could carry them out.

I left Lucius talking rapidly into the deskcomm.

Flavius and I hurried down to the locker rooms to change, ignoring curious stares. My head was still processing the additional protocol, so I wasn't much of a conversationalist. Thank the gods my locker hadn't been cleared. I flicked out the dark contacts, cleaned off Pulcheria's heavy make-up and bathed my face. My blue eyes stared back out of the mirror above the basin like old friends seeing each other after a long time away. I bound my hair tightly and shoved it under a combat cap. At the quaestor's office, Gnaeus was waiting with our suits and equipment. He handed Flavius his ID, mouthing, 'Good to see you back.'

'Here, captain, you might like these.' Gnaeus held out a pack of knives. My carbons! I'd taken only one with me. More old friends.

'The net is fully operational again, so you can use commsets in the palace. We've digitally barred Petronax and alarmed his set. Let me update yours.' He snapped it into the dock, clicked his slim fingers across the keyboard, waited a few seconds. Nothing happened. He ejected the set, repeated the procedure. He turned to me, embarrassed.

'I don't know what's happened, ma'am, but you seem to have been deleted from the system.'

Of course, my little program had eaten everything, including itself.

He looked at me, expectant.

'Well, there was a malfunction last time I used it. Can you reinstate me?' I gave him what I hoped was a winsome smile.

'Hmm, I can give you temporary access, if the adjutant will countersign it.'

'Oh, for fuck's sake, just do it – we're in the middle of a Strat8.'

He looked shocked. But he did set it up and update my commset. His manner was chilly as he handed it to me.

Another ego to massage. Too bad.

Hurrying down to the basement, I made a call.

'Apollo, Petronax has my cousin – the little girl. I have to go to her. Your troops are safe. No casualties. They'll be on their way back to you shortly. I'll come as soon as I can.'

In the garages, we picked up our three long wheelbases, already loaded as Lucius had promised. Six other guards followed us in a fourth vehicle. More would go as back-up with DJ to pre-planned points. But the main strike force was already in the palace – my own Active Response Team.

When we arrived, Daniel looked stressed out, tired and guilty all at once. His eyes were preternaturally round, red-rimmed, his skin dull. When had he slept last? A temporary command centre had been set up next door to the palace security room. Uniforms moved in and through it, but Daniel was bone still.

He found his voice. 'Bloody Petronax is on the roof terrace with Hallie. He's made her sit up on the parapet. He's threatening to push her off.'

The grass area below was four floors down. I gulped then gathered my brains together. 'Camera feed?'

He showed me the images from the terrace itself and up from the garden border at an angle of forty-five degrees. There she was, in a light cotton tunic, feet in her favourite sparkly sneakers, short legs dangling over the stone edge, waiting to be killed by a madman.

I stared at the screen. How had Petronax become so disconnected from the normal? Why would somebody want to kill a small child despite all the taboos associated with such an act?

No way would I allow that to happen to Hallie.

'Right, get my ART in here and let's work out some kind of plan to deal with this.' How clichéd that sounded, but I had to say something to break the immobility we'd all frozen into. As I looked back at the screen, something occurred to me. 'Where's Conradus?'

'With the other two children.'

'Are you absolutely sure?'

'Guardian, Command.' Daniel spoke into his commset.

'Command, Guardian here.'

'Identify your location,' Daniel ordered.

'In the children's suite,' Conrad answered. Nothing more. His voice rasped, barely forming the words.

'Very well, out.'

Daniel turned to me. 'Satisfied?'

A signals clerk handed him a note. 'Major, the DJ are here, but they're staying on the east side.'

'Thanks. Tell them to send their commander up here.'

My ART arrived. Paula, Treb, Maelia, Nov, Livius, Atria joined Flavius and they stood there like a phalanx – kitted, booted and ready.

We'd trained, exercised and handled live operations together for over six years. If the tactical situation went to Hades, and you didn't have time to think through what to do, the team adapted as if connected by telepathy. Even Treb, the youngest, had melded well in a remarkably short time.

We walked quietly into an adjoining room, grouped around a table and started working. Maybe my eyes were reacting to not having to wear dark contacts, but the lighting was painfully strong.

'We have full authority under Strat8 rules,' I began. 'Given the parapet, we'll use Scenario Three. Atria, you go try initiating a dialogue with Petronax. When the rest of us come up, I want your assessment of his mental state. He's ideologically driven,' I said, 'so no ethical base to play with, no morality in the usual sense. I don't think we can use his conscience against him.' I grimaced.

She nodded and made for the stairs up to the roof.

What *was* his background? What had made him so harsh and single-minded? He must have some redeeming qualities – did he like animals? No, he'd probably tormented them as a child. Novius brought up Petronax's personal file on the screen. It showed a steady progression of a dedicated but efficient security man. His reports were good, but neutral. They showed a self-contained but otherwise tediously ordinary personality.

'Yeah, but we do have to remember Petronax is a very savvy operator.' Livius was a smart cookie and probably the best soldier in my unit. For him to say that was worrying. Petronax would be incredibly difficult to reason with; he'd know the book we'd be working from. But what did he hope to gain? Being brutal, if he pushed Hallie off, he had no other leverage. Maybe he gambled that we'd never allow him to do it. Maybe this was why the fallback instructions had been drafted.

Three minutes later, a knock at the door. Daniel put his head round.

'Have you got something to go with yet?'

Seven pairs of eyes bored into his.

'I know, but the child has been up there for over twenty-five minutes.'

I panned around – they all nodded. Watches synch'd, Nov, Livius and Flavius ran downstairs to unpack kit from the vehicles. Paula grabbed her pack and headed off along the corridor to the window immediately under the roof garden level. Treb, Malia and I stripped down to our black tees and shorts. No weapons showing, I packed two of my carbon fibre knives in sheaths at my back waist, another in my right boot. We gave the guys five minutes to get in place.

I walked back with Daniel to the command centre.

'Can you have the DJs plus about a dozen of our people to step up activity on the outer cordon to give Petronax something to look at? Otherwise he'll think we're up to something else.'

'Come in and brief their commander yourself,' he suggested.

'Good idea.'

Not such a good idea, as it turned out. I nearly had my head blown off for the second time that day.

The figure in DJ blues turned round, took one look at me and snatched his pistol out. He swung his arm up and shoved the barrel of his pistol to within millimetres of my head.

Lurio.

Hades.

A dozen Praetorians immediately trained assault rifles, safety off, on him.

'Whoa!' said Daniel. 'Let's not do anything rash here.' Fingers on keyboards stopped, muscles tensed. The only sound came from equipment humming. The only movement came from images on screens.

'Now, commander, whatever the problem, I suggest you lower your weapon and we talk about it calmly.'

Daniel sucked at hostage stuff.

'Don't you know a traitor when you see one, Stern?' Lurio snarled. He was as hot as a bridgewire detonator and as ready to explode.

'One or two, but I'm not looking at one now,' Daniel said.

Lurio kept his eyes trained on me, his forehead creased in concentration. I opened my mouth to deny it, but Lurio gripped his pistol harder and raised the barrel so it almost touched my skin on the side of my head.

'We were tracking her and one of her associates. They disappeared into a known criminal's lair and we lost them.'

'Why?' Daniel said. 'Why were you tracking her?'

Oh, shit. Lurio was about to blow my Pulcheria cover, and Daniel would be so mad he'd let Lurio blow my head off.

Lurio looked astounded. 'It was your lot that issued the "shoot on sight". One of my undercover people spotted them in a café down by the docks. Now she's here in the middle of a Strat8.'

My heart was thumping on maximum. I desperately wanted to take a deep breath but daren't make even that movement. Any distraction would cause Lurio to fire almost as an automatic response. Gods, my stomach was twisting like Hydra's heads waiting for Daniel to diffuse Lurio.

Daniel rubbed his fingers across his forehead.

'Look, Lurio, I don't have time for this. We're at a crucial point of a sensitive operation. If she isn't on that roof within the next minute, an imperial child will die at the hands of a madman and a real traitor. Your choice.' His tone was grim.

'Seriously?' Lurio still looked suspicious.

'Oh, for the gods' sake, man, stop fucking about like some arse-ache and let us do our job!'

· · ·

We entered the roof garden from the top floor door. It was a charming retreat, decorated by living green arches, a grassed area, pots brimming over with flowers, a teak slatted table and chairs, loungers and barbecue area. At the far end, part of the high trellis, normally dripping with white clematis flowers, had been broken away, and the ledge was visible. A small hunched figure sat with her back to us, the tips of her fingers visible each side of her ribcage from crossed arms. We froze. Atria was sitting a few metres away, on the green, her fingers playing with the blades of grass. Her hand signalled she was fine, but the situation was not.

'Well, well,' came the ratty voice. 'Look what the wolf sicked up!' Petronax stepped out of the shadow at the corner of the garden and stood in front of the gap, blocking Hallie. He carried a standard-issue light machine gun in the crook of his arm. Two pistols sat on his hips, one each side; his pockets were bulging with spare magazines.

He stood legs braced, relaxed and assured, his slim, medium-height figure projecting an imposing presence. Many people were nervous around him, maybe because of the nature of his job, but more instinctively because of some kind of innate nastiness he radiated. I grasped my lower lip between my teeth for a second but quickly plastered on a friendly smile and strode forward like I was greeting my best friend on a Sunday afternoon stroll.

'That's far enough,' he barked.

I stopped immediately, two metres further forward than Atria.

'I'm not falling for any of your little tricks.'

'C'mon, Petronax, I don't have anything up my sleeve. Look, I don't have any sleeves.' I held my hands out each side of my body and rotated my arms slowly, managing a few more centimetres forward.

Treb and Maelia had each managed to slide a few steps sideways in an arc during my performance. Atria had also shifted forward.

'The next little girlie that takes one step nearer will get a bullet in her head,' he warned us.

We stood stock still. 'Can I stay here?' I asked. Petronax needed to think he could control me. I was only about halfway between the door and him. I didn't think I could make it to where he stood before he fired or, worse, pushed Hallie off.

He nodded.

'What do you want, Petronax?''

'Oh, I think you know that.' He spoke in a flat tone, but intense, concentrated. His face was smooth, but his hard little eyes burned. 'It's quite straightforward – the end of you and your kind.'

'What do you mean – my kind?'

'You women, always dominating everything. You're not content, are you?'

His eyes started to bulge.

'What would you like us to be?' I asked gently, lifting my hands to accompany my question, easing my foot forward by a few centimetres.

He snorted. 'Where decent women should be: out of sight.'

'Well, that might be quite difficult now.' I looked to see how that went down. No change. 'We'd find it quite hard to go back, you know,' I continued. 'Apulius knew that. His way has kept us safe.'

I waited. No reaction.

'I know it's not easy, seeing things differently,' I sympathised, edging forward. 'I've been an outsider. Sometimes I've felt I never belonged, but I've gotten used to it.'

I was so disconnected from that girl in the New York ad agency, I could be on the other side of the universe. But I had to find some link to him. And I needed to buy time so I could move nearer.

I looked at him beseechingly. 'Come on, Petronax, put it all behind you and try again,' I pleaded. I managed another two steps forward.

'You keep away, you slut!' he shouted, his eyes spewing hatred. 'You're all filth, egging us on, betraying us.'

Ah, now we were there – he was afraid of women. No, he hated us. Viscerally. These "hating men" worked in many cultures to hurt or destroy women, sometimes disguised as professional rivalry, more directly as bullying, rape or plain domestic violence.

In Roma Nova, we were his worst nightmare.

And there was no hope.

His cold ideological shell was breaking down. 'Caeco and I agreed. Your precious cousin, her family, and then you and yours are next.'

Calm. I had to stay calm. I took some deep breaths. I inched a little further forward. I was around three metres away from him. I could take him.

'Well, it's over,' I said. 'We've picked up Caeco and your other friends. The DJ and our people are all around. Best give it up.'

'I might as well kill you now and push the little creep off the parapet.'

He raised his assault rifle. In the second before he could steady it to aim, I whipped out one of my carbon knives and sprang at him, slamming him down. The rifle crashed to the ground and rolled away. I shoved the blade up through his chest, aiming for the heart but his breast bone deflected it, jarring my wrist. I threw my knife down, crooked my elbow to drive it into his neck. As I shifted my weight to make the jab, he freed his arm enough to grab his pistol.

As I heard the shot ring in my ear, heat raced up my arm like a hot poker had been rammed through my flesh. The pain echoed up to my teeth. I gasped, dredging breath back into my lungs.

He kicked me to one side and sprayed the garden with his light machine gun. He was clutching his chest. Hopefully, the pain would make him collapse. But he was one of those wiry, tough bastards. He staggered towards the wall. He brought his hand back to shoulder level, elbow bent at an acute angle. Then he gave one quick shove and Hallie was gone.

23

A roar of 'Nooo!' burst out of my mouth as a flood of red clouded my vision. I sprang up straight from the ground at him, not caring this time. I knocked him down by sheer force against the inner parapet. Splinters of wood and flower petals showered down on us. I hoped I'd smashed his head open and spilled his demented brains.

Unbelievably, he struggled up, pushing me to one side. He managed to stand upright again, but swayed. Cradling my right arm against my chest, I staggered to my feet. I couldn't feel the arm, just warm liquid dribbling over the skin. I brought the outer edge of my left hand up to smash down on his throat. I heard a shot. A high velocity shot, a sniper. Petronax dropped on me like a ton of Aquae Caesaris granite, spattering warm brains and blood over me. I lost my balance and collapsed on the ground, cursing.

The brief high from the pallalgesic working its magic didn't last. I was trying to hold it together about Hallie's death, but black depression set in and I wanted to run and hide somewhere safe.

'Hold still, lady.' I heard the voice of Caecilius, Silvia's physician, like he was metres away. But he was right there, dressing my wound after removing the bullet. The lump of lead and the extraction tube lay discarded on the grass, along with pads soaked with blood. Mine and Petronax's. As he finally clicked the fastener on the sling strap, somebody thrust a hot drink into my good hand: ginger and malt. It smelled wonderful as I lifted it to my lips. I hadn't realised I was so thirsty.

No way could they have gotten there in time. I dreaded seeing Hallie's thin broken body, smashed after falling four floors, limbs turned wrong ways, a pool of blood. I bent over and threw up. Caecilius must have heard me retching. He rushed back over and wiped my mouth and face. I drew the back of my hand over my eye sockets, pushing the last tears out. I struggled upright, gave him a quick nod, and walked in the direction of the roof door. More like a waddle than a walk, my legs were cotton wool. I saw Atria sitting up, a medic treating her arm and shoulder. Maelia was lying unconscious on a stretcher, leg splinted, head bandaged.

'Report,' I said to the senior medic.

She looked at me. 'Both non-fatal, one leg wound, concussion, possible fracture, the other flesh wounds, shoulder and arm.' She spoke with that dispassionate voice they all used.

I looked Atria. 'You look pretty bloody!'

She made a face. 'Yeah, the stains'll take ages to wash out.' Her face tightened. 'What happened to the little girl?'

'I don't know. I'm...I'm on my way to find out, but what's the point? The boys didn't have time to save her before Petronax pushed her over. At least they shot the bastard.'

She quietly absorbed this and turned her head away, but not before I saw a tear roll down her face.

I picked my way through the smashed flower pots and wrecked loungers to the door. A figure nearly bumped into me as he burst through the doorway: Flavius.

'Where in Hades have you been?' I growled at him.

'Hey, settle down. I was coming to fetch you to the lower garden where the others are.'

'Is it very bad?'

'Well, it's a bit of a mess.'

A mess? Were they all as devastated and off-balance as I was?

We emerged through the side of the atrium into the main back garden. The soft lighting from overhead lamps and ground lights placed strategically along the lawn edges and scattered through the beds was designed to create an air of tranquillity and quiet dignity.

Not a sign of that now. The lawn was churned up by large-grip wheeled mini-trailers with a wide hammock-style net stretched high between them. One end was ripped away. PGSF guards milled around, several others kneeling or squatting in a group, shouting and laughing.

What in Hades did they think they were doing? Hot anger exploded through me. I bulled my way through, not caring about my arm. The talking died. I stared down at the figure lying on the ground.

Livius? His beautiful face was criss-crossed with cuts and scratches, the blond curly hair muddy and his foot flopped over at an awkward angle, but it was him. The circle around him started joshing him again, but he was giving it back as good as he got. Where was Hallie's body?

I took some deep breaths preparing to throw questions at anybody in my sights when my commset pulsed in my ear. Damn, I had forgotten to reactivate voice mode.

'Mitela.'

I listened and a heavy stone settled on my stomach.

'Of course. I'll be right there.'

Flavius's eyebrow rose in question.

'The steward. I'm requested to attend the imperatrix "at my earliest convenience".'

Right at that moment, I'd rather have gone to my own funeral.

I was completely at a loss. Silvia was safe now, but her child was dead. I would be exonerated under the Strat8 rules.

Screw the rules. For a second, I thought about running. I shifted my weight onto the balls of my feet but then relaxed it back onto my heels, No, that would be the easy way out. Not this time.

I stared at Flavius. He knew me so well he must have known how useless and anxious I felt. And how guilt-ridden. The old hackneyed farewell fell into my mind: *'Nos morituri te salutamus'*. I took a deep breath and went off to confront my own version of death in the arena.

I was dressed perfectly for an audience with the imperatrix: hair sweaty and falling in wild strands, black tee and shorts muddy and torn, blood and other dribbles down my neck and arm, and the rest of my flesh scratched and bruised. The only clean part of me was my sling. One of Silvia's staff handed me a towel to wipe my face, then let me through into her private drawing room.

Silvia looked unfazed. Her brown eyes were clear, no red rims, no dried tears. Her neutral casuals were neat, her red-brown hair carefully dressed, all in place. I knew she could hide her emotions well, but this was weird.

I bowed, my stomach hurting and stiff from Petronax's kick. Before I could stand up fully, she came over, hugged me and murmured, 'Thank you.'

What?

I expected to be arrested for *laesa maiestas*. At best, I failed to stop the murder of a member of the imperial family; at worst, I was an accessory to child killing.

'For Diana's sake, come and sit down, Carina. You look exhausted.'

I hesitated. I studied her face for any sign of hysteria, denial or other imbalance. She continued smiling at me, gesturing me to sit. I perched on the couch next to her. It was blue, soft and comforting. I prayed I wouldn't leave any stains on it. I shook my head to clear it and steadied myself. Why was she so calm? Where were her attendants? Conrad? Anybody?

She paused, looked at me, her eyes full of concern. 'You don't know, do you?'

'What?'

'Hallie's safe. She's alive.'

'She can't be,' I croaked. 'I saw him push her off.'

'He went to push her off, but Conradus grabbed her off the ledge at that exact moment.'

Conrad?

'Tell me everything!' I said.

While Livius, Flavius and Novius had been inserting the safety net and Paula setting up ropes from the upper windows, Conrad – the supposed invalid – had been busy. Once the two additional PGSF guards had arrived in the children's quarters, he'd slipped out and made his way to the top floor corridor below the roof garden.

'There's a sub-parapet that runs around the top of the building,' Silvia said. 'The maintenance people use it occasionally. It's less than a metre wide, so they don't if they can help it.'

I'd never heard of it. Or seen it. It must be hidden from normal view by some clever recessing. Even with safety harnesses, it wouldn't be a popular job going up there: nothing would break your fall for four storeys. Of course, Conrad had known it was there. He would have explored the palace thoroughly from his first day there with Silvia, let alone when he was on more formal guard duty. When he'd found it, he'd probably sat on the edge, admiring the view. I closed my eyes for a second or two.

'He brought her back down. She was gripping his neck as if strangling him. Her eyes were bulging and full of tears, and she was shivering. Conradus handed her to me without a word. He grabbed a throw and enveloped her and me in it and pulled us down onto this very sofa. After a few minutes, he stood up, bent over to kiss her head and left.'

I turned to one side. The tears fell down my face. It was sheer reaction. I felt Silvia's arm fold around my shoulders.

'I thought we'd lost her.' I took the handkerchief she offered. It was exquisite – fine lawn edged with lace. The fragile curls and whorls hardly touched each other except by a single thread – a world away from the blood and brutality of the last few minutes. I couldn't blow my nose on this piece of delicacy. I sniffed instead.

'No, she's fine. A bit cold and dazed. Caecilius has given her a mild sedative and she's sleeping now.'

'I'd like to see her.'

She held her hand out and I took it in my left. We went down the hallway, arms linked, closer than we'd ever been. We passed the two armed guards stationed outside the children's suite. They immediately came to attention, but Silvia waved at them to stand easy. I smiled at her casual attitude. While she could be dignified on formal occasions, she was very relaxed in her own home.

The dimmed light was soothing, a soft pleasure after all the action. Silvia gently pulled me through Hallie's bedroom door and we snuck in through long drapes that separated dressing from bed area. A guard was sitting in the far corner, but she didn't have any weapon showing. She stood up as we entered. A nurse by the bed looked up. She half-rose, but Silvia waved them both back down.

I crept over to the bed. Hallie was fast asleep, arm curled around a yellow rabbit sporting a vapid grin. Her face was a good colour and relaxed, no tension lines. Well, we'd see in the morning. I bent and kissed her forehead, wondering at the resilience of children.

Silvia touched my arm. She smiled and mimed that we should go.

Outside in the corridor, she turned to me. 'Come back in the morning. She wants to see you. Conradus caught her, but she knows it was you who faced Petronax so bravely and led the rescue.'

'I thought I'd killed her. I tried so hard to reason with that madman. But ideologicals are rigid, almost impossible to manipulate—'

'Shush! Stop being so angst-ridden! I know.'

I gaped at her. She was the mother who'd seen her child on the brink of death, the ruler who'd nearly lost her second heir, but her eyes were full of sympathy for me.

She looked straight at me, her brown eyes hardened into agate, and lips set straight as a mailbox slit. 'I am as bound by the covert protocol of Strategy 8 as the operational leader is. If you'd been compelled to let Hallie go, I'd have been compelled to accept it.'

I swallowed hard. I couldn't come close to imagining how difficult her life must be on these occasions.

As if a switch had been thrown, she shifted personas. She smiled warmly and took my good arm. 'Come on, drink. I certainly need one and you look as if you do, too.'

She brought over two crystal glasses with generous measures of dark gold liquid. Before I swallowed the first drop, I had to ask, 'Silvia, where's Conradus? I must go find him. Climbing along that parapet in his condition must have exhausted him.' I set the glass down and stood up.

'Sit down, Carina. He's resting, probably asleep now. I told the doctor that, as soon as he'd finished with your people, he was to check Conradus.' She sipped her brandy. 'I hope Caecilus gave him a strong sedative. Conradus was an idiot to go up there, but...' She looked at me gravely. 'It finished years ago between us, and he is still a good father to the children, but I'll never be able to forget that he gave me back Hallie tonight.'

We swallowed the rest of our brandies in silence.

An attendant came in and whispered in Silvia's ear.

'Ah! Of course.' She turned to me. 'You're wanted in the Operations Room?' She raised an eyebrow.

'The Red Dining Room,' I smiled.

'Well, I hope they haven't trodden muddy boots all over the Aubussons. The French Ambassador will have my hide if they have! When you've finished, go and sleep in the Antonia Suite. They'll wake you up in good time to see Hallie.' She smiled in dismissal, lent over and kissed me on both cheeks. I stood up, bowed and set off back into the chaos.

24

'Glad you could join us.' Daniel greeted me at the doorway. I saw lines of exhaustion and stress around his eyes, but a certain peevishness in his expression. He leaned in to me. 'Have you been drinking?'

'Yes. And?' I cocked my head and threw some attitude at him.

He didn't bite. 'How is she?'

'Fast asleep, sucking a plush rabbit.'

We sat around the table in the Red Dining Room. I'd glanced at the floor and seen that somebody *had* taken the Aubussons up. In real life, setting up a temporary command centre doesn't happen like in Hollywood films where they all dash in shouting and stomping around. It's more like a quick and efficient office fit-out. Furniture and rolled-up rugs had been stacked against the walls, utility tables and workstations set up in the required pattern, commsnet installed within minutes by the electronics group. Nobody shouted, rushed or clucked about nervously. The whole machine glided into place, operators slid into their seats and it was all up and running in under thirty minutes.

Now the Strat8 operation was terminated, natural order was back so, as senior rank, Major Daniel Stern took the head of the table. I sat at his right, ignoring Lurio opposite me, the fit members of my ART clustered around the rest of the table. The guard commander sat on a chair at the side with one of her sergeants, along with a medic of some sorts and a support service staffer. They all looked dishevelled in one way or another, except Flavius who, irritatingly, never seemed to look untidy or dirty, even when crawling around in mud. How did he do that? He'd just shrugged when I'd once asked. He sat there, drawing aimlessly on a clean pad of paper as if he was at a PTA meeting.

'Report,' Daniel pounced on me.

'The objective is achieved – Hallienia Apulia is safe and under protective guard. She is resting and I will speak to her in the morning. Petronax is dead. No fatal casualties on our side: four injured, three with gunshot wounds, all good prognoses.'

'Very well. Full written report on my desk within forty-eight hours, please.'

'Sir.' I groaned inwardly.

'Commander?'

'Perimeter held, diversions successful, no casualties.' Lurio kept his voice neutral. I didn't know how he had the balls to look me in the eye after trying to blow my head off.

'I would value a copy of your report, please,' Daniel requested, a distinct frost in his voice.

'Of course, major, my pleasure.' Lurio smirked.

'Guard commander?'

'Nothing to add, sir. We've stood down to orange level. We're doubling, but with no known threat.'

'Thank you. Medics?'

'All evacuated and team stood down,' came a neutral answer.

'Support service, let me know when you finally clear the site, please.'

A nod.

Daniel looked round. 'Any comments, observations?'

Nobody cared to make the obvious one.

'Very well. Find some food and get cleaned up and rested. Back on duty at 18.00 tomorrow. Thank you, everybody – a good night's work. Dismissed.' And that was that.

I nodded to Paula, Treb, Nov and Flavius to come with me. Out of the corner of my eye, I saw Daniel watching us. I thought he might come over but I badly wanted to speak to the others alone. Luckily, the support service guy ambushed him.

'Through here,' I whispered, and led them through a couple of corridors and into a small service room off the atrium.

I perched on the edge of the table. The others took up position around the walls of the tiny room and waited.

'So what really happened?' I demanded.

Paula and Flavius did the obvious thing and exchanged glances. The others looked down. Nobody spoke.

'Somebody draw the short straw and dish, please,' I said.

I saw Paula shrug as she volunteered. 'The boys were positioning the safety net and lifting the platform to snatch the child and bring her down. I was readying the lines and harness at the fourth-floor window for Livius to come in that way if he had to. But the platform held, he reached the parapet and shot Fabius.' She looked at me, carefully evaluating my reaction. 'Couldn't really miss at that range,' she snorted. 'Petronax looked stunned already.' She turned to me. 'Was that you, Bruna?'

'Yes, I was showing him a new way to breathe directly into the lungs.'

Good diversion attempt, Paula, I thought.

But Nov chimed in, spoiling Paula's hard work. 'The next thing we knew, he'd lost his balance, landed in the nets at an angle, and flipped off into the garden.'

'Lost his balance? Sorry?' Livius was one of the most agile soldiers I knew.

'I rather think he was surprised by what he found on the sub-parapet,' added Flavius.

'In what way surprised?'

I was momentarily distracted by Paula and Flavius doing that eye thing again.

'It was the legate,' Novius blurted out.

Flavius's mouth turned down in disapproving lines, and Paula frowned at Nov. Silvia told me Conrad had caught Hallie before the shot that killed Petronax.

'What was the legate?'

'Bruna, you're not going to like this,' Flavius started.

'Yes, I have that feeling. Just say it. I'm tired and hungry and don't have the whole night.'

'Very well. The platform lift had taken Livius almost up to visual level, when he suddenly saw the legate on the sub-parapet. He'd crawled out from a service access. Livius signalled him to stay still and silent. But the legate stood up and mouthed "Jump" at the child, which she did.'

I closed my eyes and nearly stopped breathing.

'He caught her and clung to the building edge. We'd dismissed it as far too dangerous for the child – it's not even a metre wide. Livius stood, made the shot and crouched down. He was spitting anger like Vesuvius. He mouthed something to the legate, shook his fist and arm. The legate's arm shot out and, the next minute, Livius was crashing down into the net then bounced off into the roses.'

I flicked a speck of dust off my arm sling. A mistake. Caecilius's shot was wearing off. The whole arm was acutely sensitive, and pain washed through it.

'That's it?' I asked calmly.

The four of them looked surprised and relieved. Really, I doubted I could say anything printable at this point, so I didn't.

Operating on automatic, I saw the others off on their way back to barracks in the long wheelbase and checked with the medics about Atria, Maelia and Livius. I also had them give me another shot for my arm. Noble suffering is such a crap idea when you can have it relieved. The problem was it made putting one foot ahead of the other in a forward motion a lot tougher.

At the Antonia Suite, near to Silvia's own apartments, I fumbled with the silver handle and opened the door. I'd despised the pastel insipidity when I'd stayed before, but tonight it was soothing. Emerging from the short hallway, I heard a background hum but saw the main room was empty. With hardly a moment to process anything, or to decide what to do next, I was interrupted.

'Good evening, lady. My name is Petra. I have prepared a bath for you and something to eat.' She looked like somebody's mother – efficient, caring, anticipating. She led me into the enormous, warm bathroom, peeled all the dirty and torn clothing off, not blinking at the knife holsters at the back of my waist or the sharp blades in them. She gently removed the sling and helped me into the bath. She washed me as if I were a five-year-old. The water was so soothing I didn't want to leave the warm cocoon, but somehow I was sitting on a chair, wrapped in towelled luxury, having my feet rubbed.

I sagged with tiredness, but I couldn't give in before I'd seen Conrad. Shuffling along to the third bedroom, I eased the door open, but it scuffed over the thick carpet. Conrad didn't wake. Lying on his side, one arm, still bruised but now with a few more surface scratches, lay outside the comforter. He was snoring lightly, from the effect of the medication, I guessed. The skin was sunken over his face bones, and brown shadows surrounded his eye sockets. I pulled the cover over his arm, and bent over and kissed his forehead. He didn't stir.

Back in the living room, Petra made me swallow some soup but I couldn't hold up much longer. Half asleep, I was led into another bedroom, fell into bed and dropped into blissful nothingness.

The next morning, I woke up groggy and heavy-eyed. It felt like emerging from a pit of liquid lead. I wiped my eyes and blinked at the morning sunshine suffusing the room. Who had opened the drapes? I grunted and turned over into the soft, thick comforter. Right onto my shot arm. That woke me fully. I stretched my legs. Big mistake. My whole middle section felt like a soggy, sore lump of wood. Hades.

'Cup of tea?' Petra stood at the side of the bed, steaming mug in hand. I saw her more clearly this morning. She was all brown – eyes, hair, dress. But the concerned look was the same as last night.

'What's the time?' I didn't have the least notion.

'It's still early, just before seven. Caecilius will be along in fifteen minutes to see about your arm. I'll make some breakfast for you in, say, half an hour?'

I nodded, my head still heavy with tiredness.

The doctor dressed my arm, gave me a shot and fussed around. He made me drink another cup of the malt and ginger restorative, which I had to admit tasted good. Petra eventually booted him out, gently bullied me into eating a mountain of food, and extracted the infernal dye from my hair. I watched the brown-stained water and solvent foam disappear down the plughole. The final trace of Pulcheria vanished along with it.

I pulled on a robe, flicked my damp hair behind my ears, and shuffled along to the far bedroom. Conrad's hair was damp from the shower. He was in his robe eating breakfast at a small table, watching the morning newscast like it was a normal day. How could he sit there so calmly? He looked around slowly, deliberately. His thumb on the remote cut the television.

'Hello,' he said and stood up.

I couldn't reply – I just walked into his arms which closed around me. As I hugged him, he winced. I pulled back and searched his face. He looked a lot better than I felt.

The bruises had dulled to faint yellow patches; in between, a healthy pink was showing. The puffiness had receded around the eyes – I could now see their normal tilted shape – and his mouth had healed leaving a vertical scar.

He kissed my forehead and gave me a lopsided smile.

I couldn't work out where to start, what to say. I knew he'd risk anything to save any of his children. He loved them all, unconditionally. But he'd risked himself and Hallie unnecessarily, and it was a miracle Livius wasn't dead. Whatever his feelings as a father, he knew as a commander he'd made the wrong decision to go up on that parapet.

I didn't say anything, just looked at him. His smile faded and a dull red spread across his face under my steady gaze. Maybe my expression showed my thoughts. Eventually, I said it. 'You were wrong.'

His face closed up and all softness disappeared. He raised his head to look down his nose at me. He looked awkward, caught in an impossible situation. 'The operation was successful. That's all that counts,' he said tersely. 'How we did it is irrelevant.'

Crap. He was going to pull rank. I pressed my lips together. I was too angry to speak. He was being incredibly unfair, but I'd have to swallow it. But it didn't stop me glaring at him.

The sun was climbing the sky, throwing its bright light into the room, but none into the space between us.

'I'm going to see Hallie,' I said.

I paused by the door.

'What really bugs me is that you didn't trust us to rescue her. You've always said to keep the personal out of operations. It's the Roman way, you said. This time you failed spectacularly. Great example.'

25

Hallie was sitting up in bed, eating porridge. Eew! Silvia had been raised by a Scottish nurse, then an English tutor, so was happy to indulge in this kind of stomach-churning practice. I would opt for eggs and bacon any day.

Hallie's face broke out in a smile when I came in. How glorious to give somebody such pleasure. 'Auntie Carina!' she shrieked.

I was humbled by the intensity of her feeling. I hugged her fiercely. I loved her so much. She was such an open and friendly child, a reflection of her mother's nature. That she oozed charm came from Conrad.

She looked me over, disappointment plain on her face. 'Why aren't you in your uniform?'

'Well, princess,' I began. Her eyes rolled at that. I grinned back. 'I got a little messy, running around the roof garden chasing the bad guys, so I had a bath and a change of clothes.'

'Yes, but you're wearing a *dress*!'

'It's a very nice dress,' I protested. Dark green silk, shot with gold and a gold belt, gold earrings and fine leather gold sandals. Petra had also part-braided my hair and drawn up it into a chignon. She'd passed make-up brushes and pads over my face in a few rapid strokes and fitted me with a clean white mesh sling. 'I think it's one of your mother's, so it must be all right.' I grinned.

'Oh, I see,' she said. Then she went quiet and looked down.

I looked her full in the face. There was never any point dodging the issue with children. They could always spot a phoney.

Her brown eyes met mine after a few moments. 'Thank you for saving me,' she said in a thin, stricken voice. Juno! If Petronax weren't already dead, I'd beat him to death for the hurt his vile actions had put on this child.

'Darling, I'd do it again ten times. He was a very nasty man.'

She looked glum.

'Do you know, Hallie, I was really scared of him, but I kept thinking of you being brave on that ledge. So, you see, I couldn't let you down.'

'Were you really scared?' She stared at me with wide eyes.

'Oh, yes.' I paused. 'I'm sorry if that's spoiled any illusions you had about me!'

I tried to keep it light. And then the surprise in her eyes changed to something else more lively. She winked at me.

'Okay,' she said, 'I won't tell Papa, if you won't.'

'Phew! That's a relief – I don't want to lose my job. Okay, deal.'

We clasped forearms to seal our bargain, hers barely reaching halfway along mine, but she had a firm grip. She looked at me with a mischievous grin, and we both burst out laughing.

I registered my exit with the guard commander who gave me a speculative look. I was a little too polished, I guessed. Conrad had gone straight to the barracks, so Silvia arranged my ride back. I would have happily caught a lift with the next vehicle going down the hill into the town, but her new Mulsanne was pretty neat so I sat back and enjoyed its luxury. What would happen if anybody put a muddy shoe on the cream leather seat? Probably have their foot chopped off.

Driving through the home park and out through the palace gate, I worked out my immediate plan: sneak into the barracks, dive down to the locker room and change, visit the guys in the infirmary, grab a quick meal in the mess room, and start the infernal report. I should have it finished before evening roll-call. I might even find some time to chew over some of the other problems I had lining up.

Good plan. Too bad it didn't reach the starting block.

At the PGSF barracks gate, I turned my face to the screen, spoke my name and stretched my hand out to the bioscan reader. A tiny beep replied and the gate swung open.

To my surprise, a full guard complement was on duty. I thought we'd reverted to orange level. Why weren't they training? They had plenty to do on that front. To my surprise, Lucius the adjutant came down the steps to meet the Mulsanne as it glided to a halt with my door precisely at the midpoint of the lowest step. A guard leapt forward and whipped my door open.

As I stepped out, Lucius threw me an enormous grin and clasped my shoulders. 'Welcome back.'

A flood of beige and black poured down the steps. Flavius, Paula, Treb, little Nov in the front. There must have been a couple of dozen more. Then I heard a well-known pattern of boots clattering down the steps and a distinctive voice reached me.

'Oh, for Jupiter's sake, clear out the way,' Daniel shouted as he barged through. He stopped in front of me and looked me up and down. 'Gods, you look tarted up ready for an orgy, or have you just come from one?' He grinned, glancing at my sling.

As the mess doors opened, the noise slammed into me. The acoustics were lousy. But I heard a cheer go up as I entered. A glass of champagne was thrust into my good hand. I felt humbled. These tough soldiers rarely showed such open approval. People milled around, gossiping, talking shop, a little too frenetically, I thought. Julia Sella smiled at me like she was a proud big sister.

I spotted Paula and waved her over. She hesitated, her face blank as she assessed my polished appearance. I knew what she was seeing: patrician, cousin to the imperatrix, heir to one of the great houses of the Imperium, not her comrade in arms. I'd seen it in other people's eyes. I cursed under my breath as she stopped a little distance from me.

'Hey, Paula, it's me. Bruna.'

She blinked and shook it off, her shoulders relaxing.

'How are they?' I asked.

Her normal expression reappeared. 'All on the mend. Atria and Livius will be discharged tomorrow. Maelia came round quite quickly, but needed a procedure on her leg, so she's stuck in the infirmary for a while.'

I grimaced.

'She'll be all right. Just weeks of physio.' Paula adopted a pragmatic approach, so coped with most things that came her way. Maelia would suffer or make those around her suffer during her convalescence. I looked around. 'Let's get out of here. I feel awkward in these clothes.'

Paula nodded towards the far end of the bar area. 'Kitchen service door?'

'Perfect.'

We smiled our way to the back edge of the drinkers and made for the far end of the bar counter, blanked off by a short wall. In the corner, a service door opened onto the back kitchen corridor. We paused for a second or two by the door. I could only hear the buzz of talking, some laughter, a shout or two, clinking of glasses. Until I picked up Conrad's voice. He must have stopped at the far end of the bar, away from the others, just around the corner from us. Crap. I really did not want to talk to him in front of the others. I touched Paula's shoulder and shook my head. If we moved, he would hear us. We were stuck.

'Well, Lucius?' I heard Conrad ask crisply.

'Legate. I missed you when you arrived.'

The two men had been not merely friends, but comrades for ten years, saving each other's backs literally and figuratively many times. While Conrad was the nervy risk taker, Lucius held everything together. Lucius had been the first of Conrad's fellow officers he'd introduced me to when I arrived over seven years ago, and I was reasonably well tuned into him.

'You've recovered well,' Lucius said. His tone was awkward and tense.

'Yes. The body heals when it's not being continuously abused for days on end.'

'Look, Conradus, I'm sorry we didn't do anything more quickly than we did. After Galla, well, you know...'

'I'm visiting her mother tomorrow.'

I heard a glass placed on the bar.

'After a while, your only existence is pain,' Conrad said. His voice was low, mechanical almost. 'When they start again, all you feel is pressure and points of exquisite agony.' A pause. 'I stopped caring after a while. If Carina's gangsters hadn't extracted me, I would have died within a day or two.'

I edged up to the corner and risked a peek. Only a metre away from us, they were looking back to the noisy crowd.

Lucius looked agonised. Conrad met his gaze. The unsaid message that passed between them was blurred, both men breaking contact after an uncomfortable exchange.

After a few minutes' silence, Lucius coughed. 'You'll let me know how you want to set up post-action meetings tomorrow? I've cancelled today's evening report.'

'Whatever you think best, Adjutant,' came the cold reply.

Next morning, back in uniform, my hair contained in a serious plait, I felt more collected, more structured. I looked in my mirror and saw a soldier, ready for at least light duty (despite the sling). But the eyes were full of strain and red around the rims.

There were only a few in the mess hall, the night shift mostly, eating before they slept. I nodded to them as I passed between the tables on my way to the hatch.

'Eggs and bacon, ma'am?'

Bless him! 'Yes, thanks, Glavus.'

'You go and sit down – I'll do some fresh. Here, take this,' and he thrust a plate with a warm roll and preserves at me and balanced a cup of steaming coffee on the plate. It smelled delicious.

I munched the roll and drank my coffee, trying to organise my thoughts. I must visit Maelia in the infirmary, and find Atria and Livius. But the main part of my day would be my report for Daniel. Then I would be free to go home. When I called, Helena had said they were all recovered, but her voice was muted. I desperately needed to see them. Especially my children.

Just as my eggs and bacon were delivered, bacon sliced up, Conrad slid into the chair opposite.

'Well, you are privileged.' He mocked gently, watching the cook retreat back behind his hatch.

I saw he'd had to grab his own breakfast.

I shrugged. 'Depends who you know.'

We concentrated on eating. After around five minutes, he drained his coffee mug, carefully set it down and studied the table.

'You know you'll have to undergo a long debrief.'

'Yes, I suppose.'

'Then there'll be a disciplinary hearing,' he added.

'Great. Something to look forward to.'

'You know it's not personal, just procedure.'

'Presumably I'll still have a job afterwards?'

'Fifty-fifty odds, I reckon,' he said and looked up at me. At last.

I dropped my knife and fork on the plate, the clatter drawing a few curious looks.

'Fifty-fifty!' I shrieked. A few more heads turned.

He frowned at me.

'Is that it? After I saved everybody's skin?'

'Well, they'll take that into account.' He looked up at me. 'Fishing for a commendation, are you?'

'No. Just some recognition.'

I knew I reacted badly when I thought I was being treated unfairly. Not very mature, but that's how it was. He was joshing me – or was he? His face was unreadable. Sometimes he was a complete mystery.

But what he said hit a tender spot. I *had* acted like a cowboy when I'd run off. But if I'd done the proper thing and stayed, we'd have both been dead along with Silvia and her family. Now, I was facing the possibility of being thrown out. Daniel would have told me to stop being a drama queen and wait, but a streak of fear ran though me. I would lose the life I loved.

It took me less than a minute to strike back. 'If it's all too much for you, and you throw me out, I'll go back and work with Apollodorus,' I said. 'We didn't have all this ass-busting procedure there. We knew when somebody had done well.'

'No.' His face was stretched with fury.

'What "no"?' I glowered at him, but inside I was nervous of his mood.

'I will not permit it. I'd rather see you in prison than you go back there.'

'Really?'

'Watch yourself. You may think you've saved the world, but you are not immune to the consequences of your actions. Insubordinate doesn't begin to describe it.'

I stood up, turned my back on him and stomped out.

26

Where did my knack for self-destruction come from? I jumped into the elevator up to the infirmary before they found me and locked me up.

'Morning, captain,' the duty nurse greeted me. 'What can I do for you?'

'I've come to see Maelia – she was brought in yesterday. No, night before – sorry.' I'd lost track of time.

She scanned my badge and looked at her screen. 'Ah! You're due another restorative. Please wait here a moment.'

Didn't they have anything better to do?

She came back in a few moments with a cup of the familiar ginger and malt drink. The gods knew what else was in it, vitamins or something, I suppose, but it accelerated the healing process. The swelling on my arm had almost gone, although the wounds were still seeping. Of course, it ached.

Like a true officious medic, she watched me until I'd finished. I put the empty cup down, leaving a ring-mark to make her over-tidy counter messy.

'Follow me, please,' she said.

She swept me through the swing doors. The hospital smell hit me. Even in this small facility, it ruled. It bounced off the inhabitants as well as the cream walls. There were only half a dozen rooms, and I was ushered into the second one along the short corridor.

Maelia grinned weakly. She was plugged into a monitor, and her leg was encased in a plastic brace. She looked trapped in the white bed. I pulled up a chair.

'Well?' I enquired.

'Well, what?'

'When are they discharging you?'

'When my hair grows back.' She turned and showed me the bald patch with a deep but healing graze. Poor Maelia; she loved her beautiful hair. It was normally a shiny, plentiful waterfall of glossy dark brown. At the moment, it was like a bunch of dark straw, too embarrassing for a scarecrow.

'Yeah, bummer,' I sympathized. 'Is it very hard for you now, with the leg, I mean?'

She gazed at the vase of flowers on the bedside table for a few moments and put a lot of energy in scrunching up the edge of her sheet. She eventually drew her gaze back to me. 'They see no reason for it not to heal fully, but I won't be back to full strength for a few months. I have to lie still for two weeks.' She looked so despondent. Maelia was one of those active fidgets who couldn't bear to sit still, let alone lie still. Maybe I could bring her into the strategy office when she came back to light duties.

'Too bad. You'll have to knuckle down and do what they say for once,' I said.

'Just like you do, Bruna.' I couldn't mistake the malicious gleam in her eye.

'Yeah, well, the least said about that, the better.'

'Ah, ha! Do I detect the golden girl is in trouble again?'

'You mind your business, Maelia.'

'How bad?'

I told her about the row.

'He won't let you go, you know. You might have a rough time for a short while, though.'

'You know what, Maelia, you are starting to sound like Paula. She thinks she's my mother.'

'Well, perhaps you need one.'

I said nothing. My mother had died when I was three.

We moved on, our conversation rising back up to the superficial.

'I'll come back tomorrow if I'm not up on a charge.'

'Nah, you won't be.'

I tracked Livius and Atria down to the games room. He was half-lying on a couch, beer in hand, cushions supporting his back, the good foot on the ground. She was sitting on a dining chair. Both held controllers and were intent on the screen, alive with movement. The screen flashed bright yellow then cleared completely.

Livius threw his remote on the floor. 'For fuck's sake, how did you do that? You are such a cheat.'

'Don't be a bad loser,' came her soft voice. 'I just used the advantages I had.'

'Yeah, right.'

She just laughed.

'Rematch?' he challenged. I saw him watching her, carefully evaluating her reaction – or was it more than that?

'Glad to see you're practising your theoretical combat skills,' I interrupted them.

Atria rose to her feet, moving awkwardly, her sling matching mine. I waved her back down and dragged up a chair.

'Hello, ma'am, how are you?' asked Livius. He looked completely at ease, as if he were hosting an exclusive literary salon.

'Good, thanks. Arm's a bit stiff. You two?'

'Well, I've felt better,' replied Atria. 'It's so itchy!' She moved her elbow out a little way from her body in a circular movement. 'The gods alone know what drugs they've given me to take the pain away, but I expect I'll pay for it.'

'Well, take your mind off it by choosing the next game,' Livius instructed her. As she stood up and did so, his gaze followed her.

'So what's the prognosis on your ankle, Livius?'

'I have to have physio for a couple of weeks, then light duties to the end of the month. If I pass the medical, I can go back to non-strenuous training.' His mouth turned down at the thought. He watched Atria coming back. She said, too smoothly, she was going to fetch some more drinks.

Livius turned to me. 'I wanted to say something private to you.' His usual cheeky grin disappeared. His scratched and cut face was serious. 'Up on the parapet...'

I went to interrupt him.

'No, let me finish,' he insisted. 'I was furious at the time when I saw the legate and swore at him. I almost knocked him off.' He looked away.

But it was Conrad who had reacted and Livius who had fallen.

I felt uneasy at what was coming. What was Livius thinking? As a member of one of the Twelve Families, he was perfectly entitled to challenge Conrad on equal terms, according to the Families' Codes. He was younger, fitter and quite deadly. Conrad was no slouch, but Livius was in peak combat condition – well, apart from the ankle, of course. But he was my comrade in arms, part of my personal team, so he couldn't challenge a member of my family. Gods, what complicated connections we made for ourselves!

'You could have been killed,' I said. 'And we were on a Strat8, which would have been successful anyway.'

He shushed me, taking my hand. 'We *did* succeed. That's all that's important. Don't give him a hard time. He was only trying to save his child,' he said softly.

This was from the man who'd been pushed off four floors up by Conrad.

'I know, but—'

'No, finish it here or it'll sour everything. For both of you and for the unit.'

He looked at me steadily. I was disconcerted by this serious Livius, but he was right. In the end, I looked away and hunched in the chair, not knowing what to say back to him.

'Captain Mitela?'

We looked around and saw one of the custody guards. Had he come for me?

'Yes?'

'We've had a, well, you could call it a special delivery, for you.'

'What kind of delivery?'

'The driver said it had to be handed to "Bruna" or "Flav". He said he needed a receipt from either of you.'

Few, very few, outside knew my *nom de guerre*. I flicked on my mouth mic. 'Flavius, Mitela. Meet me in the custody suite in five.' Pause. 'Some delivery or other. Either you or I have to sign for it.' Pause. 'Not a clue. Out.'

Atria came back at that point, with a steward in her wake carrying a tray with drinks and sandwiches. She was one of those people who always had immediate, sparkling service from an assistant, a waiter or a steward when the rest of us couldn't even see one.

'Hope it's not a bomb,' Livius commented and grinned.

'You'll know when it goes bang,' I said.

I hadn't been entirely honest with Livius. If only Flavius or I could sign for this delivery then there was only one possible sender.

When I met Flavius on the stairs leading down to the custody area, he didn't say anything, just looked at me.

'Well, I don't know either,' I said. 'But let's not make a big production out of it.'

We emerged into a wide, cream-painted hall. After negotiating the security gate which slid shut behind us, we passed through the body scanner which hummed but did not beep.

As we approached the desk, the duty sergeant deigned to look up and nodded. 'Ah, Captain Mitela, Sergeant Flavius, please come this way.' He handed over to his deputy and led us through another secure gate into the garage area. A standard long wheelbase occupied the far end where the sloping driveway flattened out to enter the garage, but there was no sign of any driver, just a door gaping. Not good. We all tensed – maybe Livius was right.

'Back. Now!' shouted the sergeant. We fled to the other side of the security gate, and the impact shutters crashed down.

An EOD bomb squad appeared within minutes of the alarm call. They wore Nomex bomb suits, with only their faces visible through the polycarbonate masks. They waited for five long minutes while their commander assessed the vehicle, then opened the small shutter door and gingerly entered the garage, keeping to the back. A small robot deployed, circling the vehicle with extended camera, sensors and bioscanner. The EOD commander frowned into his el-pad. *No reading for explosives, gases, mechanisms, plastic – nothing,* his disembodied voice reported, *only five life signs on the bioscan readout.*

I grabbed a spare helmet and mask. I left the body armour – didn't fit around slings – and stepped through the shutter door.

Sure enough, five glowing bio signatures showed on his screen. He sent the robot around again. Same result. Breathing more regularly, he signalled a couple of his troops in to look closer at the vehicle. Kevlar shields held in front, they scanned for electronic traps as they advanced centimetre by centimetre. All it needed was a perimeter sensor to trigger and they would be scattered in shreds of flesh across the garage. The robot's arm lifted the canvas cargo cover and slowly pulled it back. The robot camera arm snaked in over the metal tailgate and swung slowly around.

There were five men in the back, manacled and secured to the floor. Their mouths were taped and they were blindfolded with sleep masks.

I gasped as I saw them on the screen. 'Jupiter's balls!'

'Friends of yours, captain?' the EOD commander's voice buzzed through his headset.

'Definitely not!' I replied. 'But a friend may have sent them.' I smiled to myself.

The commander looked at me as if I were deranged.

'I leave you to do your body checks,' I reassured the EOD leader. 'But I think you'll find they're clean – so will the long wheelbase be.' Philippus would not have served me a dirty trick on this. Nice of him to return our vehicle.

Half an hour later, the custody guards were let in and took our new guests into their tender care. Stripped, searched, examined by the medics, they were found to be in reasonable condition, but truculent. I formally arrested them and read them their rights before they were locked in individual cells. They'd keep until the morning, I thought.

'I don't suppose you'd like to tell me who exactly they are, would you, captain?'

'It would give me the greatest pleasure in the world, Sergeant. Just find me a decent cup of coffee and a sandwich and I'm all yours!'

I finished all the paperwork by just after 14.00 and felt a little smug as I walked back upstairs. Apollodorus had behaved impeccably, whatever Conrad might have thought. Right now, I needed to find to my desk and start Daniel's damned report.

I opened the door to my office and walked into a palace. The piles of boxes, racking struts, cupboards, chairs, cabinets, screens and cabling reels had been transformed into a sleek, humming strategy centre with a large transparent polycarbonate situation screen at the end. A bank of desks and screens lined the two walls with a command station at the end of the run, facing into the room. Even my sandbox was there in the corner with bright lighting over it, illuminating every grain. The dividers between the office and lecture hall had also been renewed with pale birch panelling. On the command station top, there sat my old scratched desk organizer and cube-pad block.

I saw Fausta and Drusus, chirruping into headsets, playing some deep strategy game. Drusus turned around only to see who had interrupted them.

'Captain!' The impatient look on his face dissolved instantly, replaced by goggling eyes and an open mouth, but he quickly recovered. Fausta's head snapped round. She was equally amazed.

'What? Didn't you expect me back?' I tried to look crestfallen, but couldn't manage it. I grinned instead. They bubbled around me, like a couple of playground rivals, each intent on showing me something new and wonderful. At last, I arrived at the command station, a very streamlined affair, unlike my old, stained, wooden utility desk. Still, a keyboard was a keyboard, so I logged on and started typing.

After an hour, I stopped and stretched my legs. My arm was also protesting by then. I needed to take some medication. 'Okay, where's the coffee machine?'

They glanced at each other.

'Um, we haven't unpacked it, ma'am,' confessed Fausta.

'Because?'

'Well, we both drink mineral water.'

I shut my eyes for a moment.

'Very commendable, Fausta, but please get the coffee machine on, stat,' I instructed.

I found the fridge in the tiny side kitchen. As suspected, no milk or cream. I sighed.

'On it, captain,' Drusus almost put his finger through the deskset in his haste.

'And sugar,' I added. They looked appalled.

I finished my report and hit print. I liked to read the final version on paper with a red pen in my hand. I couldn't hear a thing.

'Okay, where's the printer?' I was obviously still thinking in old office mode. Perhaps it was something else they hadn't unpacked.

Fausta leapt up and slid out a unit from the row of wall storage.

'We keep it in here, to prevent any cross-signals with the game system.' The whole compartment was lined with grey pyramid-patterned radio absorbent material. Impressive. I collected my sheets and skulked back to my seat like a dinosaur. Amendments done, I mailed the report to Daniel. I also messaged Colonel Somna about our new guests, copying in the legate, the adjutant and the operations officer. I sat back and waited.

Inevitably, my terminal beeped with an alert for an urgent meeting: legate's office.

Although 19.00, the sun's warmth hadn't diminished much. It was only late August, after all. But a few red streaks had slashed across the yellowing sky. In an hour, it would be dark, the time when bad guys came out to play. I was sitting in the corridor outside Conrad's office looking through the sliding glass doors to the little internal garden. Long limbs of two birch trees stretched up, chased by a photinia in hot pursuit. Lavenders and rosemary added scent and, somehow, bees made their way in there. And out again.

Somna arrived with Lucius, who looked sour. I stood and waited quietly behind them. Sella appeared next and we exchanged brief smiles. There were a few minutes to go. Daniel would cut it fine as usual and he didn't disappoint. Summoned by the legate's EO, we traipsed in. He invited Somna, Sella and Lucius to sit on the couches and waved Daniel and me to find a seat somewhere.

'We appear to have acquired the core plotters,' the legate said in a neutral tone. 'Naturally enough, you will wish to interview them, colonel.' He nodded at Somna. 'Please liaise with Major Stern and Captain Mitela for operational information. They will be detailed to you for as long as you wish.'

Wonderful.

He scanned around. 'I require detailed diaries and reports of all actions you each took part in over the past three weeks. I include myself, of course,' he said. 'These will be examined by an internal security board, and appropriate disciplinary or commendation action taken as necessary.'

Nobody said a word. He rubbed the first two fingers of his right hand on the hairline at his temple – the stress sign. 'I will have to think exactly who will make up this board – none of us here are fit to sit on it, except perhaps Sella. For the time being, everybody will continue as usual. Daniel, could you step up the training schedules – please hand over to Colonel Sella on this while you are detached to the Interrogation Service.'

He looked down at the coffee table. To me, he looked pinched and pale. 'You realise the legal team will be all over us as they prepare the trials. It is therefore imperative that you complete your accounts as soon as possible.'

The dejection in his voice permeated the room. He wasn't only thinking of the past weeks, but trying to prepare us and protect us from the inevitable fallout.

After the meeting broke up, I hung around.

'Do you really want everything?' I asked him.

'Yes.'

'You'll kill my legend. I've kept it alive for seven years.'

'I know.'

'I could use it again. If I could come up with an alternative—'

'Don't try. I want it finished.'

'Is this to do with pushing me out? Should I go voluntarily?'

'I think you have to make a decision where you belong.'

I couldn't believe he was putting me in this place. I was trying to stand on both sides of a crevasse that was opening up under me. The two sides were parting at an increasing pace. I looked at my wristband. 'I'm due at the palace very soon. After that, I'll have to take a couple of days, maybe less.'

His face was neutral, but the voice was clipped and cold. 'Very well. But this is the last time.'

'I— I don't—' I couldn't say any more. I swallowed hard. I resented being forced to abandon a part of my life I felt strongly about. Apollodorus had helped me grow up. He was my mentor, my colleague, my friend.

Conrad stood up, came over to me, laid his left hand on my good shoulder, and gently stroked my cheek with the other.

'Go and do what you have to do,' he said quietly, 'and then come back to me.' He kissed me lightly on my forehead and gave me a sad little smile.

27

Flavius picked me up at the palace and we drove to Apollodorus's house. In the cooler evening, I was grateful for the black fleece uniform jacket over my shoulders. We approached the gate with its graceful stone arch. The gatekeeper would be tucked up in a warm hole somewhere, so I tried the coded entry system. I was surprised and, in a strange way, wary when it worked. The vidcamera swung in our direction as the gate opened. Flavius drove in and parked in the visitors' area at the front. By now, they would have ID'd us and be ready. To say I was apprehensive was an understatement. I was trembling inside and out.

Flavius gave me a sympathetic look. He jumped out, came around and opened the passenger door for me. He held out his hand. 'C'mon, Bruna. Let's get on with it.'

Our boots crunched across the gravel. The inner metal barred gate with its Venetian scrollwork opened almost silently for us. We continued up the path, all twenty metres of it. The sound would have alerted the house even if we weren't already being tracked on the cameras. As we reached the house door, it was swung open by a servant I didn't recognise. His outstretched arm invited us into the covered courtyard.

Waiting for us with grim expressions were Justus and Philippus, plus two bodyguards carrying compact assault rifles, angled ready for use. We were the opposition – that was obvious. Our uniforms reinforced it. Both men made a show of looking at us indifferently, but I could see wariness in Philippus's eyes. I looked across at them, a vast chasm between us now. These were comrades, loyal friends as close to me in some ways as my ART. Maybe not Justus.

'Against the wall,' Philippus said, pointing at me. His tense face, his whole manner silently begging me not to do anything stupid so he'd have to shoot me. 'Please.'

I placed my left hand at shoulder height on the cold stone. My right arm stiff, but no longer painful, just hung in its sling. One bodyguard stood a metre away to my side and glued her weapon to a point fifteen centimetres away from my head; the other covered Flavius.

Philippus lifted my jacket off, handed it to Justus who searched it. Next my belt and side arm. Philippus gave me the most thorough frisking I'd ever had. I'd never before appreciated how inquisitive his strong hands were. He unclipped the sling and eased my arm out, lifting the dressing to inspect the entry wound. I gasped as the skin pulled. The wound was still weeping a little liquid and blood.

'Sorry,' he muttered. 'Where are the knives?'

'I left them behind.'

Justus snorted. Fair enough. Pulcheria always carried her knives. 'Take off your boots. Slowly and carefully.'

Not so easy one-handed. It took forever. The silence was oppressive. I didn't even hear the birds that normally flew around here. I went to hand the boots to Justus, but he pointed to a spot on the ground a metre away. He picked them up, searched them, grunted and threw them back at me. As I brought my good arm up to catch them, and missed, the two bodyguards brought their weapons up. Gods, they were tense. What had they expected me to do?

'She's clean. You next.' Justus gestured at Flavius. Philippus couldn't meet his eyes as he moved forward to search Flavius. He took Flavius's side arm, belt and nightstick.

I couldn't retie my boots – the fingers on my right hand were nerveless and throbbing by now. Despite the weapons trained on him, Flavius threw a look of concentrated hatred at them both, knelt down and fastened them for me. Philippus couldn't look back at him.

'Follow me,' Justus said, as if we didn't know where to find anything in this so familiar house. He sounded resentful – no, bitter.

This was going to be ten times worse than I thought.

Philippus peeled off somewhere with our weapons, and Justus led us to the meeting table in the atrium where Apollodorus sat with his senior staff in exactly the same formation as our operations meetings. Hermina and Albinus scrutinised us coldly. Cassia smiled. It was the most animated I had ever seen her face. If we came out of this alive, I would find out exactly why she had left the Censor's office and if there was anything prejudicial we could bust her on. Justus came to roost by Hermina. He looked satisfied for some reason. We weren't invited to sit.

Apollo and I stared at each other. I looked into the black pits and thought I saw hurt, fury, cynicism all mixed up. I could never work him out. Who knew what he saw? Perhaps my profound sadness. He'd known I was PGSF and had been DJ before; he'd kept it hidden from the others until now, but he'd known from the very beginning. He was angry for different reasons.

'Always a pleasure to see you, captain,' he began. Gods, if the chill in his voice could go lower, I didn't know how. I waited. He was obviously deriving some unhappy pleasure from our uncomfortable situation.

'I do hope this is not an official visit – I fear you may have come a little light-handed if you wished to succeed on that path.'

Cold washed over me. We couldn't have been more vulnerable.

'No, this is not an official visit, as I'm sure you realise.'

Hermina started at the sound of my normal voice. Of course, she'd only heard me as Pulcheria who had an incredibly irritating nasal whine. Albinus looked more interested than before.

Flavius and I were walking on a very fragile surface. One click of Apollo's fingers and we'd be gone. Philippus was standing less than a metre away. Justus wouldn't even take the space of a breath to think about pulling the trigger. It would bring down repercussions of fifteen on a scale of one to ten, but I didn't have a doubt Apollodorus had some exit strategy already in place in case he chose to terminate us. I scared myself thinking so clinically when I was seconds away from a bullet through my head. I should have been shitting bricks. My blood was pumping chemicals around my body, but it wouldn't help. Even together, Flavius and I couldn't take them all, but neither could we try running. We'd be dead in seconds. I felt a tremor of fear trying to crack my shell but I pushed it back. Maybe I was going to die, but I wouldn't give them the satisfaction of seeing me afraid.

I cleared my throat. 'I must thank you for the special delivery we received this afternoon.'

Justus and Hermina exchanged glances, and Justus flicked his gaze towards Apollo who didn't respond or even make any kind of movement. He just stared at me like he was trying to bore into my soul. I felt powerless and trapped. What did he want? After a full two minutes, I caught on – he was going to make me beg. At that thought, I felt both relieved and humiliated. A pilot light of anger lit up in the back of my mind. Then it flared up to full strength. The hell with that and to Hades with him.

Nobody said a thing. Waiting for time to pass, I listened to the faint sound of a vehicle moving a short distance away and the hum of some kind of machine nearby. I would stand still for as long as it took. After a quarter of an hour, Justus and Cassia started to fidget and I heard Philippus's boots as he flexed his feet. Hermina looked uncomfortable and moved her head from side to side. Flavius and I just stood there. We'd endured hours' long parades – a favourite trick of the tribunes when they became bored with nothing to do in the barracks. It was mostly a case of making your mind adapt to the inaction. I looked straight down at Apollo, daring him to do something. Because there was no way I would.

I started counting the pores on his skin, on his nose and under his eyes. I moved on to the brows. Then I counted the eyelashes on each edge, upper and lower of each eye. That took up a good twenty minutes. Then the grains in the floor tiles I could see just off the edge of his head. When I'd finished half an hour later, Philippus was sitting at the side, defeated; one bodyguard was sitting on the floor, the other gone; Justus was walking up and down; Hermina and Cassia had disappeared.

'Enough!' Apollodorus shouted, banging the flat of his hand on the table. He stood up abruptly and strode over to stand in front of me. Very little space separated us. He glared right at me with an angry intensity I'd never seen before. '*Sacra flamma*! I'd forgotten just how stubborn you can be,' he growled.

With my peripheral vision, I saw Justus, mouth open, feet frozen to the flagstone. He couldn't believe his eyes – he'd obviously never seen Apollo lose control.

Apollo still stared at me. He didn't blink once; his face had returned to impassive.

'Philippus, take Flavius with you and get lost somewhere. You,' he said to me, 'come with me.'

Flavius looked towards me. I nodded. The crisis had passed, thank Juno. But we couldn't relax yet. I signed Flavius to use a significant amount of care. Even signing with his fingers, his reply was unrepeatable.

Apollo abandoned his usual languid stroll and strode ahead of me. As I coaxed my stiffened legs into action to catch up with him, I noticed how set his shoulders were, how rigid his neck was.

We were on the way straight to his *tablinum* – not very private, but I had no choice. To my surprise, we went past the open-ended room. To the left, he opened a plain door outward. It had always been locked, and I'd thought it was a cupboard, or steps to a cellar. It was dark inside, and I hesitated.

'In,' he commanded, holding the door open.

I sighed. I was sure he wasn't going to kill me now. I just hoped Conrad would pay the ransom. I took three steps and encountered a cloth curtain, soft and thick like velvet. He pulled the door shut behind him and all light vanished. It didn't smell cold or damp like a cellar. The floor under my feet was springy like wood. I sensed him right behind me and jumped when he put his hand on my upper arm. A tingle ran across my shoulders.

'Have you lost all your wits? Pull the curtain back.'

I did and stepped out into another century.

The first thing I saw was a walnut fireplace carved with leaves curling around each other along the top edge. Below, flames flickered behind a decorated wrought-iron grill sending warmth into the room. Over the fireplace hung an enormous mirror with lotus leaves and irises in gold-painted wood around the rim. Apart from my shocked face, the mirror reflected sinuous ivory and jet female statues standing on top of the mantel. Dull gold and crimson brocade drapes hung down the walls. Two carved wood couches, padded with red velvet mounds, and gold glass-shaded lamps shedding soft light reinforced the voluptuous style. This was a room for seduction.

The intimacy and unrestrained sensuality unnerved me. Not for itself, but because it conflicted in every way with the austere, controlled man standing behind me.

'Sit,' he commanded.

I did, both entranced and stunned. My eyes adapted to the dim light. On the left hung a print of an unclothed river nymph with flowers in her long, wavy tresses. Such women always had "tresses", never just hair. On the opposite wall was a painting of a tall, slender woman with long black hair, and wearing a pseudo-medieval robe. The artist had made her beautiful in the style of the age, but there was no mistaking from her black eyes who she was related to.

'Who is she?'

'My grandmother.'

In all the years I'd known him, I'd never thought of Apollo in the context of a family. That was ridiculous, I knew; even he must have had a mother and father. I'd never known his real name nor his age – they weren't questions you asked serious criminals. Despite his studied old-fashioned ways which I thought he used to distance people, he couldn't have been more than late forties or early fifties.

He handed me a glass of wine. I'd recovered enough to be able to hold it without spilling. I took one sip then set it down on a side table that had swan neck curved legs.

'This is my grandmother's boudoir – well, a copy of it,' he explained. 'She was French, you know, a well-known *salonnière* after the Great War. My mother, who was from Castra Lucilla, insisted that her mother-in-law came and live with them when she married my father. Although my grandmother was a *parisienne*, born and bred, she moved perfectly willingly. She feared for her son who had fatal weaknesses.' His face hardened. 'She was right, but as a small boy I didn't know that until one very bad day.'

He looked at the painting with longing. 'She gave me unconditional love. She was my anchor during the nightmare that followed.

'I won't bore you with the rest of the sordid details, *ma chère*. Nobody likes to hear about an addicted father pimping a child, a mother reduced to thieving. He even beat and terrorised his own mother when she no longer had any money left to service his addiction. Not exactly edifying examples, are they, as parents?'

So that was why he'd so hated the drugs trade when it had threatened us those years ago.

'I clawed my way through my adolescence and eventually rid my family of my parasitic father.'

I wasn't going to ask what he meant by "rid", but the hate must have boiled long and hard. It was heartbreaking. I nearly forgot to breathe.

'I became a mildly successful criminal and maintained my mother and grandmother a few rungs above poverty. My mother I honoured and was sorry for, but I have loved no woman as I have my grandmother...until seven years ago.'

We sat silently, the only noise a clock somewhere on the side. After a few minutes, I pulled myself up and went to sit at his feet. I stretched my hand up to lie on his. His other hand touched my hair, and I rested my head against his knee. We had never been so physically intimate. Nor so emotionally in tune.

I felt myself slipping away in the warmth of the room. Almost before I realised it, Apollo had scooped me up in his arms and was carrying me. I was so tired and overwhelmed I didn't care what he did. I felt my boots being removed, my uniform following, my hair released, the soft sheets, the slender hands, then no more.

When I woke, I was by myself. A thin line of light outlined the window frame. It was early, around half seven, I guessed. I switched on a light and found a green silk kimono lying on the bed. As I tied it on, I caught my reflection in the cheval mirror. I looked like Madam Butterfly. I didn't know if the past twelve hours had been a series of scenes from a comic opera or the deepest tragedy. Tears welled in my eyes as I realised what I'd found and lost all at once. I closed my eyes and shook my head to try reset my mind, but was interrupted by a knock at the door. Flavius's face appeared around the edge.

'May I come in?'

I burst into laughter, maybe a little hysterically. He was dressed as a house servant and carried a tray. I smelled the ginger and malt and groaned.

'Don't overreact. You love the stuff.'

'But how?'

'Philippus blabbed about your shot arm, and the cook made it up for you.'

'So Philippus is talking to you again?'

'Well, he thawed out a bit when Apollodorus lost it. He wanted to know what you'd done to him to make him react like that.'

I said nothing.

'Fine,' he said, and paused for a few moments. 'Well, we had a couple of beers and talked about this and that. Even Justus came and sat in. We packed up after an hour or so, and they found me a room but confiscated all my kit. So, I pinched this tunic from the laundry room this morning, then went and saw the cook.'

He sat on the edge of the bed and looked down.

'I don't know what happens next. If we come out of this alive, it's the final break, isn't it?'

He'd grown up with Philippus. They'd worked together for Apollo since they were teenagers, before I'd nudged Flavius into the PGSF. I knew he'd seen Philippus from time to time, but I'd never dreamed of reporting him.

I laid my hand on his.

'Yes,' I said, 'total rupture.'

A knock at the interconnecting door broke the silence. Then Apollo came through, also dressed in a kimono and smiling. Flavius's eyes didn't quite come out on stalks. He looked at me briefly, murmured an excuse and left. As the door shut behind him, I turned to Apollo.

'Thanks, Apollo. That was really helpful.'

'You didn't think you'd escape without paying a price of some kind, did you?'

I threw him a cold look.

'Actually, I came to see if you would join me for breakfast.' He held his hand out.

We sat alone in the small *triclinium* by the garden. Open in the summer, large glazed panels were inserted in the cooler seasons. We talked of old times, people we both knew, his roses. The barrier had dissolved between us; we no longer needed to be guarded with each other. Our link was about to break, and I realised I'd never see him again.

He leaned forward and wiped a tear off my cheek. 'I won't see you leave. I want to remember you as you are now, here, sitting with me in the garden.'

'Apollo, I—'

'Shh.' He laid a finger on my lips.

Eventually, he turned to me and said almost casually, 'I've always loved you. From the first moment I saw you.'

I searched his face. His eyes were warm and liquid, but his face was composed.

'I've always known, Apollo,' I replied.

He smiled, took my hand, kissed it and left.

Our uniforms were returned to our rooms, clean and pressed, boots shining. Flavius and I kitted up and made our way down to the atrium in silence. The reception committee was waiting for us. No Cassia – that was a relief.

Hermina spoke first. 'I don't know what to say to you. Pulcheria was my friend. I see her in you, but you are not her.' Her eyes were full of resentment and doubt.

'I'm sorry, Hermi, I—'

'Don't call me that! That's her name for me.' She looked away.

'I apologise, Hermina. I would not wish to cause you distress,' I said formally. 'I valued your friendship, and I thank you for the good things we did together. But we have to part now.' I held my good hand out. The way she looked at it, I thought she'd refuse to take it, but she did, and then embraced me briefly. Albinus nodded to both of us, and walked away with Hermina.

Justus. He just looked pissed with himself and resentful of us. 'I'll say this, Mitela, you're one hell of an operator. I never imagined you were the law. Far too maverick. I bet they love you – you're probably on a charge most of the time.' He sneered at me. Flavius took a step towards him, but I signalled him back.

'I'll take that as a compliment, Justus. Actually, I'm considered very good at what I do, very imaginative.' I grinned and added, 'Only in the cooler from time to time!'

'Ha!' He relented and half-smiled. 'So I suppose we'll now all have massive files on your system?'

'Well, you might have a mention here and there…' None of them knew it, and I certainly wasn't going to tell them, but I'd set up a personal alert seven years ago that, if they ever registered on any law enforcement radar, a report would automatically be sent to me as their contact. I wouldn't necessarily be able to get them off, but I'd ensure they had good representation and a fair hearing. I wouldn't be adding Cassia to that list.

Philippus had been talking quietly to Flavius but, seeing Justus had done, he approached me.

'I feel privileged to have known you, captain. You always were an exemplary leader and good soldier. I can see why you're such an asset to them. I shall miss you.' He held his arm out and we grasped forearms in the old Roman way. To my utter surprise, Justus followed suit.

I wasn't going to do anything lame, but I was moved by their words and actions. One of the guards brought our weapons and belts to us. After strapping them on in silence, Flavius and I nodded to Philippus and Justus, turned about and marched to the door.

Flavius, bless him, drove up to the heights over the town and stopped by the ruins of the old fortress. I sobbed my heart out. He just stared into the distance. Then we cleaned ourselves up and drove back to the barracks in silence.

PART III

ENDGAME

28

I walked through my office on automatic. There was a day-old terse message from Daniel about the interrogations and where in Hades was I? I sent an equally terse holding reply and then mailed the legate's EO for an appointment. Five minutes later, I was instructed to report immediately.

As I walked along the corridor, I focused on keeping my head in professional mode. I doubted I could go near the personal for some time. I had my hand on the doorplate to go into the outer office leading to Conrad's when Daniel came out of his own door.

'Where the hell have you been?' he asked. 'I've been stuck in with Somna for the past day and a bit. Now they're hassling me about you being AWOL.'

I couldn't deal with this now.

'I was tying up a loose end.'

He snorted. 'What loose end?'

'Need to know. And you don't.' I glanced up and down the corridor. Thankfully, it was empty.

'Bullshit! Tell me.' He grabbed my good arm.

His normally smooth olive face was contorted by harsh lines. He radiated anger and resentment. Like a kid who'd been left out of the gang. But I was late. I didn't have time to massage his ego.

'Get off my case, okay?' I heard my voice growing shriller.

'Don't you talk to me like that – I outrank you,' he bellowed at me.

'You're confusing me with somebody who gives a shit!' I shouted back at him and pulled my arm out of his grip just as Conrad's outer office door opened.

'Enough!' Conrad's voice cut through the bedlam. 'Is this a military office or the fish market? He glared at me. 'Stop shrieking this instant! You're not some sixteen-year-old tart whose punter ran off without paying. Find some dignity.' He swung around to Daniel. 'Go away and calm down, Daniel. If you can't, go for a long run. I will not have you shouting like some barbarian.'

He held his inner office door open for me. 'Sit there,' he said, pointing to the chair the other side of his desk, 'and take some deep breaths. Don't speak for five minutes.'

He scribbled something on a paper report and tapped rapidly on his keyboard. The muted staccato rhythm on plastic was strangely calming.

'I apologise for that scene,' I said after two minutes. 'I lost it when Daniel kept going on at me. I should know better.'

'Yes, you should, but I understand the strain you are under.' He shot a quick glance at me. 'Do you want to tell me about it yet?'

'No, but it's all over.'

'Very well. Now, you must go back to work. But first, I think you should go home and see Aurelia and the children for a few hours. They're recovering well, but she's worried about you. I'll schedule you for the night watch so you don't need to be back until 20.00.'

I waved my thanks to the driver as she dropped me off at the gate, passed the bioscan and trudged up the steps.

Junia's son, Macro, greeted me. 'Are you ill, lady? Let me fetch somebody for you. Would you like to lean on my arm?'

I shook my head and started through the vestibule towards the hallway. Unlike his mother, he didn't know how I hated a fuss. Where *was* Junia? The *imagines* looked particularly disapproving tonight, but I ignored them. Two were missing; coloured ceramic and marble shards lay in neat piles to the side, underneath a torn wall tapestry. A lobby door hung off its hinges. I was diverted from the vandalism by a familiar figure trip-tripping down the hallway.

'Juno! You look like Proserpina after her three months in the underworld!' announced Helena. Her voice was high and tight, and a little too cheery. One of her elegant eyebrows, each hair normally plucked and arched into submission, now soared above a black eye. Below, her cheek was swollen with red and blue bruising which made her little smile lopsided.

I swallowed hard. 'How bad is it?'

'Everybody's fine now, but Aunt Aurelia's taking us all into the country next week, to the farm. She says we need to be away from the city. It'll give the staff a chance to clean and refurbish the whole house.'

Her voice was brittle with false reassurance. She glanced around nervously, unable to let her eyes settle on my face.

'Helena, tell me.'

She looked away.

'Well?'

She shuddered. 'It was the most frightening thing I've known. Aurelia was dignified and tough. I was scared stiff, but petrified for the children.' She gulped.

I pulled her onto a couch and gently drew her to me. 'Tell me from the beginning.'

'They came first thing, before breakfast. A load of military police, they ran into the house and dragged us out into the back of a dirty truck. Conradus hadn't come back the night before; I assumed he was still on duty. I called and called him. I tried your office phone in case anybody was monitoring it, but was diverted to voicemail. I kept trying to reach somebody, anybody, until they grabbed my phone. It had to be a horrible mistake.' She glanced up. 'I know now that was when they'd taken him off to the Transulium. One of them smacked my face when I tried to help Aurelia.' She made a moue and briefly touched her damaged face. Her hand was shaking. 'The twins cried, but we managed to calm them, but Allegra just stared at everything and didn't make a sound.'

I felt a chill, and it wasn't anything to do with the stone walls. My fists balled up. I would make sure I traced that MP detail. Their regret would be long and painful. 'Anything else?'

'Well, you saw Macro was on duty? Junia's in hospital with a broken arm and concussion; Galienus has a dislocated jaw, cracked ribs and a fractured foot. They tried so hard to defend us. The rest of the household staff were held at gunpoint and then locked in a cellar. Macro came back from the early market and found his mother unconscious on the floor.' Her voice rose, shaky and tighter. She grabbed my arm. 'Carina, they had the access codes.'

'That bastard, Superbus.'

'Juno! Of course, we'd just sent the codes out for the Family Day,' she said. She gulped, trying hard not to let tears escape.

I said nothing, but pulled her to me and let her shake her sobs out.

After a minute or so, Helena drew her head back from my shoulder, looked at me and blew her nose. 'You'd better see Aurelia first – Allegra is having a nap.'

'Allegra. She's not – she wasn't…hurt?'

'No, apart from rough handling, they didn't really injure us.'

I shut my eyes and breathed out.

'Was it likely?' she asked, doubt growing on her face as she realised what I was saying.

'Unfortunately, yes. You're a teacher, Helena. Think back to your Republican and early Imperial history,' I said, roughly. 'Remember exactly how they killed female children and relatives of political enemies? How they couldn't kill virgins? What they did first?'

She stared at me, horrified.

I reached the atrium and found my grandmother on a couch by the glass wall giving onto the garden. The fall sunshine painted the walkway columns and gravels a delicate gold. Unlike Apollo's cosseted roses, the flowers were looking overblown and turning brown, on their way to becoming corpses. The grasses waved around, their ears full of seeds, but looked stalwart among the failing summer plants.

Speaking of stalwart, Aurelia Mitela sat upright on the couch reading a newspaper, new gold-rimmed glasses perched halfway up her nose. She looked like an old-fashioned English headmistress, especially as her expression so evidently disapproved of what she was reading.

'Tchah!' She half threw the paper down on the oak table in front of her and, sensing me, looked up. She opened her arms and I fell into them.

We sat there, talking quietly together. She insisted I tell her everything, interrupting now and again to ask a pointed question or when my brain overran my mouth.

'What about you, Nonna? Pretty terrifying for you.' I scrutinised her face, but she looked exactly as usual.

'Don't be soppy. I've been through a great deal worse. I'm not a little old lady out of some genteel novel.'

No, she truly wasn't. She'd been PGSF in her time, even led the attack to retake the city during the civil war. Although now in her mid-seventies, she definitely belonged to the "tough gals" league.

She gave me a close description of the arresting party. What a difference it made when the victim was a trained professional and could give you precise, detailed information. She'd printed off her statement and signed it already. They hadn't been detained long – just locked in an interview room for a few hours. Unlike Helena, Aurelia had kept her cellphone in her inside pocket when they were arrested and, once locked up, she'd simply texted Silvia. From a detached professional viewpoint, that custody sergeant needed shooting – sloppy not to have searched them.

Silvia had been told by two of the renegade senators that the Mitelae were behind a coup. She couldn't consult with her chancellor, Conrad's uncle, Quintus Tellus, as he was away in Geneva and "there was a communications problem", the PGSF signals office had claimed. Superbus, now lording over the PGSF – the treacherous bastard – had ordered the arrest of Conrad, Aurelia and the children.

Silvia hadn't believed a word, and ordered the women's and children's immediate release. She'd reluctantly agreed to Conrad's detention, not dreaming what they'd do to him, but insisted on no more than house arrest for Aurelia and the children until the situation clarified. I guessed Superbus obeyed, thinking it didn't matter as, within a few hours, Petronax would have launched the real coup and Silvia would be permanently out of play soon afterwards.

'I was more worried about Helena,' my grandmother said. 'Oh, I think she's been to some slightly risky parties and there was that kidnap business with Renschman six years ago...'

Jeffrey Renschman – my father's first-born child who'd grown into a psychopath and hunted me down in retribution for the misery he thought my father had caused him. I shuddered at the memory of how he'd threatened to kill Helena. I remembered the sense of betrayal and, to be honest, anger at my father for never having mentioned I had a half-brother. That came later when I was recovering in hospital from my near-fatal fight with Jeffrey. Would I have acted any differently if I'd known? It was theoretical; Jeffrey had cracked his head as he'd dropped to the ground and went into a deep coma, dying not long after.

'… but she's never been touched by this kind of brutal political conflict,' Nonna continued. 'Like a lot of professional people, she hasn't a clue about what I did and you do.' She smiled at me, one soldier to another. 'Shame they don't still do compulsory service.'

I let that one go. I couldn't really see Helena in a uniform.

I hadn't analysed why I did what I did. It seemed so natural for me. Service to the state was a complex idea. Some clever political scientist could say it a lot better than an ex-advertising account handler. It wasn't always desperately comfortable; we had to make some harsh decisions and slog on through impossible situations. Serving your team, building relationships that literally saved your life, submitting to discipline, going into situations no sane person would – this was all part of it. Anyway, the uniform was cool, and you were given a free drink now and then.

'Do you feel better now you've told me?' she said.

'To be honest, I'm not sure. We still have all the clearing up to do – just think of the paperwork!' I glanced away. 'And I'm dreading the fallout amongst my colleagues when the whole story comes out.'

'And Superbus?'

'Oh, gods! What an embarrassment for the family. He'll have some fancy lawyer who'll spin it out and our name will be dragged through the courts. I'm so sorry about that, Nonna.'

'It's not your fault, darling. Unfortunate he wasn't caught in crossfire, but never mind. However, I think the family may be able to help if he proves intractable. Do you know Dalina Mitela's daughter?'

She smiled like an Egyptian sphinx and outlined a possible idea…

• • •

Back in our wing, I changed into jeans and tee and went up to the children's dayroom. Helena was clearing up the morning's activities. She gave me a tight smile and nodded. Allegra was sitting at the table finishing some writing. She looked up and saw my face, smiled and walked over to me, far too calmly.

'Hello, Mama,' she said, her face serious.

'Hello, darling.' I gently folded my good arm around her.

'What happened to your arm? Did those men hurt you as well?'

'I'm fine. I'll tell you over lunch.'

She just hugged me. As I pulled back, I saw two tiny tears roll down her face.

We ate our macaroni and cheese, Gil and Tonia being messy and showing off, Allegra giving them disapproving looks. I sympathised with her.

'They are pretty disgusting, aren't they?' I whispered to her. 'But they'll get better, you know.'

She looked at me doubtfully.

Helena carted the twins off to clean them up before their nap and Allegra and I talked some more.

'Have you killed all the bad guys?'

I swallowed hard. 'One, but the rest are in jail, and will stay there for a long time. As well as punishing them, we have to teach them to change their minds and not go around being nasty to other people just for what they are.'

She absorbed that. 'So they were thinking bad things?'

'Well, everybody's allowed to think anything they want. Most people have a lot of different thoughts, and that's fine. But it's not allowed to act on bad thoughts if it's going to hurt other people. Sometimes, soldiers like Daddy and I have to stop and catch these people.'

'Oh, I see.' She glanced down and sideways as she twisted her fingers around each other. She brought her eyes back up and searched my face. 'But they were unkind to hurt you. Is your arm very poorly?'

'It's a lot better than it was – better every day.' I grinned at her. 'They all keep making me take my medicine.'

She made a face in sympathy.

Right on cue, a knock at the door and a beaker of the damn

restorative appeared. I couldn't believe it. More than that, it was Marcella, Nonna's assistant, carrying it.

'The Countess's compliments and you're to take this after you've finished your lunch, which I believe is now.' She looked pointedly at the empty plates.

'Thank you, Marcella.' I tried to sound sarcastic, but she was being kind, that stifling kindness that people who've known you for several years feel they can exert on you.

Allegra was watching me, as was Marcella, so I had to swallow it all down.

Marcella started to go but, as she reached the double doors, turned. 'Welcome home, lady. We're all delighted to see you back safely.'

I took Allegra down to the swings in the garden. We perched on the seats, idly pushing at the worn patches in the grass with our feet, Allegra's legs at the perfect angle, mine bent back almost on themselves. Helena's assistant brought out some milk and biscuits which we ate sitting side by side at the picnic table with the blue and white segmented umbrella shading us from the strong sun.

I sought my daughter's hand and held it in mine. 'Allegra, do you want to tell me about when the men took you all away?' I cringed inside, not knowing what to expect.

'They were cruel and noisy. The twins cry at anything, so they don't count.' How hard children were to each other.

'Why did they push Nonna and slap Helena?' she asked. 'We hadn't done anything wrong – I always try to be good. So why did they hurt us?' Her face didn't show distress or upset, just bewilderment. 'Helena said they were bad men obeying bad orders from that smelly Superbus. But they looked like soldiers, like you and Daddy.'

'Oh, darling, they were a different type of soldier. Not very good ones. I'll show you some pictures of different sorts, if you'd like, so you can see the difference.'

'Yes,' she agreed. 'So I know for next time.'

I hugged her tightly to me. After a few minutes, I released her and said, 'Allegra, I'm going to do my very best to make sure there won't be a next time.'

'I know you will, Mama, but, as Great Nonna says, you never

know.' She looked straight at me. 'Will you punish the ones that were cruel to us?'

'Yes.'

'Oh, well. That's all right then.'

We walked back, hand in hand. In the dayroom, we kissed and I left her with Helena.

I was far too incensed to start my report. I had to calm down first, so I went and talked to Aurelia again. I told her about my conversation with Allegra. One of Helena's friends, a cognitive counsellor specialising with children, had started sessions with Allegra, but Nonna thought Allegra would get over it reasonably quickly now that I'd started the healing process with her. I wasn't too sure that was what I'd done, but Nonna seemed confident.

I tried for an hour and a half to draft the bones of my report for Conrad and managed to flesh out part of it as well, but it was a struggle. I had an ergonomic desk in the office in the apartment, a comfortable, personally-contoured chair, perfect lighting – everything of the best. Normally, I could sit there forever. This evening, I found I had to stretch, rub my neck, stare out of the window, and flex my legs. I let my arm out of its sling and made it attempt a few picking up exercises around the rest of the office. I drew the drapes, filed some papers, played with the paperclip pile. Eventually, I ground to a halt, saved my draft, password-protected it and messaged it to my secure storage box at the barracks. After a quick sandwich, I put my uniform back on and went on duty.

29

Before reporting to the Interrogation Service, I checked in at my strategy office for mail and requested a couple of slots with Julia Sella for the next day. An email from outside pinged in. Jus@pf.improm.com.

Justus! Crap squared. I was toast.

Knowing I should know better, I opened it. It was very formally worded and had numerous attachments. A second one pinged in. More attachments. He'd sent everything we'd uncovered – statements, recordings, reports, photos – all of it. I stared at the screen, unable to move. It had penetrated the security check system. Albinus was a real smart Harry. The internal security section had been disbanded. What was I supposed to do with this bunch of stuff? My finger hovered over the Delete button. How easy to tap and erase the two emails and save myself a shovel-load of trouble. Except, of course, there'd have been copies saved automatically on the central registry.

I closed down, locked up and reported to the interrogation centre, as requested.

Unfortunately, Somna was on duty. She was a professional soldier of many years' standing, extremely effective at her job as senior interrogator. Conrad had enormous respect and liking for her. I was biased, having been on the receiving end several years ago. I'd always felt nervous around her.

Despite the name, the Interrogation Service mostly used

psychological techniques, persistent questioning, hours of it, sometimes the odd chemical, but that was strictly regulated. They just sat there, going on and on at you. They didn't interact or show a flicker of emotion. One favourite of theirs was when three of them sat in a circle around you and just stared. Didn't sound too bad but, after an hour, most people start gibbering.

Somna had been a captain working with Conrad on the Pulcheria case when I'd first encountered her seven years ago. I'd been brought in as the chief suspect. The interrogation had taken a dangerous turn, and I'd ended up holding Somna in a threatening death grip. When the DJ had identified me as their agent and had me released from PGSF custody, she'd simply nodded at me and said, 'My respects,' and walked away. She was one of the few who knew the full story. Her only reaction when I joined the PGSF was a tiny jolt of recognition in her normally expressionless eyes. Nothing since.

The duty sergeant directed me to her door. I swallowed hard, which was difficult with a dry mouth, and knocked.

'Enter.'

'Good evening, ma'am.'

'Ah, Captain Mitela, glad to see you.' She smiled at me. 'How's the report coming along?'

'Um, quite well, ma'am. I'd hoped I might be able to work on it tonight. However, something's come up.'

Her grey eyes showed a flicker of interest.

'I've had a couple of emails with some sensitive attachments. I would have reported it to the internal security office, but there isn't one now.'

'No,' she said dryly and glanced at my sling.

'So who would I inform?'

'Sepunia and I are combining forces for the present. Our teams are working their way steadily through their whole set-up and work history. Why don't you run it past me?'

'May I log on to my account here and show you?'

'Please.' She moved aside from her keyboard and waved me to it. Wired as I was, sitting closely to her made me even more hot and uncomfortable. I forced myself to breathe evenly and slowly while downloading everything from Justus. Somna stared at the screen, her eyes darting in synch as if they were interacting directly with the information and images on it. A smile grew on her face like some alien construct. She looked like she'd been taken on a world tour of interrogation conferences, all expenses paid.

After she'd seen everything once, her hand darted out and she jabbed a button on her commset. 'Longina, get in here. Stat.' She didn't shout, but it was on its way there.

A tall brunette, slender beyond skinny, came in; another one with a smooth, expressionless face. Was there a special factory turning them out? But, as she leaned over to the screen and absorbed the contents, she was moved to say, 'Fuck me!' which I thought was appropriate, but entirely unexpected from a robot.

'Right, Mitela, start telling us about this lot.'

It went on for hours. True to type, they were relentless. Not in a hostile way, but like thirsty vampires, natural to them. I felt sucked out by the time we'd finished. Almost everything was acceptable. Somna regretted that I'd stamped on Pisentius's foot and kicked Cyriacus, but it didn't invalidate it.

'Although a little crude from a professional point of view, for an untrained interrogator I think you did very well,' Somna commented. I ignored the patronising tone and almost passed out with surprise at her praise.

'I didn't realise Jus— they were making recordings,' I said. Sneaky bastard.

Longina took me to find a drink. Thank the gods. I was gasping.

'That's a goldmine, captain.' She held her hand out. Her handshake was dry and unbelievably firm.

I reciprocated and smiled back at her, relieved that it was mostly legal as well as useful.

'The colonel will want your report even more urgently now.'

'Well, there's quite a bit more to go in. It may take a few days.'

I was trying to put off the inevitable confrontations. Now, not only Conrad was on my case but Somna as well.

'Let me know if you'd like to observe any of the sessions,' Longina said.

She smiled, and I think she meant it kindly, like she was conferring a favour, but I passed for that shift. My nerves were still jangling from talking to Somna, and I needed to give them a break.

Instead, she gave me a quick tour of the service's work and

organisation. I was fascinated by the analysis and compilation facilities. I saw now there was much more work in this function than in the physical interaction with the prisoners – the iceberg syndrome, I guessed.

'So how are the interrogations going generally?' I asked.

'We've wrapped up Aburia now. Her hearing before a military tribunal is scheduled for next week. Obviously, you'll be called, so I'll get a legal staffer in to brief you tomorrow or the next day.'

She consulted her screen. 'Sextus Cornelius is wrapped. He's being transferred to the remand centre for psychological reports. Ah! There's a new note – the Cornelia Family legal officer is to support him. Lucky boy! They'll bring a top-rate lawyer in for him. Not that it'll make any difference.'

I didn't want to shatter her illusions. Sextus would probably tell the legal officer to go stick herself.

'Caeco, Pisentius, Trosius and Cyriacus were work in progress but, with your material today,' she raised her head from the screen and smiled, 'we've made a quantum jump.'

I seemed to have made somebody's day, at least.

I finished just after two in the morning, pleased with the progress I'd made on my report. As she was also going for sleep, Longina introduced me to the early shift supervisor, Porteus. Somna was still welded to her desk but would probably nap for a few hours later, Longina said.

It was quiet in the IS general office: just the hum of computers, a vidscreen on low volume, and a few people working at desks. Desks were arranged open-plan in continuous worktops with a generous space for each workstation. I thought it resembled mission control in Houston. A meeting table and chairs occupied the corner opposite the entrance to Somna's office. It looked like any boring workplace, but, of course, it wasn't.

I tapped on the door frame of Colonel Sella's office at 08.30 next morning. 'I'm sorry to have made such a short-notice appointment, ma'am, but I wonder if you could do me a small favour.'

'Well, you can certainly ask,' she said.

That jarred. Her usual friendly tone was gone, her expression neutral with no smile. Nevertheless, I had to get this done. 'I have a young cousin, Lucilla Mitela. She's a student at the Central University, and she's been working at the library over the vacation, down in the archives. She's finished there now but still has three weeks to fill. I wondered if I could use her for some routine input work here?'

'Fill in an application form online and I'll approve it then.'

'She's filled it out. I have her CV and character affidavit right here,' I said. 'And her security form.'

She looked at me with a sucked-in face. 'Do I get the impression you're trying to steamroller me?'

'Not at all, ma'am, but she only has three weeks, and it can take a week to process these things, at best. I promised her.' I smiled with what I hoped was an appealing expression.

'You're not going away until I approve it, are you?'

I judged it better to say nothing.

She tapped on her keyboard, accessed the application and signed it off. 'Drop the paperwork off with my clerk. She can start tomorrow.'

She looked down at her folder and slid the next sheet over. I closed the door quietly as I left. What was that about? Was she put out with me or was it something else?

The IS office was buzzing like a beehive that morning. I found my workstation, sipped my coffee and looked around. I was about to work on my report when Somna came up to me with a smile on her face like she was Fortuna with a sackful of gifts.

'Ah, Carina, come with me.'

So we were on first name terms now?

We made our way downstairs and entered a control room with three sides covered with large screens. Pairs of IS were sitting at five of them, headphones on, scribbling on pads or tapping into netbooks. Fright Central. Well, maybe that was too harsh. I must have been watched on these screens for the two days I was down in one of those cells. I shivered. Somna gave me a rueful smile. It was scary how sympathetic she was. If I wasn't too careful, she'd soon become my best buddy.

I stood silently while she listened to the supervisor's report. Trosius was now wrapped up, and he thought Pisentius would be by the end of the day. The supervisor looked at me with a question in his eyes, but Somna didn't introduce me.

'Shall we listen in?'

Pisentius was on a chair, hands cuffed behind him. The interrogator was standing very near, one boot nudging Pisentius's bare foot. He bent down and said softly, 'Now you don't want me to break the top of your other foot, do you?' Pisentius flinched, his shoulders rolling inwards. He let his mouth drop open a few millimetres and I heard him catch his breath.

The other interrogator repeated her question in a bored voice. And again. Then the first one pulled up a chair right by Pisentius, crowding him, and repeated the question. And so it went on, unrelenting. Pisentius started sweating.

Two minutes later, he shouted, 'Screw you! Of course we did!' and he hung his head.

I almost found myself sympathising with Pisentius, the fundamentalist traitor who wanted to kill my cousin and destroy her country. I took the headphones off and walked away from the screens. I waited by the table. When Justus and I had questioned the conspirators, it was in anger and with urgency. I respected what the IS did, probably more than I had before, but I was too emotional to do their job in this depersonalised, methodical way.

Back upstairs, I grabbed another coffee and settled down to my report. I heard snatches of conversations around me, but kept my head down. Sober slogging calmed my nerves. By lunchtime, I was finished, but I didn't share that piece of information. I had something to do first.

Longina was back at her desk.

'What's the situation with Superbus?' I asked.

Her face fell. 'Well, we've only done preliminaries with him, but even then he wanted his mummy, sorry, his lawyer. She's a tough nut, so I think it's going to drag out.'

'Will you let me know if it reaches deadlock?'

She looked at me, puzzled but interested. I left it at that.

I knocked on Somna's door and put my head around it to ask her to excuse me for my meeting scheduled later with Julia Sella. Although it was in the diary, I thought it polite to check in. Daniel was in with her and, as I tried to withdraw, Somna called me back.

'Carina, Major Stern was wondering if he was needed any longer now you're here. I rather thought not, unless you feel otherwise?'

Daniel looked incredulous and threw a load of questions at me with his eyes.

'No, I don't think so, ma'am,' I replied with a smile.

'Very well, you're released, major,' said Somna. 'Thank you for your help.'

Daniel and I walked back together to the general PGSF office. He'd completely forgotten our fight yesterday.

'So now you're best buddies with Somna? I thought you hated her.'

'I think "hate" is a little overstated but, sure, I was nervous of her. But I have to say I'm finding it easy to work with her now, and her team are very nice.'

'"Nice"!' he exploded. 'Are you listening to yourself?'

'Yes, *you* should try it some time.'

'So what more can you help her with? All the arrest reports are in.'

'Oh, this and that.'

'Hmm. Now you've crossed over to the dark side, I suppose you're not going to tell me where you disappeared to before you showed up at the palace.'

'No.'

Eating lunch, we speculated about the general fallout; who would head the security unit; whether Sepunia would be confirmed as Intelligence. Daniel wasn't fooled and, between poking at his food, he continued to needle me about my down time.

After a while, we ran out of words.

Daniel was one of my staunchest friends. We were both risk-takers, strong-headed, ready to act. We'd done some insane things together in the past. After hand-climbing the inner courtyard wall – five storeys high – for a bet, even though it was strictly against orders, we were thrown in the cells for a week. But we both thought it had been a good laugh. It sealed our friendship and we got totally smashed the day we were released. We'd penetrated and destroyed a dangerous network together; trained allied personnel; been lent to other governments; broken active service units; trained hard; lived hard.

Our bond was strong, but would it survive the next forty-eight hours? I'd deceived him about Pulcheria. Sure, it had been for operational reasons, but Daniel had been humiliated and defeated by Pulcheria and her people several times. He'd taken it really personally. The one time he'd had complete advantage over her, at the end of the tunnel, and could have terminated her, Conrad had stopped him.

I dodged it – I couldn't bring myself to tell him.

So I tried a different tactic. 'Daniel, suppose, hypothetically, somebody had maintained a long-term legend very successfully but, for various reasons, had to kill it off.'

'With you so far.'

'No, listen! I'm serious. Some of his colleagues would need to know now for recording, intelligence and training reasons. They'd be surprised. Some would be outraged as they'd come up against this person in the line of duty. How would *you* react?'

He looked at me, his brown eyes curious now. 'Why are alarm bells going off in my head? Who is it?'

'No, really, just tossing the idea around,' I said. 'Spending too much time with Somna, I think.' I laughed.

'Sooner you're out of there, the better.'

But I could see from his face, I'd set something off.

30

Colonel Julia Sella's office was like all other senior staff lairs: cream walls, bookcases, desk, workstation, a couch and easy chairs, but much tidier. It was feminine without being pink: her pictures were landscapes; she had a cluster of personal photographs at the side; and a tray of clean crockery and silverware by her kettle. It was serene and civilised – pretty much like I thought its occupant was.

'Come in.' She glanced briefly at me as I appeared at her door; then looked back at her screen. I saw her eyes flicker over to the printed sheets I had in my hand and her face tighten as if she knew what was written there. She pointed a remote at the window to the general office and the smartglass clouded instantly. We were entirely private from the outside world.

'So, what do you have for me?'

I gave her the stapled sheets. 'I'd like you to read these first, please, Julia Sella. Then I need your advice.'

She looked surprised at my use of her civil style, but didn't say anything. She sat and read the six typed sheets that could change my life.

I fidgeted. I stood up and wandered over to the outside window. I looked down and saw a centurion drilling troops on the parade ground. In the far corner by the garages, mechanics in black coveralls were climbing all over a couple of long wheelbases. People walked across the courtyard, stopping to talk briefly to colleagues or just waving to them in their haste. I sighed at the normality of it all.

Sella took her reading glasses off, sat back and looked at me. 'You're never boring, are you?'

I didn't know how to answer that, so I said nothing.

'The legate gave me a summary yesterday of your activities, but this is worse than I expected.'

Damn. But it explained her frosty attitude this morning.

'As a friend,' she continued, 'my first reaction was to hope you'd consulted a lawyer. Then I saw you'd had an advance indemnity for the legend. As a soldier, I'm lost in admiration. As your colleague, I'm not at all sure how I regard you now.'

She let the stapled sheets slide from her hands onto her desk.

'For a mere mortal like me you seem to be an exotic creature. You're undoubtedly a successful, no, a brilliant field officer, but I sense a lack of stability. Perhaps a calmer period with the regular Praetorians might not be a bad idea.'

I felt the bottom drop out of my world.

'Is it really that bad?' I said.

'Let's look at it piece by piece. Very few people know the full story, so we have to consider who needs this update. But the update without the reason for the original use of the legend will look quite strange. Who knows what about what?'

'I haven't submitted it to the legate. He knows the first part and a lot of the second, but not the intelligence that came out of it. Somna knows the first part and all about the intelligence, but not the rest. Major Stern knows nothing.'

'I see,' she said.

'Flavius knows everything, from the beginning of the first operation to now.'

'Sergeant Flavius? In your ART?'

'Yes, he came with me from the Foundation into the PGSF.'

'Gods!' Her eyes reflected deep shock and her jaw slackened. She recovered and looked furious. 'Would you care to enlighten me how many other criminals we are harbouring?'

I flushed and felt my own anger rising. 'Flavius is *not* a criminal. He's served the PGSF loyally all these years. As it says in my report, he severed all links when I did. In this recent crisis, he acted resolutely under dangerous circumstances. Both the legate and Hallienia Apulia were saved as a direct consequence. He was material in preventing a rebellion and death of the imperatrix.' I paused for breath. 'At least he got off his ass and did something, unlike others who just kept their heads down and were rolled over by Petronax.'

She flinched. Her soft features tensed, pulling her face into angles. Not looking at me, she picked up her pen and pecked at her desk with it.

'I think you'd better consider your future options, captain,' she said.

Was this reaction a precursor for the rest? If Julia Sella, normally a gentle person, was resentful and offended, what were the rest of them going to be like? She instructed me to submit my report under secret cover as soon as possible to the legate, adjutant, Colonel Somna, Captain Sepunia and Major Stern. She locked my report in her safe; didn't say another word to me apart from 'Dismissed'.

I messaged Flavius to start building back protection.

The next one was Conrad. At least he knew most things; he'd been involved in a good deal of it. The problem was the intelligence. Too bad. By now, Somna had integrated it and was on a good way to wrapping everything up, no small thanks to it. No doubt she'd advised Conrad at some stage, so I felt a glimmer of hope that she'd paved the way for me. Consulting Sella had been a big mistake. Somna, on the other hand, was a long way inside the loop. Maybe I could use her as my Trojan horse.

Back in the IS office, Porteus gave me an update. 'I've talked to our legal staffer, and we consider that your and Sergeant Flavius's personal contributions will make an unassailable case against all the conspirators. And, of course, there's all that additional intelligence that was sent to you.' He smiled.

Well, somebody appreciated me. Perhaps I'd better transfer here. Or not, on second thought.

'When do you think the hearings will start?'

'We're pushing for them within the next week or so,' Porteus said, 'unless the Public Defender's Office or any of the lawyers are hanging out for the statutory twenty-eight days. Unlikely, I think.'

'So what happens then?'

'We'll request Flavius to be assigned to IS, and both of you will be given additional personal security. All the hearings will be *in camera* and your identities will be concealed from everybody except the accused and the judges.'

I thanked him and made my way to his chief's office. Luckily, Somna was in her office and alone. She read through my report without making a comment. I told her about my interview with Colonel Sella.

'Hmm, unfortunate. Your remarks were perhaps intemperate, but quite true. Of course, I have enormous respect for Julia Sella and her team, but I wonder if they are a little divorced from the harsher realities of our world.' She regarded me gravely. 'Galla's murder impacted on our desk-based support colleagues more than the front-line operators. Petronax was able to terrorise them with less effort than, say, my team.'

Somna hadn't mentioned one word of her imprisonment by Petronax, but the Interrogation Service was right at the opposite end of the toughness scale from HR and training.

'Let's take this to the legate together before you distribute it formally.'

I was never going to let anybody say anything against Somna ever again.

Conrad didn't see me at first as we entered his office.

'Ah! Decima,' he looked up from his screen, obviously pleased to see Somna.

I stepped out from the shelter of Somna's back.

'Carina?'

'Sir.' He looked surprised to see us together.

'Well, sit down, both of you. How're the interrogations going? Are you getting anywhere?'

'I am delighted to report, legate, that, apart from Caeco and Superbus, we have them all wrapped up. And I don't think we'll be long with them either, although Superbus is proving a little awkward.'

Conrad looked stunned. 'That's excellent news, the very best! How did it happen? You were nowhere near this point yesterday morning.'

'No,' replied Somna smoothly and smiled at me. 'But we had an unexpected and rich gift of first-class intelligence fall into our laps. It unlocked virtually all the doors.'

'And the source...?'

My muscles tensed.

'One of Carina Mitela's contacts sent recordings, photographs, reams of financial records, and a great deal besides. Ninety-six per cent of it is admissible. Even the group of senators supporting Caeco is all on video and stills. We're drawing up a list for submission to the Senate president,' she added drily.

Conrad looked at me, stone-faced.

Somna came to the rescue. 'I think you would find it very helpful to read Captain Mitela's report which will provide context for this information.' She placed it on Conrad's desk, and sat back completely unruffled. That made one of us.

Tick-tock, tick-tock. Why weren't there any quiet clocks in this building? What was wrong with a silent digital clock? I practised deep breathing, concentrating on relaxing my muscles while trying to sit upright on a chair with a slippery leather seat. Conrad had picked up my six sheets almost reluctantly. Why? He'd been chasing me for the damned report almost non-stop. He made no remark, nor did his face show any reaction as he read down the pages.

'I see,' he said and laid the sheets back on his desk.

Somna tilted her head towards me. 'Perhaps you would excuse us for a few minutes, Carina?'

I was out almost as she'd finished speaking.

I sat on the bench outside and looked at the little garden. Late afternoon sun lit up the bark of the two birch trees. The lavenders and rosemary waved in a breeze that made it in there somehow. How easy to be a plant.

'Hey, Bruna!' It was Paula.

I was so pleased to see a friendly face.

'Not on the carpet again?'

'Smart-ass.'

'Sorry, ma'am, I'm sure.'

But I smiled back at my friend.

She nodded towards the sling. 'How are you, really? How's the arm?'

'Progressing. I have to go see the medics tomorrow about it and to have my tracker refitted. Fabulous!'

'Well, if you will run away…' she said, grinning.

'Maybe that wasn't such a good idea.'

'What? How did you get there?' She sat down beside me. 'You've become more of a legend than you were before. Where's the problem?' She searched my face.

'I've ruffled a few feathers, and I'm going to cause more mayhem soon.' I bowed my head so she couldn't see my face.

'You mean with being Pulcheria?'

Astounded didn't begin to describe my feeling. How in Hades had she figured that out? Had I screwed up somewhere with my security?

I attempted a blank look.

'I worked it out,' she said.

'Not sure what you mean…'

She rolled her eyes at me. 'Back when I was your minder, you know, when you were seconded from the DJ after the first operation, I overhead a snatch of conversation you had with Commander Lurio. It was an extremely covert operation so I held my tongue.'

Ever the pragmatist, I thought.

'When Pulcheria came through the tunnel with the legate a few days ago, I was one of the three PSGF with Daniel.'

I hadn't recognised her.

She read my mind, as usual. 'Not surprising you didn't see me – the light was very bad down there. When the legate stumbled, and you caught him, I recognised your body signature.'

'Crap, was I that careless?'

'C'mon, Bruna, I've known you for seven years. I know every move you make. You were very good. If I hadn't got that memory in the back of my head, I probably wouldn't have made the connection.' She laid her hand on my arm. 'He must be desperately proud of you.'

'There are a few complications,' I ventured.

'Oh?' Then she leapt to a conclusion. 'You weren't screwing somebody there, were you?'

'Juno! What a question!'

'Your choice.' She shrugged her shoulders.

It was my choice, as ever, and I remembered the intense emotion of that last night.

'I don't think Daniel Stern will ever speak to me again.'

'And the problem is?'

I laughed, but only for a second or two. We talked a bit more. She'd taken Nov and Treb out on a simulation exercise in the backwoods and they'd camped overnight. Tension was the main flavour in the general office at the moment. All ranks had been requested to evaluate their behaviour and performance during the recent crisis. That would be an interesting set of reports.

Somna came out and signalled I was to go in. Conrad was standing looking out of the window, arms folded across his chest. His head was flexed downwards, but fractionally more than the angle of view required; the cords on his neck stood out as they disappeared up into his blond hair; his shoulders were hunched.

I took up position in the centre of the room and waited. I looked around, taking in nothing in particular, but I noticed his books were all out of order as if stuffed back on the shelves in a hurry. A few things were missing, including a small gold eagle I'd bought for him at Christie's in London and the silver-framed photo of Allegra with a tiny butterfly of diamonds. That bastard Superbus! I'd bet he had them. Something else to sweat out of him. I looked forward to it.

'Do you love him?'

I was startled back into the present.

I went up to him, laid my hand on his left hand half hidden in the crook of his right elbow. I rested my fingers on the gold betrothal ring I'd given him seven years ago. His face was still, he looked indifferent even, but I could see muscles trembling lightly under his skin. The tilted eyes were half-shut now, squeezed with pain.

'I'm not asking if you slept with him. Your choice,' his voice rasped. I could see he hated saying that. Like he was eating funeral ash straight from the pyre. In a society that put the procreation of the tribe first and sexual fidelity low, we were an unusual pairing – we had contracted for life. But he was Roma Novan enough to concede my freedom of choice.

'I have only truly loved one man, body, soul, heart and mind, in my life,' I said. 'And you know you are that man.'

He opened his eyes a fraction and swung them down to stare at me.

'But if you ask if he has a place in my heart, then, yes. It's a small place, locked up now, but I can't say it doesn't exist.'

31

After he'd let me go, Conrad had my report circulated later that afternoon. I'd escaped to my room for the rest of the evening, not wanting to face anybody. Cowardly, I knew.

With the pre-trial security hung on me, it was easier to sleep at the barracks. Besides, at home, they were making ready for a week in the country. It would have been the opposite of restful with all the packing and fussing that entailed. Or so I convinced myself.

I'd stared myself dizzy at the wall of my lonely room last night trying to forget how the green in Conrad's eyes had been flushed out by a hard agate brown. His face had closed down and he'd withdrawn into neutral professional. I'd winced as he'd said, 'Very well,' in a cold, clipped tone and effectively dismissed me from our meeting. I hoped, with all my heart and being, not from his life.

So, after a night empty of sleep, I was first to arrive in the morning for the senior staff meeting. I sat on the bench outside, forcing myself to read my el-pad, glancing occasionally at my bodyguard.

Somna was next. As I stood up, she greeted me, smiling. Perhaps Daniel was right and I *had* crossed to the dark side. I nodded curtly in reply to Julia Sella's half-smile, when she appeared. Very rude of me, but I was still smarting from the disappointment of our meeting. She looked taken aback but went to talk to Sepunia. Lucius merely nodded to Somna and said nothing. Daniel stood as far away as possible and ignored me.

Rusonia, the legate's EO, ushered us in, and sat at the back to record the meeting; the electronic and vid recorders had been switched off. I hoped she'd put on protective clothing. And could duck quickly. Unusually, the chairs were arranged in a circle. What was this: a séance?

'Thank you for attending at short notice,' Conrad began. 'There's only one item on this morning's agenda – Captain Mitela's report.'

Except for Somna and Lucius, they all avoided looking in my direction.

'You've all read it. Firstly, does any participant in the action wish to comment on the factual content relating to their own part?'

Not a peep.

'Or relating to any other participant?'

Some coughing and shifting.

'Well?'

Nothing. My reports were normally accepted as accurate. This one had been painful to write in places, though. But we were only in the opening skirmishes stage of this meeting, so I waited.

'Very well, open forum,' he said.

To my surprise, Julia Sella started. 'How do we stand from a legal point of view, legate? Weren't the vast majority of these actions illegal or, at the least, entrapment?'

'You'll be relieved to hear, Julia, that the first operation was fully sanctioned by the Minister of Justice herself, acting on Imperial Order.' Quite a few gasps and raised eyebrows at this stage. Lucius half-smiled to himself. 'The second falls under the Emergency Order umbrella, although there are some minor infractions which will be dealt with under military disciplinary codes.'

Somna went next, telling them about her early Saturnalia presents. Sepunia supported her on the intelligence, but was meticulous in not mentioning me by name. You'd think it'd dropped out of the air like a miracle instead of Apollodorus's organisation pulling out all the stops.

Daniel crouched, tight-lipped, and volunteered nothing, so Conrad forced him.

'Operations? I'm sure you have some comments.'

'Sir, I have several points to make, but I would like to formally record my disappointment that Operations was kept completely in the dark both times. How anybody thought this deceit would help, I can't imagine. I shudder to think of the resources wasted when the agent in place was supposed to be one of ours. It's a mercy there were no fatal casualties on our side.'

Everybody stared at me now, not all in a friendly way.

'I understand your point of view,' Conrad replied, 'but, if it helps, neither was I aware of the first operation until the end.' He smiled wryly at the memory. 'Two factors here: firstly, you were very new at the time, only five weeks into your period of detachment, so while you took part in the standard surveillance and arrest operations, you were held out of the intelligence loop.'

'Yes, I understand that, sir, good security and so on. But I fail to understand why the then Head of Operations wasn't informed and why there's no report included in the file.'

'Need to know, and Operations didn't qualify.' Conrad's voice became clipped. 'It was a sensitive time with considerable internal security problems. And the operation was led by our colleagues in the DJ.'

Daniel didn't look at all mollified, but he couldn't dispute Conrad's authority.

'Secondly,' Conrad said, 'I agreed that we should save the Pulcheria legend, so the decision was mine.'

He didn't look at me as he spoke the deliberate lie. Was he trying to protect me?

'I'm sorry if that was uncomfortable for you, Daniel,' he continued, 'but I am sure you understand operational necessity. Unfortunately, it turns out that we won't be able to keep the legend this time as we must prioritise prosecution of these traitors over operational assets.'

'Legate, if I may?' Lucius spoke up. 'I think some of us in this room have missed a crucial point. Both operations were spectacular successes. The first prevented the drug trade penetrating the Imperium. And, of course, it brought us the charming company of Carina Mitela to swell our ranks.' He nodded in my direction.

Juno! Shut up, Lucius.

'The second, not to put it too finely, saved all our skins, stopped a rebellion, and secured the imperial family. I may be a traditionalist, but I count these as positive outcomes. At least, Colonel Somna appreciates the value of the information Mitela has brought in.

Perhaps Sepunia will think the same when she's had time to reflect, and act in a more collegiate way.'

Sepunia squirmed in her seat.

He gave Julia Sella an almost brutal look. 'I'm convinced there are enough training lessons to learn to keep your department busy until the next millennium, colonel. I suggest you concentrate on them rather than on matters outside your competence.'

She blenched, flushed and looked down at the floor. Despite her lack of support for me earlier, I felt sorry for her.

'As for Operations, that's what you're there for, major: to operate – to carry out the orders given to you. Period.'

Daniel didn't have a cardiac arrest, but I figured he was pretty close.

'Thank you, Adjutant,' Conrad said, poker-faced. 'Anybody else?' He turned to me. 'Carina?'

I shook my head violently.

'Very well. I'm sure I don't need to remind you, but I'm going to anyway. Absolutely not a word outside this room. You'll wish to work together on matters relating to the two operations, but select your additional personnel judiciously and work discreetly. Dismissed.'

They all filed out, except Rusonia, but Conrad grabbed my arm, holding me back. 'Have you had any breakfast?'

I shook my head.

'Can you bring us a selection, please, Rusonia? And some coffee.'

She was the perfect EO, quiet and efficient. People were often deceived by her slight frame and pretty good looks, but she was a tigress at protecting her principal. She must have known more secrets than anybody else, probably including Conrad.

She slid out and we were alone. I didn't know what to say. After yesterday, I was too scared to touch on the personal. I was going to stay in my uniform, in my head as well as my body.

'Did you put Lucius up to that?' I asked suspiciously.

'Absolutely not! He said he had some strong opinions on what people thought of you, but that's all. And Somna has taken quite a shine to you. You seem a lot more relaxed with her.'

'Oh, didn't you know? Daniel says I've gone over to the dark side. That is, when he was speaking to me.'

I was more than dismayed by the loss of Daniel's friendship. I not only felt grief at having killed our bond, but also guilt. Sometimes I hated my job.

'I think Lucius was too severe on Daniel,' I said.

'Perhaps, but Daniel was being self-indulgent. I love him like a brother. He's a first-class operations officer, but I can't quite work out why he was so…so petulant. Any idea why he took it so personally?'

'I *did* give him a bad time whenever he encountered me as Pulcheria. Not very comradely, I know, but I was in deep cover. I thought we'd be able to laugh about it together, but was I ever wrong!'

'Time to arrange a major training exercise, I think,' Conrad said. 'A winter warmer, up in the eastern hills.'

A week of numb fingers and waking up in the morning with frozen eyelashes. Sometimes I forgot what a tough nut Conrad was.

'But let's headline your strategy training first. We have to give them something mentally intensive to distract minds from recent events.'

A tray of breakfast arrived which we attacked with enthusiasm. I was starving. We ate in silence. It was almost a relief when my commset bleeped with a message from the security guard announcing Lucilla Mitela had arrived – please attend.

'What's that about?'

'Oh, I fixed three weeks' clerical work here for her.'

'Dalina's daughter?' He smiled, an appreciative look in his eyes. Few of the Mitelae were homely, some not bad-looking and many handsome, but Dalina was magnificent. The male members of the Mitela tribe – and I used that term advisedly – were one hundred per cent struck. Dalina was very tall, with long, wavy chestnut hair, the usual Mitela blue eyes, flawless skin and figure, but the stunner was her plentiful sexual charm. She'd just passed forty, but had men of all generations drooling over her. Ironically, only one of her children had inherited the same beauty and attractiveness, but he was only twelve. Lucilla, her eldest at eighteen, was a clever cookie, currently on the advanced list at the Central University, but she was pretty normal in the looks department.

'Well, I think Lucy will learn a lot and she's bright enough to be discreet about anything she does or sees here.'

He raised an eyebrow. 'Is this another of your clever schemes?'

That stung. I said nothing.

'Well? The truth, please.'

I explained exactly why she was there.

He shrugged. 'It could work, I suppose.'

'The only tricky part is having a recorder here on the day,' I said, hurrying on. In previous ages, recording family events was a full-time, prestigious post. Now it was symbolic. 'I know we have three in the family, plus some assistants but, besides old Publius Mitelus, I can't remember who any of them are. And they're all bound to find some excuse saying they're too busy. I'll have to ask Nonna for their names and pressure one of them.'

He smiled at me. At last.

'What?'

'Have you forgotten?'

'Forgotten what?'

'You have,' he said. 'I'm one of the assistants.'

I hurried down to the vestibule, trailing my bodyguard, and found my young cousin standing by the reception counter with a scruffy backpack.

'*Salve*, Countess Carina,' she said formally, sounding slightly apprehensive.

'Hello, Lucy, how are you?' Lucilla Mitela had my red-gold hair, but frizzier, and the blue eyes. She also had that half-starved student look, but I'd put my money on her having a good appetite. All teenagers did.

I signed her in and took her to the quaestor's officer for a civilian uniform, pass, and commset. As we walked there, she stared at the yellowy-cream walls and polished wood floors. There were a few action pictures, flags, and insignia display cupboards.

'I've never been in an army barracks – it's very businesslike, isn't it, Countess Carina?'

'Lucy, you should call me "captain" or "Carina Mitela", whichever is easier for you, but not Countess Carina, unless I ask you to.'

'Okay,' she replied laconically.

Gnaeus put her on the system and tried out his charm on her. 'I expect you get up to all sorts of wild stuff at the university.' He half-leered at her. He thought he was the young maiden's dream.

She looked him up and down, fished the gum out of her mouth, threw it in the bin and said, 'Well, I guess it's too long ago for you to remember.'

Gnaeus was so taken aback he didn't attempt anything else. When she was trying on her uniform, he remarked she was a true Mitela and he'd know next time. We dropped her bag in the room she'd be sharing with three other young clerks, and I took her up to the strategy room to introduce her to Drusus and Fausta. They gave her a drink – another water drinker, I noticed. Drusus had her set up at a terminal within minutes. I left them to it.

Back at the IS, I saw Flavius in the general office, looking a bit lost. Of course, he had to report here for the duration.

'Hi, Flav, welcome to the dark side.'

Longina looked at me as if I'd stepped on her cat, but Flavius grinned back. His shadow looked as bored as mine.

'Sergeant Flavius?'

He turned round. 'Yes?'

A petite brunette wearing silver-rimmed spectacles had appeared at his side, holding a file under her arm.

'I'm Staff Zenia from the legal branch. You've been assigned to me. I'm going to brief you for the arraignments. Come with me.' As they walked off, I heard her say, 'Have you ever been to a court hearing before?'

I smiled to myself. Yeah, juvenile court, but he'd always got off…

Longina reported that they were nearly there with Caeco. Somna had moved him on considerably: Caeco was now confessing in sporadic chunks. But Superbus refused to say anything without his lawyer. Even then, he was mostly saying no, or remaining silent. When I outlined my plan to Somna, it put a smile on her face.

That afternoon at the infirmary, I had my tracker reinserted. The wound was a little sore but the plus point was that, unless I went outside the building, I could lose my bodyguard. The sling went, at last, but the medics scheduled me for half an hour's physical therapy each day for the next week. The dentist reinserted my tooth mic which gave me a sore gum. I awarded myself the afternoon off.

Back in my little room in the officers' mess wing, I pulled the drapes halfway across to reduce the sunlight, then stretched out on the bed and closed my eyes. I couldn't stop the thoughts rushing in. Since

Conrad had asked me about my feelings for Apollo, he'd closed me out and retreated into professional, treating me like a colleague and nothing else. Was this the future?

Letting Pulcheria go and parting from Apollodorus had torn a hole out of me. I'd deliberately kept myself busy since then. I hated the quiet moments now.

Worse, although the operation was finished and the mop-up going well, something was still unresolved. It gnawed away at me, but I couldn't identify it. It was like that nagging buzz that had haunted my head after interviewing Mossia all those weeks ago. Was I overtired or was there something else I'd missed?

32

I spent two days trying to figure out what was bothering me but gave up in the end. There was too much other stuff to deal with. The following night, at home, I asked if Daniel had been back, but Macro said he hadn't seen him. Daniel had slipped out of both my professional and private lives.

Back at the IS office, Flavius and I had an awkward session with the legal team. They thought operations guards were strong-arm thief-takers; we thought they were legalistic bureaucrats. New Roman law was complex despite the clean outs and reforms over the centuries; even the big one in the 1700s. Like members of most law enforcement and intelligence organisations around the world, I wondered whose side the lawyers were on. But we promised to behave during the arraignment hearings.

The following morning, Superbus was due for an interview, with his lawyer in attendance. An hour before it started, I asked Fausta to find Lucy some regular smart clothes and have her report to the IS office. I grabbed my garment bag, changed into my civilian suit in the restroom. I'd done my hair in a formal chignon that morning in an attempt to look authoritative. I lifted the gold myrtle leaf and flower badge with its gold-embroidered purple ribbon out of the velvet case and looped it around my neck. The original junior badge had gone missing in the fourteenth century, so this was a seven-hundred-year-old catch-up.

Longina and others nearby stared at me when I came back in, wondering what was going on. I smiled, said nothing, and sat at the table in the corner. When Conrad appeared shortly afterwards, in a business suit, carrying a long thin velvet bag and pad and paper, most work stopped. Somna came out of her office.

'Welcome, legate.'

'Better to call me plain Conradus Mitelus for this.' He gave a half-smile.

'What do you need us to do?'

'Nothing for the moment,' Conrad replied. 'We're waiting for our second witness to arrive, but I think there's plenty of time.'

Somna glanced at her watch. 'The lawyer isn't due for ten minutes. Would you like to wait in my office?'

'Thank you, but it's better if we're seen by as many witnesses as possible.'

I spotted some movement at the other end of the office which turned out to be Lucy arriving. In a dark suit and with her hair contained in a ponytail, she looked older than her nineteen years. I nodded my thanks to Fausta.

Lucy glanced up shyly at Conrad. She patted her hair nervously. 'What are we doing here? I mean, what's this about?'

'Well, Carina and I have to interview Superbus under the Families' Code, and we need a third Mitela.' He paused. 'It's a bit archaic, but don't worry. You don't have to do anything; just watch and listen. At the end, I'll ask you to sign the record to confirm you were present. Can you do that for me?'

'Yeah, sure,' she said. 'I remember doing it in history at school. Um, there's no fee for this, is there?'

I frowned at her, but Conrad just laughed. 'No, you do it for your family. And no giggling.'

'Okay, cool.'

Leaving Conrad to his role as cool friend, I turned to Somna. 'We're ready to start. Would you please have somebody take a handwritten record of the next few minutes?'

To everybody else's amazement, she bowed to me. Had she seen a Families' Code interview before? Well, that was fine by me. I'd never done one before.

'Paulina Longina will make a record.'

Longina closed her mouth, grabbed a pen, and scrabbled around in a drawer trying to find a pad of paper.

Conrad took a gold-tipped ivory staff out of the velvet bag. Around forty centimetres long, it had a rounded point one end and a flattened semicircle at the other: a symbolic stylus. He tucked it under his arm parallel to the floor, turned to me and bowed. I nodded in acknowledgement and waved my hand in Somna's direction.

'Colonel Decima Somna, I am Conradus Mitelus, Assistant Recorder of the Family Mitela. I present Countess Carina Mitela, junior head of Family Mitela.'

'I am here to exercise my right as set out in the Twelve Families' Code,' I said, 'to question a delinquent member of my family, Gnaeus Mitelus Superbus. I demand that you hand him over to me for private interview with strangers excluded. The Recorder will make a written account of the proceedings. The second witness is Lucilla Mitela, here present.'

'Countess Carina Mitela, I recognise your right under the Code and cede to you. I trust you will allow me to provide a suitable room.'

I nodded.

'Please follow me.' We traipsed down to the interrogation suite and Fright Central. Longina checked everything was ready. The lawyer had arrived and the IS staffers were setting up the session.

I laid my hand on Lucy's shoulder. 'Totally off the record, Lucy, if this gets too rough, you just have to suck it up. I think we'll only have to scare him a little, but there may be a bit of shouting. Okay?'

Her eyes bulged like tennis balls, but she accepted it. 'This is the bigs, isn't it?'

'Yep, nothing bigger.'

We reached Interview 4. Somna released the bioscan lock, I grasped the handle, pulled myself up to be as tall as possible, opened the door and swept in.

I focused all my attention on Superbus, signalling Conrad and Lucy to the side with a wave of my hand. 'Strangers out,' I ordered.

The two IS staff goggled and looked at Somna. She jerked her head. They picked up their paraphernalia and fled. Superbus sat there, transfixed.

'What the hell is this?' a voice squeaked.

Somna spoke from the doorway, addressing the lawyer. 'You are required to leave the room immediately. Please comply.'

'Over the Styx!'

I switched my eyes to the hopping little irritant. 'And you are?'

'Claudia Vara.'

It always had to be a Vara.

'I am here representing my client,' she said. She looked at us, panning round and glaring at our faces, as if looking for potential threats.

Her instincts were, of course, quite correct.

'You can't order me out. I'm this defendant's legal representative. Now, if you don't get the Hades out, I'll sue you in the High Court, the Senate Court and anywhere further north.'

'Look at me, Vara,' I said in my coldest voice. 'I am Mitela, here under the Twelve Families' Code to question a delinquent member of my family. Strangers are excluded. If you do not comply, the head of your family and you personally will be subject to penalties. I'm sure Livilla Vara will be thrilled to pay. Currently, I understand it to be up to two years' exclusion from the Families' Council and ten thousand *solidi* fine. In any event, you are going to be reported for insolence to a family head.'

I looked at Conrad. 'Recorder, ensure that is noted.' Conrad duly scribbled away.

I saw it dawning on Claudia Vara that she was playing in fast traffic and had crossed a big fat lane line.

'I didn't know. I—'

'Out.'

The door shut and only the four Mitelae remained. I sat down and studied the unlovely Superbus. The flesh in his face rolled in greasy folds over one another. His blue eyes were shrunk in terror. Sweat beaded on his forehead.

We waited a full five minutes. Lucy wisely stayed near the back wall. Standing behind Superbus, Conrad turned around to give her an encouraging smile.

Predictably, Superbus broke first. 'You can't treat me like this! This is illegal. My lawyer will nail your hide to the side of the courthouse,' he blustered.

'Yes, she can. No, it isn't. No, she can't,' came Conrad's voice a centimetre from Superbus's ear. Superbus's whole body spasmed. His eyes puffed up. I thought he was going to have a seizure.

'Superbus, look at me and concentrate.'

Gods, he had foul breath. It oozed like a miasma from his thin lips, poisoning the air in front of me. I took the shallowest breath I could survive on and continued. 'Firstly, as junior head of your family, my duty is to provide you with legal support. I'll appoint a team to represent you at all hearings and at any other meetings. They'll carry out any legal or administrative measures relating to your case. All costs will be paid by the family.' His eyes lit up at that.

Then he looked wary. 'You'll only appoint one of your own who'll report back to you and sabotage my case. You'll fix it to go your way.'

Like a professional lawyer would do that, unless she wanted to lose her licence. I sighed. 'So that you're more comfortable with it, I'll contact the Legal Guild and they can choose one and send them directly to you. Or you can even have Vara back, if you want. Is that satisfactory?' I hated having to be polite to this vicious little turd, but remembered Nonna's words about obligations and responsibilities. Just about. He nodded his head and I asked him to agree out loud to this so it could be recorded. He looked sullen, like a child, but complied.

'Now we've agreed the support for you, it's payback time, Superbus. We can do this the easy way or the hard way. You know from a few days ago that I'm very efficient at dealing with tiresome sludge I find under my feet.' I hoped he remembered how hard I kicked him with my steel-capped boot.

'Our little cousin here looks innocent, but she adores cutting limbs off small animals. She's good with a blade, and a bigger animal will be much more fun.' Poor Lucy, that wasn't very nice of me.

'S'right. Where can I start?'

I could hardly believe what I was seeing. Naïve little Lucy had darted forward and was pressing her nail file slowly up the side of Superbus's neck. Suddenly, she jabbed the end in just below the skull line. She didn't even break his skin, but he screeched like a banshee.

'That's for sticking your hand up my skirt last Family Day.' She stamped hard on the floor right next to his chair. He flinched and threw his hands up in front of his terrified face. She smirked at him and walked calmly back to the corner of the room. Out of Superbus's view, Conrad grabbed her and shook her, nodding his head violently. Then spoilt it all by grinning at her.

'Now, Superbus, are you ready to talk?'

'Keep that little fiend off me!'

'Depends how talkative you are.'

Once Superbus started, he wouldn't shut up. Conrad wrote as fast as he could. Superbus had met Caeco in a men's baths, and they'd talked about how horrendous women were and progressed from there. Superbus complained how he would have headed the Mitelae if there'd been any justice. I hated to disillusion him by telling him there were fourteen other heirs, including males, with better claims. He would have served in the military, except he was the victim of a medical condition. He'd been thwarted from displaying his obvious leadership abilities. Besides, women were always given priority. He'd been cheated in business, he claimed. His own daughter was disruptive; he put this down to marrying his first cousin. Her brothers were just jealous and ignored him, et cetera, et cetera.

Gods! It was boring.

Caeco had seen a Grade A bully and coward, vain and easy to manipulate. The jewel in the treasure box had been that, although on the fringes of the family, he was a Mitelus. Gold strike for Caeco and Petronax.

After the renewed threat of Lucy being let loose, Superbus admitted he'd had Aurelia and the children arrested by a military riot squad; a bunch of tough primates trained to face hostile crowds attacking them with razor balls, Molotovs and baseball bats. Perfect for a senior, a bunch of small children and their tutor.

Eventually Superbus shut up. Silence dropped like a winter dusk. Conrad stood up, I thought to release some of his physical tension. He walked over to Lucy leaning against the far wall and gave her a vague smile. She placed her hand over her mouth and mimed an exaggerated yawn, then pinched her nose and made a face. I watched her. I was fascinated by her antics and her confidence.

I dragged my eyes away and resumed my questions. 'Now, Superbus, she's still there and beginning to get a little restless. I want you to think very carefully about these next two questions. You see, Conrad might join in. He's mighty pissed with you, and it's only me stopping him.'

To reinforce the point, Conrad came back to stand by Superbus's right side and leaned into his face. If I was on the receiving end of that look, I'd be shaking in my sandals. I signalled him to back off. He rejoined Lucy.

'Did you order the beatings by the Transulium guards?'

He shook his head.

'I need you to say that out loud.'

'No.'

'Who did it?'

'Specials, ordered in by Petronax.'

I saw Conrad's eyes glint and take a step back towards Superbus.

'Their names?'

'I don't know – I really don't.'

'But you signed the access authorisation, didn't you?'

Conrad hovered behind Superbus like a starved vulture, claws and beak ready. For a long moment, Conrad stared at me. I understood how he felt. He wanted to pound Superbus into the ground, to smash every bone and snap every tendon in his body for all the hurt the conspirators had done him and his – both family and unit. Keeping my stare fixed on him, I shook my head. I couldn't allow Conrad to challenge my authority as head of the family, especially in front of a heap of crap like Superbus. His stare intensified as if pulling in every bit of willpower to override me. After several tense seconds of locking eyes, he backed off. He sat down, hunched over the table, glanced at me once and wrote. I released my breath slowly.

'Answer me, Superbus. Did you sign the access authorisation?'

'Yes,' he mumbled, looking down at the table.

Conrad stopping writing, the pen immobile on the paper in mid word. Superbus glanced sideways and met Conrad's eyes, and looked back down immediately. If a look could incinerate, Superbus would have been a residual pile of funeral ash. He slumped forward and covered his eyes with his pudgy fingers.

But I hadn't finished. 'Lastly, where are the gold eagle and the silver frame from Conradus's office?'

'Sorry?'

'Look at me, Superbus.'

He peeled his fingers away from his face. I nodded as if to Lucy.

'No!' he gulped. 'They're in my safe at home.'

'Combination, please.'

That was all I needed. I leaned back in my chair and took a deep breath from the side. 'Now, Superbus, it wasn't so bad, was it?'

'You're not going to kill me?'

'Don't be ridiculous – you're not worth the paperwork.'

He grabbed my hand, bleating gratitude. Tears, dirt and sweat ran down his face. Just to complete a perfect session, the smell of faeces spread from him through the room.

After he'd finished writing, Conrad read the statement aloud to Superbus as the law demanded. Conrad's voice was even, but terse and full of repressed energy. He thrust the document across the table at Superbus and told him to sign. Superbus flinched. After glancing at Conrad's face, he signed it with a hand that trembled like a Parkinson's case.

I countersigned, Lucy witnessed, and Conrad completed the document, adding the wax seal. He picked up the ivory staff, writing kit, took Lucy by the arm and stalked out.

Superbus was pitiful – a petty thief as well as a bully and a coward. He didn't have a scrap of dignity. It was embarrassing to think he shared blood with me.

'You were a total dumbass, Superbus, getting mixed up with those people.'

'You don't understand a thing, you and the old lady. Even that Cassia woman—' He sucked his lips in and shrank back.

Juno! Cassia?

'What about her?' I asked in the most casual tone I could muster.

He bent his head down and muttered, 'Nothing, nothing.'

'C'mon, Superbus, you can't tease me like that. What about this Cassia? How is she involved?'

He shook his head. He wouldn't look at me.

I waited for some minutes, but he stayed slumped in his chair, terrified and silent.

Somna and her team stood back as I exited. I thanked her formally and apologised for the mess my family had left. I asked if she would kindly have Superbus cleaned up and checked over by a doctor. The

Mitela Family Recorder would appreciate a copy of the medical report and photographs. She bowed once more and we were done.

I leaned against the grey plaster wall for a few moments breathing in the clean air. Upstairs in the IS office, Longina said nothing as we appeared, just thrust a cup of coffee into my hand.

'That went well,' Conrad said, and perched on the edge of desk. He looked calmer, but not completely relaxed. 'Your first legal act as head of family. How do you feel about it?'

'A lot better than I thought I would. Superbus is a miserable piece. It was almost too easy.'

'I'd be in dangerous waters if I said you were so like Aurelia that it was uncanny.'

I glared at him to make the point, but secretly I was flattered.

Aurelia had executed legal acts, made Families' Codes judgements and been a true family head since she was in her late twenties when her mother had been unwell. To me she was a natural: she had presence, decisiveness, authority. I was definitely the junior partner, always afraid I'd be found out and be dismissed as a light-hearted insignificance. But maybe, today, I'd convinced myself I *could* do it.

'No, I'm wrong,' he said, and smiled. 'You've found your own authority. I realised it when you forbade me to attack him. It felt like a strong wave about to flatten me.'

'It would have ruined it all.'

'I know.'

He'd had such a lousy time in the Transulium that I felt bad about cheating him of retribution, but that was how it had to be. It was a shock to realise that I'd put the interests of family and state before those of my love. He understood why – he'd been raised here in Roma Nova – but to me it was a revelation, one of those moments when you scared yourself.

Conrad kept his gaze on me, oblivious to the interested stares of others. I tried a smile and received one back. A huge weight seemed to fall off my back. He left the edge of the table and came to sit in a chair beside me, his leg not quite touching mine. He said nothing.

'Where's Lucy?' I asked to break the silence.

'She says she has to fix her mascara. It ran down her face,' Longina said from across the room.

Oh gods, had she had hysterics and was now traumatised? I

remembered I'd heard a strange noise in the background. I'd never be able to look Dalina in the face if I handed her back a shocked and damaged daughter.

'She's fine – really,' Conrad added. 'She says she's never laughed so much as watching Superbus. She held it in, as promised, until we finished, then couldn't stop.'

I frowned at him. I'd involved her because I thought she was mature enough to keep a level head, but young enough to keep clear of the serious part. Instead, I'd released Lucrezia Borgia on the world. 'You didn't help, egging her on.'

He attempted an innocent face, but I wasn't fooled.

'My respects, Countess,' interrupted Somna. I jumped, almost spilling the last of my coffee. Her lizard eyes had a strange shine, almost animated. Crap, I realised she'd seen it all.

'I hope, colonel, you haven't made a recording.'

'No, but we watched.' She must have seen the black look on my face. 'For training purposes.'

Yeah, and I'm a dancing monkey.

Lucy reappeared, face repaired. Longina took her out of my reach and handed her a bottle of water and a frown. Lucy threw a baby face back at her. I'd talk to Lucy later. She'd crossed the line, but helped us significantly in producing an excellent outcome.

But who was the woman Cassia whose name Superbus let slip? There'd been no mention in the records, unless she'd been entered as C. It was a common enough name, but I didn't believe in coincidences.

33

Released from my temporary posting to Colonel Somna's IS team, I was back in my strategy office. Conrad had prioritised the training programmes. I delegated the strategy one to Drusus and Fausta. They were perfectly capable of producing the first draft and we'd refine it together.

Bur before anything else, I needed to find Daniel. Herding cats would have been so much easier but I eventually tracked him down in the field equipment room.

'Daniel.'

'Major Stern to you, captain.'

'Don't be like this, please.' I could see the hurt in his eyes and the harsh lines of tensed muscles in his face and neck.

'I don't know what game you're playing now,' he said. 'But then I don't seem to have known anything, do I?'

'It was a long-term legend, built up layer upon layer.' I sounded like I was making excuses. 'Your antipathy to Pulcheria was essential and couldn't be simulated.'

'Oh, great, now I'm an incompetent patsy!'

'You know how it works.'

'How can I believe anything you say to me now? I've always told you everything. Now I find out the little tart I'd most like to take down is the other half of my best friend.'

Rage spiralled off him, hitting anything it touched, mostly me.

'Let it go. Please.'

I held out my hand to him, but he said nothing, shoved past me and stomped out.

I was due at the courthouse at 11.00 the next day. Dressed in my number one uniform – grey skirt, black jacket with silver buttons and insignia – I grabbed my side cap and made for the mess hall and some breakfast. As I chewed and swallowed, I couldn't stop the bitterness of losing Daniel's friendship rising to defeat my appetite. I pushed the rest away and drank my equally bitter coffee.

Flavius and I gave our testimonies before the examining magistrate. It took all day. She warned us that the defence would no doubt submit a long list of questions, so we should be prepared to come back to make further depositions. If they were being especially picky then we'd have to be prepared for a live cross-examination in closed chambers. That was something to look forward to.

We collected our bodyguards afterwards and drove back through the evening gloom and rain. I was mentally exhausted and not a little depressed, and went for an early night. Propped up in bed, not watching the newscast, my mind returned to Superbus and how he'd clammed up when he mentioned a woman called Cassia. How could a woman have been part of their patriarchalist conspiracy?

A knock at the door jolted me. Conrad.

He smiled his crinkly smile. 'I didn't know if you were asleep yet. How did it go?'

I waved him in and closed the door. 'Long and boring,' I said. 'And it's going to be another one tomorrow.' I grimaced. Family Day. Juno!

He helped himself to a beer from the tiny fridge and sat opposite me. 'You don't need to worry. Aurelia and Junia had it all organised before they went to the country. All we have to do is turn up and smile. You were scary yesterday with Superbus.' He smiled. 'I can't think you'll have a problem with anybody else.' He raised his bottle to salute me.

I wasn't so sure.

He looked down and spent a few moments studying the bottle. The laugh had fled from his face.

'Carina, I—' He swallowed, but not the drink. 'Don't stay away from me.' He set the bottle on the desk and stretched out his hand. Mine was already there to meet it. He pulled me up to him and his mouth crushed hard on mine.

A little later than planned, we set off early next morning to go home, complete with my bodyguard. I asked Conrad why he couldn't count as my guard over the weekend.

'I know we have Superbus in custody, but can we guarantee he hasn't corrupted any of the other Mitelae?'

I guessed he didn't want to trust anybody at the moment.

'Surely not?' I said. 'Superbus was an anomaly, wasn't he?'

'You tell me.'

So Trebatia, the chatterbox in open country fatigues, trotted along behind us.

In the car, I activated the smartplex privacy screen. Conrad tilted his head to one side, smiled and raised an eyebrow.

I smiled back, but shook my head. 'It's Superbus,' I said. 'I'm not sure it's anything but after you and Lucy left, he said something weird. When I told him he was stupid to have gotten involved with Petronax, he said none of us understood, "even that Cassia woman". Then he just dummied up. He was too scared to say another word.'

'Ah.'

'Oh, please,' I said, 'it's a common name. It can't possibly be *his* Cassia. Wrong side, remember?'

He didn't reply. We rode the rest of the way home in silence.

The hairdresser came in to do artistic things and tutted at the condition of my abused hair. But, when he'd finished, a completely different person stared out of the mirror: formal, elegant and unreal. He'd inserted a gold filigree band across my head with diamonds and sapphires caught in gold webs. It matched my blue gown and gold palla. My nails and face were next. I usually resented all this pawing, but this time I submitted passively.

Helena, looking like some model out of Vogue, brought Allegra to see me. She was so lovely in her first formal outfit, I almost burst into tears.

'Hello, Mama,' she said looking up at me. 'You look beautiful.'

'Hey, you're pretty wonderful yourself!'

'Some are arriving already,' Helena informed me, 'but you don't have to go down quite yet. It's only just eleven.'

'Where's Aurelia?'

'In her sitting room, fortifying herself with French brandy.'

I took Allegra's hand, and we went up the back stairs to the level above our wing and along a narrow service corridor. I knocked on the door at the end and surprised Aurelia's assistant.

'Sorry to startle you, Marcella,' and we barged in.

My grandmother, dressed in her finery, was downing a generous glass of Remy Martin.

'Hey, Nonna, going to share?'

She chuckled and poured me a glass. Allegra took up position on one of Aurelia's gilt chairs and watched us set a bad example.

I swallowed mine quickly and put my glass forward for another. Aurelia looked at me sharply, but said nothing. The three of us sat there, sharing a quiet moment. Nothing could start without us, anyway.

After making appropriate speeches of welcome, i.e. short, Aurelia and I mixed, smiled and talked with the swarm of relations assembled in the hall. Trebatia, now in a calf-length gown Marcella had found her, trailed around in my wake. With her slight figure and fresh complexion, she looked more like somebody's kid sister than a bodyguard, but she scanned everybody and everything, her hand fixed on the gold-embroidered purse containing her semi-automatic.

Around four hundred Mitelae packed the atrium, a little under two-thirds of the recorded number of cousins to the second degree. It was a tribal meeting, supposed to remember the links of blood and loyalty across nearly sixteen centuries. That was a romantic idea. In reality, those here today were because of careful, often conniving and sometimes bloody manoeuvring to protect and promote the family so it survived over those years. Like most organisations, it was the pedantic, boring people who kept the records and sat on the family council, but you had to give them their due: they'd held it all together. Over centuries and against the odds.

We spilled out from the atrium into the back garden to eat – a huge relief as the noise was way above reasonable. Junia had mobilised the household to produce so much food that Abundantia could have refilled her cornucopia from it. Once the drink started flowing, the noise and testosterone levels had ramped up. Despite the mobile crowd, I managed to find Superbus's wife. I'd sent a car for her earlier that morning. She and her two children were sitting alone, largely ignored by the rest.

'Hello, Valeria. Fabia, Caius.' I waved over one of the older house servants, who I knew had grandchildren, to take Fabia and Caius to find Allegra.

'Please tell Allegra that Mama has asked her to keep special care of these two.'

Watching them go off, Valeria turned to me. 'Countess Carina, how can I thank you?'

'Oh, Valeria, none of this is your fault.' She looked pretty miserable, though. 'What do you want to do? Can I help with anything?'

'Oh, I'll divorce him. He's a waste of space.'

Excellent plan.

'He was so stupid. I didn't know he was up to anything special until two weeks ago when that man appeared.' She looked down the garden at the chattering crowd.

Petronax, I'd bet, come to finalise his plans.

'I was crossing the atrium after seeing the children to bed and saw Superbus on the far side with a visitor. They looked like cartoon characters: Superbus fat and fussing, and the dark man tall and calm. Then the man's head swivelled round – he must have heard me. I'll never forget those black eyes.' She caught her breath. 'They bored into me. I don't think I've ever been so frightened in the whole of my life.' She gave me a tight smile. 'Perhaps it's nothing. I haven't seen him since.'

The noise buzzed around me like a swarm of angry wasps on adrenalin.

No.

Nearly one million people lived in the city. Amongst a people descended from Romans, there must be a high proportion with dark eyes. There was no way it could be him. I batted it out of my mind. I had other stuff to concentrate on today.

Valeria glanced at me, then stared down at her hands. She seemed uncertain what to do next. I jumped up, pulled her arm through mine, and took her with me. As we circulated, I made sure people saw us together. I left her talking to some cousins of her own age, including the magnetic Dalina.

I saw Allegra queening it over a children's party area, watched over by Junia's deputy, Galienus, recovering from his injuries. They had magicians, games and races laid on, so they probably had the best time. The weather was outstanding, warm for early October. Most of the teenagers disappeared, probably to the maze. Whether they'd emerge intact in the strict sense was anybody's guess.

The band left off easy listening and started playing some classical dance music, and the middle-agers stampeded onto the temporary wooden dance floor. The trellis over it was decorated with swathes of silk, white flowers, ribbons and fairy lights, and looked pretty in a kitsch way.

But, almost surprising myself, I'd discovered for the first time how much pleasure there was in reinforcing and nourishing these family links. I wanted to hear about problems, perhaps even throw in an idea or two to help. I laughed and smiled at the gossip; I rejoiced about the triumphs, whether a child's school success, a business deal or a published novel. I relished making connections between two cousins, introducing unknown ones, finding a useful contact for somebody.

Around six o'clock, parents started gathering their children up, who by now were sick, crying or sullen, and their elders who were maudlin about "the olden days", and carted them off home. The professional middle-agers started "networking" over generous amounts of champagne. I saw Conrad, having gotten rid of his heavy toga, escort more than one to a hedge or shrub where they could quietly throw up. I sighed. We were down to the hard core.

My grandmother had taken up position on the terrace with a group of cronies, Allegra had gone, and Helena. I evaded Trebatia and made my way down to the walled garden for some peace. I let myself in and sat under the myrtle tree. I could hear faint shouts and giggling from the maze. The odds against Lucy not being in there leading the mayhem were pretty slim.

I shut my eyes and breathed in the last myrtle scent. But, when I did, I only saw black eyes set deep in a fine-boned face and projecting an ironic expression. As I brought my hands up to my face, I saw they were shaking.

34

The temperature had dropped along with the light. It was half past nine. I hurried back and found my grandmother indoors, saying goodbye to half a dozen of her contemporaries.

'Thank the gods, that's the last of the oldies. Fancy a nightcap?' She picked up a bottle of champagne from a bucket and two glasses and pulled me along to the small back office. There was some kind of dubious card game going on in the main sitting area off the atrium and rather too much flesh was emerging for her liking, she said. Best to leave them to it.

'A successful day, don't you think?' She shucked off her sandals. They were gorgeous: silver with large pearls and semi-precious stones.

I emptied my glass in two gulps and was watching the drops clinging to the inside surface struggling to join and split from the others. Nothing stayed the same for more than a few moments.

'Carina?'

'Sorry, Nonna. Of course, a really good day.' I set my glass down. 'I think I'll go up now. I'm tired.' I leaned over and kissed her cheek.

'Everything all right, darling? You look upset, not just tired.' She scrutinised my face, looking for the least thing. I flushed, but didn't reply.

'Well, go and have a good night's sleep. When they've all gone tomorrow, we'll have a proper talk.'

• • •

When I reached our apartment, I was so wired I made busy work by taking time to clean off my make-up, moisturise, brush my teeth, unbraid my hair, brush it out, hang up my gown, put away my shoes. This was pure displacement to stop my furious brain and jangling nerves making connections. I made a hot milk drink, I rubbed my feet, I found a cooling eyemask which eventually irritated me so much I threw it on the floor. When I did fall asleep, all I saw were a pair of black eyes.

The hands were warm, stroking my neck, then my breasts, one across my stomach, the other over my hip, along the top of my thigh and gently into my groin. His warm masculine scent, slightly earthy, enveloped me. Warmth flowed through me, slowly building to heat. I wasn't going to open my eyes. He held my wrists in his hand, pulled them over my head and entered me. I gave myself up to the glorious pleasure of sex. Conrad knew every inch of me intimately. He was as purposeful in ensuring we reached an explosive and mutual peak completion as he was in everything he did.

We lay together afterward, he nuzzling my ear, me hiding in the curve of his body. I could feel the tears trickling slowly across my cheeks.

'Hey, what's up?'

I sniffed.

'You've been a little busy recently. You've led a successful operation, saved the world generally, and even survived Family Day. Our children are safe, Allegra made us so proud yesterday, and we've discovered a possible new recruit in the fearsome Lucy. Did I miss something?' He smiled at me, but had a rallying tone in his voice.

I shook my head. I couldn't speak.

He got out of the bed and came back a few minutes later with two steaming cups of tea. What a gift this drink was. No wonder the British had conquered half the world. I'd heard they'd given it up for soda and coffee these days. Bad move.

He settled back in the bed, plumped up the pillows, and encircled me with his arm. We sipped companionably in silence for a few minutes.

'You have something fairly weighty to say – I can see that.' He looked down at me and briefly touched the tip of my nose with his finger. 'You're worried about discussing it with me, so it doesn't take a logics professor to see that you think I'll react badly.' He smiled gently and kissed the back of my hand. 'I promise I'll try to behave myself.'

I lay my head in that perfect place at the base of his neck and closed my eyes. It felt so warm and safe there.

'After I came back from Apollodorus,' I began, 'you were very upset when you thought I loved him. Even after the rupture with him, I don't think you liked it that I kept good memories of those times.'

'Doing well so far,' came a terse reply.

'I've had to go undercover at other times, sometimes making new friendships, establishing myself in other environments. You've had to do the same. So why was it different with the Pulcheria operation?'

He didn't say anything for a few moments. I didn't know whether he was composing his thoughts or himself.

'I hated the idea you might have been permanently attracted by the values, the way of life, as well as the man. I thought I'd lost you.'

I swallowed hard.

'You're not going to tell me he's a DJ long-term sleeper,' he said, 'and one of the good guys, are you? Please not!'

'No, no…of course not.'

'Well, I never know with you.'

'No, it's a lot worse, if I'm right.'

35

A sweet-sour smell of stale humanity and alcohol was mixed with citrus astringent cleaning product battling its way through the atrium. Picking my way through people wandering aimlessly, nursing heads or sprawled still in the arms of Morpheus, I went to find Trebatia. Macro, hurrying along armed with a brush and bucket, pointed me down to the basement.

My lovely pool was full of bodies, jumping in from the sides, spraying water at each other, throwing inflatables about like hooligans. Scattered around the edges lay sodden towels, clothes, shoes and things I dreaded to identify. In the middle of it was Trebatia, supposedly my bodyguard. The noise was deafening.

'Enough!' I shouted in my best parade ground voice.

They looked up in surprise at the spoilsport. Trebatia made for the edge immediately, pulled herself out and stood at my side, dripping.

'Sorry, ma'am.'

'No problem, Trebatia. You have fifteen minutes to go get dressed and grab some food. We have a situation.'

I turned my angry attention to my rampant family. 'Right, clean this pool up. I want it empty of bodies in one minute, trash removed, the inflatables down and drying, and all this crap on the poolside gone in ten.'

They looked at me open-mouthed.

'Starting now.'

One or two smiles of bravado, but most made their way to steps or edges. Except for two.

'If I have to come in and throw you and your brother out myself, Crispus Mitelus, you'll be spending an uncomfortable few hours in the city emergency room.'

There was a feeble attempt at eye-staring from the two of them, but they surrendered after the minute was up. Maybe seeing me in my uniform they remembered what I did for a living. I stood there for five minutes, arms crossed, foot tapping now and again. I caught a few pulled faces as they walked past. When I pretended to look over imaginary glasses at them like Nonna did, it was remarkably effective: some of them actually scuttled out instead of walking. With the pump running at full, it would be clean and crystal clear again by the evening. Unlike the rest of my life.

Upstairs, Junia and Macro were running a buffet service for the massed hordes – there must have been nearly a hundred of them. Gods! Where had they all slept? I dove between two cousins, startling them, and grabbed a bacon roll – I was starving. Gulping down a mug of coffee, I scanned the room and spotted Trebatia, back in her uniform, and beckoned her over.

'Have you had something to eat in this madhouse?'

'Yes, thank you, ma'am. I'm sorry if I was negligent – they're such a fun crowd to be with. I didn't know families could be like that.' She sounded wistful. 'Well, a bit wild, I suppose.' She glanced at me.

'Apology accepted. I'm sorry to have curtailed your fun, but we have to go back in.'

'You have the floor.'

Conrad's voice was neutral, but his eyes were still full of anger. I shuffled to my feet and described my findings to the others around the table. The banks of computers in the strategy room hummed, but the only screen alive was the situation board.

'This is disappointing, of course,' Somna said. 'To be fair to Captain Mitela, there wasn't a hint of this during all the interrogations. I have to conclude that none of the conspirators apart from Petronax and Superbus knew about this connection.' She fixed her gaze on Conrad. 'Obviously, Petronax is dead but, if you authorise it, legate, we can use a chemical stimulant on Superbus to encourage him.'

Conrad tapped his fingers on the table, all four fingers moving together like a leaf-catcher.

'What's wrong with raiding the house and terminating this criminal?' said Daniel. He looked down his nose out of half-closed eyes and smirked at me.

I folded my arms across my chest to stop myself marching over and slapping it off his face.

'Legalities,' said the adjutant. 'We don't have any proof. Look at it: we have four words from Superbus after a stressful interview carried out without a lawyer present.'

'It was a perfectly legal procedure,' I objected.

Lucius gave me such a cynical look. 'Sure, the Families' Code interview is fine as an admission of guilt for the conspiracy. I don't see any argument with that, but in respect of this new development, Superbus made his remark *after* the formal interview was concluded, so it doesn't count. Valeria's conversation with you is circumstantial. If we *can* nail that down, it's enough to send the scarabs in.'

'For Mars' sake, is that the best we can do? The scarabs!' Daniel thumped the table with the flat of his hand.

Lucius shrugged.

'Sepunia?'

'I've started a search on this Cassia.' She looked at her watch. 'I'll have some results for you within an hour or two.'

'Very well,' Conrad said. 'Captain Mitela will go with you and put el-fits together. Adjutant, send somebody to fetch Valeria Mitela in and another guard to stay with her children. I want everybody to have reread the operational reports when we reconvene in three hours. Dismissed.'

'Here, drink this.'

I saw Sepunia's hand through the crook of my elbow. I lifted my head off my hands and gave her a weak smile as the arabica smell wafted towards me.

'Lifesaver. Thanks.'

'You must be feeling quite depressed at the moment. Hellish, probably. Hardest for those who've always been stars.' She laid her hand on my upper arm and pressed lightly. 'It'll work out – don't worry.'

I'd spent two hours compiling el-fits of Cassia and Apollodorus. Sepunia had dredged all her sources and was only waiting for the Censor's office to come back. They worked at their own pace. Their investigators' branch was notoriously close.

One of Sepunia's staffers came in, glanced at me, then spoke to his chief.

'Message from Lieutenant Longina in IS, ma'am. Valeria Mitela is here and requests support from the head of her family.' He coughed and glanced again at me.

'We're finished here until the tax people deign to reply, so Captain Mitela is released.'

Longina greeted me and took me along to Interview 1, the "friendly" interview room where I'd questioned Aidan several weeks ago. It seemed like several years ago now. Valeria was perched on the edge of a plain green couch, opposite Porteus and Somna. She looked very nervous, one hand playing with the fingers of the other. A mug of brown liquid and plate of untouched cookies were on the coffee table in front of her. She looked up as we entered, and jumped up as she recognised me. She clung to me as we exchanged kisses.

'Carina—' Her hand fluttered.

'I know. I'm here now. It's okay.' I nodded at Somna and Porteus and pulled Valeria back onto the couch. 'Have they explained what's happening? Do you understand why you're here?'

She nodded. 'I want to help, of course, but I don't know how.' Poor woman. She was a food technologist. She probably didn't even have a parking fine on her record.

'Well, I can't ask you anything during the interview, but I can explain things and protect your interests and rights. When they ask you a question, just answer it straightforwardly. Take your time. If you think of anything afterward, don't worry. Just say it, even if it's trivial.' I smiled at her. 'Or even sounds stupid.' I looked at Somna. 'Have you begun yet, colonel?'

'Only to take ID details.'

'Play it back, please.'

She was right, but I wanted to be sure.

Valeria repeated what she'd told me, pretty much word for word. She was a scientist and precise. By the end, she was calmer, and her voice had steadied. Somna thanked her formally and asked me to take Valeria upstairs to do the el-fit. I left her working at it with one of Sepunia's experts.

Sepunia looked up as I returned to her office. She didn't say anything but handed me three printouts with the Censor's seal. I read them through in silence and handed them back. I took several deep breaths before I spoke.

'I didn't like her then and I still don't. Have these people never heard of the joint watch protocols?'

Sepunia's desktop peeped. Report meeting in ten minutes. I took a moment to go see how Valeria was doing. I dropped my hand on her shoulder.

'I've done my best, Carina,' she said. Her eyes looked strained, the result of staring intently at a screen without a break.

It was good. Too good.

I arrived at the strategy room a few minutes early. Fausta was tapping on the transparent board setting it up to enter the data as the meeting progressed. I walked up to her, but didn't have time to say anything as the door opened and Daniel for once in his life arrived early.

'Huh! Trust the girl blunder to be first here. Trying to make up for your massive error of judgement?'

'This is not an appropriate time for personal remarks,' I said, fixing him with a solid stare.

'Well, your mistake was personal as well as gross.'

Warmth flushed up my neck into my face despite all my efforts to calm it by breathing deeply and slowly. I ignored him and took my place at the table. He sat opposite and grinned at my discomfort. How could he have turned like this? Life was full of disappointments, and he was one of them. Sepunia was next and sat by me, pushing some printouts at me. We stood as Conrad, Lucius and Somna appeared. Conrad looked especially grim as he began without preliminaries.

'There is no doubt Apollodorus was Superbus's visitor that night.'

He glanced at me. 'I can personally confirm both el-fits are accurate.' He held his hand up at the murmuring. 'Before we jump in heavy-booted, we need to develop our process.' He nodded to Fausta who was hovering ready, her fingers at the green starting point.

'Sepunia, please.'

'As the legate says, we have confirmed IDs on Apollodorus and Cassia. I was considerably taken aback by the Censor's office admission that Cassia was a long-term undercover investigator. We had no idea. They should, of course, have advised us via the joint watch protocols.' She looked down at her el-pad. 'I strongly recommend a liaison meeting without delay.'

'Stupid bastards,' said Lucius. 'What did you make of her, Carina?'

I glanced over at him. He smiled like he still wanted to know me.

'Cold and heartless. And snotty. I would hate to be a subject of her investigation. I had very little to do with her, to be honest.'

'Sounds like a normal investigator, then.'

But I hadn't seen past her outward manner. I studied the table. How could I have been so blind?

'Well, according to their report,' Sepunia added, 'Cassia is one of their top investigators. She didn't find any trace of evasion or misconduct. Everything had been filed, submitted or recorded right up to last month by their administrator.'

I smiled to myself. Hermina was too efficient, and too proud, to make any mistake there.

'What's so funny?' Daniel asked, frowning at me. 'You're a bit too pleased she found nothing. Didn't want to erode your share of the profits, eh?'

'Daniel,' said Lucius.

'Sir?'

'Shut up.'

Sepunia coughed. 'I can't find any match for Apollodorus. His image is not on the PopBase, there is no record of his presence under his name. No DNA, no fingerprints, no optical scan, voiceprint, health record. Nothing. So I assumed he was operating under an alias. Using the el-fits and the information from Carina's report about the French immigrant side of his family and the mother coming from Castra Lucilla, I ran a probability analysis and got nowhere.' She grimaced. 'Well, 27.2% which is statistically equivalent to nil.'

'But that's well below the minimum of forty per cent,' Conrad said.

'Indeed. My conclusion is that PopBase has been, er, amended by a highly skilled hacker.'

'Are you sure?'

She looked back at Conrad with her steady green gaze. 'Yes.'

Nobody could speak. Apart from our own system, PopBase was the most protected digital asset in the Imperium. The only sound was Fausta's long lacquered fingernails scratching as she updated the situation board. I glanced over at her, more to reassure her than anything. She stared back, pink blotches on her cheeks, and I knew.

Crap.

'Very well,' Conrad said, his tone clipped. 'We send the DJ scarabs in to arrest Apollodorus. Light back-up on standby, please, Daniel. We can hold him for questioning, take some biological data and find out who he really is.' A red border surrounded Apollodorus's image in the centre of the board. The interconnecting lines sprang into life, connecting to me and Flavius. Once you'd said or thought something, it seemed obvious afterwards. The truth glared out at me.

'Even if it proves innocent, which I doubt, we can't have people like him unrecorded. Sepunia, liaise with Interior about their leak in PopBase. Somna, leave Superbus where he is. I'll speak to him myself. Dismissed.'

I stood up with the others, pushed my chair up to the table. I felt remote from the whole surreal meeting. Strange, nobody had worried about Apollodorus before – a pragmatic acceptance that there *were* people in Roma Nova who weren't pure and innocent. We owed a huge debt to Apollodorus. Maybe Conrad had forgotten he owed his life to him.

'Carina. A moment.'

Conrad's voice was as remote as I felt.

We watched the others file out. Fausta switched the backlights off, logged out and went to follow. As she passed by me, I stopped her with my hand on her arm. She glanced up at my face then dropped her gaze as quickly.

'Well done. We'll talk in the morning.'

Her face was tight, but she nodded. When she'd closed the door, Conrad waved his hand towards the table.

'Sit down.'

He sat beside me, but tilted his chair at an angle.

'I didn't want to do this in front of the others, especially bloody Daniel. Jupiter, if Lucius hadn't got there before me, I'd have taken him out and thumped him.' He looked over at the blank strategy board. 'I'm sorry, but you're off the case. It's standard procedure. I don't have a choice.'

'Don't you?'

'No, and you know it.'

The way he looked at me – through me – I knew the delicate personal links we'd been rebuilding had been severed in one cut. I suppose I was lucky I wasn't being thrown out.

He shot a look at me then studied the table. His mouth was drawn in a tight grim line. Crap, there was more.

'On a personal level, you're going to have to fight a full disciplinary investigation, so it's not in your interest to stay involved.'

More damned standard procedure.

He stretched his hand out, but withdrew it before he touched mine. He lowered his voice. 'I tried to deflect it, but I couldn't argue her out of it – the senior legate has insisted you and Flavius are suspended with immediate effect and confined to barracks.'

36

Stripped of the right to wear my uniform, I pulled on my oldest jeans and plainest tee the next morning. I reported to Lucius's office in the admin block and surrendered my badge. He handed me a white plastic card with an embedded optical chip.

'You'll be able to access most of the building, but not the working areas, including the guard zone. Don't lose it, or a security detail will be on you within minutes it splits from your biosignature. Ditto if you talk to Flavius. No Internet, no phone calls out.'

The early morning headache started throbbing harder. I'd never been white-carded. Now my colleagues would drift away, little by little, conversations about work – the thing that bound us together – would stop when I was near. Pity, embarrassment, even fear of contamination.

'What am I supposed to do with myself?'

'Keep out of everybody's way, mainly.' He leaned back. 'Start preparing your hearing. You can access the library.' He glanced up at me. His eyes narrowed as if giving me a message. 'It's neutral ground.'

Word hadn't got around in the mess hall, so it was no different from a normal day, except that when Flavius came in, he spotted me and instantly went back out. The proximity alarm was five metres so I hoped it was only him being careful. In the library, I logged on to my internal account and tried not to include "error of judgement" too many times in my draft defence statement.

But had it been an error? If the circumstantial evidence did lead to nailing the case against Apollodorus, the worst was that I'd been blindsided by him. And Cassia. I had no control over their movements. Obviously, I'd tried to hack into Cassia's account, but she'd locked it down. I'd managed to physically search her office once. Not easy when she was glued to her desk most of the time. But I couldn't find anything out of place, let alone incriminating. Although Apollo sometimes worked in his study, the *tablinum*, he most often sat in a recess in the atrium. I hadn't known about his private retreat until after the operation. I didn't deserve to be under this semi-ostracism. I wasn't in a cell, but I might as well have been. Just a larger one, with people in it.

In the ancients section in the library, I searched for examples of generals who'd been duped or made an error of judgement yet were still considered "great". Not that I considered myself in any way great, but I'd be able to show that even the best made mistakes. I was searching through Caesar's Gallic Wars and pulled out a heavy, purple, leather-backed volume, frayed and scratched on the spine and corners. I nearly jumped out of my skin when I saw Fausta's anxious eyes in the space.

'Juno!' I hissed at her. 'Don't do that. What do you want?'

She glanced to her right, but we were deep in a recess, practically invisible.

'Are you going to report it, ma'am?' she whispered.

'I don't know.' I scratched the back of my neck. 'Do you remember any of the, er, original data?'

'No, he told me to access Po—, the program I mean, asked me to show him how to change it and seal the system. Then told me to leave the room. I tried to go back in out of curiosity, but the program had locked that entry. I couldn't bust it.' She shrugged. 'I guessed I was safer not knowing.'

'Undoubtedly.'

She stared at me, her face miserable. She grabbed a book off the shelf, pretended to look at it. Even from where I was, I could see she was holding it upside down. She closed it and went to put it back, but her hands were trembling so much they let it slip off the shelf. The loud smack on the wood floor brought the librarian around to investigate. I darted along the row and hid at the far end. Fausta was apologising like she'd been caught stealing the book instead of dropping it. Eventually, the librarian went back to his desk.

'Fausta! Here.'

She glanced back; then sidled up to the end where I stood.

'Look, thanks for telling me. I'll protect you if I can, but you have to go back to your desk and act like nothing happened. And don't, for the love of Juno, say anything to Drusus.'

I had no appetite for lunch, but couldn't sit still. I went for a run on the indoor track and back to my room. I lay on the bed, staring at the ceiling. And this was only day one.

I woke with a start as my commset peeped. It had been silent since last night which, for a few hours, was a novelty, then spooky. Apart from alerts throughout the day, I must have gotten upward of ten operational or command messages on a normal day. I grabbed my el-pad which synched with my commset and wiped the screen to access the alert. I stared at the images. Philippus and Hermina had been entered on the watch net.

I almost ran down the corridor of the sleeping areas, through the admin and domestic zones, and reached the guard area where I was stopped by a flashing red light and an alarm.

Crap. I couldn't pass through. I slammed the wall with my palm. I had walked through the automatic barrier each day for seven years without thinking. I was taking deep breaths to calm myself, trying to convert the anger into energy, when Lucius appeared.

'What the hell are you doing? Trying to wreck the place?'

'Sorry. Sorry, I can't do this.' I folded my arms across my chest, bent forward slightly, and jammed my mouth shut.

'I knew you'd find it hard, but I didn't expect you to crack so soon.' He snorted. 'Come with me.'

He stalked back along the corridor, studded sandals clacking and echoing. I deeply envied him the sound: I wanted my own back on. He opened the door to his office and gestured me to a chair.

'One, don't fight it. Two, don't destroy my building. Three, stop bleating sorry. Now, what's the problem that has you behaving like a barbarian?'

I swallowed. 'Two personal alerts have come up for me.' I showed him my el-pad.

'Hmph.' He tapped on his keyboard, and I saw the edge of the joint watch screen load. I jumped off my chair and went to stand behind him as he scrolled down.

'There!' I jabbed the screen. When he opened the first, Philippus's face and profile stared out at me. The next showed Hermina.

'Arrested this morning after raid on a riverside house out on the Brancadorum road. Detained under conspiracy to treason for standard twenty-eight days,' he read out. 'Friends of yours?'

'Yes,' I said sullenly. I walked over to his bookcase, then back again and once again. 'I have to help them. It's a question of obligation. Normally, I'd pick up the phone and have some smart-ass lawyer in here for them before Somna could open her dossier.' I sat down. 'Now I can't even make that simple call, can I?'

'No.'

'They gave me loyal service; they helped save Conradus's life; they were crucial to throwing Petronax out of this building; and you won't even help them have the legal representation they're entitled to?'

He was silent.

'One call home. My grandmother or the steward can do it from there.'

He looked out at me from under a frown. 'You're doing it again.'

'What?'

'Never mind. This is your one call. If you squander it on these criminals, you won't get another.' He flung himself out of his chair and waved me to his desk. Ten seconds later, I had Junia on screen. And five after that, Aurelia.

'*Salve*, Nonna. I only have time for a short call, but could you do something for me?'

I went early for my food so people wouldn't feel obliged to sit with me or be embarrassed about avoiding me. My spoon overflowed with a large scoop of my favourite dessert, honey island, when two guards with security badges entered the mess hall and found me.

'You'll have to wait.' The honeycomb foam dissolved in my mouth.

'The legate says you are to come immediately.'

'I'm sure he does,' and I stuffed another mouthful in.

I got to my feet, one hand holding the dish and the other the spoon with the last mouthful. I gulped it down, smiled sweetly and went with them.

'What in Hades did you think you were doing? I should throw you in the cells!' His face was livid, the skin tight. His eyes were like agates.

'I didn't know arranging a lawyer was a disciplinary offence,' I said, 'or a criminal one.'

'Don't split hairs. You've just made our job twice as difficult.'

'Well, too bad.'

'Oh, come on, you were the one who suggested the Families' Code interview to work round Superbus's lawyer. Now you've put the same block up for these two.'

'One big difference – Superbus was guilty as hell, a main actor in the conspiracy intent on destroying us, but Philippus and Hermina are innocent.'

'Innocent,' he snorted. 'Hardly.'

'Yes, of this, I'm sure.'

'And since when did you become a judge?'

'Fair point,' I said, 'but they deserve a chance.'

'Your sense of right and wrong is too flexible for me.'

I shrugged.

He picked up a sheet with a DJ logo. 'The scarabs want you to go to Apollodorus's house to see if you can point out anything missing or different. You'll be escorted the whole time, but I want your word you won't violate the CB order again.'

'I didn't see it as a violation...'

'You wouldn't.'

'...but if it makes you happier, you have my word.'

37

We approached the entrance of Apollodorus's house with its graceful stone arch, the tall gates now wide open with *custodes* porting machine guns each side. We parked on the gravel area alongside a truck and two patrol cars. I jumped out the rear door of our wheelbase. The wind was rising this evening. I stopped for a moment to zip up my fleece. The inner metal barred gates with their Venetian scrollwork and graceful finials hung off their hinges, their lockwork smashed and distorted.

Another armed *custos* checked our ID as we stopped under the portico. He grunted and signalled us to proceed. The atrium was cluttered with figures in white suits running hand-held scanners everywhere, cartons being packed with papers, blue figures speaking their reports into el-pads. Two *custodes* were carrying computers out, cables trailing. I looked up at the large glazed bull's eye in the roof but saw only dark sky.

A *custos* pointed us to the large recess where Apollodorus used to sit. Now it was occupied by Lurio. He made me wait by the table he was working at. 'Captain.'

'Commander.'

'Your monkeys can leave.' He waved my two guards away.

'No disrespect, sir, but we are under the legate's instructions to stay in close contact,' said the *optio*.

'Two choices: with or without force.' He fixed them with a genial smile. 'You choose.' The *custos* who had been sitting with Lurio stood up and approached my guards. Another two joined her. She tilted her chin at the two PGSF and they conceded. We watched as they retreated to the other side of the atrium and sat opposite, but kept their eyes fixed on me.

'What happened to you? You look like a piece of street trash.'

'Don't be a smart-ass, Lurio. You know I've been CB'd.'

'Mitelus throw his pens off his desk?'

I said nothing.

'Come on then, let's go for a viewing tour.'

For some reason, the disorder left in every room by the *custodes'* search saddened me. Even in my bedroom, the closet had been emptied and clothes thrown in a heap on the floor.

I knelt down and picked through a few things. 'I'll take these back, if that's okay.'

'Nothing doing. Everything's going to be examined. You can buy them back in the public auction when it's all finished.'

'You're all heart.'

'C'mon, you know the rules of evidence as well as I do, or has your brain dissolved?'

On the table, the little blue vase still had the half-dozen blooms I'd picked in the garden, but they were all brown, desiccated and weary. I dropped the clothes back on the floor and reached into the top of the closet. On the inside of the door frame, between the moulding and the frame, was a cell chip with a blue logo and miniscule parts number.

'Yours, I think.' I handed it over to Lurio.

'Mars! That's from seven years ago.' He turned it over, squinting at the number. 'But you never used it.'

'I didn't need to.'

Apollo was a powerful, dangerous man. No question. But I'd rarely felt in danger from him. Not enough to use the emergency chip Lurio had given me. Maybe I should have been more frightened. A heavy lump settled in my heart. My legs turned to rubber and I sank down on the bed. I braced myself with my arms to stay upright. I bowed my head as tears trickled down over my face.

Apollodorus, why did you do this? Why did you double-cross us?

· · ·

277

I couldn't see anything else remarkable or different. I wandered through, touching the furniture, fingering the cushions, stroking the velvet and linen drapes. A bowl of rotting fruit on the immaculate dining room table was drawing flies; the veranda was desecrated with recent cigarette butts. I was angry on Apollo's behalf. He would have been coldly furious and snapped his fingers to have it remedied. But it would never have gotten to that state in the first place.

I led Lurio to the older part of the house behind the atrium where the floor turned to flagstones. Two *custodes* were packing up the contents of Apollo's *tablinum*. The door to its left was ajar, outwards. My pulse rate rose as I remembered that last emotional evening with him. I opened the door wide, bracing myself to see the lovely room dissected and dismantled. All I saw was shelving, piled with dusty domestic plates and bowls, the kind you only use if extra people come to stay. The dust was undisturbed. I knocked on the back wall of the cupboard. A dull thunk. I tapped in several places but the same solid, reassuring noise came back.

'What is it?' said Lurio.

'Help me take this stuff out.'

We worked methodically, setting the crockery to one side. I ran my fingers over the edges of the door frame, the back wall, everywhere. Nothing. I stood back and searched the surrounding stonework, scrutinising each ripple and curve, each mortared joint between.

'Tell me what we're doing here,' he said. 'I do have other things to get on with.'

'Wait. I'm looking for the way in.'

'What to? It's a cupboard. Come on, we've got upstairs to look through yet.'

'No, wait. There's a room here.'

He lifted his arm and spoke into his commset. I was still feeling the stonework when another *custos* arrived with a woodsman's axe.

'Stand back,' Lurio said to me and nodded to the axeman who hefted his axe back in both hands, ready to strike.

'No, I'm sure the catch is here somewhere.' Then I felt it – a too-smooth stone to the right of the door jamb. It slid down to reveal a number pad.

Lurio had one of the white-suited forensic drones run his scanner over to reveal the code. The shelves swung open noiselessly to the left and then backward into a recess. A velvet curtain slid across in front to camouflage the shelving. Lurio dismissed the others and followed me in. He aimed his flashlight into every corner, throwing the strong beam around the room. I bent down and switched on one of the exquisite Lalique lamps. The soft gold and crimson room glowed into life. I swallowed.

'Jupiter's balls!' He whistled. He moved around the room, examining everything, captivated for a minute or so by the grandmother's portrait.

'I want this room sealed. I don't want some soulless forensic cutting it all up. I'll help pack it up and box it myself,' I pleaded.

'He really got to you, didn't he?'

'I...I owed him so much. He helped me grow up.'

'But now?'

'Now we have to find him. If he did backstab us, I promise you I'll personally hunt him down.'

Lurio worked with me. We took down, boxed and crated everything within three hours. He helped me enclose the tall portrait between two large sheets of cardboard. I wasn't sure why I felt this responsibility for keeping these things safe. Maybe they meant more to me than I would admit. I worked my hurt out pushing and taping the bubbled plastic and wrapping fleece.

I ran my hands over the inlaid top of the small table with curvaceous swan-neck legs. I saw the crystal glass half-full of pale yellow wine that Apollo had poured to steady my nerves after the shock of entering this room. I batted that memory away, grasped the table by the shallow carved skirt to lift it into a box, when my index finger found a tiny half-circle depression on the underside. I glanced over at Lurio. He was busy packing some lamps. I knew I'd found a concealed compartment. My dad had an old table with one in our New Hampshire house. When I was a kid, I'd loved making up stories about imaginary secret documents hidden there. I let my breath out. I pushed and it slid open. My fingers touched paper. Lurio had his back to me, so I carefully extracted a small bunch of sheets. I glanced at each one of around a dozen, but the most interesting were four stapled together and folded lengthways. As Lurio turned, I stuffed them into my fleece pocket.

It was gone two in the morning when we finished the rest of the house, but I'd lost my concentration. I didn't tell Lurio I'd discovered where Apollodorus might be. If I'd guessed right, it had now become personal. Once I was free, I was going to bring him down myself.

38

After a poor five hours' sleep, I woke to a summons to report to the
guard zone security gate at eight. The code was from Somna's IS team.
I guessed they were going to grill me further on the extent of my
involvement with Apollodorus. I chose dark casuals and applied
subdued make-up. Going into battle appropriately dressed and
warpainted worked for me.

Longina greeted me formally and buzzed me through. Maybe I
was paranoid but nobody, even close colleagues, looked me in the eye
as we walked along the corridors. At Somna's office, Longina
knocked, opened the door for me and left without saying another
word.

Somna looked up from the file she was studying on her desk.

'Good morning, Carina. Thank you for coming.'

Like I had a choice. Still, Somna had supported me all along, so I
shouldn't grump. Maybe I was in for nothing more than an informal
chat with her.

'I think you may be able to help us.' She addressed me as if I was a
civilian witness, not a member of the same unit. I felt uncomfortable,
no, apprehensive.

'Of course, ma'am, if you think I can,' I said, far too cheerfully.

She stood up, picked a book off the shelf, but laid it on the desk
without opening it. 'On the facts, I think you've been misjudged. The

difficulties and pressures of operating undercover are not always well-remembered by those who have attained higher rank.'

I hoped I wasn't staring at her with my mouth open. Did she mean Conrad or the senior legate?

'Well, let's get on. I know you formed friendships with the Pulcheria Foundation associates. I presume this was why you are funding legal representation for the two we have in custody.'

'I...'

She held her hand up. 'It's more demanding for us, but you were perfectly within the rules, and I applaud you for your sense of responsibility.'

Was she softening me up for something bitter? She was a psychologist, so had all the techniques.

'I know from your report you found it awkward to deal with them when you went back there with Flavius. I think meeting the two detainees now would be even more trying.' She fixed me with her more familiar grey lizard stare. 'But I need you to do it.'

'Why?'

'They refuse to say anything. Even when their lawyers suggest they might compromise or answer simple things. It reminds me of somebody else just as stubborn.' She smiled as she perched on the corner of her desk. 'We could undoubtedly crack them within the twenty-eight days, but the legate says we need the answers urgently, preferably yesterday.'

'I don't think either of them will talk to me.'

'You realise the seriousness of your own position, I presume?'

'What do you mean?'

'Failure to cooperate could, of course, lead to formal arrest and detention.' And she smiled.

I sent Somna a hate-filled look as the security detail pulled my hands behind my back and cuffed me. I was marched down to the cells, protesting all the way, but powerless to do anything. I refused to cooperate as they strip-searched me, prodding and pulling, and piled on the complaints louder and louder. The door to the open-barred cell block was ajar and the noise must have carried through. When the custody sergeant told me to can it, I spat at him. He slapped my face. I laid every curse I could think of on him. Two guards pushed me none too gently through the door to the cell block and shoved me in the end one. I cursed the Hades out of them. One turned around and gave me the finger.

I kicked the base plate on the front wall of the bars, but forgot my feet were bare. This time the swearing was genuine. I rattled the bars and shouted they couldn't do this. I demanded release. I wanted a lawyer. After ten minutes, I gave up shouting, sat on the bench, my back to the other cells, and muttered about the unfairness of it all.

Half an hour later, I had my first visitors: Paula and Livius.

'Are you trying to earn bonus stupid points?' Livius shouted at me. He projected anger and concern in equal amounts as he jabbed his index finger at me.

'You forget yourself, optio.'

'Don't pull rank on me. Besides, you have none now. Mars help me, if you were a grunt in my squad, I'd run you around so hard you'd be too knackered to misbehave.'

'Well, thanks for your visit. You can piss off now.' I turned my shoulder on him.

'Bruna, calm down,' said Paula. She laid her hand on Livius's arm and shook her head. 'Tell me what happened.'

I glanced up and down as if checking that nobody was overhearing and caught a glimpse of Hermina and Philippus two cells up. She was standing, obviously listening, he in the further cell, sat looking unconcerned, but the side of his head turned in my direction.

'Somna threatened me again, tried to push me about Apollodorus. I don't know. I really don't. Then Conradus, I mean, the legate, clambers onto my case, insinuating my loyalties were split.'

'Aren't they?' Livius asked. 'I mean, we're chasing a known criminal who's a traitor. Case proven.'

'No, it's not. But I was as shocked as anybody at the accusation. I can't believe he's crossed us like this.' I hung my head down. 'It's become personal with Conradus.'

'Has he any reason to think it's justified?' asked Paula.

'None of your business, or his!'

'I see,' said Paula. She looked like a mother whose kid had a term report with straight Ds.

'If I could find Apollodorus and talk to him—'

'Fat chance,' said Livius. 'But I'm sure they'll arrange to put you side by side when they catch him.'

'Go away, Paula. I can't think. And take this idiot with you.'

'Pulcheria?'

Hermina.

'I know that's not your name, but I can't think of you as anything else.'

'What?'

'Thank you for arranging the lawyers.'

I twisted around, grasped the bars and knelt up on the cell bench. 'It's the least I could do. You didn't deserve this.'

'I don't understand why we're here. I thought we'd helped. Now they think we're part of the conspiracy.'

'Don't I know it!'

'So what happens next?' Philippus.

'Me, I catch a court martial. If they prove I'm more involved than I said or that I'm protecting Apollodorus, probably twenty years in the central military prison. If I were you two, and you truly don't have a clue where he is, I'd make a full statement. The lawyers will get you off.' I paused. 'You don't have an idea, do you?'

Philippus looked up at the CCTV camera, shrugged. 'No, not a clue, but I wasn't giving them the satisfaction.'

I gave a short laugh. He grinned back.

'Hermi, is there anything you can think of that might help?'

'Nothing. I find it impossible to think of Apollodorus betraying us like this. He had so much to gain with you, I mean, them being in his debt.' She shook her head.

I believed them both. Would Somna?

Around half an hour later, Hermina and Philippus were taken away, hopefully on their way out of here. I reckoned three hours passed – they'd confiscated my watch in the custody suite. When the guards shoved a bowl of soup through the door slot, slopping half of it on the floor, I didn't touch it. Juno knew what they'd put in it. Traitors, even suspected traitors, had a rough ride. I remember Robbia seven years ago when she appeared at her hearing: pale, subdued and nervous. And she'd been a confident and sassy officer before her arrest for treason. I'd wait until the official rescue party came.

But it wasn't until early next morning after a tense night that Longina came and fetched me. She looked embarrassed and twitched while my cell door was unlocked.

'I'm so sorry you were left here. Please believe it was a mistake. The colonel will be furious. I wouldn't care to be the overnight shift leader when she gets hold of him.'

'A mistake? How can it be a mistake? Do you realise I've eaten nothing since breakfast yesterday?'

'Why didn't you ask for something?'

'You ever been a prisoner where all the guards think you're a traitor?'

She stared at me, not understanding.

'I didn't think so.'

She signed my release and stayed with me while I changed. The same custody sergeant was back on duty. I apologised for my behaviour, explaining I had to make it realistic so the bait would be taken. He didn't change his dour expression.

I insisted on getting fresh clothes, showering and eating a full breakfast. Longina sat with me in the mess hall, and I saw she was shocked by some of the hostile looks.

Somna had gone to a round-up meeting so Longina showed me Hermina's and Philippus's statements. As predicted, they'd been released conditionally, pending formal discharge.

I'd done some hard thinking last night about my own future. No formal charges had been brought, and the disciplinary hearing might yet clear me. I'd helped Somna unblock the logjam with Hermina and Philippus, so I guessed that counted in my favour.

Despite his concern, Conrad had retreated into formal and official, Sella regarded me as an unstable maverick, and I'd lost Daniel's friendship. Lucius and Somna would support me, but they were part of the system. I wasn't sure I could see a way back from where I was. Maybe I'd talk it through with Conrad. He couldn't refuse me as my commanding officer. But I came to the conclusion I was on my way out.

• • •

Lucius buzzed me later that morning, but when I reported to his office the only person sitting at the desk was Conrad.

'Well done for encouraging those two to talk. You're quite remarkable when you operate.'

'I'd prefer a less hostile environment another time.'

Somna had messaged me with her thanks, regretting the "unfortunate misunderstanding" about not extracting me earlier.

'I've just sent a circular out so you shouldn't get any further trouble. I think I'll be able to persuade the senior legate to relax her attitude now after what you did at Apollodorus's house as well as unjamming the interviews. It's obvious where you stand.'

Although he wasn't to blame for my CB order, he looked contrite.

'I had a lot of time to think last night in my cell,' I said. I couldn't look directly at him. I didn't know if it was embarrassment or apathy underneath, but I'd lost my ability to be bothered about anything. 'I don't think I'm following the same road as everybody else. I know I produce results, but it's not enough. I want you to accept my resignation.'

He looked appalled. 'No.'

I sighed. 'You can't refuse. I feel so wrong here, as if something's broken.' I looked at him. 'You have to let me go.'

After I wrote and delivered my resignation letter by hand, copied to Lucius, the adjutant, I cleared my locker, messaged my comrades, posted a drinks date two weeks later for my ART, if they wanted to come, and left. I felt depressed, alienated. I wasn't glad or sorry about leaving; just numb.

39

I went home and slept for a full ten hours. The next day, I moped around the house, grumping at everybody. By mid-afternoon, I'd made the children cry, quarrelled with Helena, and infuriated my grandmother. I retreated to the atrium to sulk to myself.

'I want a word with you, my girl.'

I looked up at my grandmother but didn't say anything.

'I don't know what's going on, but I won't have you flouncing around here like a brat having a tantrum.'

I shrugged and looked down at my magazine. I knew it was rude, but I couldn't be bothered to apologise. The next minute, the magazine was across the other side of the room and my face was stinging.

'Nonna.' I gasped and struggled up.

'Sit down.'

She looked like the Furies on a bad day. With hangovers. I shrank back into my seat.

'Now tell me.'

'I've resigned. I don't belong there.' I gave her the short version.

'So you made a mistake and ran away. I thought you had more backbone.'

I looked down at the marble floor.

She snorted. 'What about your promise to Lurio? To bring Apollodorus down?'

'He won't expect me to go hunting now. I'll tell him what I suspect. He'll take it from there.'

'So you're going to complete your self-misery by letting down your oldest colleague and turning your back on a challenge you're perfectly capable of dealing with because you can't face the fact that you made a mistake?' She raised her eyes to the ceiling. 'Juno grant me strength!'

She took both my hands in hers. 'If you don't do this, you will never be able to look inside yourself and like what you see. You made a mistake. You think it's the end of the world. Believe me, it's happened before. I've made some horrendous foul-ups in my time, so I know.'

She gave my hands a little shake and me a little smile.

'The way to work through it is to recognise your mistake and swallow the embarrassment. Be honest, catch your breath, and pick yourself up. Then you have to get on and do something about it.'

She fixed me with a steady, uncompromising look. After a few moments, she let my hands fall, went over to the drinks table and poured out one small and one standard measure of her French brandy.

'Here.' She handed me the small one. 'You may be driving later and you don't want to be picked up for drunk-driving.'

I called Lurio and asked if he could let me have a small item.

'I'll call by with it in about an hour.'

As I sprayed the mouse-brown dye into my hair, I wondered what in Hades I was doing. Inserting the contacts to dull my eyes to grey, I blinked back excess liquid, not sure it was tears or saline solution. By the time I was pulling on old jeans and a threadbare top, I was resigned to it. Closing my apartment door and walking into the atrium in worn sneakers and carrying a thin cotton jacket and canvas backpack, I was as ready as I could hope to be.

Lurio's bulky figure sitting on the couch was bent in conversation with my grandmother. He rose as soon as he saw me and strapped the ID I'd asked for onto my outstretched wrist.

'Got your knives?'

I nodded.

'Got your head together?'

The nod was briefer.

'Come on, then.'

I had him drop me at a shuttle stop on the city south-east periphery.

'Sure you don't want to go to the car rental or the interrail terminus?'

'No, this is fine. And no, I'm not telling you where I'm going. But thanks for the ID.' I leaned over and kissed his cheek, then pulled myself out of the car as if I carried twice my own weight and trudged down the steps into the dark tunnel.

I spent a few moments in the restroom picking the back off the ID and removing the tracker chip. I smiled as I flushed it down the pan, a journey which would give Lurio a few minutes' grief. The train south left in ten minutes, and I hung around behind the luggage carts until the door warning sounded. I jumped on, catching a frown from the guard. She checked my ticket there and then. I shrugged and plunked myself down on a spare seat next to a suit. I stepped off at each of the next two stops, walking a few cars further up or down the platform each time, turning my coat inside out and putting my hair up or loosening it. I couldn't see anybody following. Nobody paid any attention: they just wanted to get home after work.

I finally quit the train at Castra Lucilla. Although we came here every summer and in between, I'd never been to the train station: we always travelled in Aurelia's Mercedes. I checked the town map for the nearest *mansio*. Only three streets away. After grey soup and roll in the dining room, I found my place in a four-bed room, tied my shoes together to one of the legs at the head of the bed, pulled the cover over my fully-clothed body and went to sleep.

I was first in line at the door of the employment centre at eight next morning. I registered for casual outdoor work, specialism horticulture, knowing that at this time of year estate labour would be pressured by olive and grape harvesting. And the Mitela home farm was the largest one around. The steward ran it efficiently with a lean team, calling on casuals twice a year during harvest and pruning to take over the routine stuff and free up the more skilled permanent staff.

Sure enough, I was called forward and told to assemble for a transport that would take us up there. We passed the shaded plane-treed drive I knew well and bumped up the service entrance. As soon as the truck stopped, we were told to hurry up and climb out. A farm assistant I didn't know allocated us each a dormitory bed. After a plain lunch in the farm hall, we collected coveralls, gloves, tools and task sheets.

Next day, I asked if I could work in the gardens as I had experience. The assistant looked over her glasses for a moment, but agreed and gave me the herb garden which looked straggly at this time of the year, all six metres of it. I forgot just how boring weeding was, but the upside was that I was getting nearer to my goal. I didn't want my quarry to hear the whisper of a hint I was anywhere near him. I wanted him to feel totally secure.

I graduated to the main driveway the next day, strimming the edges and weeding the bases of the trees. Near the main gate, I stopped and leaned back to ease my shoulder. I glanced across the fields on the other side of the road to give my eyes a break. Then I saw the skinny figure loping from one of the privately let farm cottages towards a utility. He pulled himself into the cab and drove off. It trundled along parallel to the main road, raising little dust whorls behind each wheel. As it made a right turn, it came towards me, and I was sure then.

After the evening meal, I checked I'd left the shower block far window catch open. I glanced at the group of smokers outside the accommodation and made a walking sign to them. I blinked at one off-colour reply, but carried on towards the back of the farm. Dusk came down fast and with it a new moon. I double-backed to the main road perimeter. I knew exactly where the thinnest part of the hedge was and pushed out with minimum tearing to my jacket. I darted over the road and crouched in the ditch for a few minutes checking nobody was following.

The fields were open with a few shrubs scattered along the boundaries. I crouched behind the cover provided by hedges, resorting to crawling along the open ground between them by pulling myself along by my elbows. As I edged up the side of the track, I saw lights shining through the window of one cottage. Built nearly two hundred years ago for older, often poorer, cousins who had lost the ability to make enough to support themselves, only two were occupied now by Mitelae; the others were rented out to city people.

I reached the hedge twenty metres from the cottage, fished out my pocket field glasses and scanned to see if I could see anyone. I zoomed in on the windows, pushing the digital focus to maximum. At that moment, the window was flung open. I stabbed the auto button which fired off a series of shots from the built-in camera and threw myself back on the earth. I heard the squeak of the wooden shutters as they were swung shut and the metal hasp rammed home into the internal catch. The sound was repeated several times before it became quiet again. But I had glimpsed the ratty little face as it turned in profile to talk to another person in the room.

Justus.

40

I was trimming shrubs at the far side of the villa next afternoon when I heard a car stereo blasting away in the distance. It gained in level relentlessly. I heard, but couldn't see, a car racing up the drive, passengers bawling their heads off to the music. The brakes screeched, no doubt depositing rubber on the driveway that one of us would have to clean off. The music cut with the engine, followed by laughing and shouting. Sounded like three, no four voices. I heard car doors slam, the steward's calm voice, then silence.

I wheeled the barrow full of green clippings back to the composting bin in the yard, hoping that the arrival of this noisy weekend party, undoubtedly some of the younger Mitelae, wouldn't interfere with what I had planned. Thinking about it, they could be a great diversion, keeping the steward's team too busy to follow what a casual outdoor worker was up to.

My backpack had been upended, my pathetic collection of tees on the floor with boot marks, my notebook torn, the plastic baggie with my wash kit split open, the contents scattered over the bed. The sponge was making an increasing wet patch in the centre. Two women at the far end of the dormitory stopped talking as I started gathering things back together. I sensed more people circling around. I glanced up, but said nothing as I repacked my things.

'Oh dear. Had an accident? That's what happens when you keep to yourself.' A coarse face, framed by long black and grey hair tied back with an elastic tie, topped a broad unforgiving figure. 'We too good for you, ay?'

'She goes off on little walks by herself in the evening, spying on the rest of us having a good time.'

Another, younger version said, 'Look what I found.'

Crap. My field glasses. I held my hand out. 'Give them back, please.'

'Oooh! "Please". Little Miss Suck-Arse who bags garden duty while the rest of us are scrubbing in the fields.' She smiled at me, revealing gapped, stained teeth under mean little eyes. 'Come and get them.'

I reached her in two strides, kicked her fat stomach, winding her, grabbed the field glasses as she fell, and whirled round to face the older one. She had a knife in her hand. I threw my glasses on my bed, praying nobody else would feel tempted. My knives were too safely hidden inside the mattress. I shucked off my jacket, held it in my left hand, ready to use it like a *retarius* net. We circled. My opponent's breathing shortened. She tried a few jabs and slashes, but I dodged them easily: she moved too slowly.

Time for a lesson. I flicked my left wrist and my coat shot out, slapping across her face. She lunged towards me, I shot my leg out, and she went over, landing hard. The knife skittered away. Her younger friend had recovered enough to rush me from the other side. I jabbed my right elbow into her face with the whole force of my upper body. The crunch of breaking bone was easy to hear in the silence surrounding us. She collapsed on the floor, clutching a bleeding nose.

The older one grabbed my ankle, pulled me over, but I rolled as I fell, tearing my leg out of her reach. I was on my feet in seconds. Crouching. Waiting. She pushed herself up, put her hand out toward the audience, fingers commanding somebody give a fresh weapon, but they shrank back. Breathing heavily, she lunged at me, a good eighty-five kilos of solid flesh, mouth wide open and roaring. As she bent her head to bite, I jumped sideways, thrust my covered arm into her jaws and brought the edge of my right hand down in a hard jab on the back of her bent neck. She stopped dead, her eyes rolled up, and she fell, unconscious, slumped in a heap.

'Anybody else?' I unwrapped the coat from my arm, but nobody looked me in the eye. 'Okay, then somebody take out the trash on the floor.'

I was in the laundry room an hour later pulling my washed tees out of the machine when a young boy came with a message that the farm assistant wanted to see me in the dormitory now. My things were spread out on the bed again, but tidily. A number of other workers loitered in the background.

'Please explain why I have two previously able-bodied workers in the infirmary.'

'They'd stolen something that belonged to me. They wouldn't give it back. I recovered it.'

'How did you acquire such an expensive pair of field glasses?'

'I didn't steal them, if that's what you're saying.'

'I'm not. Please answer my question.'

'I saved up.'

'And why do you have them?'

'Why not?' I shrugged.

'I seen her writing things in her book,' said one of the audience.

'Show me,' said the assistant.

I handed her the torn notebook.

She took it and leafed through. 'I see. These notes go back two years. How long have you been watching?'

'Several years.'

'Well, you might try the far shore of the lake. It's a good spot for grebe, greylag geese, black-headed gulls and sometimes kingfishers. The rise the other side of the road near the cottages is where migrating populations gather.' She stopped smiling. 'You're a good worker, so I don't want to lose you. But I won't have brawling. You're deducted three days' pay to cover medical costs for the two injured, and you're reassigned to field work for a week. Do you understand?'

'Yes, ma'am.

'Ex-military?'

I nodded.

'Try to remember the "ex" part.'

I looked away.

• • •

That evening, with my knives under my tee, I set off as soon as I could after the evening meal towards the cottage. I'd pulled a muscle that afternoon, but nothing important. I had the strangest feeling of not being alone. I stopped and waited for ten minutes, extending every sense to its furthest stretch, but I heard and saw nothing. I couldn't smell much beyond grass, sheep dung and hedgerow plants.

I found a better vantage point to observe which had sight of the front door. I glimpsed Justus talking to somebody else but, irritatingly, couldn't see the other person. But I knew in my heart who it was. Twenty-five minutes after I'd arrived, a car pulled up with a rental plate. My throat constricted as I saw the driver step out, lock the door and approach the cottage.

Philippus.

No.

Justus answered the door and, within seconds, the two men were waving hands around and shouting at each other. I had to hear this. I had no distance mic so, scanning left and right, I crept across to the wall and pressed myself against it. I took a quiet deep breath and edged along to just before the corner.

'...be so childlike. He was protecting our interests.' Justus's voice was terse, impatient even.

'You knew! You knew all along!'

'As a matter of fact, I didn't. But I'm so relieved he dumped that little tart and her national interest crap.'

'But he backed the wrong side.'

'No, he played both.' A pause. 'Good tactics.'

'Yeah, but they know,' retorted Philippus, 'and they're hunting him.'

Justus's laugh. 'They'll never guess where he is and now Mitela's contained in jail, even she won't be able to do anything about it.'

'So why did he want to see me?'

'He'll tell you himself. Turn round against the wall.'

I heard the movement of Justus's hands over Philippus's clothes as he searched him.

The door opened and closed. I shut my eyes. Thank Juno, Philippus wasn't involved.

I edged back to the window. I always thought it was too obvious in spy movies when the window was left open, so I nearly laughed when I saw the gap. But the voices overrode my bizarre thought. Apollo's rich, cold voice and Philippus's hurt and angry one.

'My dear Philippus, this really is unlike you to be so overwrought. It was a matter of pragmatics.'

'I thought we were doing the right thing when we helped Pulcheria, and I thought you did. I don't understand.'

'It's always wise to make, er, arrangements with other players, you know. Do tell me, just how did you find out?'

I shivered with fear. What would Philippus say? I dreaded he would go too far and give Apollo no option but to terminate him.

'Hermina and I were dragged in by those PGSF bastards and given the full treatment.'

'I trust Hermina has recovered?'

'Do you? I always thought you cared for your people, Apollodorus. Now I'm not so sure.'

Shut up, Phil. Don't get him riled, I begged silently.

'But you still haven't told me how they found out,' Apollo said in his softest tone.

I shut my eyes.

The jab of a barrel rammed under my jawline woke me up.

Shit.

'Nothing smart. Hands on the wall above your head.' Justus kicked my feet apart. He punched me in the small of my back, so I collapsed against the stone wall. I couldn't stop a grunt escaping. I was helpless with pain as he wrenched my wrists down and circled them with a cable tie, pulling the plastic band tight. I sagged to my knees and fought for my breath. He hauled me to my feet and dragged me round to the front entrance, each step a jab of pain. He shoved me through the door into a rustic living room with an open fire blazing and pulsing out heat.

My head swam but I planted my feet on the tiled floor. I willed myself to stay upright. Sitting at his ease on a high back couch was Apollodorus. But I knew him too well. The skin around his mouth was tight, a sure sign of tension. Was it anger or guilt shining in his eyes? Or some other emotion? Philippus stood back facing him, fury all over his face.

Both men stared at my dramatic entrance. Apollo was first to recover.

'My dear Carina Mitela, so kind to drop in.' He gestured to Philippus. 'A chair.'

I dropped down onto it, catching another jab of pain, but a relief from standing. Philippus sent me a desperate look, but I closed my eyes and shook my head.

'I think, Philippus, you should sit down opposite me where Justus can see you. I would be disappointed if you did anything rash.' Apollodorus's face had regained its usual praeternatural calm. 'Now, I would like very much to hear what our other guest has to say for herself.'

'First, I need some water.'

Apollo lifted a jug and tumbler.

'From an unopened bottle.'

'Dear me, you don't trust anything, do you?'

'No, as I've found out.'

He stood up, disappeared into the kitchen, came back with a small blue bottle, and with an ironic bow handed it to Philippus to serve me. It was liquid heaven. And, apart from the occasional crack from the fire, my gulping was the only sound in the room.

'How did you know?' Apollodorus asked at last.

'Oh, you were very careful. I knew in the back of my mind something didn't mesh together but couldn't put my finger on it. Superbus let slip something after I interviewed him. He mentioned Cassia.'

'Cassia?' His brows drew together.

'Common enough name, but it worried me.'

'I thought a descendant of the Twelve Families would know how to hold his tongue, how to behave.'

'Then you're kidding yourself. He's an amoral little shit.'

'Very well, I admit I was not overly impressed.' He shrugged. 'I did warn Petronax to keep a close eye on him, but I was too far in by that stage.'

My back was aching like seven levels of Hades, the breath was circulating my lungs on minimum running, but I couldn't help myself. I smirked at him.

'Cassia,' I said, 'turned out to be a Censor's Office investigator. An undercover one. She went through your organisation like a ferret on a high.' Apollodorus and Justus exchanged nervous looks.

I gave a quick laugh. 'Don't worry on that score – Hermina had everything in wonderful order. Cassia found nothing. You don't deserve Hermina. She was fantastically loyal to you. She's devastated by your treachery.'

Apollodorus rose off the couch, his hands balled. I tilted my face up, daring him.

'But the key was a witness at Superbus's house,' I carried on. 'She saw you the evening before the coup and has identified you.'

He sat down again, his face sombre.

'Why did you do it, Apollodorus? Why did you deal with Petronax?'

'Pragmatism, my dear. My father was weak – it was humiliating. Although I loved my grandmother, I sometimes hated her for sneering at him, her son.'

'That's sentiment, not pragmatism. He was a druggie pimp who prostituted his own child.'

'Petronax winning would have settled that for me. I would have become one of the richest men in the new order.'

'You knew it was wrong.'

'I never said I didn't.'

'We worked so well together against the drug dealers all those years ago.'

'Yes. You were so useful to me then and it never hurts to have the establishment owing one a favour.'

'Is that all it was?'

'You know it wasn't.'

I was trying to puzzle out this complex and damaged man. The hard ruthlessness was genuine, but so was the sensitivity. A crack from a log breaking up on the fire made me jump.

'Why did you help Flavius and me when we were shot in front of your gate?'

'Petronax hadn't made his big move then. It could have gone either way.'

I shivered when I thought about when he'd had Conrad at his house. Out of Transulium into the traitor's trap.

'How did you know I was here?' Apollodorus asked.

'You told me.'

His brow creased.

'You always said you'd finish where you began, so I guessed you'd return to Castra Lucilla. I found the rental contract you took out five years ago in the concealed compartment in the swan's neck table.'

'And what precisely were you doing in my private room?'

'Didn't Justus tell you?' I smirked at him. 'I would have thought he would have the answer off pat. Or is he hiding something from you?'

Justus swung his hand up in an arc to smash his semi-automatic down on my face. Pleasure and anticipation shone out of his eyes.

'Justus,' Apollodorus's soft voice chilled the air. Justus's arm came down slowly. He was only centimetres away from me. He waved the Glock in my face, but stepped back.

Apollodorus turned his black gaze on me. I couldn't read it, but I tried very hard not to shiver.

'If you attempt to provoke him again, I won't stop him. Now answer my question.'

'You know the *custodes* raided the house. They brought me in to help with their search. I found the panel into the room.' I shrugged. 'It's been stripped out, and the contents will be sold off at public auction when you're convicted.'

His lips turned almost white in a mouth pulled into a tight line. Pink blotches gathered in his cheeks. I had never seen him so angry. I was pleased to hurt him: it eased my own hurt. I knew I was going to die now. And he would kill me himself.

'Why didn't you terminate us when Flavius and I came back after the operation?'

'I don't know. I had you in my hand.' He sighed. 'I should have known you would work it out eventually. You are so persistent.'

'Did none of the good work we did mean anything to you?'

'Yes. My bitterest regret was betraying your friendship.' His eyes drilled into mine. The lines at the corners of his mouth pulled down. 'You're so single-minded, Carina, so sure of yourself, aren't you?'

'Never believe that. I've had my struggles, but I know the difference between right and wrong.'

Justus broke the silence. 'What happens next?' He spoke directly to Apollodorus. 'You can't let them go.'

Apollodorus put his hand in his inner pocket, drew out a mother of pearl box. He flicked open the lid, extracted a tablet and swallowed before anybody had time to react. He drained his glass and replaced it on the table.

I stared at him, not believing what he had done. I pulled at the plastic binding round my wrists, to get to him, but I couldn't move. 'Apollo, you— No!'

'I will not face the public humiliation of a trial. I am satisfied I have chosen the time and circumstances of my own death.' He closed his eyes. 'I'm sorry. Truly.' A spasm rode through his body and he was gone.

'No!' Justus moved forward, bent over Apollo. He swung around, his face contorted. He brought his semi-automatic point-blank to my head. As his finger went to squeeze the trigger, a crack sounded, his eyes bulged, a red jet exploded from his forehead. His legs folded and he fell.

I rocked my chair off balance and threw myself to the ground in the same split second Philippus dived for the floor.

41

Livius had made the shot that killed Justus. It seemed obvious now but, at the time, all I took in was Justus's blood and brains everywhere; warm on my face, a spreading pool of blood on the tile floor.

Philippus was crawling towards me when something thumped heavily on the door. The lock exploded away from the wood. I screwed my eyes closed and turned my head away from the flying debris. The door was smashed back on its hinges. I opened my eyes to see Paula and Flavius burst in, semi-automatics in their hands. Conrad on their heels. From the floor, I heard more than saw Paula and Flavius run toward the kitchen and hallway doors. Half a second later, they shouted, 'Secure.'

Conrad pushed Philippus out of the way and dropped to his knees by my side. We stared at each other. My heart was still thudding hard from the fall but seemed to speed up. He closed his eyes for a second, then shook his head like he was rebooting his brain. He leaned over my body and slashed the plastic tie around my wrists.

The pulse rocketed through my wrists, swiftly followed by pain as blood started circulating through my flesh.

'Ah, ah, Juno.' I bit my lip. Pain shot through my arm that had gone numb from taking my weight when I crashed to the ground. Conrad shoved the fallen chair away. Although he carried out the standard vitals check swiftly and surely, I felt his fingers tremble as he pressed my wrist for my pulse. He was silent as he focused on my arm.

'Nothing's broken, thank the gods,' he rasped after a few moments, then wrapped his arms around me. He bent his head down onto my chest, and I brought my good hand up to touch his hair.

'Conrad, I'm so—'

'Shush, relax. It's over.' He glanced up at Flavius who was standing over Apollodorus's body. 'And?'

'Dead.'

Conrad grunted. 'Get the first-aid kit.'

Ever practical, Flavius raised my head and wedged a cushion under it. He strapped a cold pack onto my bruised arm and gave me a shot. The cold liquid curled through the flesh of my arm. Conrad gently wiped my face clear of Justus's blood and flesh with a stericloth. His smile faded as he packed it in a plastic waste baggie. When he'd finished, he took my hand in his, stroked it, then cupped it in both of his

'There are so many charges I could bring that you'd be immobilised in prison for years, safe where you couldn't get up to anything remotely dangerous.'

I studied his face. It wasn't anger but anxiety.

'No, too tempting to start a riot,' I whispered back.

His grip on my hand became more intense. 'Gods, woman, don't ever do this again to me.'

I gave him a little smile. 'No guarantee of that.'

But he smiled back, bent over and kissed my lips.

I didn't remember much of the ride to hospital, but I felt his hand on my face and the warm pressure of the other one holding mine.

They'd been the noisy group arriving that morning. Conrad had asked Aurelia for permission to track me, but they took a little while to realise exactly where I was on the estate. Livius had followed me up to the cottage with Conrad, Paula and Flavius behind. They'd gotten every word on a distance mic.

Conrad hadn't processed my resignation further than his in-tray. He knew I'd be back.

· · ·

Apollo was identified at last: his mother had been a moderately successful businesswoman's daughter from Castra Lucilla. His family history tied up with everything he'd told me. He'd leased the cottage for years. I left hospital in time for his funeral at the Castra Lucilla public burning ground. Philippus, Flav, the public recorder and duty priest and I were the only attendees.

Philippus threw his libation on last – a woven leather belt. 'It was the first thing he gave me the day he scraped me off the street. He said none of his household, his family, would ever wear rope around their waist. I'd never owned anything so good. It doesn't fit any longer, but I kept it to remind me of that moment.' He tipped his head toward the burning body. 'It's right it should go back to him.' And he threw it in an arc into the middle of the flames.

After a surprisingly short trial, the conspirators were given long sentences, all hard labour, except Superbus, who was sent to a state farm where he flourished. Leaner and fitter, he ended up managing it and making a profit for the state. He still had bad breath.

Aidan was tried for complicity but escaped with a public censure after we'd entered a plea citing his co-operation. But Aburia's hearing was awkward and the tone terse. The senior legate giving judgement spoke like she was eating gravel. As Aburia was being taken away to the central military prison for the next five years, she shot a venomous look at me, the only sign of animation from her during the whole ninety minutes.

On the day she was released, Aidan was waiting for her outside the prison. I had no contact with them after that, but Mossia reported a year later that they were happy and had a young son.

I had the accommodation blocks for the casuals on the Mitela farm refurbished to include partitions and lockable cupboards in the dormitories, a games room and quiet common room. I caught some strange looks from the farm manager, who asked me why I was so concerned, but I turned her questions aside.

After I was passed fit for duty, I took a two-month secondment to the regular Praetorians. The disciplined routine was tough but predictable. I enjoyed my shifts on the palace guard. I saw Hallie recover her joy as well as her grit. The rest of my life had calmed with the regular hours. Julia Sella had been one hundred per cent correct about that. A good lesson to learn.

I went to Apollo's house for the last time a week before I went back to the PGSF after my secondment. The dozen or so rows of chairs set out in the middle of the atrium were half-filled; scattered with neutral-faced professional dealers, excited private collectors and the curious. The public auctioneer rapped his gavel to stop the murmuring filling the atrium. A latecomer slid in the back row as it began. I bought several lamps and furniture, including the swan-legged table, but waited until the last lot. After a tussle, including with a phone bidder, I acquired the tall portrait. For its black eyes.

I left my under-steward to handle the paperwork and walked over to the glass doors leading to the veranda. The winter frost had persisted until this afternoon, making the grass look like plastic white turf, but pale sunshine struggled through. The river looked like skeins of white and grey silks.

A movement to one side. Nonna's chauffeur put his arm out to block a figure approaching me.

'It's okay, Nic.' I gave the blonde-haired woman a tight smile. 'Hello, Hermina. So you couldn't resist coming either?'

'I thought I'd pick up some bits and pieces cheaply for the new office.' Her casual tone didn't fool me. The tense eyes gave her away. 'Philippus told me what happened out at Castra Lucilla. Have you recovered?'

'Oh yes. A boring week in hospital until I discharged myself.' I grinned at her.

She gave me a slightly more relaxed smile.

'Well, I'd better go,' she said and nodded at me. 'I have a Foundation to run.'

And I had a job to go back to. Whether I wanted it as much as before, I didn't know.

***

The story continues nine years later when Carina must defend her family and Roma Nova against the most malicious enemy she has ever faced. And where the next generation plays a vital role... SUCCESSIO

WOULD YOU LEAVE A REVIEW?

I hope you enjoyed PERFIDITAS, the danger, adventures and passions.

If you did, I'd really appreciate it if you would write a few words of review on the site where you purchased this book.

Reviews will really help PERFIDITAS to feature more prominently on retailer sites and let more people into the world of Roma Nova.

Very many thanks!

HISTORICAL NOTE

What if King Harold had won the Battle of Hastings in 1066? Or if Julius Caesar had taken notice of the warning that assassins wanted to murder him on the Ides of March? Or the Spanish Armada had defeated and conquered England in 1588? Suppose Christianity had remained a Middle East minor cult? Intriguing questions, indeed. Alternate (or alternative) history stories allow us to explore them.

PERFIDITAS focuses on one main character, Carina Mitela, and her struggle to defeat a conspiracy entwined with personal and professional betrayal. The whole concept of a society with Roman values surviving for fifteen centuries is intriguing, but I have dropped background history about Roma Nova into the novel only where it impacts on the story. Nobody likes a straight history lesson in the middle of a thriller!

But if you are interested in a little more information about the mysterious Roma Nova, read on...

What happened in our timeline

Of course, our timeline may turn out to be somebody else's alternate as shown in Philip K Dick's *The Grasshopper Lies Heavy*, the story within the story in *The Man in the High Castle*. Nothing is fixed. But for the sake of convenience I will take ours as the default.

The Western Roman Empire didn't 'fall' in a cataclysmic event as often portrayed in film and television; it localised and eventually dissolved like chain mail fragmenting into separate links, giving way to rump provinces, local city states and petty kingdoms. The Eastern Roman Empire survived until the Fall of Constantinople in 1453 to the Muslim Ottoman Empire.

Some scholars think that Christianity fatally weakened the traditional Roman way of life and was a significant factor in the collapse. Emperor Constantine's personal conversion to Christianity in AD 313 was a turning point for the new religion. By AD 394, his several times successor, Theodosius, banned all traditional Roman religious practice, closed and destroyed temples and dismissed all priests. The sacred flame that had burned for over a thousand years in the College of Vestals was extinguished and the Vestal Virgins expelled. The Altar of Victory, said to guard the fortune of Rome, was hauled away from the Senate building and disappeared from history.

The Roman senatorial families pleaded for religious tolerance, but Theodosius made any pagan practice, even dropping a pinch of incense on a family altar in a private home, into a capital offence. And his 'religious police' driven by the austere and ambitious bishop Ambrosius of Milan, became increasingly active in pursuing pagans...

The alternate Roma Nova timeline

In AD 395, three months after Theodosius's final decree banning all pagan religious activity, over four hundred Romans loyal to the old gods, and so in danger of execution, trekked north out of Italy to a semi-mountainous area similar to modern Slovenia. Led by Senator Apulius at the head of twelve senatorial families, they established a colony based initially on land owned by Apulius' Celtic father-in-law. By purchase, alliance and conquest, this grew into Roma Nova.

Norman Davies in *Vanished Kingdoms: The History of Half-Forgotten Europe* reminds us that:

> *"...in order to survive, newborn states need to possess a set of viable internal organs, including a functioning executive, a defence force, a revenue system and a diplomatic force. If they possess none of these*

things, they lack the means to sustain an autonomous existence and they perish before they can breathe and flourish."

I would add history, willpower and adaptability as essential factors. Roma Nova survived by changing its social structure; as men constantly fought to defend the new colony, women took over the social, political and economic roles, weaving new power and influence networks based on family structures. Given the unstable, dangerous times in Roma Nova's first few hundred years, daughters as well as sons had to put on armour and heft swords to defend their homeland and their way of life. Fighting danger side by side with brothers and fathers reinforced women's roles and status.

The Roma Novans never allowed the incursion of monotheistic, paternalistic religions; they'd learnt that lesson from old Rome. Service to the state was valued higher than personal advantage, echoing Roman Republican virtues, and the women heading the families guarded and enhanced these values to provide a core philosophy throughout the centuries. Inheritance passed from these powerful women to their daughters and granddaughters.

Roma Nova's continued existence has been favoured by three factors: the discovery and exploitation of high-grade silver in their mountains, their efficient technology, and their robust response to any threat.

Remembering the Fall of Constantinople, Roma Novan troops assisted the western nations at the Battle of Vienna in 1683 to halt the Ottoman advance into Europe. Nearly two hundred years later, they used their diplomatic skills to forge an alliance to push Napoleon IV back across the Rhine as he attempted to expand his grandfather's empire.

And in more recent times?

Prioritising survival, Roma Nova remained neutral in the Great War of the 20th century which lasted from 1925 to 1935. The Greater German Empire, stretching from Jutland in the north, Alsace in the west, Tyrol in the south and Bulgaria in the east, was broken up afterwards into its former small kingdoms, duchies and counties. Some became republics. There was no sign of an Austrian-born corporal with a short, square moustache.

Thirty years before the action of PERFIDITAS in the early 21st century, Roma Nova was nearly destroyed by a coup, a brutal male-dominated consulship and civil war. A weak leader, sclerotic and outmoded systems that had not developed since the last great reform in the 1700s and a neglected economy let in a clever and ruthless tyrant.

But with characteristic resilience, the families' structures fought back and reconstructed their society, re-learning the basic principles of Republican virtue, while subtly changing it to a more representational model for modern times. Today, the tiny country has become one of the highest per capita income states in the world.

THE ROMA NOVA THRILLER SERIES

The Carina Mitela adventures

INCEPTIO

Early 21st century. Terrified after a kidnap attempt, New Yorker Karen Brown, has a harsh choice – being terminated by government enforcer Renschman or fleeing to Roma Nova, her dead mother's homeland in Europe. Founded sixteen hundred years ago by Roman exiles and ruled by women, it gives Karen safety, at a price. But Renschman follows and sets a trap she has no option but to enter.

CARINA – *A novella*

Carina Mitela is still an inexperienced officer in the Praetorian Guard Special Forces of Roma Nova. Disgraced for a disciplinary offence, she is sent out of everybody's way to bring back a traitor from the Republic of Quebec. But when she discovers a conspiracy reaching into the highest levels of Roma Nova, what price is personal danger against fulfilling the mission?

PERFIDITAS

Falsely accused of conspiracy, 21st century Praetorian Carina Mitela flees into the criminal underworld. Hunted by the security services and traitors alike, she struggles to save her beloved Roma Nova as well as her own life.

But the ultimate betrayal is waiting for her…

SUCCESSIO

21st century Praetorian Carina Mitela's attempt to resolve a past family indiscretion is spiralling into a nightmare. Convinced her beloved husband has deserted her, and with her enemy holding a gun to the imperial heir's head, Carina has to make the hardest decision of her life.

The Aurelia Mitela adventures

AURELIA

Late 1960s. Sent to Berlin to investigate silver smuggling, former Praetorian Aurelia Mitela barely escapes a near-lethal trap. Her old enemy is at the heart of all her troubles and she pursues him back home to Roma Nova but he strikes at her most vulnerable point – her young daughter.

INSURRECTIO

Early 1980s. Caius Tellus, the charismatic leader of a rising nationalist movement, threatens to destroy Roma Nova.

Aurelia Mitela, ex-Praetorian and imperial councillor, attempts to counter the growing fear and instability. But it may be too late to save Roma Nova from meltdown and herself from destruction by her lifelong enemy....

RETALIO

Early 1980s Vienna. Aurelia Mitela chafes at her enforced exile. She barely escaped from a near fatal shooting by her nemesis, Caius Tellus, who grabbed power in Roma Nova.

Aurelia is determined to liberate her homeland. But Caius's manipulations have ensured that she is ostracised by her fellow exiles. Powerless and vulnerable, Aurelia fears she will never see Roma Nova again.

ROMA NOVA EXTRA

A collection of short stories

Four historical and four present day and a little beyond

A young tribune sent to a backwater in 370 AD for practising the wrong religion, his lonely sixty-fifth descendant labours in the 1980s to reconstruct her country. A Roma Novan imperial councillor attempting to stop the Norman invasion of England in 1066, her 21st century Praetorian descendant flounders as she searches for her own happiness.

Some are love stories, some are lessons learned, some resolve tensions and unrealistic visions, some are plain adventures, but above all, they are stories of people in dilemmas and conflict, and their courage and effort to resolve them.